the itofit

David Anirman

iUniverse, Inc.
Bloomington

The Itofit

iUniverse books may be ordered through booksellers or by contacting:

iUniverse
1663 Liberty Drive
Bloomington, IN 47403
www.iuniverse.com
1-800-Authors (1-800-288-4677)

ISBN: 978-1-4759-3910-1 (sc)
ISBN: 978-1-4759-3911-8 (e)

Library of Congress Control Number: 2012912887

Printed in the United States of America

iUniverse rev. date: 8/7/2012

FROM SWAMP to POMP

Saturday morning
A beautiful day, sunny
With fresh, moist air, clear as the first day ever
(Which it almost seemed to be)
And new flowers bursting out
With the palette of spring shading to summer
And yellow-striped bees and opalescent hummingbirds
Choosing their favorite colors to sip from,
And Toliver Manfellow loosed for the day
Found Toonie, his friend
From long ago and far away, and tomorrow too
(Whose mother only called her Petunia Petalpaper
When she was very angry
About this or that or something else)
And together they went off to the woods
With Toonie's orange-yellow tabby cat with green eyes and a
    swooshing tail
Who had his own name but answered to Boogie
When people fed him
And Toonie's little cousin from the city
Who usually spent Saturday morning playing computer games
In his apartment on the 26th floor

Of a very large building where the doorman and the janitor
And the neighbor's Pekinese knew him as Whizlet,
And when the four of them left the road behind
And came to the gnarly old elm tree
Where Mrs. Mudfinger's African gray parrot, Hobnail
(Whose bright red patches looked like flames on his shoulders)
Sat on a branch whistling Mr. Copeland's *Outdoor Overture*
To the robins and sparrows and wrens
And waiting for them
And the adventure they probably brought with them
(Because they always did)
They knew the day was perfect.

"Let's go this way," said Toonie.

"That's a good idea," said Toliver.

"It looks scary," said Whizlet. "Like the swamp in *The Abysmal Adventures of Okefenokee Okie*, where the crocopotamuses and the hippodiles hide in trees and under things that look like rocks but aren't."

"There is a swamp in here," said Toliver, not meaning to frighten Whizlet but telling the truth like he always did, or almost always.

"And a lake too," said Toonie. "With beavers in it."

"And a stream to the lake that goes through a huge tunnel under the highway," added Toliver.

"Where Trolls live," said Toonie who didn't mind frightening people if they didn't frighten back.

"Me-ow," said Boogie who went off in a different direction.

"Gone-away. Gone-away," said Hobnail who fluttered to another branch and pointed after the cat with his pretty gray wing.

"Let's go that way too," said Toliver.

"All right," said Toonie, "but we have to go my way later."

"It's kind of dark," gulped Whizlet, "and those trees have awfully big roots, and those vines hanging down could have nasty things swinging from them, and those bushes are funny looking."

"And there are stickerbushes too," added Toonie.

"That get huge black berries later," added Toliver.

"Hurry up. Flutter down. Fly in circles 'round 'n 'round," squawked

Hobnail grabbing a vine with his feet and hanging upended over their heads.

"Me-ow-ow." said Boogie impatiently from some distance away.

"Let's go," said Toliver who took Toonie's free hand, and pulled a little bit because her other hand was being held very tightly by both of Whizlet's hands, and Whizlet was mostly pulling in the other direction.

And so they followed the cat, or rather the cat's me-ows, deeper
    and deeper into the woods
With Hobnail flying above them
And things getting darker and darker
And the air getting danker and danker
And the ground getting wetter and wetter
And even slippery
And the trees getting closer together
With their roots all tangled and covered with dark green moss
And a spider web with a furry black spider with orange eyes in the
    middle
Watching them pass beneath
Till they got to a place where Toliver had never been before
And Toonie didn't like
And Whizlet couldn't say anything because his heart was caught
    up in his throat
And even Boogie came back and rubbed himself around Toliver's
    legs
And Hobnail hid in the leaves of a tangly green bush, listening…
Listening…
Listening to what Boogie had heard that made him come back
And now Toliver heard and made him swallow hard
And Toonie heard and made the hair on the back of her neck
    stand up
And Whizlet heard and made his eyes get so big they almost
    bumped into his heart
Which was still in his throat
And they all listened…
Listened to a very strange sound that seemed to have a peculiar
    voice attached
Kerumph and kerbibble, kerboomer too
Klickety-klack and I haven't a clue…
Knobbely knubbely knibbely knock

I'm lost in the woods without kandle or klock…

"W, wh, what's that?" quivered Toonie

"Yi, yi, yipes-a-doddle!" stammered Whizlet who clung to her even more tightly.

"I don't know," admitted Toliver, who nevertheless tried to sound like he knew (or at least like he knew what he was doing), but couldn't because he didn't. But since he was the biggest and not supposed to be afraid of scary sounds in the forest, he peered around the tree in front of him; parted the branches of a bush, and looked out into a little grove where a strange, furry apparition was sitting on a mossy rock holding its hat in its hands and scratching its ear with its foot.

The apparition paused in its scratching, its nose twitched, its head swiveled atop its long neck, and its eyes, very large and shaped like Brazil nuts with purple pupils, looked directly at Toliver. Then, as though ignoring him, the creature turned its head so only one eye was looking at Toliver, then, much to Toliver's surprise, the whole side of its face seemed to become one huge eye staring at him curiously. Then, quicker than a wink (which it was), a transparent shield with a strangely colored iridescence slid over the whole eye whereupon the fur seemed to relax and fold down from the top and up from the botto, both at once, leaving only a purple Brazil nut in a head that then turned to face Toliver.

"Well at least I'm not lost alone," said the creature who, while its head now remained fixed in place staring at Toliver's very wide eyes, twisted the rest of its body beneath until the whole of itself was facing that way, and its nose twitched again and one whisker reached up and brushed its eyebrow.

"Come, come," it continued in a voice that sounded like a melodious French horn. "Don't just look there standing. Come out and we'll make a glass of shrinking violet tea with chamomile flower froth. You do have folding glasses, don't you? and a shrinking teapot? like any civilized…" It paused, staring even harder at Toliver, then added questioningly, "…person?"

Toliver let go of the branch, which snapped up and clipped his nose making him tumble backward in surprise. He fell into Toonie, who still had Whizlet attached, so they all tumbled over and landed in a heap with Boogie on top and Hobnail fluttering above saying: "Strange bedfellows. Strange bedfellows."

Before they could untangle themselves, the head of the creature appeared in the very same place where Toliver's had been the moment before, and surveyed the heap of furry and skinny limbs until one eye swiveled out and looked up at Hobnail who cocked its head and stared back quite at a loss for words.

"A pandemonium of persons," said the creature, "posing as a pile of perplexity. 'Twont do. 'Twont do at all. Up, up! All of you! It's tea time, you know, or it should be, or it must be, or it is, or it isn't."

Toonie poked her head up with the cat clinging on top. "What are you talking about?" she asked, somewhat peevishly, since she was otherwise still under the pile of Whizlet's and Toliver's arms and legs and bodies and heads, and that would make anyone peevish when meeting someone new for the first time.

"I'm talking about tea. I'm talking about me. I'm talking about you. I'm talking me blue. Talking, talking, talking! It's one of the things I do when I'm not thinking."

Toliver rolled out and sat up. "You talk a great deal," he said, "so you must not think very much."

"I only talk when I have nothing to say," said the creature cutting him short. He then pulled his head back smartly and disappeared the way he had come.

There was a moment of somewhat stunned silence while the three friends and their parrot and cat companions sorted themselves out. Then, as soon as their curiosity won out over their befuddlement, they followed Toliver around the tree and into the grove. The creature was again sitting on the mossy rock with its chin on the back of its hand which looked like a paw with six fingers, or rather four fingers with a thumb at either end, and retractable nails (one wouldn't say claws as they were rather longer than that but not as sharp and, as the creature demonstrated by bending one into an upside down J while scratching his cheek, flexible too.) Its nose was twitching rapidly and the purple pupils above were gazing at all five of them with a good bit of unabashed speculation and, perhaps, just perhaps, even a touch of trepidation.

"Who are you?" demanded Toonie from over Toliver's shoulder

"I," said the creature rising majestically to his full height that put his shoulder somewhere between Toonie's eyebrow and Toliver's earlobe, "... am the Itofit."

"The who?" asked Toliver.

"The what?" said Toonie.

Whizlet just hiccupped, which he often did when he couldn't think of anything to say.

"I'm the It," said the creature trying to sound as dignified as he could but with a certain quiver in his voice. "And I'm from It." He looked away and sighed gently. "Therefore, I am the Itofit."

"And where's that?" asked Toliver.

"Well," replied the creature thoughtfully. "It is not here." He tilted his head and pointed his nose toward the treetops. His ears swiveled in little circles and his tongue jabbed out like a pointer. "And It's not there. So it must be someplace else."

"And where might that be?" chimed in Toonie who didn't like people being coy with her although she didn't mind being coy with people, at least every once in a while, but only when absolutely necessary, and then for a reason, although maybe just a little reason.

A tear welled up in the Itofit's eye. "I don't know anymore," he said. "I'm not sure if I don't remember, or if I'm confused, or if someone turned everything around while I was napping, or if maybe I changed my mind when I wasn't thinking, but I just don't seem to recall."

"You must remember something." said Toliver who didn't like to forget things unless they weren't very nice.

"Nothing. Nothing at all. Not even anything else either."

"Me-ow-sniff," said Boogie, slipping forward on his belly and stretching out like an accordion to sniff at the Itofit's toe.

"O, yes," said the Itofit to the cat. "Thank you. I remember now. I came out of a flower."

"A flower!" exclaimed Toonie who knew flowers came out of the ground but didn't know anything except bees that came out of flowers.

"What kind of flower?" asked Toliver who always liked to be sure about what he was talking about even when he wasn't.

"I don't know. I never smelled one like it before."

"Was it a weed?' asked Toonie who knew that nobody sniffed weeds so that someone sniffing one for the first time wouldn't have smelled it before either.

"What is a weed?" asked the Itofit.

"That's a flower big people don't like," replied Toonie.

"Big people? What are big people?"

"It doesn't matter," answered Toliver, "except when they're around." He scratched his head and sat down at the foot of the Itofit. "Do you remember what the flower looked like or where it was?"

"Why yes, of course. It was white and blue tinged with vertul, and had yellow streaks that looked like lightning bolts on it, and it was pink and xoc inside with long stamens with eyes on the end flecked with golden pollen, and it was shaped like a big, beautiful horn on a long xaalu colored stem with huge dark green leaves tinged with purple." He pointed off to the side where only a lone brown toadstool stood. "And it was exactly right there, but now everything has changed all around."

"Things don't just change around like that," said Toonie who sat down next to Toliver and pulled Whizlet down to sit next to her. "Things stay like they are until they change."

"Exactly like I was saying," said the Itofit. "After the flower dropped me on the ground, I sat down on a mossy rock and looked all about and things were very different than they are now. It wasn't shady like here and there were no big tree all around and the flowers were standing in different places and had different colors, and look!" He swung his arm around the glade, "Even the peculiar flower has disappeared."

"I never heard of a flower like that," said Toliver. "Maybe you bumped your head and wandered here by mistake."

"No, that didn't happen," said the Itofit, "because I remember everything perfectly. I was down by the bumpergrass glade below the It's-Fine, which is below our talapalodion tree basket house, playing my twistle with my friend Snorf, who's a snigglesnorf."

"What's a twistle?" asked Toliver.

"What's a snigglesnorf?" asked Toonie at exactly the same time so it sounded like they said: "What's a sniggletwistlesnorf?"

"I've never heard of one of those," replied the Itofit. "But a twistle is what you twistle on, and a snigglesnorf is...well, let me see...I suppose you could say a snigglesnorf is a snorf who sniggles. Anyway, Snorf and I were just whiling away the morning wishing Is was with us with Snorfa and her cloth harp when I noticed this wonderful new flower I'd never seen or even thought about before, so I went right over and smelled it and it had the most wonderful fragrance, and when I put my nose closer to smell it again, why, it pulled me right inside, just like a vacuum flish sucks up snibbles."

"How amazing!" said Toliver.

"Maybe you ought to have your nose checked," said Toonie.

"Sweet flower. Pretty flower," said Hobnail who swung by clutching a vine and peering closely at the Itofit's large wiggly ears as he passed.

"And when the flower spit me back out, I was here," continued the Itofit with a bit of perplexity. "or at least near here, because I haven't sniffed a single flower since I got here, so I must still be here, or if not here, close by."

"You must have gotten some pollen in your eye," said Toliver who always liked to make sense out of everything. "And walked here while you couldn't see."

"Or more likely in your nose," added Toonie, "and sneezed yourself here."

"I haven't taken more than three steps," declared the Itofit. "One when I looked around at all the water, one when I sat down on the mossy rock, and one when I stood up. Of course I was quite confused, but there were some pretty flowers and bulrushes all about so I asked them where I was but they wouldn't speak at all. I supposed that they must have been sleeping so I decided to nap myself and talk to them in dreams, but even then they just seemed surprised and didn't seem to know how to talk at all. And then when I woke up, why I wasn't even here anymore."

"How do you talk to flowers?" asked Toonie who'd never heard of such a thing and wasn't at all sure if the strange creature might be fibbing to her or, at least, stretching the truth just a trifle.

"The same way you talk to trees and bushes," replied the Itofit. "But you usually say different things because flowers aren't very interested in larger issues."

"But how do you do it?" persisted Toonie who considered this a large enough issue to get to the bottom of.

"Why just like this," said the Itofit and he took three deep breaths and stared off into space. His face softened into a smile, his eyes crossed just a little, and his ears began to swivel around.

"I can cross my eyes," said Whizlet doing just that, "but I can't wiggle my ears. Does that matter?"

The Itofit said nothing in reply until a quite a few moments later when he seemed to wake up all of a sudden. "No," he said. "The ears don't matter at all. Nor do your eyes for that matter. All you have to do is see with your mind and listen with the inside of yourself, but there's nothing to listen to here. These flowers don't seem to speak at all. I'm sure they do among themselves, but they don't appear to know how to talk to others. It's all very peculiar."

"Flowers are for picking," said Toonie whereupon she did just that and held the blossoms to her nose.

"Ouch!" said the Itofit.

"What?" asked Toliver ,who had been watching everything very carefully, not at all sure what to make of it.

"The flower said Ouch!" said It. "You shouldn't surprise it like that. They loved to be picked, you know, but not all of a sudden without warning. They liked to be asked first so they can pretty up their perfumes. But at least I'm glad to see they do know how to speak. They just don't seem to get much practice." He stood up again and looked at the rock on which he had been sitting, "This rock is as peculiar as the flowers. It has changed too. It's still mossy, but when I sat down on it, it had a splinter at one end and a blob at the other. And it had pretty designs all over it. And it wasn't sharp like it is now, and he put his foot on the rock and ran over it with his toes."

"And you left your shoes somewhere," said Whizlet, who always wore shoes in the city and figured they came with being smart.

"Shoes?" asked the Itofit somewhat puzzled until he noticed that Whizlet was standing on one foot and brandishing the other in front of him. "You mean those toe-traps you have on your feet so you can't feel the it of It under you or walk upside down along branches? That's very peculiar."

"You're very peculiar too," said Toonie who generally supported her cousin unless it was important.

"No, I'm not," said the Itofit. "You are."

"But you have big, flappy, pointy ears," said Whizlet.

"And teeth like a squirrel," said Toonie.

"And thick white hair that looks like…like…like the inside of an oyster shell," said Toliver who hadn't learned the word 'opalescent' yet.

"With red and yellow patches," added Whizlet.

"That's not hair," said the Itofit. "That's my fur, at least the silver and xaalu is. The xoc and yellow is my tunic." And while he was speaking a long tail whisked out from behind him and brushed across the top of his head, smoothing the fur that had, though he would never admit it of course, become somewhat ruffled from the fright he had felt on first seeing such an unusual thing as Toliver's head peering through the bushes at him.

"AND A TAIL!" exclaimed Toliver, Toonie, and Whizlet all together.

"Everybody has a tail," said the Itofit indignantly. "How else can you walk right, or talk correctly, or swing by in the trees, or even brush your face?" He pointed at Boogie who was even now peering around Toliver's side and swooshing his own tail just like tigers often do when ready to jump or run away. "Now there is a smart creature. He knows the value of a fine tail!"

"Me-e-e-ow-w!" answered the cat proudly.

"His name is Boogie," said Toonie. "and he belongs to me."

"I know that," said the Itofit. "But he is of the opinion that you belong to him."

"I do not!" exclaimed Toonie reddening her cheeks with lady-like outrage. "He belongs to me. I belong to my mother!"

"He thinks your mother belongs to your father," continued the Itofit. "But sometimes the other way round."

"How do you know all that?" asked Toliver who was genuinely curious since he didn't think anybody belonged to anybody else anymore.

"Why, he just told me. Didn't you notice? Do you have a noisy caterpillar in your ear that makes you look sideways so you can't see what he's saying?"

"All he said was me-ow," said Toonie. "That's all he ever says."

"That's not all he said," said the Itofit. "He also said: My name's Spitpurrkoff but they call me Boogie and I'm an orange-yellow tabby cat with green eyes whose great-great-grandfather was a Bengal tiger, and I like to talk with my tail too, and bat people with it when they're being peoplish, but I never swing through the trees because it's undignified."

"He did not!" said Toonie. "He just said me-ow and nothing else."

"Little you know," said the Itofit. "You just don't listen very well and you weren't watching either. Between the 'me' and the 'e', he said Sptprkf with his nose, toes, and tail; and between the 'e' and the 'e' he said 'Boo', and between the 'e' and the 'ow', he said 'gie', then gave a flourish with his whiskers while his pretty yellow-orange fur stood up, and his eyes flashed like the emerald orbs of a Bengal tiger, and his tail lashed out, pointed at those vines over there, said 'no-no-no-never', and dotted the 'i' in Boogie just like that!" And the Itofit poked his finger right at Toonie's forehead so dramatically that Toonie flung out her arms and fell over backward, knocking Toliver and Whizlet with her, and Whizlet exclaimed "Yipes-a-doddle!" as he did a backward somersault.

"Wow!" said Toliver getting to his feet and pulling Toonie up with him. "I'd like to be able to hear like that."

"It's not very difficult," said the Itofit. "All you have to do is know what you're doing and then practice a lot. But first of all, you have to find creatures to practice with". He looked about and fixed his gaze on Hobnail who retreated to a branch on the other side of the tree, from where he poked his head out to keep one eye on It, and the other on an escape route behind. "She'll do."

"She's a boy!" said Toonie firmly.

"No, she's not!" said the Itofit, just as firmly. "You didn't see her feathers ruffle or her tail twitter."

"I did too," said Toonie, "and he did it just like a little boy bird, which he is."

"She isn't either," persisted the Itofit. "She just said she's been fooling everybody all along but any day now she's going to lay an egg and surprise Mrs. Dirtytoes."

"Mrs. Mudfinger," corrected Toliver.

"Humph," said Toonie, eyeing the Itofit speculatively, not sure whether he was telling the truth or just talking to say something else, but he seemed so sure of himself, she decided to be as bold as he was. "I've known he's a girl all along. But we girls stick together and don't give away each other's secrets. But he already talks too much anyway so we can't practice with her."

"And she only says silly things," added Whizlet who finally felt comfortable enough to say something silly himself.

"Do not!" screeched Hobnail. "Smart bird. Smart bird." And she grabbed a hanging vine and swung by wiggling her rear end and fanning her red shoulder feathers dramatically.

Toonie had to duck and Whizlet jumped out of the way but the Itofit was delighted by the feisty parrot and did a pirouette-like swivel with his tail by way of applause. "She says her real name is…" and here he whistled a beautiful tune that sounded like * * * * * "and she's not really a bird at all. She's a dinosaur, or at least her great-great-grandmother was an archaeopteryx."

"And she's very well educated too," added Toonie. "Mrs. Mudfinger lets her listen to classical music all the time so she minds her P.D.Q.s and Bach."

"* * * * *" said Hobnail with a marvelous trill, then added: "Singing bird. Singing bird!"

"My goodness," replied the Itofit. "That's certainly wonderful indeed. But if you already speak we'll just have to find someone else to practice with." He looked all about and since his eyes were very sharp, he stopped when his head had only swiveled about halfway around. "Let's see now... How about that creature under the bush behind you?"

"What creature?" asked Toonie somewhat puzzled because she hadn't seen anyone else around.

The Itofit looked slightly puzzled himself. "I'm not at all sure what it is. We certainly don't have anything like it on It, but it looks very much like a tail without a creature attached to it."

"There's no such thing," announced Toliver firmly.

"And if there was," added Whizlet, "who would wag it?"

"SNAKE!" screeched Toonie jumping two feet into the air and coming down behind Toliver.

"Hsssssssssssssss!" said the snake.

"Yipes-a-doddle!" gulped Whizlet, who jumped behind Toonie but finding her shaking as much as he was, ran to the Itofit instead, and hid behind him.

"O, poof!" said the Itofit to the snake. "You can't fool me. You're a pretty tail but how you get around without a creature to hang onto is surely a mystery. And I don't know why you're trying to scare everybody since you certainly wouldn't hurt anyone."

"How do you know that?" demanded Toonie, "since you don't even know what a snake is, and have never even seen one before, and you don't have any on It, and all he said was Hssssss anyway?"

"I told you already," replied the Itofit, stretching up to add a touch of haught to his height. "Tails talk just by being there. And this one is definitely there, all coiled and quivering like a pretty vertul and red and yellow banded circus rope with one end sticking straight up, and sticking its tongue out at us on top of that, and the other end slapping on the ground like a thom-thom drummer drumming thom-thoms on his thom-thom drum. But it isn't attached to anyone at all! Very curious indeed. It is the most wonderful talking tail I've ever met."

"That's silly," said Toonie. "It's a snake, not a tail, because a tail has to be attached to something. It just couldn't talk all by itself."

"O, yes it could," continued the Itofit. "Mine does it all the time. Sometimes it says things I'd never dream of saying myself." And then, as though to punctuate his utterance, the Itofit's tail moved out in front of his face, made a rather magnificent flourish, and settled its tip upon his shoulder. "You don't say!" said It.

"What did it say?" asked Toliver.

"It wouldn't say," confided It. "But I know it has something up my sleeve or it wouldn't be so smug about it." With that his tail swished out in front of him, drew three quick circles in the air, and ended up pointing at the snake.

"Hsssssssssssss," said the snake moving its head ever so slightly to look from the Itofit, to Toliver, to Toonie, to Whizlet, to the cat, and the bird, and then everyone all at once, so it seemed to be taking them in, and even tasting them all at the same time. The long, brightly banded body swayed from side to side, beaded its eyes and flicked its tongue, hissed again, and managed to look thoroughly sinister.

"You're scary!" exclaimed Whizlet from safely behind the Itofit's leg.

"Of course I'm scary," said the snake. "All snakes are. We're long and skinny and easy to step on, so if you weren't afraid of us, you'd never look where you were going, and you'd step on us all the time."

"But some of you are poisonous," snapped Toonie, not sure if she was more angry than frightened or maybe both, but definitely sure she knew what she was talking about.

The snake slapped his tail on the ground in no little bit of exasperation. "So are some plants," he said peevishly. "And don't forget insects, and clams too or at least sea shells, not to mention mushrooms and spiders, and even you people have poisoned tongues when you're being stupid."

"You talk too!" exclaimed Toliver who was only now awakening to the fact they were actually conversing with a snake.

"Everything talks," said the snake. Then he rose up two more inches and turned just a trifle to show his best profile. "But few with the eloquence of a forked tongue, darting out beneath hypnotic eyes, supported by an undulating body, slithery torso, and an exclamatory tail, all of which is imbued with scaly elegance, coiled cunning, and serpentine reasoning."

"If you talk like that, you must have a name," continued Toliver, utterly fascinated by the swaying form in front of him.

"Of course I have a name," replied the snake. "I'm Hissofer Booshocks, direct descendant of Adam's amanuensis and Eve's effrontery." He rose a bit higher and turned to look directly into Whizlet's eyes, which were still somewhat larger than usual. "And I'm a king snake which, though certainly true, is something of an unfortunate understatement."

"Don't you miss being attached to a creature?" asked the Itofit who was genuinely curious and very sympathetic.

"Now that you mention it," answered Hissofer Booshocks, "I'd never even thought of it, except, of course, when I'm hungry. But I suppose it could be interesting, and the creature, if he was halfway intelligent, might even learn something." He looked apprisingly at the Itofit and darted his forked tongue in his direction. "Perhaps I should try you."

"Why of course," said the Itofit. "I'd be delighted if you would. We might even learn something from each other."

Hissofer slid over and inspected the Itofit's tail, then wrapped himself three times around it so that the bottom end of his body disappeared into the fur of It's tail while his top half stood out like another, completely separate, tail waltzing with the other.

"Wonderful!" exclaimed the Itofit looking over his shoulder. "I've never had a forked tail before. But now I do and it can even talk to itself to set things straight between us!" And he was so excited he did a little dance around the mossy rock while both tails wove in unison behind him as if they were two Cossacks, arms crossed, kicking at each other. Toliver, Toonie, and Whizlet hurriedly backed up against the bushes at the edge of the grove, Boogie climbed a tree, and Hobnail fluttered to a higher branch from where she called down: "Weird beans. Weird beans!"

When the Itofit finished his dance, he took a little bow with both of his tails poked around his left side staring at each other, then at their audience. He took off his hat, spun it on his finger, and threw it into the air so it twisted and turned over seven times before landing smack on top of his head, just like it was supposed to.

"How interesting," remarked Hissofer, looking up at the tall hat. "You carry a penthouse with you and it even has a circular verandah for sunning oneself in the sunny sometime!" He detached himself from the Itofit's tail, slid around his belly, over his chest, and up to his shoulder, went twice around his neck and once over his ear, all the time inspecting the wonderful hat. He slid around the back of It's head, returned over the other ear, then slipped underneath the hat's brim and disappeared within. A moment later his head poked out of the little flap in front, which the Itofit had to open occasionally to cool his head when he had been thinking so hard he overheated his brain. Hissofer pushed out so he could see over the brim, looked down at the Itofit, then up at Hobnail, and around at the others, and announced: "I like it here. Let's go someplace!"

"Where should we go?" asked Toonie.

"Let's find It's flower," suggested Toliver

"Or at least the other mossy rock I was sitting on," said It. "Because it was close to the flower but far enough away so you couldn't get tricked by it unless you wanted to."

"Over here. This way. That way," said Hobnail letting loose of her branch and swooping down through the glade, then heading off through the trees whistling Mr. Elgar's *Imperial March*.

"No, no, that won't do at all," said the Itofit somewhat dejectedly. "We can't go this way or that way, because there's water everywhere we go."

"No, there isn't," said Toonie. "We came that way and there isn't any water there, or we'd have fallen in."

"And we'd be all wet," added Whizlet who liked to draw all necessary conclusions whenever they explained things that hadn't happened.

"There's water there, too," responded the Itofit with a touch of obstinacy, "because I looked all around before I sat down and there was water everywhere. In fact, that's why I decided to take a nap. There's no water around the bumpergrass glade, so I knew I must be sleeping and dreaming all this, and the only way to wake up was to go back to sleep, so I did just that and woke up here."

"You can't wake up by going to sleep," said Toonie stamping her foot on the ground.

"Or else you'd dream you were awake and then you'd never know if you weren't or not." stammered Whizlet.

"Wait a minute," said Toliver who had been thinking things through without listening to everybody else. "If there was water all around you, you must have been on an island. And if you were on an island, you must have been in the swamp. And if we weren't lost, we'd know where the swamp was and could take you there. But we don't, so you'll just have to remember how you got here, then we'll know where you came from."

"But I can't remember," sighed It. "When I sat down I went to sleep."

"You can't sleep sitting down, or sitting up either," said Toonie who needed her jamies and teddy bear in her own bed with Raggedy Ann on the nightstand and the door open just a crack and the hall light on to go to sleep lying down with two sheets and one blanket and her daisy yellow pillow with the cloud-cherubs on it.

"Of course I can sleep sitting up," responded It. "Can't everyone? I can sleep standing or sitting, lying down or hanging by my tail, eyes open or closed, whiskers either tucked in or out, fur smooth or ruffled, wet or dry."

"Me-ow-ow," said Boogie who'd gone off behind Hobnail and was now some distance beyond the grove and growing impatient with people who said one thing and then talked instead.

"Spitpurrkoff's found something," announced the Itofit, noting the treble of excitement in the cat's call, and he hurried off in that direction, quickly disappearing in the forest.

"We'd better go too," said Toliver.

"We'll just get more lost," said Toonie.

"Maybe we'll get unlost," said Whizlet who was beginning to find the woods almost as interesting as the Cyberspace Outback in *Uncle Aussie's Upside Downunder*.

They had only gone twenty or thirty yards when they caught up with the Itofit who was backing out of some bushes and shaking his tail. When he turned around, he looked very perplexed and his head was shaking just like his tail.

"What's the matter?" asked Toliver.

"Spitpurrkoff found the mossy rock I was sitting on," replied It, scratching his chin with his sixth finger (or second thumb), and smoothing his ruffled eyebrows with his whiskers. "But it is a very peculiar rock indeed. It seems to be rolling uphill". He pushed the branches of the bush aside and pointed behind him with his tail.

"That's not a rock." said Toliver.

"It's not rolling." said Toonie.

"It's a turtle!" exclaimed Whizlet. "And it's running away!"

"Rockbutt. Rockbutt," screamed Hobnail from a branch in the bush.

"What in the world is a turtle?" asked the Itofit who couldn't imagine why anyone would call a rock a turtle, even if it was rolling uphill.

Hissofer Booshocks slithered out of the vent in the Itofit's hat, curled three times around the brim, then peered over the front, first at the turtle, then by turning his head upside down and looking backward right into It's eyes. "A turtle," he said, "is just like me in your hat, except he has his own hat, and he's been in there so long, he's stuck."

"Maybe we can tell where's he's been by where he's going," said Toliver who ran up the hill in front of the turtle and looked back in the direction from which it had come. The commotion, of course, startled the turtle; or rather, since turtles don't startle very easily, alerted it to possible unpleasantness in the vicinity, so he drew his hands and feet and tail and head back inside his shell and closed all his doors.

"What do you see?" asked Toonie.

"More trees," replied Toliver somewhat disappointed since not one of them looked familiar and none of them had water around it.

"Can't we follow his trail?" asked Whizlet who knew one had to do just that to get to the treasure in *Bluebeard's Bestiary*.

"Turtle's don't leave trails," said Toonie. "They just stir everything up so it looks like it always does when it isn't all stirred up."

"Couldn't we just turn him around while he's inside and not looking," asked It, "so when he comes out he'll go back the way he came?"

"He's pretty big," said Toonie.

"We'll probably need sticks," agreed Whizlet.

"And ropes too," said Toliver who pulled a piece of string out of his pocket.

"Turtles like skunk cabbage," said Hissofer Booshocks, "which proves they're reptilian rejects, but there is some right over there." He came six inches off the Itofit's hat brim and pointed to the side with his snout. "If you sprinkle some around his side and down the hill behind him, he'll come out for lunch and turn around all by himself while he's eating."

The Itofit was delighted with his new friend's suggestion. He pulled off a large skunk cabbage leaf and tore it into little pieces, which he carefully put around the turtle just as Hissofer had suggested. And they all sat down to wait. And they waited. And they waited. And they waited, until, finally, a brown snout appeared, followed by a head and a long neck which reached out until the mouth in front opened and plucked up a tidbit of skunk cabbage. And then, as all the sitters watched with bated breaths, the turtle slowly turned about eating each piece as he came to it until he was finished and pointed back down the hill in which direction he lumbered off. The others followed a little bit behind being careful not to frighten him again, and he led them back through the grove where they had all met, and past the other mossy rock (which didn't have as much moss on it as the turtle, but the turtle spent more time in the water so that was understandable), and out the other side, and over roots and under bushes and around trees until he passed close by a whole patch of fresh, new, shinny skunk cabbage which a little breeze caused him to smell and he turned aside and began to graze.

"This won't do at all," said Toliver sadly. "We'll be here all day before he finishes."

"And then he'll probably nap," added Toonie who yawned herself in order to make her point.

The Itofit rubbed his cheek with his tailtip and studied the situation carefully. "Maybe, if we pick that really big, juicy leaf and hold it in front of his nose, we can lure him away from the skunk cabbage patch and back the way he was going."

"He'd see us standing in front of him and go right back inside his shell," said Toonie who didn't want to be a spoilsport but figured she'd better explain that anyway, and when she got everybody's attention, continued: "And Slam-Bang-Boom! He'd close up, and we'd have to sit down and wait all over again."

"We could put it on the end of a stick and hold it in front of him so he would see it but not us," explained Whizlet who remembered that that's what you had to do to get the donkey back in the barn in *Farmyard Fandango*.

"We can tie it on with my string," said Toliver who again pulled a piece of twine from his pocket. "And hang it in front of his nose."

"What a good idea!" exclaimed the Itofit who plucked the big, juicy leaf and found a short stick lying in the grass, and tied the leaf to it with Toliver's string so it hung down like the worm on a fisherman's hook. He crept up behind the turtle and tried to suspend the cabbage leaf right in front of him, but the stick was too short to reach all the way, so he very carefully climbed up on the turtle's shell and sat there dangling the prize in front of the turtle's nose. And while Toliver picked another skunk cabbage leaf and put it in his pocket, just in case, the turtle sniffed the big, juicy leaf in front of his nose. Once. Twice. Three times. Then slo-o-o-owly pushed his neck out further and turned his head to look up on his shell. "You again!" he said to the Itofit. "I thought you dropped off when I climbed over that mossy rock in the grove."

"Oh, I did indeed," said the Itofit who wasn't sure whether the turtle was noticing the beautiful skunk cabbage leaf that was now dangling behind his neck. "But the view from your roof is so nice, I just had to climb back up. You know, it's very smart of you to take your house with you when you go anywhere, because then you're never far from home and can sit on your porch whenever you want to rest."

"And you can't get lost," added Toonie who was very aware they were, and wished she'd brought her house with her, and maybe her mother too.

The turtle turned to see where the other voice was coming from and just then happened to notice the juicy leaf above his nose, so he stretched his neck to take a big bite out of it. But the Itofit pushed the stick forward just a bit so the turtle snapped on air and had to take a step forward to try again. But every time he stretched and snapped, the leaf floated still a mouth-watering moment away and he had to step ahead to try again, and again, and again until he was back on course walking the way he had come that morning, stretching and snapping and stepping onward, with the Itofit on his back, and Toliver, Toonie, and Whizlet behind, and Boogie ranging to the side in case there were any mice lying in ambush, and Hobnail above jumping from branch to branch and humming *Syncopated Rhythm* under her breath. And everybody, except the turtle, were hoping they wouldn't stumble on another patch of skunk cabbage, when suddenly they came out onto the grassy bank of the swamp covered with pink and purple and yellow and red flowers, and even some dandelion seed balls just waiting for a little breeze or someone like Toonie to puff them every which way, even into people's faces. Ahead of them, half fallen into the water, was a huge, broken branch from an oak tree that looked like an old fashioned sailboat except the withered leaves on the smaller branches sticking up made very tattered sails indeed.

"Look out there!" exclaimed the Itofit stabbing his stick like Cyrano de

Bergerac's sword past the fallen branch. "That little island looks like I ought to remember it, and if that's what I smell, it smells very familiar." He was so excited the leaf swung way out in front, then right back, and hit the turtle in the snout. But before the turtle could bite a piece off, it swung forward again, and hung there just out of reach.

"That's not fair!" stammered the frustrated turtle, looking back at the Itofit. "I brought you all this way for nothing more than that little piece of skunk cabbage, but all you do is slap me on the nose with it and then take it away again."

"I'll give it all to you," said the Itofit, still very excited, "if you'll take me back to that island out there…" and he again poked the stick forward to show what he was talking about, and the leaf once more slapped the turtle, but this time in the back of the head because the turtle was now staring angrily at the gesticulating apparition perched on his back, "…where that beautiful flower is growing on the little rise above all that swamp grass and those tangly bog bushes."

"Hrrumph!" coughed the turtle, who swung his head around quickly, or quickly for a turtle but rather slowly for the rest of us, especially Whizlet who could be quick as a wink when he wanted to, and snapped at the leaf, but missed it completely and stepped forward to try again.

"Aweigh we go!" laughed the Itofit as the turtle slipped into the water. "What wonderful creatures you turtles are! Why, you're a houseboat too!"

"What about us?" yelled Toonie from the shore.

"We'd like to go too," called Toliver.

"I can't swim," cried Whizlet, "but I can paddle and kick if somebody'll hold me."

"Oh, my goodness, yes!" exclaimed the Itofit, looking around frantically. "We all started together so we have to stick together or it won't be any fun at all anymore." He had to duck as the turtle went by the huge branch with all its withering leaves hanging out like tattered whatjamacallits, which gave him an idea, and he called back: "Quick! Jump on this log and we'll pull you behind us!"

Hobnail flew down and landed on top of one of the sticking up branches, flapped her wings at the others, and flayed her tail. "Yo-ho-heave-ho, matie!" she cried to the Itofit. "Billow yer mains'ils and flug me scupper. We're off on the briny for treasure and supper!"

The Itofit wrapped his tail around a branch in front (one that poked forward at an angle just like the bowsprit on a Spanish galleon), while the turtle (who was still walking in the shallow water) dug in his hands and feet and pulled harder. The big branch quivered and quaked and shook and rattled, and very slowly started to pull away from the shore.

"Hurry!" cried Toliver running down and jumping onto the log.

"Quick!" yelled Toonie running after him and pulling Whizlet so hard he tumbled over and had to be dragged the last few feet.

"Help!" screamed Whizlet who wasn't at all sure he wanted to be pulled upside down into a swamp, but really had no choice since Toonie was going scatterbrains for battlesprains downhill, and only at the last moment did he manage to grab a tree fern and pull himself upright.

"Me-ow-ow-ow-ouch!" called Boogie who waited behind, quite discombobulated by the water, but determined not let it show. And being a quick thinking and quintessentially cool cat, he sat down to wash under his arm so everyone would know he could be as nonchalant as the Prince of Wales in a public water closet when he had to be.

"Come on!" cried Toonie.

"Hurry up!" called Toliver.

"Run away and hide!" yelled Whizlet who was clinging to his branch with all his might.

And Boogie washed and waited. And hesitated. And me-owed again. And waited some more, until the log was a full three feet from the bank when he knew he'd either have to jump or be left behind, so he widened his eyes, stuck out his fur, puffed up his tail, and ran like a streak to the edge of the water where he launched himself into space, and landed a harrowing moment later on the very end of the log. As soon as he landed, he ran forward through legs and between arms to the tallest branch that was sticking up, and ran up it like a shuttle launch until he got to the very top (which was as far as possible from the water) where he wrapped his arms and his legs and his tail around the branch and pretended he was the captain on the bridge of his ship.

"'Fraidy cat. 'Fraidy cat," screeched Hobnail clutching her topsail perch, which was waving wildly as the log settled further into the water. "Scared o' water. Scared o' water." (Of course, she didn't mention that she was as high as she could get on her branch too, and only really liked water to drink or when Mrs. Mudfinger put out a lukewarm tray of it for her to take her bath in.)

Pulled by the turtle and the Itofit's tail, the log moved slowly out into Swamp Lake weaving its way toward Strangeflower Island, but before it got halfway there, it stopped dead in the water like the hulk of an old derelict foundering at sea. The turtle turned his head and looked at the Itofit just like a conductor on a train would look at someone whose lost ticket he wanted, and no more excuses and no funny business either. "Let me have that leaf right now," he said. "I've gone long enough ferrying you around without even a morsel to sustain me."

"As soon as we get to the island," replied the Itofit not unreasonably, but not too smartly either, "I'll give you the whole thing."

"That's not soon enough," replied the turtle who pulled his head back and began swimming again, but this time straight down into the depths of the swamp.

"Oh!" exclaimed the Itofit as the water came up around the turtle's back and wetted his furry feet; then, "Oh! Oh!" as his trouser cuffs got all wet; and "Oh! Oh! Oh!" as the water passed his knees and wetted his seat and climbed right up past his belly to his chest.

"You're going down!" cried Toliver.

"Hang on!" encouraged Toonie.

"Hold your breath!" gasped Whizlet as the water bubbled up past the Itofit's neck and kept going right over his startled face.

"Burble-glurp!" responded the Itofit as he disappeared until the only thing left above the water was his hat, floating on its wide brim, and Hissofer Booshocks coming out of the flap in front and coiling up on top where he looked like a puff of black, red, and yellow smoke rising out of a chimney.

"Squawk. Squawk. It's sinking. It's sinking," screeched Hobnail pointing a gray wing at the Itofit's tail which was unwinding from the bowsprit branch and being dragged down under the water.

"Hang on!" yelled Toliver hurrying forward.

"We're adrift!" screamed Toonie.

"At least he's not pulling us under," sputtered Whizlet remembering the terrible fate that awaited the unwary in *Octopus Otto's Grotto*.

Before Toliver could get to the front of the log, the Itofit's tail pulled completely free, and only its tip remained quivering above the water. But just before that disappeared behind the rest of him, Hobnail flew down, grabbed it with her feet like a bald eagle (or, actually, a feathery eagle) snagging a salmon, and tried to pull it up again. But the Itofit was too heavy and rather than fly up, poor Hobnail was pulled down until the Itofit's tail was completely under water, and Hobnail's feet too, and then her pretty gray tail feathers, and soon her frantically flapping wings were flailing the air and splashing lots of water too, and she was on the very verge of foundering, when Toliver reached out and grabbed her by the scruff of the neck and managed to keep her out of the water, and almost managed to pull her back, when he started to slip off the log himself, and would have done so except Toonie grabbed his legs, and Whizlet grabbed her ankles, and Boogie ran down from his captain's perch and grabbed Whizlet's shoes with his paw claws while jabbing his feet claws into the log and wrapping his tail around the branch. And everybody held on for dear life. And held on. And pulled. And the Itofit's hat floated away toward the beaver dam with Hissofer coiled on top wondering where he was off to, and if he should swim to shore, or maybe go back and pull with the others. But before he could make up his mind, Hobnail broke free of the water still holding onto the Itofit's tail, and Toliver pulled her back to the log, and the Itofit came up, tail first, until his head came out of the water right under his hat, and he coughed and sputtered and sneezed and took a great big gulp of air and wheezed: "My goodness! That was very wet down there and I didn't even know I was thirsty!"

He floated on his back for a moment, took off his hat and apologized to Hissofer for not warning him of the impending soaking, then clamored aboard the log and shook himself from head to toe to tailtip while holding his hat above himself so as not to get it wet but wetting everyone else except Boogie who saw what was coming (having had a lot of practice with wet dogs) and ran back up to his captain's perch and hid in the leaves.

Off to the side, floating on the water, was the Itofit's stick with Toliver's twine still tied to it and the juicy leaf of skunk cabbage. And while everybody watched, a brown snout appeared below the leaf, opened, grabbed it from the bottom and pulled it down into the depths of the swamp, followed shortly thereafter by Toliver's string and the bobbing stick.

"There goes Toliver's string," sighed Whizlet.

"What can we do now?" asked Toonie who had no idea herself but noticed they were marooned in the middle of Swamp Lake with their motor fallen off and everybody else looking every which way except smart.

Toliver sat down with his chin in his hand, and the Itofit, who was carefully bending his ears forward to wipe the last drops of water off them with his whiskers, said: "I think we should think about it because wonderful things happen when you think about It, especially, if you're far from It and trying to get back home!" He sighed and sat down next to Toliver and began to think.

Hobnail, back on her branch, shook her head and tail, and flapped her wings as hard as she could in order to dry them off, and sent a breeze down on top of all the others.

"That's it!" exclaimed Toliver jumping up and snapping his fingers. "We'll make a sail."

"But there isn't any wind," said Toonie.

"Hobnail's making one," said Whizlet.

"And I can blow," said the Itofit who took a great big breath and blew it out all at once right at the branch where Boogie was still hiding, and all the leaves around him rattled and spun about and he had to dig in with his claws to keep from blowing away. "But we'll need sails."

"We can use my shirt," offered Toliver.

"And mine too," added Whizlet.

"And I can hold my hair out like the cape of a maiden in distress who's out on the moor on a dark and windsome day," said Toonie who quickly stood up and pulled her beautiful long hair out to arms' length on either side of her head so she looked like a bat landing on a cornstalk.

Toliver took off his shirt and tied one sleeve to the branch by his side and held the rest out at arm's length, and Whizlet did the same except he had a short sleeve shirt and couldn't tie it very well."

"We need some thumbnails," explained Toonie.

"I have some thumbtacks, I think." said Toliver reaching into his pocket and rummaging around until he came out with a little board sprinkled with red and blue and green tacks.

Toonie tacked Whizlet's shirt to the branch and he held it out to the other side of the boat and Toonie stood in front holding out her hair, and the Itofit got behind them all and took a deep breath, and Hobnail flew to the branch above the Itofit's head (where Boogie just happened to be still captaining the whole enterprise) and squalled: "Give it up. Let me down. Cat's in the crow's nest. Bird's in the crown." And in the face of the determined parrot, Boogie had to scramble down two branches and hang on with his toenails.

Then Hobnail flapped her wings and the Itofit blew as hard as he could (which was very hard indeed because he had powerful lungs and strong lips which even made the wind whistle as it came through), and Toliver's and Whizlet's shirts billowed out, and Toonie's hair caught the breeze, and the big oak log started to move. Except it wasn't going anywhere in particular except around in a circle.

"I think we should go back to shore," said Toonie being very practical about the whole thing, not to mention a bit nervous, "and wait for the turtle to come back for more skunk cabbage."

"We have to take It to the island first," said Toliver who always thought of other people before himself except when he was tired or going someplace else.

"We're not going anywhere now," moaned Whizlet whose arm was getting tired from holding his shirt out.

"We need somebody to steer," pointed out the Itofit who had been thinking the whole time, "and we're all busy except Spitpurrkoff."

"Me-ouch!" groaned Boogie who knew exactly what the Itofit had in mind and didn't like the idea one little bit.

"You can do it," encouraged It. "And it's the only way we'll get anywhere at all, and if you don't we'll be out here on the water all day and maybe tonight too."

"Me-ow-oh-no!" moaned the cat, who knew the Itofit was telling the truth and was afraid he might never get off the log if he didn't do it. So very reluctantly, he did what the Itofit had in mind (and had explained rather quickly with his tail). He backed down the branch and very, very carefully made his way to the far end of the log, sniffed it thoroughly, then turned around and straddled it, digging all twenty of his claws into the wood, and lowering his tail very, very slowly into the water so he could steer with it like a rudder.

The log straightened out and pointed its bowsprit branch toward Strangeflower Island. Hobnail flapped her wings, and the Itofit huffed and puffed (though not like a bad old wolf but rather like a good ole It), and Boogie growled at the water spraying in his face, and Toliver, Toonie, and Whizlet caught the breeze, and the log lumbered across the water and into the shallows and ran aground on the sandy shore of the island. Boogie pulled his claws out of the wood and his tail out of the water, and ran straight ahead, right through the Itofit's legs and past Toonie who was trying to straighten her hair just so (and without a mirror either) and between Toliver and Whizlet, and up and over the bowsprit branch, and jumped to the shore and ran up the beach until he felt safe enough to roll on his back with his feet and paws stabbing erratically at the sky and his tail swirling circles in the sand.

The Itofit slid off the log and waded ashore while Whizlet jumped off and Toliver stepped off and turned around to help Toonie because he knew boys were supposed to help girls except when they scratched.

"What's that wonderful smell?" asked Toonie who had her hair back in place and liked the feel of the sand underfoot but wasn't yet ready to let go of Toliver's hand.

"It smells like a garden," said Toliver

"Or my grandma's bedroom," said Whizlet.

"It's the flower," said It, "the peculiar flower I came through to get here. See! It's right up there on top of the hill."

And there it was indeed, just where the Itofit was pointing with his finger and his tail and his nose. The flower was standing as innocently as Willie Sutton in a bank vault, standing demurely in a bed of bright green grass with its big, shiny leaves, and its long, thick stalk, and its beautiful, horn-shaped flower, glistening white and blue with streaks of yellow looking like lightning bolts, and pink inside with long, golden pollen covered stamens staring at them like wide little innocent eyes.

"It looks awfully small to swallow someone as big as you," said Toonie who could be both observant and critical when she wanted to.

"I think it shrunk me too," replied the Itofit, "but I'm not sure of that because I wasn't watching me at the time. I was watching everything else which seemed to get bigger and bigger as I disappeared inside."

"What do we do now?" asked Toliver.

"I don't know," admitted the Itofit, "but the last time I didn't know either and look what happened! So maybe if we don't do anything again something wonderful will happen all by itself."

"Yipes-a-doddle!" stammered Whizlet who noticed something that nobody else had seen. "What's that?" His finger was quivering but still managing to point at the bog full of cattails and cranberries behind the Itofit, where what looked like three eyes on periscopes were pushed up through the thick swamp grass. No sooner did everyone turn around, however, than the eyes disappeared and immediately thereafter something streaked through the grass so quickly nobody could see what it was even though everybody saw it racing along the ground. It struck the Itofit just above the ankle and ran up his tunic like an undulating bulge until it stopped between his shoulder blades. A moment later, the three eyes which were at the end of flexible stalks reappeared looking over the Itofit's shoulder, one looking at Toliver, another at Toonie, and the third, as might be expected, directly, and somewhat reproachfully, at Whizlet who'd first spied them, and then, just as everybody noticed them, disappeared again. "You've been torpedoed by a submarine!" exclaimed Whizlet who was in a tizzy because he knew what terrible things could happen when the underwater missiles in *Submarine Sultans from Atlantis* zeroed in on you. "And now it's in your shirt aiming at us!" And he quickly ducked behind Toonie who was the closest thing to duck behind.

"Oh no," said the Itofit reaching over his shoulder and down into his tunic. "It's not a submarine. It's just my friend Snorf, the snigglesnorf I told you about." And with a little coaxing, the Itofit drew forth, or rather encouraged to climb up his hand and arm, a very strange and terribly shy creature which, as the Itofit's arm came forward, wrapped itself around it three or four times, and twisted as it did so, so sometimes its back and sometimes its front were up, and it didn't make any difference because they both looked exactly the same. The Itofit scratched Snorf under its chin, which was either above or below his snout, which was short and pointed and looked exactly like his tail, which was also short and pointed (except pointed in the other direction). His body was as flat and as pretty as a Persian carpet, only long and narrow so it looked like a Persian carpet carpeting a long hallway, and both sides of him were identical and had twenty-four sets of hands-feet along both lengths.

"How did you get here?" exclaimed the Itofit with a bit of astonishment even though, had he thought about it for a moment, he'd have known the answer to his question, or at least guessed it.

The snigglesnorf emitted a cacophony of squeaks and clicks and thrubbles and fluvvers, to which the Itofit answered: "The very same thing happened to me, but I didn't fly through the air except when I fell out of it here and rolled down the hill." The snigglesnorf gesticulated again which it could do very well, in fact better than anybody else because it had so many arms, or maybe they were legs, up and down both sides of its body. "Well, I certainly didn't mean to go anyplace else either," replied the Itofit. "I just sat down on a creature called a turtle which looks all the world like a mossy rock, and took a nap, and when I woke up my new friends here were peering through the bushes at me, and brought me back, or rather the turtle brought me back, but they helped." And then, because he was always polite when he remembered to be, the Itofit introduced Snorf to Toliver and Toonie and Whizlet and Boogie and Hobnail and was trying to remember who else, when the snigglesnorf glurped excitedly, dashed up his sleeve and came out at the throat where all three of his eyes were staring at the brim of the Itofit's hat over which a very curious Hissofer Booshocks was staring back.

"And that is Hissofer Booshocks who's older than Adam but has never eaten an apple in his whole life, and he likes to scare people, so don't let him frighten you, because he's really nice, and make friends with him instead 'cause he's long and skinny too."

While the snake and the snigglesnorf eyed each other warily, Toonie, who'd already had quite enough adventure for one day, thank you, sighed a bit louder than she had to, but just loud enough to get everybody's attention. "Well," she said rather more casually then she felt, "I suppose we should be getting home now."

"Home?" exclaimed Whizlet who realized they were only at Level 2 or 3 of at least a 10 Level game and nobody in his right mind would turn it off until they got to Level 7 or 8, and then only if groblets were threatening to come out of the machine and bite your kneecaps.

"We have to get It home first," announced Toliver. "And Snorf too. So lets everybody think about it and see what we can decide."

"I suppose we should talk to the flower," said the Itofit after a moment's reflection, "and find out what heshe thinks about all this."

"Flowers can't talk," stammered Toonie, seeing her opportunity to escape slipping away and herself being hornswaggled at the same time. "They just smell pretty and drop petals on the floor."

"Of course they can talk," persisted the Itofit. "How else would we know how to cook them or make salads or tie bouquets for pretty Isettes? On It, flowers and us do all kinds of nice things for each other and you certainly can't do nice things for one another if you don't talk it over beforehand...unless, of course, it's a surprise party."

"Pretty flower. Pretty flower," swooned Hobnail who loved its fragrance and began singing a madrigal as she fluttered past Boogie who was still rolling on his back and thumping his tail on the ground. She circled the plant once looking at its sweetly smiling flower (If flowers can be said to smile sweetly just because their petals tilt upward at the ends) whose little eyes were looking at her, but as she came around the second time, she seemed to stop in midair. Her wings were still flapping, in fact she even flapping them harder and faster, but she wasn't going anyplace at all, neither up nor down nor to either side. She was completely at a standstill (or flystill) in the air. Her pretty tail feathers were toward the flower and she was looking down the hill at the others with a very peculiar expression on her face.

"Hobnail's learned a trick," cried Toonie.

"She's flying backwards," agreed Whizlet who noticed the bird was now drifting away from them and floating toward the yawning mouth of the flower, even though she appeared to be trying very strenuously to go the other way.

"And she shrinking!" exclaimed Toliver.

"I think she's in trouble," cried Toonie who noticed Hobnail's beak was chattering even though she wasn't saying anything, and her large eyes were getting bigger and bigger even though she was getting smaller and smaller.

But before anybody could do anything at all, poor Hobnail zoomed backward right into the open mouth of the flower, and just managed to squawk "Pirates!" before she was swallowed up. A great big bulge appeared at the top of the flower's stem which moved down rather quickly, getting smaller and smaller all the time until, just as it reached the first shiny green leaf, it disappeared completely. The flower burped, wiped its petals with a leaf, and turned its dreamy little eyes on the rest of them.

"The flower ate Hobnail!" exclaimed Toliver.

"Vacuumed right up," agreed Whizlet who then make a sound like his mother's Hoover upright: "Whoosh! Quick as a wink!"

"You awful weed!" stammered Toonie rushing up the hill at Boogie who, still on his back, had caught the whole episode upside down over his head, and didn't know what to make of it that way either. "You won't get my cat!" She grabbed for Boogie but he, startled by her running at him, twisted quickly to his feet and started to run away. Toonie caught him by the back left leg, but fell on her face as she did so. Boogie, of course, tried to pull away (since cat's can't stand to have people pull their legs) and noticed that someone was helping him, but too late realized it was the strange flower sucking him toward it. Since she was flat on her stomach with both hands above her head, Toonie couldn't dig in her heels, but refused to let go because she was loyal to the end (or maybe just stubborn), so she was pulled along too.

"You can't steal my cousin!" screamed Whizlet, who ran up the hill and grappled Toonie's shoe. But he was already too late. The flower bent to the ground, sucked harder, and gobbled the cat before he knew what was happening, then quick as another wink pulled Toonie in too, and Whizlet behind her. Three bulges appeared in the stem, one right after the other, all of them getting smaller and smaller until they too disappeared completely.

Toliver charged up the hill like the Light Brigade (the ill-fated Light Brigade, that is, of which he knew nothing although he'd have been right there in the thick of things if he had) and tried to grab the flower by the stem. He wanted to squeeze it really hard and force it to cough up his friends, but the flower pulled back and burped, not once but three times, in his face. And before he could burp back or say anything else either, he felt his hair standing straight up on his head, his head being pulled up on his neck, his whole body being straighten out, his feet leaving the ground, heels first then toes, and the whole kit and caboodle being sucked into the flower with an ear-rattling 'whoosh!'

"Gulp!" exclaimed the flower as another bulge appeared in its stem, shrinking to nothing as it disappeared among the leaves.

The Itofit watched all these events in amazement. Snorf retreated to his back with only one eye peeking over his shoulder, and Hissofer Booshocks slid out of his flap and wrapped himself round and round around the Itofit's hat as tightly as he could until he encircled it five and a half times and held on for dear life. He stuck his forked tongue out and hissed at the flower (as a professional courtesy) then asked the Itofit: "Where has everybody gone?"

"I don't know," said It, "but they've certainly gone somewhere, or maybe sometime, and definitely somehow. Perhaps we ought to discuss it man to man, or It to it, with the plant." And he started up the hill.

"I don't think this is a very good idea…" began Hissofer, but before he could explain why it wasn't, he felt a peculiar force pulling on his nose. He hissed again and squeezed the Itofit's hat even tighter but that didn't do any good because the hat began to turn on It's head. Hissofer felt his long, slender (incredibly handsome, lithe, and tenacious, or so he maintained to all his snake friends) body start to unwind like a kite string on a spool. The hat spun faster and faster and Hissofer rolled out longer and longer until he flew off like an arrow right at the strange flower who caught him with the finesse of a shortstop fielding a line drive. He was so skinny there wasn't any bulge at all in the stem and the flower seemed merely to slap its lips and utter a very throaty, "Slurp!"

"That wasn't very nice," said the Itofit crossly shaking his finger and his tail and sixteen of his upper whiskers at the flower. "And it's all my fault for letting them be nice to me, so hang on Snorf! We've got to help them!" With that he lunged forward and dove headfirst into the startled flower who gulped anyway and swallowed him whole, whereupon he quickly became a bulge in the upper stem, moving downward, and becoming smaller and smaller and smaller.

The flower burped, smiled, and settled back to enjoy a well-earned sun bath, but just then a bubble appeared in the water by the beached log, followed by a nose, a mossy covered shell, and a pointed tail. As the turtle came up for air, he sissssed (as turtles do when they exhale) and pulled himself onto shore, wondering about the strange group of creatures he had tricked into feeding him a luscious skunk cabbage leaf. And he was also hoping that the flustered furry person (who needed to ride everywhere) would take back his stick (which was dangling inconveniently in front of the turtle's snout) and maybe even pull the tasteless piece of string out of his throat.

Toliver had not felt himself getting any smaller but he did notice the horn of the flower getting bigger and bigger until it looked the mouth of Mammoth Cave, and every bit as gaping and scary, and then he was inside spinning about and shooting ahead like a rocket to the moon (except he was going down instead of up.) At first the flower had been white and pink with blue streaks and yellow blurs (which were probably specs of pollen in his eyes) which smelled like wildflower honey and tasted like candy, but when he looked again it was all dark purple with twinkling lights like little stars rushing past him, and it seemed to be singing because he heard voices, or what he thought might have been voices if he could have heard the words a little better, and other pretty sounds like whippoorwills and morning doves cooing among themselves with violins and saxophones in the background played by people he couldn't see, and smelling like salt air by the foggy ocean and damp forest freshness with mushrooms growing thickly in the entrance of a humid cave into which he wasn't going but coming out of, and it was getting lighter everywhere and the dark purple was becoming pink and white again, and just as he saw the first blue streak streaking past, he popped out of the flower into a very peculiar world. But before he could really see how peculiar it was, he saw Toonie and Whizlet on top of whom he tumbled, and off to the side was Boogie with very large eyes staring at him with all his hair (and his tail too) standing up. And sitting on a something that might have been a branch behind the cat was Hobnail preening her pretty tail feathers as if she hadn't a care in the world, if this was, in fact, the world. And hearing a whoosh above him, Toliver turned in time to see Hissofer Booshocks shooting out of the flower like Moses' staff and swizzling down through the bright green, velvety grass (if it really was grass) and sliding to a stop some feet ahead. Above Toliver's head, Toonie and Whizlet suddenly saw another head poking out of the flower with furry ears and whiskers and purple eyes which didn't seem startled so much as very, very curious like whatever was behind them was thinking very, very hard and maybe even cogitating about It's trip home. The flower bent down to earth, if that's what it could be called, and the Itofit with Snorf peeking out of his tunic front, rolled onto the ground doing a somersault so he ended on his feet by Hissofer's tail.

"Well, my goodness," said the Itofit, standing up with great dignity and shaking himself just a bit while wiping his forehead with the end of his tail. "Welcome to It. How nice of you to come."

"Thank you," said Toliver getting to his feet.

"Where are we?" wailed Toonie.

"Wow!" exclaimed Whizlet who hoped this might be the gorgeous grimbled garden of *Wizard's Paradise,* but suspected it was probably someplace else.

"We're back to It," replied the Itofit, answering the only question directed at him. "Right where I was this morning when I discovered this brand new, completely different, strange flower and decided to sniff it."

"There are no brand new, completely different, strange things," said Toonie crossly as she let Toliver pull her up anyway. "Everything's been here forever, otherwise it would be scary, and nobody would know what to make of anything." And then for good measure: "And we haven't changed either."

"Oh no, we haven't," replied the Itofit. "Or if we have, at least we've changed from something else and gotten better and better all the time."

"Or worser and worser," opined Whizlet who remembered what his mother had said when he broke her flower vase after he broke her porcelain pitcher which happened on the afternoon of the morning he broke her teacup.

"Or just different," said Toliver who didn't like to waste time arguing about things that weren't important.

"Look!" exclaimed Toonie pointing at the flower, which was beginning to wiggle and shake as a long narrow, transverse bulge followed by a short fat bulge worked their way up the stem. The plant weaved, then waved; then started to shake its flower violently. Toliver, Toonie, and Whizlet jumped away and ran to the side of the Itofit while Boogie meowed loudly but didn't move because everything around was so strange he didn't trust anyplace except where he was, and Hobnail stopped preening her tail and stared at the flower which coughed and wheezed and finally, with a loud Ker-plopp, spit out what was caught in its throat.

"There's my string," exclaimed Toliver who always knew his things even when somebody else had appropriated them (or even when meeting them for the first time, for that matter.)

"And there's my stick," added It.

"And there's the turtle," cried Toonie pointing to a pretty carapace which had landed upside down at their feet whose owner was trying to turn himself over with his snout but couldn't do it because of the stick stuck in his mouth.

"Dumb brute. Dumb brute," called Hobnail from the safety of her perch.

"Am not either," growled the turtle. "Just momentarily inconvenienced by circumstances."

"If you let us have my stick," said the Itofit coming close to him, "we can use it to topple you right side up."

"And I can get my string back," added Toliver who hated to lose anything that was his, and sometimes other people's things too, but not as much.

"Take it," said the turtle opening his mouth. "But first use it to chase away that garrulous, gossipy parrot."

"Belly up. Belly up. Soup in the half shell. Time to sup," gloated Hobnail who knew that nobody was going to swish at her with a stick, and if the turtle tried, she could fly circles around him.

Toliver took the stick and carefully pulled his string out of the turtle's throat, then slid the stick under the round shell. He and the Itofit pushed on the stick while Toonie pushed on him and Whizlet pushed on her, and with a loud flop-plop! the turtle popped over, right side up. As Toliver rolled up his string and put it in his pocket, Toonie picked up the stick and shook it at the flower, which had developed a nasty case of the hiccups. "Serves you right," she said, "and I hope you have indigestion too." Then, seeing the flower was in no condition to retaliate, added: "I ought to bop you on the bazooka!" She had no idea what a bazooka was but it sounded too good not to say, so she said it, and stuck her tongue out too.

The plant lifted its flower and pointed it to the sky just as if it was sticking its nose up. It hiccuped again, then wheezed and burped but managed to ignore her completely while doing so.

"Don't make the flower angry," said Toliver, touching Toonie's arm so she'd stop shaking the stick in such a threatening manner. "It's the only way we have to get back home."

"Oh, my goodness" gasped Toonie coming to her senses, then, smiling crookedly at the plant, continued demurely. "I'm not trying to make the pretty flower angry, I'm trying to help it by scaring away its hiccups."

While this was going on, the turtle stuck out its neck and inspected its shell for scraps and bruises, then looked at the Itofit who he suspected was the source of his troubles. "Do you have another skunk cabbage leaf for me?"

"I forgot to bring one," explained It. "I should have put some in my pocket but we were so busy, it slipped my mind."

"Not very thoughtful of you," replied the turtle. "I suppose I'll just have to fend for myself."

Hissofer, who felt like he'd been chiropracticly crinkled, rolled himself into his accustomed coil, one vertebra at a time, hissed twice to check his breathing, then slithered to the Itofit and started winding up his leg. "Your hat is on backwards," he said.

"So it is," replied It, who turned his hat around so the snake could peek out the front while safely seated on his head.

"Me-ow-wow!" said Boogie who had decided to investigate the strange bush Hobnail was sitting on and discovered it smelled like a cross between a mouse and a piece of cheddar cheese and had bite sized cones hanging there for the taking.

"Don't you run off," said Toonie turning to the cat. "We have to go home right this minute and you can't stay here without us no matter how good it smells."

"Can't we stay just a little while?" asked Whizlet who was sure they were wrapped up inside some game he'd never played before but wanted to more than anything else he could think of.

"No, we can't," said Toonie firmly. "We said we'd help It, and we did, and now we have to go home."

"We could go to the It's-Fine for a glass of spinach and parsnip tea," said the Itofit who could see that Toonie was upset, and knew the perfect tonic for her and precisely where to go to get it. He was not only being polite (he knew, of course, how to be a very good host when people dropped in on him, especially when he dropped in on them first) but he also wanted to show off his new friends to his very best friend. "And you could see our talapalodion tree basket house, and Is will be there."

"Who is Iswill?" asked Whizlet who often got his tenses mixed up himself.

A serene look came over the Itofit's furry face. "Is is my special friend," he said, "who plays the cloth harp when I play the twistle, and likes to intertwine tails, and wosker whiskers, and wonderful things like that."

"Is that your talapalodion?" asked Toliver who wasn't listening very carefully and only caught the strange word the Itofit had said. He was staring at a deeply polished and beautifully crafted something or other made of reeds and bamboo with brass frets and little flexible tubes hanging off which was hung by its strap from a branch of a lovely old bojum tree (or something that looked like a lovely old bojum tree, a tall orange-blue carrot with only its nose stuck in the ground and wiggly arm-branches hanging off every which way and a marvelous crown of ferns on top.)

"Oh no," replied the Itofit, "that's my twistle, but we can play if for you if you'd like to hear us." And no sooner had he said that then his tail raised up and twirled like a lasso above him until the knot on the end slammed down and bonked him on the top of the head with a resounding Bonka-onka-n'ka-ka-a echoing like a happy bull frog calling to the moon.

"We?" asked Toonie just a bit apprehensively because she felt like something peculiar was watching her although she didn't know who, what, how, or why but did know the where and when were right here and now.

"I can play it alone," continued It, "but it sounds better and it's much more fun when all my friends play too."

"Your friends," asked Toonie looking about carefully but feeling quite relieved that whoever was watching were at least on their side.

Whizlet ran over to where the twistle was hanging. He looked at it curiously for a moment then reached up. He was just going to touch it, not take it down since he wasn't sure how he was supposed to hold it anyway, but just as his finger was about to run itself over the polished surface, something whizzed through his legs, up the bojum, grabbed the twistle's strap, and whisked it out of reach three bojum-branches up.

"Yipes-a-doddle!" cried Whizlet leaping backward, and he would have said it again except he was swallowing so hard he couldn't. Above him, Snorf had wrapped part of himself around the branch, the rest of him hanging down and holding the twistle lovingly in fourteen sets of upper (or maybe lower) handsfeet. His snout was pointed at Whizlet and his eyes, two of which were pushed out on their stalks on top of his head, and one below, were looking every which way but back, and his mouth was either grinning or frowning depending on whether the top was on top or the other way round, but when he chortled and licked his snout with his furry tongue, Whizlet could see he was grinning and figured he'd maybe found a new friend, albeit one he'd have to keep a wary eye on. To prove the point, Snorf lowered the twistle down by its strap just like bait on a fish line. And Whizlet, who could never pass up well-crafted bait, reached for it again, and once more the snigglesnorf pulled it out of reach, but this time, while Whizlet was all stretched out, Snorf did a somersault between his arms, ran back down the bojum, and out between his legs.

"Yipes-a-doddle' yelled Whizlet again, this time jumping up in the air and turning around at the same time so he wouldn't lose sight of the snigglesnorf who was streaking along the ground on his bottom handsfeet while holding the twistle aloft with the upper ones. He ran straight to the Itofit, up his tail, and didn't stop until he was on It's shoulder, looking over at Whizlet with a very pleased expression on his face. But as the Itofit took the twistle from his friend, Snorf's expression changed, his snout wiggled, and all three eyes swiveled up to gaze at Hissofer who was hanging down from the Itofit's brim and tasting the air around the snigglesnorf's head with his forked tongue. Poor Snorf, who for some reason had forgotten all about Hissofer, was so startled he did a backflip off the Itofit's shoulder, curled up into a ball that seemed to roll down It's arm (although it was really grabbing handsfeet of cloth as it went), and back up his sleeve as quick as a sneeze. A moment later, three eyes accompanying a snout, followed by the rest of a snigglesnorf face, appeared in the v-neck of It's tunic and peered cautiously upward at what appeared to be a tail hanging off the Itofit's hat, but a tail which had two fascinated eyes and a forked tongue flashing from its many-toothed mouth.

The Itofit tucked in his chin so he could look down at Snorf and tenderly stroked his snout. "I told you Hissofer's job was to scare people so they remember who they really are, but Spitpurrkoff told me we can soothe the savage snake with music, so as soon as the balooms come…"

"What are balooms?" asked Toliver.

"Well, let's see," replied the Itofit, "balooms are…how can I explain it? Well, among other things, they're incurable romantics and incomparable twistle players, and there was a whole flock of them here this morning." Snorf gurbled excitedly, causing It to look past the bojum trees where the snigglesnorf was pointing with his snout. "Why there they are now. They've been hiding in the bumpergrass since they saw what the flower did to us this morning, but they'll come if I…" And he lifted one end of his twistle to his mouth and sounded a call that floated out over the bojums like a fragrant morning mist. A moment later a flock of very strange, unbird-like creatures fluttered into the clearing. They looked like feathery pufferfish with wings and brightly colored tails but instead of having mouths or beaks, they had long, rolled up proboscises with which they were able to drink from deep flowers and through which they could snort, honk, and twizzle a whole medley of reed-like sounds. The Itofit's twistle was fashioned like elaborate panpipes with seven hollow tubes arcing out horizontally and a long neck with taut strings and frets hanging straight down, and a bugle-like mouthpiece which swiveled to blow air through the tubes, and the strap of course, and under each tube was a long, flexible spout going off in every direction. All the tubes had finger holes on top, and as the Itofit adjusted his fingers and thumbs to fit them, and put the mouthpiece to his lips, Snorf arranged himself on his chest so he was hanging on with one set of handsfeet and using the other to tune and strum the strings, and seven beautiful balooms, plump with excitement (and a good deal of air they'd sucked up) detached themselves from the flock, fluttered over, and attached their proboscises to the spouts coming from the bottom of the twistle.

The music started all at once. It sounded like a miniature chamber orchestra playing a sonata for flute, strings, and woodwinds, and was so utterly lovely that poor Hobnail, who had been looking at the contraption with the critical eye of the true professional, gasped and immediately joined in, not missing a beat, or intruding her own voice too loudly, but sang a high treble accompaniment which caused the rest of the flock of balooms to fritter and whizzle with excitement. The Itofit smiled happily and Snorf, who was clinging to the fur of It's chest through his tunic with one set of handsfeet, very delicately pressed the frets and plucked, strummed, and bowed the strings of the twistle with the others. One of its eyes watched the Itofit; another, the balooms; and the third, though dancing occasionally from Whizlet to Toonie to Toliver, mostly kept itself affixed to Hissofer Booshocks who was hanging off the Itofit's hat brim and rhythmically swaying with the music, completely hypnotized and oblivious of everything else.

Nor was Hissofer alone in his ecstasy, for the beautiful, happy music was the nicest the children had ever heard and caressed their ears as though it was cool lemonade on thirsty tongues. Notes seemed to talk to each other and different tunes arose from the interweavings of the chords, all forming an enchanting melody which made everybody's heart thump a little more joyfully, and Toliver sat right down with his mouth open, and Toonie put both hands to her cheeks, and Boogie slid over on his belly then rolled to his back (because he could listen better that way and even thump his tail whenever he felt a drum was called for.)

"Oops!" said Whizlet.

"Sh'ssh," said Toonie who often felt responsible for Whizlet's behavior.

"But it looks like…"

"Later." whispered Toliver putting his finger to his lips.

"But the turtle…" persisted Whizlet pointing up the hill behind the Itofit who was completely lost in the joy he felt playing the twistle.

"Sh'sh!" said Toonie again, even more emphatically, but being a curious person she couldn't help but look where Whizlet's quivering finger was pointing.

"No!" she screeched. "Stop!"

Her exclamation was so dramatic that Toliver sat up and turned to see what was disturbing her and the Itofit stopped playing right in the middle of a crescending arpeggio. "Don't." yelled Toliver

"Oh no!" exclaimed the Itofit so fervently that the balooms all detached themselves from the twistle and fluttered away and Snorf stopped in mid strum.

"Hisssss," added Hissofer loudly, hoping to scare the turtle but didn't because turtles aren't afraid of snakes in any case, first because they are cousins, and second because fangs only bounce off their shells, and forked tongues only tickle.

"Yipes-a-doddle!" said Whizlet. Then, shaking his head: "Clean as a twistle."

"Oh no!" wailed Toonie who was staring wide-eyed at the turtle who had just that moment bitten through the stem of the strange flower and was now champing it down right to the top of its pretty pistils.

"How awful," said Toliver.

"Me-ouch!" agreed Boogie.

"Stranded. Stranded," cried Hobnail. "Dumb turtle. Dumb turtle. Ate our boat. Left a hurtle!"

"Oh! What will we do now?" wailed Toonie who shook Whizlet by his shirt collar. "Why didn't you say something!"

"Chomp, chomp, chomp." said the turtle.

"The flower twisted and gurgled and, just as the last of it disappeared down the turtle's throat, gasped. "Well now. I wonder where I'm going?"

"Come back," shouted Toonie who ran up to grab the turtle by the neck, but the turtle pulled its head inside and slammed its door in both of their faces.

Toonie sat down in front of the turtle, which now looked very much like a mossy rock, and she began to weep. "How will we ever get home? What can we do? What will Mrs. Mudfinger say when she finds out we took Hobnail?"

The Itofit came over and sat down next to Toonie. He put his arm around her shoulders and his tail around her waist. "It's all right," he said. "Everything's always all right, even when it isn't."

"But how will we ever get home again?" wailed Toonie, who turned and buried her face in the warm, silky fur of It's chest.

"Well, let me see," said the Itofit scratching his brow with a long silver whisker. "I suppose we could go talk to the Wun-dur-phul about it."

"Who's the Wun-dur-phul?" asked Toliver.

"The Wun-dur-phul is our en-cyl-clo-morph," replied It. "And he knows everything about everything that can be spoken about in one syllable words like up and down, good and bad, here and there, right and wrong, yes and no, you and me."

"That won't work with the flower," said Toliver who said flow-er very carefully and held up two fingers.

"Hmmmm, you're right," responded It. "Perhaps we could call it a rose, just for today."

"But then how could we tell it about the tur-tle eating it?" said Toonie with a loud sniff.

"Or even that we're from some-place dif-fernt," added Whizlet.

"Oh my, that would be difficult, I mean hard, for him." said It. "Perhaps we should go to our talapalodion tree house instead and see what Is is ising about and what she thinks we can do. I'm sure we all need a cup of spinach and parsnip ice-erb tea in any case."

"Yuk!" said Whizlet.

"It's not far," said It. "And we can always come back when we remember what we're supposed to do."

"Do you have ice cream?" asked Whizlet perking up.

"Oh my yes. Is makes the best amaranth and rutabaga ice-yam you've ever tasted, but spinach and parsnip tea is much nicer than ice-yam in the morning, even if the ice-yam has some turnip topping on it and maybe a dab of dandelion."

"How far is your toe-tap-a-lode-on-it?" asked Toonie who wasn't too excited about spinach and parsnip tea (or ice-yam either), but always liked to know where she was going when someone gave her directions, and how long it would take to get back if she got lost.

"Not far at all," replied the Itofit. "It's through the bojum forest, and around the bumpergrass patch, and over the hill to the meadows of Kamirill, and…and…well…just follow me." And he led them off past the bojum with the balooms twittering about in front and Snorf clinging to his chest fur with all his eyes keeping a close watch on Hissofer who was hanging from It's hat and sticking his tongue out in return.

"Gribble-growl-grump-grump," said Snorf to the dangling tongue.

"Hiss-hiss-bah-siss-siss," replied the snake.

"Cantankerous caterpillars," screeched Hobnail from ten feet above Toliver's head.

"Me-owl-growl-spit-spit," added Boogie who had nothing better to say but knew he had to say something just to keep his teeth in the conversation.

The Itofit stopped so quickly that Toliver almost ran into him, and Toonie, who was keeping an eye on Hobnail, ran into him, and Whizlet, who was walking ahead but looking backward at the turtle who was wandering off in the other direction, ran into her. "We can't go anywhere together if we aren't all together," said It, "so we have to take care of this situation before we take another step. Besides, it's so much more fun to be friends than anything else that we should all make sure we are all the time." He took off his hat and held it in front of his face so Hissofer was looking right into his eyes (but would have looked off and up to the left if his eyes worked that way, and maybe even whistled a little song) and Snorf squiggled back into his fur hoping to hide a bit. "Get on my arm," he said to Hissofer, and his tone of voice was so commanding that Hissofer unwound himself from the hat and crawled up It's arm to the elbow, then down and under and back until the front of him passed It's wrist and projected six inches ahead of his hand. "Get on my other arm," he said to Snorf who wiggled around under his tunic and moved like a liquid bulge up to his shoulder and down the sleeve on his other arm until he came out at It's wrist and, gauging how much of Hissofer was projecting from the other hand, stuck six inches of himself out too. The Itofit brought both of his arms toward each other until the snake and the snigglesnorf were snout to snout. Hissofer stayed as cool as a cool blooded creature can but instead of flicking his tongue out at Snorf, which he couldn't do without hitting the snigglesnorf in the face, merely folded it back to touch his own forehead; and Snorf contented himself with his most baleful look, letting his three eyes stand out as far as they could on their stalks and stare Hissofer's two eyes down. The Itofit pushed his two arms closer together so the bottom of Hissofer slid over the top of Snorf who grabbed hold with his first four sets of handsfeet. He squeezed just a little, not enough to hurt but enough to let Hissofer know he could if he wanted to, and for the first time in his life found his hands completely encircling another creature. He was quite amazed by the scaly skin because he'd never known anyscalybody before (except flish which were always so wet they slipped away before he could hold them) and he could actually feel the little vertebrae in Hissofer's back! Hissofer, for his part, was not too happy to be thrust atop a creature who had enough feet to step on him forty or fifty times in a single pass, but when he felt the strong little handsfeet massaging his back (which was still sore from his much too stiff flight through the flower), why, it was so very nice he decided not to bite him after all. In fact, he slid ahead to let some more of the handsfeet at him, while Snorf, who was enjoying the fine textures of Hissofer lithe body more than he ever thought he would, also slipped ahead, pulling himself out as if Hissofer was a rope he was tugging on which was tugging back. A few inches later, Hissofer decided to check Snorf's underneath (or overneath if Snorf was in fact upside down to begin with) so he slid around to that side, found more willing handsfeet there, then came back to the top, and then did it again and again because it was so much fun, and gave the snigglesnorf a nice firm squeeze to let him know how he could massage too. Since he was now wrapped around Snorf several times, he actually squeezed him all along his body which Snorf discovered was one of the nicest things that he'd ever felt. Since they were now both well out in front of the Itofit's arms, It bent over and put them by his feet where they continued to squeeze and massage and twist and roll along the ground.

"Sniggle-sniggle-snorf-snorf," said Snorf happily.

"Hiss-a-tickle-he-he-he," responded Hissofer, who was delighted with what was happening. He rolled on his back with his head lolling off one end of the snigglesnorf and his tail hanging from the other. Snorf's handsfeet moved very rapidly with the snake between them going back and forth, first to the right, then to the left, just like he was a harmonica and Bob Dylan was playing *Mr. Jones* on his ribs.

Hobnail took this opportunity to land on the Itofit's shoulder (which she'd been wanting to try for some time now) and began whistling *The Chairman Dances* to the spectacle on the ground which would probably have gone on as long as that interminable (although intricate and marvelously redundant) piece of music, except the Itofit leaned down, picked up both creatures, and disentangled them. "I'm glad you see what I mean," he said to the two now fast (though momentarily separated) friends, "because it's so much nicer for everybody this way and, who knows, we might even need each other sometime sooner than we think."

A moment later Snorf was back on his shoulder happily saying "snorf-snorf-snorf-sniggle-snorf" to Hissofer, who was curled around the Itofit's hat brim and, taking the Itofit at his word, was sniffing the air in every direction with his forked tongue (which was also his sniffer of course) and seeing further than anyone else because he was higher up.

"Well, my goodness," exclaimed Toonie as they started off again in a much happier fashion, "if a snake and a snigglesnorf can become friends so easily, I should think people could too!"

Whizlet had run ahead to the top of the hill beyond the bumpergrass patch and was looking out across the meadows beyond. "What's that?" he called back to the Itofit while pointing ahead to something that nobody else could yet see.

"I don't know," replied It. "But if it's where you're pointing it must be the meadows of Kamirill and the mazeberry labyrinth or our It's-Fine and the talapalodion tree which are beyond them. "What does it look like?"

"I'm not sure," responded Whizlet scratching his head. "It might be the floating castle in *Space Gardens* or it could be the wicked witch's bubble-bound dreamscape in *Snow Blue's Ice Bubbles* except I don't see any groblets guarding it."

Toonie ran up the hill to where Whizlet was standing because she never like to be second when something was happening for the first time or people were opening presents. "Oh, that's beautiful!" she gushed. "I love your to-lip-a-luv-on-em. What is it?"

Ahead, across a lovely little stream that meandered through the meadows and beyond a labyrinth of low, flowering berry bushes, was the tallest, and gnarliest, and prettiest tree any of the children had ever seen, either in the woods or computer games about rain forests or elf-glens, which seemed to be growing out of a marvelous rock garden of great stone boulders and slabs of cliff-face, and towering high above them, with huge old branches, and deep green leaves hiding bowers and flowery recesses from which vines hung down and sprays of blossomed stalks pushed up, and what looked like roofs and terraces of a wonderful house. And before any of them could take in the whole marvel, the Itofit said simply: "That's our friend, the talapalodion tree, with the It's-Fine around its trunk which the Most Able It, who was my grandfather's grandmother's great great grandfather, built when he came back from a far away and secret place called Arigonia which is as far as he got in his search for Ludgordia. And up in the branches is our talapalodion tree basket house, and I think I can already hear Is playing her cloth harp."

Everybody stopped to listen but nobody could hear as well as the Itofit (whose wiggly ears were also very large and good at catching faraway sounds) and all they heard was the breeze through the bojums, and before anyone could be sure whether or not that was a cloth harp, Hobnail began singing Mr. Shumann's *Fairy Tale Pictures* and they started off again. The meadows were filled with spring flowers and the trail they were following led to a little stone bridge, which went halfway across a stream. It stopped at a large rock in the middle and the rest of the way wasn't a bridge at all but stepping-stones placed here and there in the water so a person had to jump from one to the next until getting to the other side.

Toonie held back a step. "Are there trolls under the bridge?" she asked.

"Of course," replied It, but when he saw Toonie whiten three shades and miss half a step, he hasten to add: "But they're very nice trolls. And they sleep through the morning so we'll have to be careful not to disturb them. But we can say 'hello' to another marvelous friend."

And before Toliver could inquire who that might be, or Toonie could say she'd just as soon they didn't disturb anybody at all, the Itofit called out: "Good morning, Kamirill."

He stopped, seeming to listen, so everyone else stopped too and were very quiet. All anyone could hear was the happy burbling of the water over the rocks (and it lapping on the sandy beach below the bridge as it passed), and the swoosh of some curious birds who were wheeling above and who Hobnail had been assessing rather carefully for some time now, and the buzzing of busy bees who were engaged in making water lily honey from the nectar of the flowers in a backwater below the bridge, and the 'chirp-chirp-chirp' of a cricket-like something under a nearby rock, and the 'glump-glump-ga-lump' of a frog among the flowers, when all of a sudden these sounds seemed to come together as a single sound which sounded very much like it said: "Good morning everyone."

"What was that!" exclaimed Toliver.

"Why that was Kamirill," replied the Itofit.

"Who's Kamirill," asked Toonie who was so enthralled by the lovely voice that she quickly decided that even the trolls of It might be worth meeting, perhaps later.

"Kamirill is the stream," continued It, "or rather, the waterspirit of the stream which lives everywhere the stream meanders and takes care of all its flish and flowers, and even looks after the trolls while they're sleeping, and loves it when Is and I come down for picnics and swim in its deep places."

"Sounds like the Whispering Wizard's will-o-the-wisp," said Whizlet as he ran up on the bridge and peered over the side at the flowing blue water below. "He must be around here somewhere."

"Kamirill is everywhere the stream is," said It. "And heshe loves to show us hisher secrets and tell us wonderful things, and even splash us when we're not looking."

"Oh look," cried Toonie who ran across the bridge and jumped from stepping stone to stepping stone behind a beautiful (and very large) wonderfully colored butterfly.

"That is a royal-regal flutterby," explained It as he followed along, "and if we follow her she'll lead us home because she's looking for Is' cloth harp to lay her egg and then she'll live in the talapalodion tree for awhile."

"Is your talap-a-luv-in-it a butterfly house?" asked Toonie who could now see more of the basket-like house built high up among the branches of the great tree which, though it was still quite some distance away, looked close because it was so tall and thick with big branches and large green leaves.

"It's an everybody house," replied It. "Flutterbys and balooms and baloomerangs live in the talapalodion tree, and there are flish in the lavatorium in the It's-Fine, and Thomey is always about because she doesn't like to go out, and Snorf and Snorfa hide everywhere, and Is and I are in the basket house, at least on rainy days, and…"

"Look!" exclaimed Toonie again, not meaning to interrupt the Itofit's telling about all his friends, but seeing a rainbow forming beyond the talapalodion tree so one end seemed to disappear among the high foliage and the other someplace over the hills beyond, she couldn't contain herself (or her surprise either because something seemed not quite right with that particular rainbow.)

"That looks funny," said Whizlet who knew a lot of games ended with rainbows but never one like this.

"What are all those extra colors?" asked Toliver who was pretty sure he'd never seen anything like that before.

"What extra colors?" asked the Itofit, genuinely confused. "There's xoc and red, orange, yellow, green, blue, purple and indigo, vertul and xaalu…"

"Xoc?" asked Toonie.

"Vertul and xaalu?" repeated Toliver.

"Of course," said the Itofit, "just like in my fur. Mine is silver with streaks of xaalu and Is' is silver with a sheen of vertul, and we both have xoc colored whiskers because we can sort of see at night with them."

The children stared at the Itofit as if they hadn't been looking at him for a good part of the morning, but now they could see that his fur, which when they first met him had seemed no more than a beautiful opalescent silver, was indeed tinged with xaalu. "That's a very pretty color," agreed Toonie who saw nothing peculiar in seeing new colors.

"And look at Hissofer!" exclaimed Toliver. "His black stripes aren't black anymore, they're vertul!"

"They're beautiful," agreed Toonie. "He looks like he just crawled through the rainbow and got all painted with poesy."

"Yipes-a-doddle!" exclaimed Whizlet. "What color is that?" He was pointing at a big, shiny xaalu and indigo-glazed bee-like insect with xoc eyes and filigreed wings, and a long, very pointed stinger hanging down from its tail.

Hobnail leaped from the Itofit's shoulder and began huzzing her version of *The Flight of the Bumblebee* which she had to do by warbling her throat strings and zizzing her beak to make it sound right.

"Oh! How lucky we are," said It. "It's a tingly-tickle bee!"

Toonie waved her arms madly in the air, suddenly realizing to her horror that It wasn't as perfect as it seemed to be. "Get away. Gget away!" she screamed, then grabbed the Itofit's leg and tried to wrap his fur around her. "Hide. Hide!" she yelled, "or she'll sting you!"

"I certainly hope so," said It, who poked his nose up and wiggled it enticingly until the tingly-tickle bee noticed the protuberance and came to investigate. She circled the Itofit's head two or three times before landing on the tip of his nose. The bee walked around in a circle, occasionally stopping to rub her back legs together and flex her stinger while looking It in the eyes which were quite crossed to follow the insect's progress.

The bee found the spot she was looking for, took firm hold with her four front feet, and lifted her stinger high in the air. "Bzzzz?" she asked.

"All set," replied It.

As the bee slammed her rear end down, her long, pointed stinger opened out like a windblown umbrella which, instead of stabbing into It's nose, squiggled out with six ticklers that poked, and pinched, and plubbled it. The Itofit jumped straight up in the air and giggled while shaking his head wildly from side to side and up and down, throwing the tingly-tickle bee head over tailtube back into the air. "How marvelously tingly!" he exclaimed. "What a fine tickle!" And he began to dance around, snorting through his nose, and laughing all the while.

Boogie and Whizlet had escaped the bee by going to the far end of the bridge and, after checking back under it to see if they could discover a sleeping troll (which they couldn't, of course, because trolls always sleep under their invisible blankets), they jumped from stepping stone to stepping stone across to the other side of the stream, and hurried ahead into the labyrinth of bushes which, though quite low, were well above their heads, with pretty little groves of tapple trees sticking up among them (because mazeberries and tapples taste so good together, there are always a few tapple trees in mazeberry labyrinths.)

"Be careful," called the Itofit from the top of the bridge where he'd finally stopped laughing and was wiping his eyes with his six-fingered handkerchief. "It's easy to get confused and all turned around in there."

"Could they get lost?" asked Toonie who was again feeling responsible for Whizlet as well as her cat and thought everyone else should know she felt that way too.

"Not at this time of year," replied It, "but when the mazeberries are ripe and fermenting just a little bit, it's very easy to do. I was once in there for a week and thought I was only gone for the afternoon." He led Toliver and Toonie across the stepping stones and into the labyrinth, through which he knew his way as well as he knew his way up and down, and round and round, and over and under, and through and through the It's-Fine and talapalodion tree house. It wasn't very long at all and they were safely to the other side, but Whizlet and Boogie were nowhere to be seen.

Toliver put two fingers in his mouth and let out a shrieking whistle that completely astonished the Itofit who had never heard such a sound uttered by a creature (except for a troll in distress, but they don't count because they're only marginally creatures.)

"How do you do that?" he asked.

"It's easy," replied Toliver proudly, "you just put your fingers in your mouth, pinch your tongue, twist your lips, tighten your throat, stop your nose from the inside, take a big gulp of air, and blow." And he let out another, even more piercing sound.

Far back in the maze an orange-yellow face appeared climbing up a tapple tree, looking at the world like it was looking for a way out. A moment later, Whizlet's somewhat red face climbed into view below the cat's while Hobnail wheeled above screeching: "Snookered boy. Cat in a tree. Puzzled persons. Amazed is me!" And much to their embarrassment, she then led them out through the labyrinth by calling down to them (and everybody else) every time they made a wrong turn.

Ahead and towering far up into the sky was the great talapalodion tree. Around its trunk and among its roots, many of which seemed to swim off like sea-dragons whose backs were above the water, was the It's-Fine, which from this distance, looked like a garden of huge rocks set among mossy hills. Small, wind-blown trees and flowering bushes bristled everywhere, and blossom laden vines hung down, and a bubbly stream flowing over a terraced waterfall burbled into one side of the garden and out the other into a little lake. The boulders which, on closer inspection, could be seen to be very carefully put together like a marvelous castle made by the loving hands of Mother Nature (since Mother Nature has dominion over It as well as Earth) were the most beautiful rocks any of the children had ever seen, being all different shades of blue-grays and roses and yellows that blended together and were banded with streaks of dark red and black and gold, and were sometimes rough and sometimes water-worn smooth but everywhere perfectly proportioned. The path rambled through the garden and took them between two of the dragon-like roots and by a great slab of silver-blue stone where a soft, fragrant breeze was coming out of a twisty hole that might have been some sort of window or maybe just a twisty hole, and there was a soft tinkling in the distance like wind chimes blowing in the breeze or water falling over syncopated stones.

"What a nice smell," said Toliver who knew that nice smells mean nice things like dinner or circuses or his Aunt Griswalda who always smelled as pretty as she looked.

"What a nice sound," said Toonie.

"What a weird window," said Whizlet who thought it might be a groblet hole.

Around the next root-knob (and under the root) and through a grove of tapple, tum, and prear trees was the entrance to the It's-Fine. The sun threw intricate patterns upon the stone through the leaves and branches of the wind-sculpted trees, and the rock radiated a pale blue light, which seemed to caress the group as they approached, warming them in a wash of many colors. Flutterbys were butterflying all about and more of the tingly-tickle bees were bumbling in the flowers of the flowering vines stretching up the rocks. The entrance itself had no door but looked like a mysterious cave and, in the darkness beyond it, a tunnel went down among the roots. To either side of the entrance was a niche in the rock. These were actually doors to smaller caves and in each an ill-formed statue was standing which looked to be of rough and weathered stone. The one to the left was short and squat and very ugly, with a terrible grimace on its face, and bulging eyes, and huge hands balled into fists. The one to the right was much taller and even graceful in a grotesque way with a great grinning mouth filled with large sharp teeth and huge ears with ornaments in them, and hair like knotted ropes atop a bulging skull. The smaller one had a big club slung over its back on a strap, and the larger one had a spear in its right hand and a chain in its left.

"Yipes-a-doddle!" gulped Whizlet, who thought they might be groblets even though groblets had big bodies and tiny heads. "What are those?"

"They're Fine Thanes," replied the Itofit. "The Most Able It brought them back from his travels to Arigonia where they guarded the other thanes, the magical Thanes of Ludgordia. And they've lived in the roots of the talapalodion tree and guarded the It's-Fine ever since."

"They look like thimble thanes," commented Toliver. "At least their skin looks a lot like by grandmother's thimble."

"And they don't look like anyone could needle them either," added Whizlet.

The eyes of the two creatures followed them as they approached, their nostrils flared, and when Toonie, who was holding very tightly to the Itofit's hand, shivered, they both snorted out little puffs of blue vapor.

"Gulp!" gulped Toliver. "They're scary."

"They're supposed to be scary," said It, "because they're here to scare away drevils and globins and other scary things who deserve a taste of their own medicine every now and then." He tipped his hat (along with Hissofer who was wrapped around the brim and surveying the thimble thanes like a general reviewing his troops.) "Good morning, Panoleon," he said, nodding to the shorter one; then, "Good morning, Lamburtaine. All these people are our guests, so help them any time they need help and hinder them any time they're liable to fall down."

"Roink!" said Panoleon.

"Ribble-ribble!" said Lamburtaine.

"Weird wonks. Weird wonks!" said Hobnail excitedly.

"Hissssss," said Hissofer to let them know he approved.

Boogie said nothing at all but slid between the Itofit's legs to be equally far from both strange gnomes as he passed their surveillance, and Snorf, who was wrapped around the Itofit's neck, greeted them as he went by, using his upper and lower handsfeet to salute them both at the same time.

The tunnel, which seemed dark when looked at from the outside, was actually well lit, with luminescent roots along the ceiling and walls. There were also clumps of moist mosses and dry lichens and ferny plants with marmalade-orange and scarlet flowers that wove tapestries on which elf-glade pictures shimmered, and the air smelled like musk-rose and damp juniper berries. The music they had heard earlier was now louder as though a wind was blowing through crinkley hedges and over tinkley sands and down avenues of resonant stalagmites and hollow stalactites dripping dribbles of limestone juice onto petrified woodhorns. As they came out of the tunnel into a great hall, the Itofit tapped his twistle on the side of his face and all the balooms started to gaggle and murmur among themselves as they huffed and puffed themselves full of air. It put the twistle to his lips and blew a lusty TA-DA! Which was immediately followed by a series of almost echoes as each baloom, in turn, did a ta-da! or a da-da-ta-da! or a ta-tata-ta-ta!

The room into which they had come was bright with shafts of sunlight pouring down through high pastel-colored windows and the near wall was a great sheet of glass (or maybe some crystalline stone for it seemed to sparkle all by itself). The water from the stream filled a large pool beyond the glass, except the water was so cool and clear it seemed almost not to be there at all, and all the strange and beautiful flish which were now coming to the glass (since they had heard It's twistle call) looked as though they were many-colored birds with translucent fin-wings floating about in fresh, morning air beyond a window.

"These are our friends who are flish," said the Itofit sweeping his arm so as to take in all the pretty waterarians at once. The beautiful creatures swam back and forth looking out at It and his new friends and blowing bubbles at each other just as if they were talking.

"What are they saying?" asked Toliver who knew they had to be saying something.

"They're saying 'good-by' and 'hello', 'good-by' to the empty room 'hello' to us, and the big one there, the queen of the lavatorium, is saying 'aren't you pretty people and aren't we glad you came,' and the accordion one with the asparagus nose and silver-blue-pink ribbonscales is asking where I found such happy-glowing companions."

"That's very nice," responded Toliver who always liked to return a compliment with another compliment. "Would you tell them they're the most beautiful flish we've ever seen…"

"Except for cannon-nose," cut in Whizlet who ducked behind It's leg remembering the frightful flowers in *Greenthumb's Garden of Horrors* and thinking they could probably live under water too, and if they shot snot through the glass it would be curtains for everyone.

"This is a wonderful place," said Toliver running his hand over a polished onyx wall. "Who built it?"

"We've all worked on it, generation after generation of Its, all adding our favorite places and things to do," replied It. "So now we have the lavatorium and the library; my shop and Is' studio; the cloth room, the music room, and the friendly room with its undulating dance floor; our playroom and climbroom and dark room and sitting room."

"Do you have a garden room too?" asked Toonie who loved all the flowers around and wondered if they had their own place to stay.

"Every room is a flower room," replied It, "because they're all our friends and do so many nice things for us."

"Like smell good," said Whizlet.

"They all smell good," continued It, "but some feed the flish, and other undulate the floor in the friendly room, and others clean and dust and mop."

"How can flowers do that?" asked Toliver.

"Why we train them to and they love it because that's what they do best: waving their leaves around and brushing cushions with their tendrils and eating dustballs."

"Wow!" said Whizlet who figured they were like the delete button on his computer. "Is Bill Gates your gardener?"

The Itofit scratched his temple with a scratching whisker. "We have duck bills and garden gates, but no bill gates though I suppose there might be such things."

"There sure are," agreed Whizlet. "cause that's what the money goes through when everybody turns on their machines."

Toonie stepped among some bushes, which began to powder her nose with perfumed pollen and brush her hair. "Where did you learn to make such a wonderful place?" she asked.

"My grandfather's grandmother's great great grandfather learned from the Thanes of Ludgordia who live in Arigonia and when he got back he started building the It's-Fine as soon as he convinced everybody how wonderful it would be to live like this. That's why we still call him the Most Able It, but he was never satisfied. He wanted to learn more and even tried to go back to Arigonia and continue his studies with the Thanes, and maybe sit at the feet of the Great Halidon of Ludgordia, but…"

"Great Halidon!" interrupted Toliver. "Who's that? And who are the Thanes?"

"We're not sure. The Most Able It always got a tear in his eye when he talked about the Thanes and just said they were wonderful, but since he learned from them, they must be the teachers of Arigonia, and we suppose the Great Halidon was their teacher, but we don't know because the Most Able It never got to meet him, and Ludgordia, of course, is where everybody is a friend of the Ludgord, and the Ludgord is the teacher of everyone."

"Where's Ludgordia?" asked Whizlet who hoped it might be on his hard disc somewhere.

"Nobody knows," answered the Itofit. "Even the Most Able It never got back to Arigonia or sat at the feet of the Great Halidon, but that's because he got bushwhacked in Alabramble when he tried to go back, and only managed to get home after some harrowing adventures and the greatest difficulties."

"Alabramble?" repeated Whizlet hoping that wasn't on his hard disc. "Where's that?"

"Beyond Glibia," said It, "but nobody goes there nowadays."

"Is it too wild?" asked Toliver.

"Well, no," continued It, rubbing his chin with his tail. "It's not wild wild anymore. It's tame. It's just that it was tamed by the wrong people, so it's wild in a different way."

"It's tame for them and wild for everybody else," explained Whizlet nodding his head sagely and scrunching his lips together like the squished end of a toothpaste tube, since he knew the Itofit was talking about a place like the sticky-stinky-spookylands in his *Demonworlds Gazetteer* where the sticky-stinky spooks sat on their potato couches drinking muddy blarys and making everyone else chase each other around with bonking sticks and zipper zappers.

Toonie said nothing at all. In fact, she wasn't even listening, because she didn't think girls should have to be distracted by boy-talk, or spooks or bonking sticks either, and she wasn't looking at the flish anymore, because her eye had been caught by the most cuddly bear skin rug she'd ever seen. It was very small, not even as long as she was tall, and it was spread out on the floor with its friendly furry face facing her. Its fur was golden in color and very thick and so silky over its cheeks and around its eyes that she knew it was softer than a swan's down powder puff. It's stubby arms and legs were spread out to either side but instead of having claws, they ended in pretty little toes and fingers with suction cups on their toetips and fingertips. It was so wonderfully inviting that Toonie kicked off her shoes and stepped right into the middle of it.

"Ouch!" said the rug.

Toonie jumped into the air and came down with a thump next to the rug's right ear. "Pardon me," she exclaimed, "but I've never seen a rug that talks before."

"I'm not a rug!" said the rug somewhat miffed and almost defiant, but not quite.

"What are you?" asked Toonie backing away just a bit since her toe was near the creature's mouth.

"I'm a grumpled-and-grizzly-golden sta-ya-thome," said the rug shaking itself all over, then pushing itself up on its hands and feet. "But you can call me Thomey."

"Why that's a very nice name, and it sounds like my name which is

Toonie, and I'm very pleased to meet you, and I'm sorry I stepped on you and called you a rug, but I thought you were and didn't mean to. But what do you do except lie around looking like a rug?"

"I don't rug at all," replied Thomey. "I hug. That is, I like to hug people who wished they'd been born with a beautiful golden grumpled grizzly fur coat on. If you'd like, I'll show you."

Toonie thought about it for a moment. "How do I put you on?"

"You don't. I do. Just sit down and I'll do everything."

Toonie sat down and Thomey raised up as far as she could on her short arms and legs and very carefully climbed up Toonie's back until she was draped over Toonie's shoulders and wrapped around her sides with her hands and feet in front holding on very gently with her little finger and toetip suction cups, and her face was on Toonie's shoulder where she could whisper in Toonie's ear.

"Look at me!" exclaimed Toonie standing up and twirling around so everybody could see her new fur coat friend. "I'm a princess and this is my golden robe whose name is Grumpled Golden Grizzly Bear Skin Hug!"

"Hi, Thomey," said It. "You certainly know how to pick a beautiful hostess."

Toonie spun again and Boogie who was behind Whizlet who was still behind the Itofit's leg came over to sniff the strange creature and compare furs, but before he could do anything at all or even me-ow his appreciation (or a challenge), a marvelous new sound filled the chamber adding depth and color to the wind and water sounds which were already caressing their ears. The Itofit's face lit up with a wonderful smile and he began to dance his little jig to the new music which was even more enchanting then anything they had heard yet, and seemed to be wafting down from far away and high above.

"What is it, It?" asked Toliver who had never heard such lovely sounds before.

"It's Is," exclaimed It, "playing her cloth harp." And he lifted his twistle to his lips again and sounded another TA-DA!

Hobnail was gliding about in a circle of sunlight, thoroughly fascinated by all the wonderful music, and answered with her own lovely version of Mr. Mozart's *Magic Flute*, hoping to home in on whoever was dueting with her, but since the wonderful sounds filled the whole chamber and seemed to be coming from everywhere at once, she hadn't a clue as to which way to fly.

The trunk of the talapalodion tree was the far wall of the chamber and a circular vine ramp wound around it to roof above. Lost in playing his twistle which called out and answered the sounds of the cloth harp (all of which were harmoniously blended with the wind and water sounds, not to mention Mr. Mozart's Hobnail's *Flute*), the Itofit danced up the ramp followed by all the others until they came out into the roof garden beside the top of the lavatorium where the flish were now jumping into the air, turning circles and smiling at the strange assortment of land and air people before splashing back down into their own element. And high above them all, the great tree spread its huge branches so its leaves speckled the beautiful blue sunlight with green reflections, and several vines unrolled out of the foliage and descended down to hang among them.

The Itofit stopped playing for a moment and called out: "We'll need a tulivator too, since most of my new friends don't have tails and aren't accustomed to hanging from vines." No sooner had he said it then a large basket (that looked like a tulip flower) hung from other vines appeared dropping from the leaves.

"Whoever is doing that is really quick," said Toliver, who liked things that worked well, and was quite impressed by the efficiency of the unseen elevator operator.

"Talapa is doing it," said It, as though that explained everything. "Heshe is very vigilant and knew we've been coming for a long time now."

"Who's Talapa?" asked Toonie rubbing her cheek against Thomey's dry, velvety nose, and thinking maybe there was another sta-ya-thome in the basket house who she could use for a pillow if she needed to take a nap.

"Why Talapa's the talapalodion tree shimself?" replied It. "Heshe does all the housekeeping and most of the chores for us, and all we do is love shim for being so wonderful, and take talapanuts to faraway nice places so they can grow there too."

The tulip basket touched down next to them and its petals fell open so everyone could walk in without having to climb over the sides. Hobnail, of course, didn't bother but hearing where the lovely music was coming from was circling up to the platforms in the branches above, completely intent on meeting the player of the cloth harp before another two bars could elapse.

By the time the tulivator arrived at the lowest sky-terrace, Hobnail was already hanging from a vine and swinging in little, ecstatic upside down circles above not one, but two persons playing the cloth harp. At one end was Is who looked very much like It except she was much prettier (whereas he was rugged and handsome) and her eyes were larger and looked like star sapphires, and her fur (just as It had explained to them) was tinged with xoc instead of xaalu, and she was smiling sweetly at the three eyes of a snigglesnorf who was at the other end of the cloth harp. The harp itself was brilliantly colored piece of thick-woven cloth stretched between them, one end being held by Is' tail threaded through loops up one edge, and the other end by the snigglesnorf who was perched on her lower four sets of handsfeet and using the upper twenty to grasp the edge of the cloth which she was methodically stretching and relaxing all along its length while Is' six-fingered hands ran over either side of it, strumming arrays of taut strings and strange little colored bumps. Is looked at them briefly, smiled even prettilier, and cooed something in a low voice and a very strange language.

The Itofit's large ears cupped toward the whisper. "Is is saying that they're playing for people who have never heard a cloth harp before so the music should be nice and soothing and quite proper."

"Is she explaining all that to the snigglesnorf?" asked Toonie.

"Oh no. Snorfa can see us perfectly well herself. Is is talking to the cloth harp which only has ears, or rather is an ear, and a tongue of course, on which flutterbys congregate and hatch."

"She talks to her harp?" asked Toliver.

"Sure," whispered Whizlet who often talked to his computer and knew that everybody talked to some peculiar thing or other even if they would never admit it.

"It is one of her very best friends," continued the Itofit. "Each bump is a cocoon with a different type of flutterby inside so each makes a different sound when she touches it, or plucks it, or caresses it, or tweaks it, or rubs it, or tribbles it, or scratches it, or twiddles it, or anything else's it. The color of each cocoon tells the notes it plays and the size tells its octave. Eventually each cocoon will hatch a flutterby who will live in the talapalodion tree and, when it lays an egg, will attach it to the cloth so the harp is always tuned although always tuned a bit differently."

Snorf stood up on It's shoulder and rubbed Hissofer with eight of his handsfeet while happily pointing at Snorfa with seven more, while the flock of balooms twittered about Hobnail who was still swinging upside down above Is with her beak hanging open.

"The balooms are asking Is to sing a song," whispered It.

"All right," said Is, smiling at the balooms and very nicely moving into a new melody which Snorfa followed without the slightest hesitation, and a moment later Is began to sing:

There's a place in my heart for you always
There's a place in my heart where you dwell
I remember the morning it opened
When a kiss put me under your spell.

"How pretty," said Toliver who could be very sentimental when he felt that way.

Toonie put both hands over her heart and sighed as Thomey snuggled a little tighter about her, and even Whizlet, who was usually pretty suspicious of girls singing love songs, cleaned his ears with his fingers so he could hear better.

We were off in the meadows by sunrise
Where the flowers were scenting the day
And the trees in the forest were pining
For lovers to come out and play

It responded by lifting his twistle to his lips while Snorf hurried into position and the balooms, who were puffing themselves up outrageously, added melodious little puffs and peepers to the tune.

We walked holding hands while you led me
Past the stream where the speckled trout lay
And the warm breeze that wafted through morning
Was perfumed with a joy that has stayed...

"Pretty song. Pretty song," said Hobnail who flew up to the roof of the basket house and pulled out a long grass fiber just like she was going to start a nest.

Your eyes shone like pools of deep water
As we sat in the sweet grassy glen
The world was alight and delighted
As we fell into love once again.

"Oh my!" said Toonie as the song ended. "You fell into love again!" Her eyes were swimming as she gazed from Is to It and back again.

"How could you fall into love again if that was the first time?" asked Whizlet who was the more practical of the two cousins.

"We've been in love forever," replied the Itofit. "From the very beginning of time…" He smiled and ran his fingers through Toonie's hair and smiled at Whizlet. "But every time we get born again into a new world, we get to fall into love all over again."

Hobnail fluttered down chirping for more, but Is withdrew her tail from the loops, and Snorfa, after very carefully folding her end of the cloth harp and putting it at Is' feet, scooted off to a wall of the basket house and disappeared through a window. A moment later, however (since all the children now knew about snigglesnorfs) everyone saw three eyes reappear peeking over the sill.

"This is Is," said It sweeping out his tail majestically and bowing toward his guests. "She is my companion in life, and for life, and because of life too."

"You're beautiful," said Toonie.

"Thank you," said Is in a voice like the Itofit's but softer and more like a woodwind than a French horn.

"Is is from Is," said It. "But she lives here now."

"Then you must be the Isofis," exclaimed Toliver who was always delighted when he was able to put things together really quickly.

"No, Isis is my mother," said Is. She went over to It; took his arm, and brushed his shoulder with the tip of her tail. "I'm the Isofit."

Everyone could see that the Itofit was beside himself with happiness, but because he was almost embarrassed, Is distracted them by picking up the cloth harp which was still vibrating and tingling as its sounds faded away into the rustling of leaves in the breeze and bees in the flowers. Very carefully, Is tapped one of the cocoons which looked like it was ready to burst, and with a wonderful twang-sang-sa-whoosh! It did just that, and a beautiful xoc, red, and blue flutterby flew out and around her head. A moment later a whole cloud of other flutterbys came down from among the branches and all fluttered about the new one, zinging and wooing among themselves until the balooms on It's twistle couldn't stand it any longer, and they all detached themselves and joined the dancing flutterbys around Is' head.

It's face was wrapped in a smile so big it made his head look three times larger than before, and his eyes were alight like stars in a twinkling sky, and he was breathing very fast, maybe because he'd been playing the twistle, or maybe because he'd danced all the way up from the flishroom, or maybe because of some other reason like seeing Is for the first time since early that morning. Is took his hand and their tails entwined, and her smoldering sapphire eyes twinkled before the lids closed halfway down, and Toliver noticed that the hair on the back of the Itofit's neck straightened up and ruffled itself, and Toonie noticed that Is turned her head just slightly to the left and dropped her chin a whisker's worth, and Whizlet noticed that Boogie was crawling along the platform behind them by pulling himself along on his belly with his claws, and then Hobnail came down among the balooms and flutterbys who hardly had to move at all to let her through, and she landed on Is' xoc-tinged, silver-blue shoulder and started to preen her cheek.

"Hobnail likes. Hobnail likes," she said then added her own bit of music by adding *****.

"Who are your friends," asked Is, who realized that It had forgotten what he was supposed to be doing.

"Oh, yes," said It coming back to himself and smiling sheepishly. "This is Toliver."

"How do you do?" said Toliver very politely, but then turned to It with a bit of consternation in his voice. "How did you know my name since I haven't told it to you yet?"

"Hmmmm," said It, scratching his chin with his tailtip. "Let me see… You look just like Toliver and you talk like Toliver and you don't have a tail like Toliver doesn't, so it's a very smart guess that you are Toliver. You're not anybody else, are you?"

"No." admitted Toliver still not sure he quite understood.

"I'm Toonie," said Toonie. "Petunia Petalpaper from Hickory Lane", and she did a little curtsy, "but all my friends call me Toonie because my father says I brought a beautiful song into everybody's life, just like a cloth harp and a twistle and a…"

"Toonie Petunia is a beautiful name," agreed Is. "You're a singing flower and that is a very nice way to go through life."

"And this young fellow is Yipes-a-doddle," continued It motioning to Whizlet who wouldn't have cared if It called him dippsydoddle if he wanted to.

"Is that another Snorf," asked Whizlet, motioning in turn to Snorfa who, since everybody was being so friendly and nice, had scuttled over from the basket house and climbed up to cling to Is' breast. She took the cloth harp from Is, and rolled it up very carefully (using only one eye to watch what she was doing and the other two to gaze at everyone else) then held it like a precious old scroll.

"This is Snorfa," said Is, taking the cloth harp from the snigglesnorf and carefully lifting her from her breast so everyone could see her better and admire how pretty she was. But Snorfa would have none of it and ran down Is' arm and jumped all the way to It's hip where she immediately began to chase Snorf up and over It's shoulder, around his neck, down his side, across his belly, and up the other side.

"Hisssss. Hel-lo, hel-lo-o-o," said Hissofer Booshocks who was hanging off It's hat watching the mad scramble below and wondering what wonderful things might happen to a snake who had two snigglesnorfs to play with.

"And this tail without an attendant creature is Hissofer Booshocks," continued It looking upward and crossing his eyes, "who scares people so they won't step on him." He uncrossed his eyes and looked down at Boogie who was on his back with Is' tail between his paws, rubbing his cheek with the tuft at the end. "And this is Spitpurrkoff who talks with his tail except when he's batting people with it, and also answers to Boogie if you share what you're eating with him. And this is…" and the Itofit whistled Hobnail's musical name again, "…a wonderfully fascinating flying-creature who, for some very obscure reason, Mrs. Dirtytoes calls Hobnail."

Is nodded very pleasantly to the cat and the snake, then turned her head to smile at Hobnail on her shoulder. ***** whispered Hobnail in her ear.

"I know," replied It. "and I love you too, and I've never seen such beautiful feathers before. You are truly lovely."

Poor Hobnail seemed to wilt on Is' shoulder and her whole body sagged against Is' neck. "Hobnail happy bird. Hobnail happy bird!" said she dreamily.

The Itofit walked to the door of the basket house whose frame was a flowering bougainvillea vine, paused (as he always did) to look out over their beautiful little valley, and announced: "We came for a glass of spinach and parsnip ice-erb tea and a bowl of amaranth and rutabaga ice-yam with turnip topping and a dab of dandelion…" He licked his lips so deliciously that everybody immediately wanted to taste what he was talking about in spite of what it sounded like, "…over which we're very seriously going to discuss the situation so we can decide what to do before we do it and then do it and see what happens."

"What situation?" asked Is who was simultaneously tweaking Hobnail under the beak and rubbing Boogie's belly with her toe.

"We have a problem," said Toonie with as much authority and decisiveness as she could muster, which was quite a bit now that she knew everybody and knew they liked her too.

"Shusssssssh!" said the Itofit putting his finger to his lips. "Not so loud."

"Oh dear," said Is to It. "You know what that probably means."

"What does it mean?" asked Toliver who knew that Is didn't know what their problem was yet, so couldn't know what they were talking about.

"It means somebody will hear what Toonie said," said Is.

"And that may be one of them now." said the Itofit pointing out beyond the mazeberry labyrinth through which they had just come.

"What's that?" asked Whizlet.

"I don't know," admitted It. "But it is probably one of them."

"Who's them?" asked Toonie who looked where everyone else was looking but really couldn't see anything except a little dot bouncing up and down.

People's eyes aren't as good as Itians' eyes for seeing little things in the distance (because the Itians' eyes can poke out and zoom in) so Toliver reached in his pocket and came out with his telescoping spyglass which he put to his eye and focused on the bouncing dot.

"What's that?" asked the Itofit.

"It's my spyglass," replied Toliver handing it to him. "It makes everything bigger."

"It must be a magic wand," offered Is, "because anything you put in it it would have to be very small indeed to start with and probably in need of biggering."

The Itofit looked at the spyglass, turned it around, and put it to his eye just as Toliver had done. "My goodness!" he declared. "Someone's shrunk the maze or moved it to the next county!"

"You're looking through the wrong end," explained Toonie, "which does the opposite of what you want it to do unless you're trying to get away."

"Hmmm," mused It, turning the glass around. "Why how marvelous! Yes, indeed! It certainly is one of them."

He handed the glass back to Toliver who felt very important (and not just a little like Captain Hornblower on the bridge.) Toliver put it to his eye and immediately saw that the little figure rushing toward them was very peculiar indeed. It appeared like a tiny human being but most certainly wasn't. It had a large round head and a belly to match, but between them were narrow shoulders (or maybe two narrow shoulders since it had four arms, two hanging off either side) and one hand was carrying a briefcase, another an umbrella, a third was waving madly to them, and the fourth was wiping its brow with a handkerchief.

Toliver scratched his jaw bone. "Is that a person?"

"No," replied Is. "They pretend they are, of course, but they aren't."

"They're creaturettes with four arms and two mouths and their ears are on upside down and point to the rear so they get everything backwards," added the Itofit, "and they have a very tight spring inside which their partners wind up every morning which is why they need so many partners."

"He looks awfully small," said Toliver who wondered if the creaturette was on roller skates because he was moving so fast on such little legs.

"That's because he's middle aged," replied It. "They get littler and littler as they get older and older."

"How curious!" thought Toliver just barely out loud.

"Not really," continued It, "since they spend all their time learning more and more about less and less, they just naturally get smaller and smaller until one day they blow away in a puff of hot air."

Whizlet ran to the railing by the tulivator to see the strange phenomenon better and Toonie followed him because she hated to be left out of anything even if it was just looking at something curious over a railing or down a drainpipe. "It's not a groblet," announced Whizlet, "because its head's too big, and groblets never have umbrellas because they always have little rain clouds over their heads so they'd wear 'em out too fast."

"They're called vawyers," said It, with a touch of resignation. "They make it their business to watch everybody else's business and then charge a lot to do something about it."

"And what they do is usually wrong," added Is.

"But always profitable, for them." concluded It.

"But what do they do?" asked Toonie.

"As soon as you have a problem, they arrive to make sure nobody else gets there first," replied Is.

"Then what do they do?" asked Whizlet.

"Well," said It scratching his ear with a scratching-whisker, "then they discuss it with their partners after which they take it to the bar, have a three tarmini lunch, and go home."

"But what do they do?" persisted Toonie.

"If anyone knew that," replied Is, "we probably wouldn't need them at all."

"Maybe the mazeberry patch will keep him away," said Toliver not sounding too sure of it but hoping so anyway.

"I don't think so," said It. "They're always in one kind of maze or another, so he'll probably feel right at home."

And It was right. The creaturette's two unoccupied arms were pumping furiously like a racing walker hoping to propel his legs even faster than a walking racer's, and he only hesitated long enough at the entrance to the labyrinth to open his briefcase and take out a pogo stick. With this he bounded into the maze and, being able to bounce higher than the low berry bushes, could see his way ahead and got quickly to the other side without missing a bounce or a turn either. He put the pogo stick back in his briefcase and hurried on along the path they had followed earlier until he came to the two dragon-roots near the entrance. He slowed there and carefully crept ahead to peek around the corner of the last root-knob. He was being very stealthy but not stealthy enough to fool the thimble thanes. Lamburtaine saw him first, let out a howl, and leaped from his perch. Panoleon was right behind him, but the strange creaturette was as quick as they, and, throwing his briefcase up like a shield, stabbed at Lamburtaine with his umbrella. The thimble thane leaped to the side, parried the blow with his chain, and let out a fearful holler that would have awakened the dead not to mention anyone sleeping within a mile or so of the talapalodion tree. Panoleon jumped to the front with flames coming out of his mouth and smoke from his ears. The vawyer danced away and having no stomach for a real fight, scurried back the way he had come, holding his hat in his third hand and sprinkling thumbtacks behind him with his fourth.

"Whew!" said Toliver. "That was a close call!"

""He's sure no groblet," said Whizlet with a touch of annoyance. "They always fight till they're kerplunked!"

"He may not be finished yet," said Is who knew nothing about groblets but knew it was next to impossible to kerplunk a vawyer.

"At least he's running away now," sighed Toonie who then yelled over the railing, "And good riddance!" because she always liked to get the last word in, even if she hadn't said anything else.

The Itofit leaned further out over the rail. "Never underestimate a vawyer," he said, "because no matter how low you estimate they are, they can always get under it."

"You're right," exclaimed Toliver pointing down.

The creaturette raced back to the twisty hole in the blue-stone rock, threw his briefcase to the ground, climbed onto it, and pulled himself through. A moment later, his head reappeared along with one arm holding the wrong end of his umbrella with which he reached down, snagged his briefcase with its curved handle, and pulled it up after him. Just then Lamburtaine reached the window but it was too high for the gnome to leap through so all he could do was gnash his teeth and shake his spear until Panoleon scuttled up and got down on his hands and knees beneath the window. Lamburtaine jumped on his back, then through the twisty hole. Panoleon leaped to his feet, unslung his club, and scooted back the way he had come until he disappeared into the It's-Fine through the tunnel entrance.

"Oh, dear," said Toonie taking Is's hand and snuggling against her fur. "That vawyer is just like a nasty old mosquito with that umbrella!"

"What's a mosquito?" asked Is, who wasn't sure she knew what that was (since there weren't any on It or if they were they were always someplace else.)

"That's an insect that sucks your blood and just leaves you a little itchy welt so you know you've met one," explained Toliver.

"That sounds about right," agreed It.

"You could use some groblets yourself," announced Whizlet shaking his head sagely. "Two at each window, four on every roof, and back-ups at the door."

A few moments later, the creaturette appeared on the roof by the lavatorium. Talapa knew he was there so heshe pulled up all sher vines.

"That ought to stop him," said Toliver who always rooted for the good guys, especially when they had roots.

"Spear him Lamburtaine!" yelled down Whizlet to the tall gnome who was just then rushing out onto the roof followed immediately by Panoleon brandishing his club. "Bonk him Panoleon!"

But the little man threw open his briefcase again and extracted a folded up balloon into which he quickly huffed and puffed and blew it up until it was three or four times bigger than he was.

"What's he doing?" cried Toonie.

"Filling it with hot air," replied It. "He's got more of that than anything else."

The creaturette scooped up his briefcase with the umbrella handle, and, using two of his other arms to hang onto the balloon, rose into the air and floated away just as Lamburtaine and Panoleon skidded to a halt beneath him. He employed his fourth hand to straighten his hat and tie and brush his mustache, while his ears, wiggling like radar antennas, zeroed in on Toliver who was watching his ascent with wide eyes, a half opened mouth, and a sense of impending déjà vu (because he had the distinct impression that vawyers, like bad pennies, worse jokes, and good boomerangs always came back.)

The balloon with the creaturette dangling below rose to their level and drifted across the railing. He stepped to the terrace and began letting the hot air out of the balloon which he used, first, to blow the dust off his shoulders and hat; second, to blow dry his forehead (which was a bit sweaty) and his hair into place; thirdly, to press the crease back into his rumpled trousers; and fourthly, to blow dirt from his shoes and off into the corner. When the balloon was empty, he folded it up with two hands and stuffed it into a pocket of his vest, while extracting a small pair of glasses with his other hands, polishing them carefully, and perching them on his nose. He was indeed a most unusual creaturette, having a very large, round head, beady eyes, and oversized ears, which were certainly on upside down. On the very top of his head was a tuft of black hair, around which was a bald ring, below which was a ring of stringy black hair hanging down to his eyebrows (which were also black and frizzy) and over the bottoms of his ears (which were, of course, on top). He had two mouths, one on either side of his face, with a long, sharp nose between and another squizzle of black hair beneath it. A magnifying glass was hung around his neck on a gold chain and another chain threaded through the buttonholes of his vest, ending at a large ornate stopwatch which he carefully pulled from his pocket, glanced at briefly, and pushed the button to start timing the interview. Another hand pulled out a large, flamboyantly pink handkerchief with which he wiped his brow while peering past it to study the group huddled by the railing watching his every move. He hurried to Toliver with his fourth hand thrust forward, grabbed Toliver's hand before Toliver could hide it in his pocket, and shook it vigorously.

"I'm Nister," his right mouth said soothingly (although a bit louder than was probably needed since his face was pushed right up under Toliver's nose), "of Phister, Blister, Nister, Twister, & Toppenbottom, the best vawyers in… let's see, where are we now?…It…that's it, the Best Vawyers in All of It's our motto. We spring to your defense every morning and take your problems all the way to the bar. Here's my card; here's my phone number; here's my fax number; here's my E-mail address; here's my references; here's my coat size; here's my Swiss Bank Ac-oops; and here's my fee schedule. Your problem is as good as fixed so you can start with the last first and the devil take the rest…"

He turned to It and his left mouth took up where the right had just left off. "He'lo, It," he said purringly, "I really like your hat band. Love that tongue, but next time, stick to black. Those colored rings are too flashy, and a nice ring of black around your head, y'know, will give you that distinguished look, maybe even get you a job in torts."

"Hissssssss," said Hissofer Booshocks.

"And next time try to get one that doesn't leak."

"Hissofer doesn't leak," stammered Toonie. "He just sounds like he leaks so everybody will think he's an inner tube sneaking up on them. Isn't that right, It?"

"Yes and no," said the Itofit's voice from somewhere behind him. "Yes if he's leaking and no if he's sneaking. But to air is human and to forget is snakey."

The Itofit was so startled to hear his own voice saying what he was just about to say, that he twirled around in confusion, only to see Hobnail, with a grin on her mischievious beak, sitting on the rail behind him.

"Hobnail can mimic anybody," said Toliver.

"Especially if they're full of sophicals," added Toonie who often knew what she was saying even when she didn't.

"Very clever," said Mister Nister's left mouth. "Very clever indeed, It. Everybody knows that two mouths are better than one but nobody ever does anything about it. Right right?"

"Right left," said the other mouth with a much more resonant tone. "If you're not among the blessed born with two mouths, any strategum to get an extra will work."

"But the trick is," confided the left, "never let the other one sound like you or people won't know you've got it. You want two distinct sounds, It, one for cajolery, one for Calliope; one for blood, sweat, toil, and tears, one for syrupwater; one for confounding the enemy, one for contorting the…"

The right mouth cut the left off. "That's sanctified information, left. Not to be given away free. Besides there's time enough for pleasantries later. Now to business…" Just then a bell inside his briefcase began to ring. Mister Nister opened it quickly with his lower two hands and with the upper two took out two telephones, one of which he put to each ear, but held the right one with his left hand and vice versa so his wrists covered his lips and no one could read them from a distance.

"Hello." said the left mouth smiling broadly.

"Nister here," said the other.

"Why yes, of course," said the left.

"No! Never!" cried the right.

"Coddle him," said the left.

"Not until he pays," continued the right, "and slap a lien on his bank account, mortgage his house, and get Slippery Sam to appraise his tootmobile…"

"But tell his wife we're sorry," said the left sympathetically.

"But if she continues to support him," advised the right, "target the kids. Mention foster care, no, make that an orphanage since they're back in style."

"Remind her most of them have nice schools nearby and accept food stamps," continued the left.

"Get on it right away," concluded the right. "Keep me advised." And he slammed down the phone.

"And tell her we're only interested in their welfare," said the left, still smiling. "Bye now."

"What was that all about?" asked Toliver, momentarily taken aback by the curious nature of the conversations.

"None of your business," snapped the right mouth. But then it smiled and a right hand ruffled Toliver's hair. "You're not in the loop so it doesn't matter, young man."

"Just a chat with Mister Toppenbottom," said the left mouth. "Nothing important, but tell me now, what's troubling you?"

"Well, we do have a problem," admitted Toliver reluctantly, "but we're going to discuss it with the Wun-dur-phul, so we probably won't need you."

"Oh, don't see the Wun-dur-phul," said the left mouth soothingly, and one of the left arms reached out and patted Toliver's shoulder. "He'll just tell you what to do and there's no contention in that, now is there?"

"You do want to be a contender, don't you boy?" demanded the right mouth and the hand still tousling his hair, squeezed his head instead.

"Well, yes. I guess so," agreed Toliver. "But Mr. Wun-dur-phul has been recommended, and, ouch! that hurts."

"Sorry, boy, but I had to get your attention," said the right mouth.

"Mr. Wun-dur-phul, indeed!" snapped the left mouth with pursed lips. "Fat lot of good he'll do you. Nothing in this world is more dangerous than free advice. You get nothing for nothing, you know, and Mister Wun-dur-phul charges nothing. So you figure it out!"

"Never trust anyone who doesn't make a dime out of his verbiage or a nickel per wink," agreed the right mouth.

"Not even your mother," added the left.

"My mother always gives good advice," stammered Toonie who, though she might not always agree with what she happened to be saying at the moment, always wanted other people to do so.

"Ha!" exclaimed Mister Nister's right mouth. "Things like 'Go to bed!' when you still want to play, or 'Don't eat any more cake and cookies!' when you're still hungry, or 'Please be quiet!' when you have a lot more to say. Ha! Indeed! I know all about mothers!"

"You seem to know an awful lot for someone who's so little," said Whizlet who usually thought of bigness as good (except, of course, in groblets) and littleness as, well, littleness.

"What's that?" questioned both of Mister Nister's mouths simultaneously. His head turned to frown at Whizlet with its right mouth, and smile at him while it spoke with the left. "Modesty compels us vawyers to shrink as we get older and become more renowned."

"You mean you're going to get even smaller!" exclaimed Toonie who was sort of wishing he'd do so right now, maybe even disappear altogether.

"Of course," said Mister Nister smiling serenely with both mouths. He rose to his full height somewhat above the Itofit's knee. "We all do. Look Mister Phister, if you can see him. Why, he's now so famous that we need a magnifying glass to see him." He pulled out the glass, which was handing from the gold chain around his neck and put it to his right eye. The eye grew as large as the glass and with it Mister Nister examined Toliver, Toonie, and Whizlet in turn. Toliver looked somewhat flustered but very determined nonetheless. Whizlet looked like he might try to kerplunk him, or at least kick at his shins, so the vawyer dropped his glass and spoke directly at Toonie who was still gaping at him hoping he'd shrink away to nothing. "Come now, little lady. Tell Mister Nister what your problem is."

"Well, ah…er…uh," said Toonie undoubtedly taken aback by the ogling of the creaturette. "We met the Itofit on a mossy rock and came here in a flower after floating across Swamp Lake where the turtle ate it after getting It's stick stuck in his throat and now we can't get home."

"A turtle, eh?" said Mister Nister right mouth as he rubbed his chin with a thumb and finger of one hand, scratched his neck with another, wiped his brow again with his handkerchief, and pulled out a little notebook with the fourth. "Nasty things, turtles. Always getting in the way, gumming things up, taking no care whatever for parties of the first part, running out in front of everybody else to eat stuff up first."

"Running?" said Toliver somewhat surprised.

"Flying?" offered Mister Nister's left mouth.

"Flying?" repeated Whizlet even more surprised.

"Well whatever," said the right mouth, visibly displeased at its left mouth's indiscretion. "What is a turtle anyway that, by a different name, wouldn't be the same thing."

"How can you know how to help us if you don't even know what a turtle is?" demanded Toonie who, now that Mister Nister's baleful stare was elsewhere for the moment, was her old feisty self again.

"Eh?" said Mister Nister's left mouth defensively. "Beside the point, my dear. 'Turtle' is a word and I know everything there is to know about words. 'Tur-tle' is made up of two syllables: 'turt' and 'tool'. 'Turt' sounds like 'dirt', and 'tool' sounds like 'pool', and, believe me, little lady, anything that smacks of 'dirty pool', I can handle."

"Funny money. Funny money." squawked Hobnail who was still sitting on Is' shoulder but was now bobbing her head up and down and pointing her feathery wing at Mister Nister.

"What's that?" said Mister Nister's right mouth, quite happy to change the subject. "Money? Funny you should mention that." He fixed Toliver with his baleful stare, then softened it to a banker's scowl. "How do you plan to pay?"

"Pay?" responded Toliver.

"Of course, pay." snapped the right mouth.

"Payrolls, pay backs, pay offs, and pillage, young man." prompted the left. "The grease that makes the vaw go 'round and 'round and down and belly-up." But when that seemed to have no effect either, continued: "Pay...money... lucre...swag...bullion...coin...booty...bank notes...stocksenbonds... rasputniks..."

"Rasputniks?" cut in Whizlet who thought Mister Nister might be referring to the greedy rapscallions in *Master Raster's Randy Realm* who always hung grenades on their money belts so pickpockets only got pin money for their troubles.

"Of course, rasputniks. How many rasputniks do you have," demanded the impatient right mouth.

"I don't think we have any of those at all," said Toliver who wanted to be truthful without being offensive or seeming to be poverty stricken either.

"What do they look like," asked Toonie who thought one might look pretty on her charm bracelet.

"Can you use them to bribe your way out of Randy Raster's Redecombobulation Redoubt?" asked Whizlet who was still trying to get a handle on the conversation.

"What! No rasputniks!" exploded the right mouth. "How dare you say you need help when you don't have any rasputniks. I can see there's no use in talking to ignorant people like you." He opened his briefcase while shaking his head and muttering to himself (or maybe his right mouth was muttering to his left ear, or vice versa). In any case, he pulled out a rope ladder, threw it over the side, and started to leave. But he'd forgotten about Panoleon and Lamburtaine and when he looked down at their fire-breathing faces, he thought better of it, and jumped back to the terrace. "Minor inconvenience," said his left mouth pleasantly while his lower arms put away the ladder, and his upper ones pulled the balloon from his vest pocket. He took a huge gulp of air with his right mouth and began puffing on the balloon, and puffing, and puffing, and puffing, and puffing, until it was considerably larger than was he.

"How did he do that?" asked Toonie who'd seen a lot of balloons in her day but never one quite this large and yet filled with a single breath.

"Vawyers go to school to learn a trick that lets them compress air in their lungs," replied Is.

"That lets them talk for ten minutes at a time without taking a breath so no one can interrupt them," added It.

"One has to be careful when explaining the vaw," snapped the vawyer, "otherwise someone else will get to explain it his way first." He opened his umbrella and hooked its curved handle to the bottom of the balloon, then stepped into its upturned lid, resolutely looked in the other direction, and floated away from them.

"What should we do?" called Toonie after him, figuring he'd confused them so much the least he could do was unconfuse them a little before he left.

"Get a court appointed vawyer," answered Mister Nister's right mouth. "They're paid to keep an eye on people who have no rasputniks and other undeniables." He pulled out his watch, glanced at it, then spun around and called back. "And that advice will cost you twenty-three rasputniks. As soon as you get them, let me know, and we'll send you a bill, a frank, a harold, or a summons, whichever comes first, depending on my secretary's day off."

"And if you don't," added the left mouth sweetly, "I know an orphanage that would just love to have you."

Boogie came out from under a table from where he'd been watching everything with the practiced eye of a connocatisseur of juicy rodents and stood up against the rail. "Me-ow-ptut-tui," he spat.

"Fan balloon. Fan balloon!" screeched Hobnail wildly beating her wings in the direction of the retreating vawyer.

"That's all right," said Is, taking the ruffled parrot on her wrist and smoothing her feathers. "He's gone now and won't be back until he smells raw and ready rasputniks, so I think we all deserve a dish of okra and eggplant sher-burr which I just made this morning."

"With turnip topping and a dab of dandelion," added Toonie who knew those things would go well with anything that Is recommended.

"An excellent idea," agreed Is. "And you and I can get it while the men decide what to do next."

"Men?" asked Whizlet looking around.

"She means us," whispered Toliver suddenly feeling very important.

"And Boogie and Hissofer too," added the Itofit, "but Toonie and Is have to help as well because it concerns us all, so all of us have to decide what we've decided and then do it together."

"Me too. Me too," called Hobnail from Is' shoulder.

Is and Toonie brought back a large tray with bowls of okra and eggplant sher-burr and even larger bowls with turnip topping and dandelion dabbings. There was a dish for Boogie who gobbled it down without any topping at all; one for Hobnail who snapped her beak, shook her head, and murmured: "Cold good. Cold good;" a banana split dish for Snorf and Snorfa; one bowl for all the balooms to dip their long proboscises in; and even a narrow little tray for Hissofer who was the only one who wouldn't eat any and turned up both ends of his tongue (which was also his nose) and said the only kind of sher-burr king snakes ate was royal mouse mousse. No sooner had Hissofer made his position clear than there was a shaking in the tree above them, the clink-clunk-bump-boomp of things bouncing from branch to branch, and a sprinkling of talapanuts rained down on the terrace, where each was caught by a leaf and directed into a basket sitting on a table by the door of the basket house, or into people's bowls, one into Toliver's pocket, and another splat into the bowl of dandelion dabbings where it splashed some onto Boogie's whiskers so he had to lick it off and find out what he had missed by being in such a hurry.

"How thoughtful," said Is out loud. "Talapa has given us some talapanuts and Hissofer can probably find one that tastes like royal mouse mousse."

"Hsssss-snap-glump," said Hissofer who snapped up one which just happened to land in the crown of the Itofit's hat.

When everyone was finished with everything, the Itofit asked if they all agreed they should visit the Wun-dur-phul for a very concise, one syllable solution to their problem.

They all nodded their heads except for Boogie who swooshed his tail instead and Hissofer who nodded his tongue, but then Is added that they'd have to be careful because the Wun-dur-phul lived on the other side of the Bad-bad Lands and they didn't want to get lost on the way.

"Oh!" exclaimed Toonie. "Bad-bad Lands sound awful. I didn't think there were any awful things on It..." She paused for a moment, looking off the way the vawyer had gone, and lowered her voice, "...except for Mister Nister and his partners."

"We also have Badder Lands," said Is wrinkling her brow and rubbing the crinkles with her tailtip.

Toonie was alarmed by Is' tone of voice. "Badder Lands too! I thought everything on It was perfect!"

"Nothing is perfect all the time," replied Is, who believed children should always be told the truth or at least as much of it as they were interested in.

"We have Worser Lands too," added the Itofit, who agreed wholeheartedly with Is, and proved it by adding: "Not to mention Alabramble which is a lot like Bambodia, Warlordia, and Thugoslavia, except closer."

"Alabramble!" exclaimed Whizlet narrowing his eyes. "If that place is anything like the terrible tangly thorny thickets in *Jungle Jinx & the Swampthomps* we'll need atomic blasters and laser bombs to get through."

"That's probably a good idea," agreed It, "because the snollygosters have all kinds of tricks to trick people with."

"That sounds very serious," said Toliver sounding very serious himself because he always liked to make his voice sound like what it was saying so he wouldn't confuse anybody, including himself.

"Tricks!" exclaimed Whizlet who was thinking of all the smoke, mirrors, and boxes inside boxes in *Whodini's Magic Top Hat*. "I love tricks."

"I don't think you'd like the snollygosters' tricks," said It. "They're all designed to hurt you, trip you up, or steal what you have."

Is shook her head and sighed. "Alabramble used to be a nice place until the snollygosters arrived and ruined it all. Everything got worse and worse and even the flowers in the jungle and roadside plants turned bad."

"Of course the snollygosters helped them along," said It. "Since everybody loves flowers and nobody ever expects them to be nasty, the snollygosters whipped them, and fed them musty-fusty fertilizers, and shocked them with lectricsticks, and locked them in dark cages until they became as nasty as the snollygosters themselves."

"They grow all kinds of awful things," agreed Is. "Weeping cryacinths and seed shooters and floating pangifrangi traps…"

"And lassoing kudzus and thorn throwers…"

"And toison pivy and mourning gories…"

"And philobopodendrons…and…" It and Is looked at each other, shaking their heads in unison,

"and giant," said Is,

"…stomping," said It,

"…clomping," said Is,

"…egregious," said It,

"…capricious," said Is,

"…malicious," said It,

"…duplicitous," said Is,

"…heinous spry traps!" said they together, and they intertwined their tail tips and banged them on the floor like a sledge hammer.

"Oh my!" gasped Toonie.

"What do these snollygosters look like?" gulped Toliver who didn't like what he was hearing one bit but knew you had to know what bad things looked like before you could avoid them.

The Itofit looked terribly uncomfortable, gazed pleadingly at Is, then hemmed and hawed: "I'm afraid they look something like you."

"Only they're bigger and not so pretty," consoled Is, who then added firmly. "But we're not going anywhere near Alabramble anyway."

"Unless we get lost, or confused, or blown off course." added It.

"Blown off course!" exclaimed Toliver. "Are we going in an airplane?"

"No indeed," replied It. "We'll take baloomerangs."

"Which are safer than airplanes," said Is, "because they're lighter than air and fall up."

"And fly by themselves," continued It.

"And always come back home." said Is.

"And should be grazing on the pangifrangi flowers upstairs right now," said It.

"Upstairs?" asked Toliver who had noticed that only vines and tulivators were hanging down from the terraces above them.

"In the upper branches of the talapalodion tree," said the Itofit pointing straight up with his tail. "I'll call them."

"Maybe we should discuss this too." began Toonie who was already having trouble keeping track of every strange thing on It. But the Itofit had already raised his tail and bonked himself twice on the head, a call which was answered immediately from above by a marvelously melodious honk followed quickly by another, just slightly less loud but even more melodious sound that was more like a honka. Accompanying the sounds was a rumbling of the upper branches that made the rain of talapanuts seem like no more than a morning mizzle. The basket house shook, the terraces swayed as though a good breeze was blowing, and the leaves above their heads parted to allow the passage of two very large and incredibly colorful creatures. They looked exactly like balooms except they were a hundred and eight times as large and had a much more serious demeanor (which was really just a front because they were certainly as silly as balooms, and, as anyone on It could tell you, every hollow bone in their bodies was a funny bone.)

"Wow!" said Toliver who had never seen anything so peculiar in his life or at least not before they had arrived on It.

"The sky's falling!" cried Toonie who didn't want Chicken Little to appear suddenly and announce it first.

"Elephants can't fly," said Whizlet with an air of finality, "except when they get blown sky high in *Safari Madness*." He scratched his head and screwed up his face. "So they must be something else."

The first of the giant creatures broke free of the lower branches and floated down, twisting as he came so everyone could see how pretty he was from every direction, and landed very gently by the Itofit.

"They look like very big balooms," said Toliver who liked to fit things into categories even if they wouldn't fit into the same boxes.

"Very, very big balooms," agreed Toonie.

"And there are two of them," said Whizlet who watched the second creature drift down to Is and put its trunk out to nibble on her ear (or maybe whisper something into it). "They must play twistles made out of hollow trees!"

"They're baloomerangs," explained Is, stroking a huge flutterby-shaped ear, "and we don't know if they're giant balooms or if balooms are tiny baloomerangs, but they're certainly cousins. This one is Rangi and she's been with me since I was an Islette, and that one is Rango and he's been with It ever since his egg hatched in one of Talapa's pangifrangi flowers."

"How do they work?" asked Toliver who was quite amazed that anything that looked like a cross between an elephant, a puffer fish (all puffed up), and a painting by Mr. Pollock (of which Mrs. Mudfinger had a copy of one hanging by Hobnail's perch to inspire the parrot, as she explained, to sing, or, as Toliver's father maintained, to scare the screeches out of her) could wander around treetops sipping from frangifunni flowers, much less fly.

"Why they just puff themselves up with air," explained the Itofit, "and keep it hot with the glotti-burners in their throats, and swim with their fins, and steer with their tails."

"And if they have to go really fast," added Is, "they can point their trunks the way they want to get away from and jet off."

"I'll get the saddlemats so we can jet off with them," said It.

"And Toonie and I can take the dishes to the waterwizzle so Talapa won't have to pick them all up," said Is.

"What can I do?" asked Toliver who always liked to help even if he didn't know how things like saddlemats and waterwizzles worked.

"You can tickle Rango under his left tuskette. Right here," said It, doing just that, "so he'll get to know you and like you a lot. And Yipesadoddle can tickle the right."

While Is and Toonie picked up all the dishes, It went to a basket-like box by the basket house and brought back two saddlemats. "They're knobbled on both sides," he said as he threw one over Rangi's back, "but their knobbled differently so one sides sticks to the baloomerang and other sticks us to it so we can't fall off…unless we want to, of course, and then we just do this:" He put his finger into the knobble and wiggled it around until the knobbles all about it relaxed and lay down.

Is came back with Toonie. "…and they're called Baloomerangs because they always take you back to where you started from," she was saying. "We can baloomalong all the way to the Wun-dur-phul's oasis and not have to worry about the Bad-bad Lands at all." She laughed as Rangi pulled on her earlobe and the flock of balooms began twittering and tittering about her head, as anxious to go as the snigglesnorfs who were chasing each other through the baloomerangs' legs and loved to fly because they got to get their handsfeet all stuck in the knobbles.

The Itofit put his hands on the side of Rango's saddlemat and vaulted up to his back. "Toliver and Yipesadoddle can come with me, and Toonie and Boogie ride with Is, and we'll be there in no time at all." Before anyone had a chance to object or offer suggestions (which nobody had any of anyway), Rango's proboscis unrolled, reached out, encircled Whizlet, and lifted him high in the air.

"Yipes-a-doddle!" cried Whizlet who didn't know if he was being kerplunked or not, but when he was deposited safely in front of It, he let out a "Wow-de-dow!" that sounded so exhilarated that Toliver didn't mind at all when he was picked up and set down in front of Whizlet. Only Boogie watched the whole maneuver with some misgivings and was about to retreat to behind the basket under the table when Toonie grabbed him and held him tightly in her arms. Is sprang to the top of Rangi and as Toonie was lifted up by Rangi's trunk, all poor Boogie could do was mutter a half-hearted "Me-ow-oh-my!"

The snigglesnorfs ended their chase with Snorf running up Rango's tail and Snorfa gliding up Rangi's proboscis while Hissofer hissed them on from the Itofit's hat brim, and Hobnail circled above whistling Mr. Gershwin's *Kicking the Clouds Away*. Thomey, however, unwrapped herself from Toonie's shoulders, ran down the side of the saddlemat, and jumped back to the terrace where she hurried to the railing and wrapped herself firmly around it. "I can't go, Toonie," she said. "I'm a sta-ya-thome, you know, and I like it fine right here. But hurry back. You're so soft and pretty I'll miss you all morning."

Rango looked at Rangi and let out a little honk. Rangi honka'ed back and, side by side, the two baloomerangs ran as fast as they could on their stubby legs, jumped over the railing, and glided out over the beautiful valley. "The Wun-dur-phul lives that way," said the Itofit pointing off to the distance, "past Pearl Rock Mountain and beyond the Bad-bad Lands."

BALOOMERANGING

The baloomerangs seemed to float through the air, moving up and down like prettily painted horses on a merry-go-round (though rather rotund and wrong-legged horses) with their small filigreed wings and large floppy ears flapping to the sides while their tails swooshed along like the flukes of whales (which they looked much more like than horses, especially if the whales just happened to have swum through a sea of brightly colored paints). On their backs everyone bounced along with them, laughing all the while, just like they were pingpong balls bounding through the air.

"Wow! This is fun!" exclaimed Toliver as he looked down at the garden-like panorama stretching away from the talapalodion tree.

"Gittyap!" cried Toonie who was very excited and delighted to be with Is, but wasn't at all sure what one yelled at a baloomerang to make it go.

"Hurufphumph!" managed Whizlet who was squeezed between Toliver and It and couldn't see anything at all and could hardly breathe.

"Oh, I'm sorry," said It who slid further back so Whizlet had more room, then pointed out the necklace of rounded peaks on Pearl Rock Mountain so he would know where they were going.

The mountains drew closer and closer and the baloomerangs, who seemed to know exactly where they were going without being told, or at least where the Wun-dur-phul's oasis had been the last time they were there, headed for a pass between two of the lower peaks. The ground with its trees and rocks and pretty lakes with green-blue water streaked with vertul waves, came up toward them and the air became bouncier so they all held on more tightly with their knees even though the saddlemats held them fast as could be.

"Wheeee!" cried Toliver who had never had so much fun in his whole life.

"Wheeee-ta-deee!" yelled Toonie who liked to answer when somebody said something, and usually added something of her own if she could.

"Look at me!" laughed Whizlet. "No hands!" He threw his arms up in the air to show he wasn't holding on at all (even though he was squeezing very hard with his knees). But finding that not adventurous enough, he put his hands on Toliver's shoulder and climbed to his feet, then lifted his hands, balanced himself for a moment, and raised one foot until his leg was stuck out like a Cossack dancer. "Watch this…" he began, but just then the baloomerangs came to the far side of the pass where all the air spilled down on the other side so it felt like the floor of an elevator had just dropped out from under them (and everybody's stomach jumped to their throats), and poor Whizlet flew up into the air, did a somersault and half-twist, and might have set a new record for the high dive except the Itofit caught him in mid air and held him tight.

"Yipes-a-doddle!" coughed Whizlet whose face was as white as the pearly snow on the peaks above them and whose eyes were as big as pizza pies with all the olives and pepperonis in the middle.

"It's usually better to hang on," said It as he twisted Whizlet right side up and sat him down again. "Otherwise you might fall into a tree and disturb some bird's nest."

"And break an egg if not your head," admonished Toonie who was very good at admonishing little cousins.

"What's that?" asked Toliver pointing toward a cone-shaped mountain with no trees at all arising from the sere and windswept landscape ahead.

"That's Pimple Peak," replied Is, "which shows we're in the Bad-bad Lands and heading in the right direction." And indeed the territory was well named for it was like a desert of shifting sands and deep gullies, but no water was flowing through the gullies and the sands, though prettily colored in the morning light with yellows and oranges and reds (and even an occasional xoc dune which the children could now see clearly and found most strange and almost ominous), were dry as the ashes of yesterday's fire. The baloomerangs gave Pimple Peak a wide berth, then followed a particularly wide gully that soon left the sands behind and cut through a gray, washboard-like land of bare stone. This too dropped behind and was replaced by low, saw-toothed hills that looked like an old wasps' nest broken and scattered about, with occasional trees like skeleton arms poking toward them and waving their tops like grasping hands in the dry wind.

"Why in the world…" began Toliver, "…I mean the world of It, does the Wun-dur-phul live out here?"

"His oasis is very nice," replied Is.

It nodded agreeably and then realizing that since he was in the back nobody could see him, added: "He says having an oasis in the middle of the Bad-bad Lands makes it even nicer, or nice-nice, as he says, because when everything around you is awful, something even a little nicer seems to be the most beautiful thing there is."

"That's very peculiar," said Toonie who rarely had to put up with awful things so didn't have much to compare all her nice things to. "I'd think it was better to live in the prettiest place around so you'd have to have even nicer things to be happy."

"That too," agreed It, who then pointed ahead to an egg-shaped depression in the crinkled gray landscape where the tops of a grove of tall green trees were poking up.

Rango honked softly to Rangi who honka'ed back, and the baloomerangs unrolled their long proboscises, blew out some of their hot air, and began to go down. The trees were growing about a pretty little pond that had a fountain in the middle from which a plume of water was splashing up like a dancing mushroom. Beyond the trees, the gray rock climbed again to the encircling Bad-bad Lands, but one of the walls had a stone house built against it (so it looked like many of its rooms were probably caves in back) and a beautiful garden in front with a lawn of flowering grass by the pond where the baloomerangs came down in front of a very large umbrella. Beneath the umbrella, sitting on a round and puffy divan, was a creature who, from the neck up, looked all the world like a horned toad, and from the neck down, at least those parts not covered by his bright pink trousers and purple bib, like a fat and florid frog. One leg was crossed over the other, one hand was fanning his face with a rippled fan, and the other holding a large book which he was studying very intently through his spectacles.

"Is that the Wun-dur-phul under the umbrella?" asked Toliver who found the figure quite imposing and certainly looked like someone they might have come all this way to see.

"Yes and no," replied the Itofit. "That is definitely the Wun-dur-phul but what he's sitting under is only an umbrella on rainy days, of which there are very few here, so today it's a parasol."

"But the Wun-dur-phul just calls it his 'lid' whether its sunny or rainy," said Is.

"Parasol is a much prettier word than lid," said Toonie. "And so is umbrella if you think about it."

"I agree," replied Is agreeably, "but the Wun-dur-phul only speaks in one syllable words and doesn't understand anything that's more complicated than that."

"So I'd better do the talking," said It as they climbed from the baloomerangs, "because he gets somewhat irritated when people say things that don't make sense to him." He reached over his shoulder and patted Snorf on the snout. "And Snorf and Snorfa have to stay hidden under our shirts because if he sees twelve of us he won't know what to make of it, but it we're only ten he'll be all right."

Toliver looked around and quickly counted their group. Beside himself and the snigglesnorfs there were nine others whose names he knew, but also a whole flock of balooms who had come with them, flying alongside except when they hitched rides by attaching their trunks to Rango's or Rangi's big floppy ears and flapping along with them, tooting happily all the while. "If we count the balooms," he said seriously, "we're a lot more than ten, maybe twenty-seven or twenty-nine."

"The Wun-dur-phul won't count the balooms," said It. "He thinks they're part of my twistle which he calls my tflute."

As it was, the balooms immediately flew off anyway to play around the fountain, and the baloomerangs, who loved to swim by filling themselves half full of water and going around like submarines with proboscis periscopes, hobbled to the water and began drinking their half-fill.

As they stepped under the parasol, the Wun-dur-phul pointed at each in turn with his fan. "Nine," he said happily.

"Ten," said the Itofit pointing at his hatband.

"What is that?" asked Phul.

"Hssssssssss." said Hissofer who wasn't sure if the Wun-dur-phul was a toad or a frog and whether or not they might be distantly related, but was sure that he wasn't at all pleased to be referred to as a 'what'.

"A hissssss it is," said the Wun-dur-phul. "Ten is right. What would you like to talk of?"

"Our friends want to meet you," continued It. "Next to Hissss, there is Tol and Toon, Yipes, Boog, and Hob."

"Hi, Tol and Toon..." began the Wun-dur-phul.

"Hello," said Toonie doing a little curtsy because she knew it was always nice to be very polite when you were introduced to someone new, even if it was a toad.

Phul's face darkened over. "What did you say?"

"Hel...," started Toonie again, but the Itofit quickly put his hand over her mouth so she couldn't get the whole word out and confuse Phul further.

"Hell is a bad place," said the Wun-dur-phul nodding his head somewhat pompously. "But Heav is a good place so they make up for each each."

"Who are you?" burst in Whizlet who couldn't decide if the Wun-dur-phul was a slippery saurian from *Dinosaur Disaster* (in which case he ought to jump into the pond and hide out with Rango and Rangi) or Freddy the Frog in *Fat Freddy's Hydrofarm* (in which case he should ask for a snail jelly donut with frog frosting and polliwogged cream.)

"Hmmmm," said the Wun-dur-phul bending closer to Whizlet and studying him carefully through his spectacles. Satisfied that Whizlet was really curious and wanted to know who he was, he sat back, closed his fan, and began to move it from side to side like a metronome:

I am the Wun who plays in the sun

I am the Dur who has no fur

I am the Phul who eats like a bull

I am the Wun who likes to have fun

I am the Dur who was born of a her

I am the Phul who pulls the wool

I am the Wun who squats to run

I am the Dur who bathes in myrrh

I am the Phul who went to school..."

"That should be 'Phool'," cut in Whizlet who thought that words that didn't rhyme shouldn't be made to.

"Shsssh," said Toonie, who was more interested in what was being said than how it rhymed.

"What did you say?" asked the Wun-dur-phul who never liked to be interrupted. "I do not fib."

"Oh," exclaimed Whizlet who'd already gotten more than he'd bargained for from the Wun-dur-phul's recital and was having a little trouble withstanding the creature's staring eyes magnified by spectacles, "I don't fib either."

"Eith or what?" inquired Phul.

"Or, or, or at least I don't think I do," replied Whizlet who knew he shouldn't fib about fibbing and was afraid the Wun-dur-phul had caught him out.

"I think too," said Phul. "But I think Wun is one. I think that is right. I think It is strong. I think Is is nice. I think It is Is, and I think Is is It, since two are one and Wun is too. I know what to think and I think what to do. What do you want to think of?"

"We have a problem," said Toonie not thinking too clearly.

"You have a prob with a man named Lem?" asked the Wun-dur-phul screwing his face up as though he wasn't quite sure who Lem was.

"No, a pr'bl'm," said Toonie hoping if she said it quickly enough the Wun-dur-phul would be able to catch on without catching her out.

"A what?" asked the Wun-dur-phul crossly.

"A thing that does not work," corrected the Itofit.

"Of course," said Phul. "All of us have such things."

"The turtle ate our flower," cut in Whizlet angrily, shaking his fist in the air in front of the Wun-dur-phul but certainly not at him.

"The what? ate who?" stammered Phul and his face grew xoc and his spectacles steamed over.

"A creech and a thing like a rose," said It quickly, seeing how upset the Wun-dur-phul was becoming.

The Wun-dur-phul took off his spectacles and wiped them carefully on his bib. "Why yes, of course, and what did the creech do that made the rose eat it?"

"Noth…" started Whizlet but found the Itofit's hand firmly over his mouth.

"No," said Toonie trying to be helpful since she knew that was the way you were supposed to be with people who didn't seem to know how to help themselves and couldn't even tell the difference between a turtle and a flower. "The creech ate the rose." She said it very deliberately, speaking each word carefully, then added as an afterthought: "The rose eats people!"

"Eats what?" snapped the Wun-dur-phul.

"It ate us!" wailed Toonie.

"Then why are you not in the creech?" asked the Wun-dur-phul who really was following what was being said.

"We were spit out," replied Toliver who wanted to get everything straight even if it sounded confusing. "And then the creech ate the rose so now we can't get back home." He let out a sigh of relief at saying it all so the Wun-dur-phul could understand, then added: "And that's what it's all about."

"A bout?" cried the Wun-dur-phul pulling his bib up and covering his nose. "A bout of what? The flu? The pox? The gout? Oh, my! How bad! A bout of the gout!"

"No, no, not at all," said the Itofit hoping to calm Phul before he had a fit. "Not a bout, a bite. The rose bit us and the creech bit the rose."

"Ah, yes! Life and death," said the Wun-dur-phul relaxing again and dropping the bib from his face. "To eat is to live; to eat is to die." He hesitated, noticing how uncomfortable Toonie looked with this line of reasoning, and being a very compassionate (though frequently hungry) creech himself, softened his words. "Food is both life and the end, small one; life for one is the end for the other. I can tell you how life makes the end but not how the end makes life."

"Oh boo!" said Toonie stamping her foot on the ground just like grown people did when they were angry or stepping on spiders. "Then you can't help us at all!"

"See the Lud," said the Wun-dur-phul pretending to ignore Toonie's outburst by staring into the distance over their heads.

"The who?" asked Toliver.

"Hear the Gord?" continued Phul, this time ignoring Toliver but cupping his hand around an ear and appearing to listen very attentively.

"What kind of gourd?" asked Toonie who had gotten over her pique very quickly and knew that gourds rattled but wondered what a rattle might be able to tell them.

"He means the Ludgord!" exclaimed the Itofit, then quickly corrected himself. "I mean the Lud and the Gord, of course Phul. But I do not think we can do that."

"You do not think of the Lud; you can not think of the Gord," said the Wun-dur-phul.

"I know that too," replied It.

"The Lud and the Gord are not two," continued the Wun-dur-phul. "The Lud and the Gord are one." While he was speaking he set down his fan and held up both hand to show two, then brought them together to show one. "Two, one," he continued opening and closing his hands, "One, two…"

Whizlet climbed on his lap and slapped his hands against those of the Wun-dur-phul. "Let's play pattycake," he said.

For a moment the Wun-dur-phul was taken aback, first by having someone on his lap, second by having someone hitting his hands, and third by a strange word that made no sense to him at all. But before he could voice his confusion, Whizlet hit his hands again, the clapped his own:

Pat-tea-cake

Pat-tea-cake

Bake her a man

Bake her a man

As fast as you can

The Wun-dur-phul was startled. "Is Pat the man or the her who bakes him to make a tea cake?"

"Don't care," said Whizlet. "Just hit hands and talk…"

"Pat-tea-cake…"

The Wun-dur-phul joined in:

"Pat-tea-cake…"

Whizlet continued:

"Bake her a man…"

And together they concluded:

"Bake her a man

As fast as you can."

They did it again and again, six or eight times, and when they finished, both laughed, and Whizlet poked the Wun-dur-phul in the stomach with his finger. "I like you!"

"Oooph!" said the Wun-dur-phul who had never been poked in the stomach before. "I like you too; thus, we like each other."

"Yes!" said Whizlet who found the Wun-dur-phul's slippery stomach scales so interesting he began rubbing them with his finger, then his whole palm.

"Ho-ho-ho-ho!" said Phul who wasn't often tickled by anyone. "I like that too." But then, as he always did when he was very pleased, the Wun-dur-phul sneezed, bouncing Whizlet up into the air until he was looking right through his spectacles into Phul's laughing eyes. The Wun-dur-phul caught him and held him for a moment, looking him carefully all over, then set him back in his lap.

"Yipes-a-doddle!" exclaimed Whizlet. "I mean, yipes a doo dull."

"Yipes a doo dull," repeated the Wun-dur-phul. "What do you do that is dull, Yipes?"

"Just yipes-a-doddle," answered Whizlet. "It means: I just had fun."

"Yes," agreed Phul. "I just had fun too."

"Not two." said Whizlet, "Just one - me! I'm a four word word."

"A four word word?" said the Wun-dur-phul sounding confused.

"Not a one word word," continued Whizlet holding up four fingers, "a four word word."

"I do not know what a four word word is."

"You mean, it does not com-pute."

Phul's brow wrinkled. "Who is this Pute who does not come with It?"

"No," said Whizlet patiently (in fact as patiently as he'd ever done anything except put pegs in *Piddley Peg's Poodley Pegboard,* when he was two and a half). "Com-pute is a two word word. It means to think fast in ones and nones."

"Oh dear," said Phul. "A two word word and a four word word, both ones and nones! I will have to think all this through with care."

"Care-ful-ly!" said Whizlet. "A three word word!"

"Oh my!" said the Wun-dur-phul so discombobulated that he picked up the corner of his bib and used it to scratch his head.

"How can we find the Lud or the Gord?" asked Toliver, who was afraid the Wun-dur-phul was becoming distracted.

"Not 'or', 'and'," replied Phul setting Whizlet by his side, "The Lud and the Gord are like Yipes." he scratched his head again, "Let me see, how do we say it, Yipes? a two word word."

"Well, how can we find the Lud and the Gord?" asked Toonie who was getting tired of philosophy (even though she wasn't quite sure what philosophy was) and thought they should stick to business.

"The place of the Lud and the Gord is hard to find," continued the Wun-dur-phul. "But I have heard from my pa who heard from his ma who heard from and so forth: there are six gates to go through:

three gates to Lud, three gates to Gord
the thanes are there and then the ford
the ground that moves, the lake that swims
the air that swirls, the flame that dims
the star that shines, the mind that slept
can not climb up the stone that steps
for where is else and else is where
the mind that wakes from there may fare."

"He must be talking about the Stepping Stone to Elsewhere which is guarded by the Great Halidon in Ludgordia," whispered Is. "It is the most precious stone in the world."

"But how do we find it?" persisted Toonie who, at least for the moment, felt the most precious stone in the world was the pebble in her fish bowl at home.

"Ope your eyes," answered Phul, "and look in. Ope your ears but hear no sound."

"He means the Ludgord can be found anywhere," whispered the Itofit, "though he is usually found in Ludgordia where everybody knows how to look and listen."

"My ears are all ways ope!" said Toonie politely, " 'cept when they have wax in them. And my eyes are ope too, but they all ways look out."

"Look out!" cried the Wun-dur-phul throwing his bib over his head. "Look out for what?"

"I think we should go," said Is who realized how overburdened the Wun-dur-phul was beginning to feel.

"But where can we go?" asked Toonie tearfully. "The Wun-dur-phul was s'posed to tell us! How can I get back to my house, not to speak of the rest of you?"

"Yes," said the Wun-dur-phul thoughtfully, "That might help."

"What might help?" asked Toliver.

"See the house that speaks," replied Phul through the bib, which was still over his head. "See the Glib."

The Itofit snapped his fingers. "Why didn't I think of that! The Glib can fix anything, and he is certainly a lot easier to find than Ludgordia."

"I'm not so sure of that," cautioned Is, "but the Wun-dur-phul has been a great help and we should all thank him. Thank you, Phul."

The Wun-dur-phul dropped a corner of his bib so that one round eye could peek out at them all. "Thank you, Phul," said the Itofit, followed by all the others who said thank you's too except for Hissofer who said Hssssssss, and Boogie who, on principle, refused to be polite to a toad and spit instead, and Hobnail who, being more exasperated than anything, began whistling *The Unanswered Question* of Mr. Ives and flew out to the fountain to tell Rango and Rangi it was time to go.

The Wun-der-phul put his finger in his mouth then held it up into the breeze. "Take care that way," he said pointing the way the Itofit was looking. "Black cloud. Black crowd. Need a lid, not a shroud. Bye bye. Come back soon. Bye for now. Trust a loon."

As soon as they had all remounted the baloomerangs, they waved good-by to the Wun-dur-phul who responded by shaking his fan and nodding his head. "We're off to Glibia," said the Itofit to Rango and Rangi (because if he hadn't said anything, of course, they would have flown right back home like baloomerangs always do) and the animals wobbled off into the air heading toward the Badder Lands.

"Where is Glibia?" inquired Toliver who liked to know where he was going even when it didn't mean anything.

"And who is the Glib?" asked Toonie who thought that sounded pretty suspicious.

"And why can't the Wun-dur-phul come with us?" demanded Whizlet who hated to lose a new friend as soon as he met him.

"Glibia is where the Glib lives when he's not in Warpington," answered the Itofit without answering much at all, "and toads don't fly, but the Glib is the glibbest of the Glibriches."

"The Glib is a person who likes to have audiences and knows how to dance in front of a microphone." added Is.

"Does he sing?" asked Toonie perking up.

"Usually, he just toots his own horn." said It.

"Which is why he's called Toot Glibrich." added Is.

"And he's not a person exactly," corrected the Itofit. "He's a politiconumdrum who drums for the Neandercans in Warpington."

"What are Neandercans?" asked Toliver who thought they were probably something you put neanders in, whatever they were.

"They're like Neandercrats," answered Is, "except that instead of spending everybody's money, they keep it for themselves."

"In Glibia there are only two kinds of people," said the Itofit.

"Boys and girls?" asked Toonie.

"No, rich ones and poor ones."

"That's not very smart," said Toliver who realized that if you had more of the latter kind (which you always did when those were the only two alternatives), then more of the former kind would have to worry all the time, so there would be very few happy people anywhere.

"That's why they keep themselves separated from each other," said Is. "The poor ones are called Glibpoors and live on the ground and the rich ones are called Glibriches and live up in the air."

"If you have a lot of money, you can fly like a jailbird," explained Toonie to Whizlet.

"Not that so much," said the Itofit. "It's just that the rich ones build their houses on the tops of poles so they're stuck up over everybody else."

"And the Glib lives on a pole!" exclaimed Whizlet. "Just like Santa Claus!"

"Yes, he's something like that," agreed Is. "Except he's only Santa Claus for some people."

"And Santa Claws for others," added It. "But if you're nice to him, and do what he wants, and never, never, never contradict him, and say 'Aye' when he tells you to, he's very nice indeed."

"But he ignores all the Glibpoors so they'll go away." said Is.

"Where to?" asked Toonie who wanted to know so she wouldn't have to go there herself.

"Maybe Alabramble," replied It, "because there are even more poor people there, and the snollygosters chain them to gangs so they can clean up after everybody else."

"What about his talking house?" asked Whizlet who thought it might be like Pleasant Palace in *Princess Pretty's Priceless Playland* in which case they could all make three wishes, spin the Wheel of Fortran, and get one of them answered backwards, or maybe like the Demon's Dungeon in *Doomsday Dominoes* in which case they might be better off in Alabramble.

"Well that's very peculiar," responded It. "In Warpington he's called the Speaker of the House so in Glibia he commissioned a huge poll and on top of that he built a house that he tries to make look just like him."

"And he doesn't paint it white because he doesn't want anybody to know he'd live in such a place." interjected Is.

"But he hardly lives there anyway," continued It. "And only goes there to juggle, play poker, and make telephone calls."

"Where is he the rest of the time?" asked Whizlet who figured they'd better go where he was and not to where he might be coming back to later.

"He stays in Warpington," said It. "But his house has cameras in the window-eyes, earphones in the ear cases, and speakers in the front door so it seems like he's right there for you even when he isn't."

"People who want to talk to him have to stand in the trenches in front and talk to a bench, and if the bench likes you, the house will shake, rattle, and roll, and finally, if you bow your head and hold your breath, answer your question." explained Is.

"As long as all you want is answers," continued It, "because if you want him to do something for you, you have to be one of the Glibriches to start with."

"But how can he help us?" asked Toonie who was feeling more and more insecure all the time.

"In Warpington, they say he can fix anything," replied the Itofit, "so maybe he can fix our flower or at least tell us how to fix it ourselves."

"What's that?" yelled Toliver who, being a bit more confused than he wanted to admit by this strange litany of facts, pointed ahead through a grayish haze to what appeared to be a town laid out like graph paper with row after row and column after column of concrete buildings all of which had huge signs on the roofs and bars in the windows.

"That's the Badder Lands," answered It. "They'll try to make us go down so they can get our rasputniks but if we stay up here we'll be all right."

"Why would anyone want to go down there?" asked Toonie who didn't think it looked like a nice place at all.

"Because they get talked into it," replied Is. "Since the people of the Badder Lands think everybody wants something, they pretend they have everything, and when you come to town they try to sell it to you."

"And then they sell you something else instead because you can't think very clearly with all the racket they make," concluded It.

"Oh, isn't that pretty!" exclaimed Toonie as a large kite that looked like a crimson flutterby climbed up toward them. "What does it say?"

"That's just a wily-willy board," replied the Itofit. "You know you're over the Badder Lands when the sky starts getting congested with them 'cause this is where everybody screams and harangues everybody else all the time."

"All they seem to do is yell and sell," added Is. "And nobody knows how anything gets done because they keep selling the same thing over and over again at higher and higher prices until nobody can afford it any more and they put it in a museum."

As they got closer Toliver was able to read the flutterby sign, which said: "*Buy Here! Our Penultimate Going Out Of Business Sale ! Today Only! Tomorrow on Consignment! Nothing Cheaper! Now or Never! Laughin' Armegiddeon's Rubies, Rags, & Rotisseries.*

"Oh my," gasped Toonie. "Rotisseries on sale!"

More kites began swimming up toward them, tethered to the ground by long strings attached to spools where people, or at least creatures who looked like very little people (because they were so far down and hardly distinguishable at all), were furiously unwinding them. Rango had to swerve to the right to avoid one that said:

MARK DOWNS
Tootmobiles with the
Classy Chassis
&
Underachievers' Overdrive

and then even more quickly to the left, where another was darting toward them:

HAPI BAZAAR'S BIZARRE BAZAAR

See
Asshe Ghoes' Purrjun Carpets
And
Tearable Kryin Towels
And/Or
E. N. Tal Rhugs

Then, as though they were bass in a lake on opening day of fishing season, a flock of balloons covered with writing bobbed up into the air before them:

Silky Selene's Hair, Fur, and Tail Stylist. Tail
Tucks & Beard Bobs, Half-Price!
HONEST ABE'S Slightly Used Carts - Nothing
Down - Everything Upfront - low daily interest
*DR. HEALTHY'S TOOTH REPLACEMENTS - specials
on Brass Bicuspids & Molybdenum Molars*
Shop at the Kitchen Sink - We Have *Everything* else too!

Suddenly a rocket burst through all the wily-willy boards and, as it roared ahead, began skywriting before them in money-green letters:

Bilbo's Bank & Wee Trust In U Co. - *Loans, Liens, Loads, & Lumps*

Soon there were so many different sizes and shapes of kites, and flocks of round, oval, square, and oddly configured balloons, with rockets squirting like tooth paste among them that Rango and Rangi could barely see their way ahead and the ground below was completely obscured as more outrageous wily-willy boards kept coming up.

"We'd better go higher," called out the Itofit as he tickled Rango with his toe.

"Honk-honk-honk," agreed Rango so quickly that Toliver couldn't tell if he was answering It's toe or blowing his horn at all the traffic. As Rangi followed the wily-willy boards dropped below, and after a while the people on the ground, seeing their quarry slipping away, reeled their signs back down. Beyond the outskirts of the town, which seemed to be an archipelago of shopping centers with interminable parking lots, was a desert that stretched into the distance toward a ridge of low rolling hills. The breeze picked up and since it created a nice tailwind they were blown along quickly and the ground was soon rising beneath them.

"Glibia is just beyond the hills," reported the Itofit, "and Rango and Rangi are taking us straight to Glibsville where the Toot Glibrich lives, or at least lives when he's home."

"Maybe his wife will be home if he isn't," opined Toonie who knew that a woman's place was in the home office, running things.

"He isn't married," said It. "His wife got older faster than he did so he had to retire her because she wasn't young enough or pretty enough to be a Speaker of the Housewife anymore."

"I think he found another one," said Is. "At least the anchorit on the vellytision said he was out bagging trophies, or bragging to fleas, I'm not sure which, so he could have someone to serve tarminis at his hentail parties."

Glibsville was just over the hill and offered a most unusual perspective. What looked like slums and ghettos were crowded on top of each other all over the land, but here and there a very large pole was stuck up into the sky. On top of each pole was a platform, and on each platform was a house and hangar, a large lawn, and a fenced off garden with a swimming pool and gazebo by the tennis court. The baloomerangs took a moment to get their bearings among the sparse forest of poles, then turned sharply to the right and zeroed in on one that supported the most peculiar house anyone had ever seen. It looked like something from a child's playbox. From the back and sides it might have been an old fashioned schoolhouse with a belfry on top and outside stairways closed in on either side. But as they drew closer, the front of the house appeared to be a pudgy, round face, with shaggy gray hair, a bulbous nose, and a sharp red tongue which, on closer inspection, was a narrow stairway covered with a red carpet leading to the front door. The door with its flanking flower boxes formed the mouth of the visage, the eyes were windows, and the nose was a dormer. The ears were the staircases sticking out to the sides, the jowls were bay windows with pink glass in them, and the roof was covered with some sort of synthetic thatch, which gave the impression of a disheveled mane. The belfry looked like a hat and behind it, no bigger than a stickpin, was the tiniest chimney they'd ever seen. A chain hung from the bell to the front steps, and all along both sides of the house, looking very much like a tight collar, were red, white, and blue tarpaulins draped over stacks of barrels and tightly tied to a railing. There was a long bench in front of the door, and smoke was pouring out of one ear.

"The house on fire!" screamed Toonie. "Call 911 and leave our address!"

"I don't think it's the house that's burning," said Is.

"It's just a smoke filled room," explained the Itofit, "where the Glib's conkniving friends play Monopoly while he plays poker with other politiconundrums, foreign indignataries, and chips off the old block so that everything can get fixed."

"It smells awful," coughed Toonie wrinkling her nose.

"Yes, it does," agreed Is. "But you're not supposed to notice or they blame it on you."

The baloomerangs set down among the trenches and foxholes in the front yard. Toonie wanted to know why the lawn was all dug up, so Is explained that Toot Glibrich wasn't above getting down in the trenches with his men where they could take potshots at Neandercrats and other fuzzy thinkers who wanted to waste money on people who weren't soldiers, prison guards, or secret agents.

"Billions for bullets but not one penny for people, is his motto," said It as he dismounted from Rango. "Because that's the way Glibriches protect themselves from ill winds or any other draft that might leave them out in the cold or in the army."

He strode to the door. Whizlet tagged along behind trying to figure out if the front of the house was a computer screen or just a canvas, rubber, and plastic facade. The Itofit pulled the bell chain by the door, but there was no clapper in the bell and all he did was disturb a bunch of bats, who flew off in a cloud. A moment later a cuckoo bird popped from the nose-window and called out: "Nine o'clock, nine o'clock, leave some money, bonds, or stock." and jumped back inside.

The Itofit waited for a few moments but when nothing else happened, he called out. "Hello Mr. Glibrich, are you speaking today?"

There was no answer to his call either, so he raised his tail high above his head and brought it down smartly with a resounding THONK-Thonk-thonk that sounded like Ringo starring on his timpani.

Again nothing happened, so Toliver, who was quite awestruck by the terribly determined visage of the façade, whispered to the Itofit. "Maybe we should go down under the platform and see if he's there."

"Down Under!" said the House and the whole front of it became animated, the plastic flowers to either side of the door curved up into a smile, the jowls glowed pink, and the eyes crossed. "Who said 'Down Under'? I love Down Under, except of course, when it's Downright Underhanded, and then I have to think about it. Who's out there pulling my chain? Step back where I can see you, but don't sit on my bench, walk on the grass, step on the flowers, spit on the floor, tread on my prerogatives, or comment on what I said yesterday."

The Itofit hurried back to where the others were standing but Whizlet remained where he was trying to determine if the facade was a somewhat bloated rendition of Father Happytimes in *Father Happytimes' Bedtime Stories* or the slightly demented gargoyle in *Gothic Gotfried's Gruesome Garret*. Since he'd never actually been inside one of his games before, this was a whole new experience for him. "Are you real?" he asked.

"Ha!" responded the House. "I'm the Glib and if you're glib you don't have to be real, just reality oriented at fund raisers. Now, get off my tongue, little boy, or you'll get a good lickin' Ho! Ho! Ho!" and the facade shook with mirth.

"What's under those tarpaulins?" asked Whizlet standing his ground.

"None of your business, Rattail. Everything there is classified Top-Top Secret Government Project - Official Eyes Only - Priority Privileges Administration - Trespassers Will Be Snookered, Snickered, Suckered, or Shot." And the House pulled its red carpet tongue out from under Whizlet so fast that Whizlet flew up into the air and came down with a thump.

"Why do you have such a little chimney," asked Toonie as Whizlet hurried back to the Itofit's side, "when you have so much smoke inside?"

"Because we don't believe in Santa Claus," snapped the House, "and children shouldn't either or they grow up to be Neandercrats."

The House sniffed petulantly. The right eye glared at Whizlet; the left at Toonie. "Boys into the trenches; girls up top where it's safer, and let's not haggle about hygiene when the nation's future's at stake. Everybody else to the front lines where you can. Don't tell for you country, and win a purple sock if you're lucky."

Toonie clung to Is' hand, Whizlet to It's leg, and Toliver, who didn't want to appear as nervous as he felt, picked up Boogie and held him under his arm. Having clearly won the first round, overawed his audience, established dominance, and put his petitioners in their places, the House relaxed and the

Speaker became very businesslike, with hardly a trace of glibness left in his voice. "Okay, my friends. Enough of these pleasantries! Which one of you is from Down Under? I have a $4 million book that will make your book factory a fortune, and if that's not enough we can do a sequel, maybe a threquel, and a fourquel too."

Toonie was nonplused. "If you publish your book down under, everything will be upside down and people will have to stand on their heads to read it, or at least make any sense out of it at all."

"On second thought," said the House, "girls into the trenches too. You! Two steps back. March!"

Is put her tail around Toonie and patted her shoulder. "I'm sure your book is very informative and timely…" she began.

"Just like me," said the House. "… And we'll make a mint off the deal. I'll live like royalties and you can talk to anybody you want to over any media you choose. After all, that's what freedom's all about, isn't it? But no favors, no intercessions with people who would fall over backwards just to get a call from me about a problem they're having trouble making their minds up over; no gratuities for being at the right place at the right time, with the right reasons to right righteous wrongs; no hints dropped in the right ears, or left ears either; no tips on the market accepted with conditions. I only help Down Under folks get down home and down home publishers get down under whatever anybody else says they should do."

"But that's exactly what we need!" exclaimed Toonie. "We've got to get home!"

"What!" said the House screwing up its facade. "How very fortunate. You only wish to get home. Renting the Queen Elizabeth, are we? No problem at all. Is that where your book factory is?"

"I'm afraid our book factory burned down…" began the Itofit who felt this might be the best way to explain to a politiconundrum why he was right in assuming they had something they didn't have without coming right out and making a mess of things before they got to say what needed to be said and give the Speaker a chance to say 'no' before he'd even heard what the real problem was.

"What!" exploded the House. "If you need post-pyro fire insurance, you've come to the wrong party. My vawyer takes care of that, but let me know as soon as the presses are rolling again. Better still, don't call me, I'll call you anything I please."

While the Glib was distracted, Whizlet (who could never leave a stone unturned, a present unopened, or a plot uncovered) went to one of the red, white, and blue tarpaulins and lifted a corner.

"Get away from there!" screeched the House. "You're messing with government secrets which could get you ten to twenty or death without…"

"Death without what?" inquired Toonie who thought death was without just about everything.

"Death without possibility of coming back as a Neandercan," said Toot.

"There are just piles of old barrels under there," said Whizlet disgustedly as he came back to the front. "And they don't say Top-Top Secret Anything, they just say Pork."

"Of course, they say P.O.R.K.," responded Toot so quickly that it appeared he'd probably had this trouble before. "That stands for Politiconundrums Only, Rattails Keepout!"

As far as Boogie was concerned, that was the straw that burst the Camel's pack, so he bristled his tail to look like a bottlebrush (or, as he thought, a cannon cleaner) and spat his name at the bench (leaving out the middle syllable, of course.) Hissofer Booshocks took up the call and not only hsssss'ed but stuck his tongue out three times in quick succession (making six times in all if you count the fork), and Hobnail leaped up backwards from Is' shoulder and, fanning her wings furiously, screeched: "Glibberish. Glibberish!"

An angry plume of smoke squirted out of the House's other ear, the shades in the eye-windows snapped shut, and the flower boxes by the door sagged to the ground (while all the plastic flowers in them appeared to wilt.) "I think we'd better leave," said the Itofit. "I don't think the Glib is feeling his toots this morning, and we wouldn't want him to call in his colleagues from the Neanders' Club who have another kind of club for people like us who do unspeakable things like speak to the Speaker before being spoken to."

Rango and Rangi, who had been patiently standing to the side holding trunks, lumbered over and hurriedly plunked everybody onto their backs, then took off like steamrollers across the trenches and foxholes (without a care in the world for whoever might have been hiding in them with listening devices) and jumped happily into the air. Toonie was downcast at their failure to get any help from Toot Glibrich and didn't perk up until Snorfa rubbed her back and nibbled on her earlobe while Is' tail patted her cheek. Toliver was disappointed but not surprised since he pretty well knew what to expect from politiconundrums anyway, and Whizlet was as happy as a clam because he'd left a snapper by the barrels for somebody to step on.

Toonie sniffed, then sighed. "I guess we'll just have to find the Ludgord," she declared. "He'll know how to help us."

"The Ludgord isn't a he," said the Itofit.

"She's a she!" exclaimed Toonie, utterly delighted with the idea.

"No," cautioned Is, letting her tail slide down Toonie's arm. "The Ludgord isn't a she either."

"The Ludgord is both," explained It. "Or rather Heshe can be anything He wants anytime She pleases."

"Even a baloomerang?" asked Toliver who definitely liked the idea of the creature they were riding on being the invincible, invulnerable, and invaluable (albeit invisible) Ludgord.

"Of course," said Is.

"Or a frog?" asked Whizlet who wanted to see how far he might push it, but also hoped the Wun-dur-phul was included.

"That too," replied Is. "The Ludgord is really everything, even you."

"Me!" exclaimed Whizlet suddenly aware he'd pushed it right over the edge. "I'm me! I'm not anybody else!"

"Yes and no," said the Itofit. "Yes you are and no you aren't, and yes you aren't and no you are too."

"Well, if Heshe's Whizzy and Rangi and frogs," puzzled Toliver, "why don't we see him right now and get it all over with?"

"The Ludgord likes people to do things for themselves," explained the Itofit. "It wouldn't be any fun if Heshe interfered all the time."

"But what about when you need help?" asked Toonie who often felt she did. "Like now."

"Well, now we're fending for ourselves," replied It.

"And we seem to be doing quite well," added Is, "so we'll have to keep our eyes open and maybe find hints along the way."

"Just like *Tops'il Tom's Treasure Hunt*," explained Whizlet who knew there were plenty of clues if you knew what you were looking for, "where another piece of the map is always someplace where you never expect it like in Pegleg's peg or Polly's cracker."

"This is all very muddley," said Toonie. "I think we should stop talking silly and just find the Ludgord and ask Him, Her, or Whoever how She, He, or Whatever can help us fix the flower and get home again before it's too late to remember where we've been, or who we are either."

"But where should we look?" asked Toliver.

"If we think about it," replied the Itofit, "we should be able to figure that out and then go there and see if we're right."

"But we keep taking you further and further away from your home and the ta-lap-a-lota-doom tree and Thomey and the thimble thanes and the troll bridge and the, the...awful flower." and Toonie burst into tears.

"Don't worry about that," said the Itofit, "we're with you from xoc to xaalu 'cause that's what friends are all about."

Is caught Snorf as he jumped over to Rangi to play with Snorfa and laughed as both snigglesnorfs disappeared under the baloomerang's belly. "Sometimes you see the Ludgord and sometimes you don't," she reflected, "but Heshe is always worth looking for. My mother told me Heshe was most easily found in Ludgordia where everybody understands the secret. And Ludgordia is somewhere in Arigonia and to get to Arigonia we would have to pass through the Ice-Capped Mountains to the Place of Wonderful Things, then cross the Bay of Beauty to the Isle of Song where a melody would waft us straight across to the Bairn of Blissful Blazes, and then... and then...let me see if I remember the rest..."

"It doesn't matter," interrupted the Itofit, "because nobody knows where those places are anyway, but if we were lucky enough to find one, it might lead us on to the others."

"What's that?" interrupted Toliver who was pointing high above them where a white crane was flying gracefully across the sky.

"It's a sacred white crane," answered Is, "flying home."

"Where does it live?" asked Toonie.

"No one knows that either," responded the Itofit. "But look! One of its feathers has dropped off and is fluttering down."

Only Is and Hobnail could see as well as It so while everybody else stared at something they couldn't yet make out, Hobnail flew ahead singing *The Magnificat*. She hoped to catch the crane (because she knew a white crane would know exactly what to do to help them), but the big bird was too high and too far away so she caught the feather instead and brought it back to Is who put it in Toonie's hair. "This is very lucky," Is said. "I think the crane is trying to tell us something."

"Maybe we should follow it," said Toliver.

"It looks like it's headed toward Alabramble," said It. "But I know it doesn't live there."

"The Ice-Capped Mountains must be somewhere beyond Alabramble," mused Is.

"I'm sure they are," agreed the Itofit snapping his fingers. "Because that was where the Mostable It was headed when he got bushwhacked."

"And it is probably still dangerous."

"But if we stay very high and keep very quiet, and Rango and Rangi fly quickly from cloud to cloud," planned the Itofit out loud, "we could probably sneak across Alabramble without anyone noticing us and see if there really are Ice-Capped Mountains on the other side."

"What does everybody else think about that," asked Is, "including Rango and Rangi who will have to do all the work?"

Hobnail answered first by fluttering her wings and singing Mr. Delius' *A Walk to the Paradise Garden* in her very prettiest voice, which Boogie answered with a Me-ow-an'-how, and Hissofer agreed to by twisting together the forked ends of his tongue into a single arrow pointing ahead, and the snigglesnorfs didn't care as long as they could play all the while, and the children all nodded their approval, and the flock of balooms twittered among themselves and asked the baloomerangs who honked and honka'ed agreeably and turned to follow the beautiful white crane which was disappearing toward the untoward Worser Lands which lay between Glibia and Alabramble.

"There's Baffleburg," said Is, pointing ahead toward what looked like a dismal swamp from which a miasma of blue fog was rising. As they drew closer, however, they could see it was not a swamp below them, but another town laid out in a grid. On every corner was a building with a peaked roof atop which a curious cruciform scaffolding was erected to which an agonized figure was attached. And rolling out in waves from the doors and windows of most of these building was the blue fog that from a distance had appeared so noxious and now seemed merely designed to camouflage what was otherwise a rather drab town.

"Wow!" exclaimed Whizlet, "that's even worse than Toot Glibrich's smoke filled room."

"They're smoke filled buildings." agreed Toliver.

"A smoke filled town!" exploded Toonie who always liked to up the ante whenever she was able to wait that long.

"Do the people in the Worser Lands try to sell you stuff too?" asked Toliver.

"Yes and no," replied the Itofit. "Yes, they try, and no, they don't, because they don't have anything anybody wants."

"Mostly they just shout a lot and try to convince everybody else they know what they're talking about…" began Is.

"And they argue all the time, mostly about who's wrong about things that nobody can be sure of anyway." added It.

"…and they don't want you to think for yourself, because it makes them uncomfortable to think you can," continued Is.

"…and if you don't agree with them, watch out!" concluded It. "It's bonkers for you!"

"You mean they harangue each other here too," said Toliver.

"No, they hallelujah each other," admitted the Itofit, "which is even worse because after it's all over, you've still lost all your rasputniks but don't have anything to show for it."

"Except promises," agreed Is, "from people who say the Promised Land is somewhere else since they haven't learned how to take care of the one they've got here."

"Why do they have those things on the roofs?" asked Toliver who thought it a funny place for scarecrows since that was where the crows were supposed to hang out after you scared them.

"I think they are some kind of warning sign," replied the Itofit scratching his chin, "to let you know what will happen to you if you lose an argument with them."

"Or more likely if you win," corrected Is.

"Oh look," cried Toonie. "More wily-willy boards are coming up."

"These aren't wily-willy boards," cautioned Is, "they're Simon-Says-Sermon-Signs."

"Which are just like wily-willy boards," explained It, "except they aren't really selling you anything, they're just trying to scare you into dropping your wallet."

"They discovered they don't have to give you anything if they can talk you out of your money instead." added Is.

"How can they do that?" asked Toonie who knew value when she saw it and could count pennies (if not rasputniks yet) with the best of them.

"They have a lot of sneaky ways," replied It. "They send up signs hanging from spider webs which say things like *Repent HERE!* or *Get Saved HERE!!* and when you go *HERE!* to see what they're talking about, they drop the net over you and pull you down."

"Where you're saved from being free and get to repent being caught," exclaimed Toliver who was very good at drawing conclusions from scanty data.

"What does repent mean?" asked Whizlet who never had to worry about things like that in the city. Then, because he liked to figure things out for himself, continued under his breath. "I guess it means 'pent again', but I wonder what 'pent' means."

"I think it means 'feel sorry for yourself'," replied It. "But only they can tell you if you're sorry enough. And they have another sign which looks like a book hanging from a balloon, which says: *Read the BOOK!* But it has glue on the cover, so when you open it up you get stuck and they reel you down like a skyflish."

"And when they get you down, you discover they'll only sell you soap to clean the glue off your hands if you give them the bottom of your foot," said Is.

The Itofit wrinkled his brow and scratched his ear with his toe, then looked at the bottom of his own foot in a most curious fashion. "For some reason, they seem to think the sole is the best part of us."

"Which is all they say is left of us after we…" Is caught herself.

"After we what?" prompted Toonie.

"After we go to discuss it with our grandfathers' grandmothers," said It who was quick as a wink when it came to not confusing children with uncomfortable thoughts.

Another sign popped up ahead which had a huge question mark on top surmounting what looked like a Don't! sign like Don't Walk or Don't Smoke or Don't Park Your Donkey Here, but in the circle, with the diagonal line through it, was a blazing fire with a ridiculously happy-seeming face in the middle, and the words curved around the circle said: Be Born Again!"

"What it really means," explained Is, "is be borne again, down to the Worser Lands because the question mark is really a sky hook."

"Hmmm," said It. "I always thought it meant 'Be Bored Again' but I suppose it means something different to everybody."

Another kite flew up to them. It had an arrow pointing the way they had come and another pointing the way they were going. Between the arrows it said: 'HELL This Way!' And the tail of the kite was actually another sign saying 'Confess! Repent! Prey in a Tent! Pay Your Taxes, Tithes, & Rent'. A moment later a balloon floated up which was shaped like a head with a leering red face and black horns peering through the business end of a pitchfork, with a sign hanging from a chain around its neck saying 'Dance, Cuddle, Kiss, & Rock 'n Roll With ME!'

"I'm glad Rango and Rangi don't seem very interested in these simony signs," said Toliver, "or they might just accidentally fly too close."

"And BAM! Just like the monster mouse trap in *Mother Hubbard's Clobbered Cupboard*," cut in Whizlet slapping his hands smartly together.

"Baloomerangs are too smart for them," said Is.

"And lucky too," added the Itofit, "because the people in the Worser Lands don't bother with them at all."

Is nodded her agreement. "They say they're dumb animals and not worth saving, even for a rainy day, because, and this is very peculiar, they say they can't think."

"Of course, only people dumb enough to believe what these signs say would believe that," added It. "But one thing you can believe is that none of them have ever sat down and talked seriously with a baloomerang about next week's weather or last month's talapanut harvest."

"Or the best seasonings for pangifrangi flower pie," whispered Is in Toonie's ear.

"Honk-blis-sa-blis-sa-honka," agreed the baloomerangs in unison as they sailed among the Simon-Says-Sermon-Signs too busy to notice and too happy to care. As a general rule, they were unconcerned with people who couldn't think very well, and thought such people were best left to their own bad thoughts, so they continued happily on their way, bobbing up and down and talking back and forth to each other and to the balooms who loved nothing better than whisper into their big cousin's flappy ears so the other balooms couldn't hear what they were saying and could only wonder about it until they got to do the same thing or the baloomerangs told on them. Beneath them the blue fog turned gray, and gradually metamorphosed into what appeared to be yellowish-brown fumes from a seething cauldron.

Whizlet noted the changes in color with some misgivings because it reminded him of the Sulfur Sea where Slimy Sam and Nasty Ned awaited the unwary in *Smorgasbord of Swampwamps*. "Is that Boobytrapped Bayou?" he asked the Itofit worriedly, "or the Fumelands where the Liquefied Lizards of Lecherous Lagoon framboozle your swampsub if you're not careful?"

"No," replied the Itofit. "It's just fumes blowing at us from a toxic old dumping grounds leaking into Mucky River, but it's a good sign, or rather a really bad sign, but good for us because it means we've almost gotten to Alabramble."

"Is that Mucky River down there?" asked Toliver pointing ahead to an oily estuary that was too wide to be an open sewer and too long to be a lake.

"Yes, it is," sighed the Itofit. He pointed into the distance where the land became bleaker and bleaker until nothing at all could be seen except a yellowish-brown haze from which, every now and then, a belching smokestack projected up. "And Smugsmog City is somewhere under it all over there."

"Smugsmog City!" exclaimed Whizlet who thought it looked like the approach to Hell Base IV in *Asteroid Prison Mines*. "We better get outa here. Do baloomerangs have warp drive?"

"Probably not," conceded It, without being quite sure what he was conceding, "but we'll go the other way and travel upriver for awhile to get away from the fumes."

"It even smells funny up here," agreed Toonie squiggling up her nose and making a face to go with it, knowing that she wouldn't be able to hold her breath until they got across Alabramble and would have to take little tiny breaths through her left nostril until they did.

"That's the saddest part," said Is. "In Alabramble nobody cares what they do to the land or the air or the water, or to anyone else for that matter, as long as they get to do whatever they please for themselves."

"And it just keeps getting worse," added It, "because nobody does anything about it. And now, nobody even cares anymore. They just want to make a pile of rasputniks and get out before it falls apart."

"Or they come down with some dreadful disease like tancer of the tung and have to give all their rasputniks to the medicrats in Warpington." agreed Is shaking her head

The baloomerangs had been listening to the conversation (and agreed whole-heartedly with everything that had been said) so they turned to the right as they drifted across Mucky River and headed away from the worst of the smog. Toliver was glad they changed direction but worried that Rango and Rangi would have to fly a lot further to take them where they were going. "Is this out of our way?" he asked.

"I don't know," admitted the Itofit, "since I don't know where we're going, but sometimes the longer way is the quicker way and the better way too."

"And it will also be prettier," said Is, "after we get past the Dead Lands and over what's left of the jungle forest."

The fumes thinned out as they proceeded up Mucky River revealing a very desolate landscape below. "Those are the Dead Lands now," commented Is. "It used to be one of the prettiest places anywhere, but the snollygosters cut down all the trees so when it rained, the land washed away into Mucky River, and when it was dry the wind blew away the topsoil that was left until nothing could grow anymore and no animals could live there."

"But the snollygosters think they're being smart when they can change land into rasputniks just by killing it," said It.

"At the time, they swore they weren't killing anything," said Is, "just harvesting trees, and they told everybody their jobs depended on them making as many rasputniks as possible."

"And since none of them would be around by the time the trees grew back, it didn't really matter whether the land survived or not since everybody would live in Smugsmog City by then anyway." concluded It sadly.

"Don't they ever think of their children?" asked Toonie feeling almost as depressed as the land below.

"Of course, they do," comforted Is who knew that everybody loved their own children even if some people only thought of them like another tootmobile or vellytision set, "but they say what the children don't know won't hurt them, and that they won't care about what they don't have any more anyway."

"Besides," said the Itofit, "they send all their children off to Warpington so they can become vawyers and make sure that nobody will interfere with what they do either."

"So it will go on and on until all the trees are cut, and nothing will grow anymore, and the land won't support any animals at all," said Toliver who could see very clearly where this line of reasoning had to end up, "and everybody will be…ah…"

"Gone off to discuss it with their grandfathers' grandmothers." concluded Whizlet shaking his head sadly.

"Can't they be used for anything at all?" asked Toonie who was so busy trying not to breathe through her right nostril that she'd missed a good bit of the conversation.

"Well, they do put garbage dumps there," replied the Itofit thoughtfully.

"And they try to get people from everywhere else to bring their garbage here," added Is. "They even came to Is when I was an Isette and wanted us to put up signs saying: 'Dump it on Alabramble', but we don't put up any signs ourselves so we wouldn't let them do it either."

The Itofit nodded gravely. "They even tried to bribe my father to put up their signs but he told them that even our silliest people wouldn't do it. Of course, he was too polite to mention that our silliest people are not as foolish as snollygosters."

"Oh dear, do they go on forever," asked Toonie who was again distracted and getting very tired of looking at such a desolate place.

"I'm afraid they do," replied It who misunderstood what Toonie was referring to. "Snollygosters are too foolish to change, too stubborn to learn anything, and too greedy to care."

"No, I mean the Dead Lands not the dead people," said Toonie.

"Yes, they end," answered Is. "Although they are getting bigger and bigger all the time as the snollygosters keep eating up the forest and spitting out rasputniks."

"Honka-honka-honk-honk," called Rangi over her shoulder.

"What did she say?" asked Toonie who didn't understand the words but did notice the note of excitement in the way they were trumpeted.

"She smells pangifrangi fragrance in the air, so we must be getting close to the jungle," answered Is.

"We'll have to be very careful," added It, "because the snollygosters are really sneaky and use the jungle to trap people who happen to pass by."

"Before the snollygosters arrived," explained Is, "all of Alabramble was a magical jungle inhabited by strange plants and animals and the native Alabramblians. But the snollygosters enslaved the natives, killed the animals, and crossbred the plants to bring out their very worst traits until everything got nastier and nastier."

"You mean they made them smell bad and taste bad and not be pretty?" asked Toonie who was very puzzled why anyone would want to do those things but couldn't think of any other way a plant could be made nasty. "That doesn't make any sense at all…" she shook her head sadly from side to side, "…but I suppose if you're a stupid snollygoster to start with, your tastebuds and noseblooms would be a little off too."

"They do worse things than that," said It. "They started by planting thorn trees which they brought with them so the natives would have to buy shoes from them."

"And they crossbred the thorn trees with toison pivy so the thorns would not only stick you but make you itch too." added Is.

"And then they crossed the thorns with seed shooters so they could throw their thorns at you too," concluded the Itofit.

"That's awful," cried Toonie putting her hand to her throat and gulping loudly.

Toliver got madder and madder and his face got grimmer and grimmer. "Somebody ought to teach them a lesson!" he growled.

"Logger John Giant could do it!" exclaimed Whizlet. "He can throw his ax ten screen lengths in fifty-five nanoseconds!"

Hobnail, who was resting on Rangi's forehead and preening the baloomerang's eyelashes. looked up and shook her head: "Dirty trickings. Dirty trickings," she said.

And Boogie (who secretly felt that even a nasty jungle would be better than a baloomerang's back, and knew with lion-like certainty that there never was a plant born that could outsmart a cat) slapped his tail on Rangi's back so hard that the baloomerang reverberated like a war drum and all the balooms were startled and flitted higher above them.

The Itofit, of course, understood Boogie's tail talk perfectly and felt compelled to caution him. "But it's true, Spit. Some of those plants can get you before you even know they're around, much less that they might have it in for you."

"Like weeping cryacinths," said Is.

"Or lassoing kudzus," said It.

"Or philobopodendrons…"

"Or musty mushroom mines…"

And then, even though they weren't meaning to do so at all, Is and It suddenly stared at each other and said at exactly the same time, "Or giant, stomping, clomping, egregious, capricious, malicious, duplicitous, heinous spry traps!"

"What's that?" cried Toonie whose hair would have stood straight up except the wind was blowing it down.

The Itofit screwed up his face and rolled up his eyes until they almost disappeared into his forehead (which he did whenever he had to remember a lot of things all at once). "Well, let me see how I can describe them: The snollygosters started with barrel cactuses because they're covered with spines and could cross the Dead Lands without needing water, and then they grafted creepers on the bottoms so they wouldn't need roots…and gave vitamins to the creepers to make them runners…"

Is helped him out. "…then crossed them with fly traps so they could eat what they caught…"

"… and grafted cabbages on top so they'd have heads…"

"… and potatoes to the cabbages so they'd have a hundred eyes…"

"… and gave them cauliflower ears…"

"… and red beet noses…"

"… and willow branches for arms…"

"… and redwood burls for hands…"

"… with stickerbushes for fingers…"

"… then grafted pulpits from Jacks-in-the-Pulpit in front right above the fly trap…"

"… and then force fed them fertilizer until they grew so big snollygosters could ride in the pulpits…"

"… and so hungry that they stomp through the jungle grabbing everything they can with their stickerbush fingers…"

"… and drop it into their gaping fly trap mouths…"

"… and chomp it down amid fits of the gurgle-giggles…"

"… and then burp!" concluded the Itofit grasping his own throat with both hands.

"Yipes-a-doddle!" cried Whizlet who had never heard of such a thing, not even in *The Green Ghoul's Galactic Creature Circus.* "We're lucky its only a fly trap and not a flying trap!"

"They have flying traps, too," cautioned the Itofit pointing ahead. "And that looks like the first of them up there."

Everybody looked where It was pointing and, sure enough, there were little clusters of flowers floating in the sky. Below them the desolate Dead Lands had finally ended and the raggedy edge of the jungle passed behind. The flowers were floating above the canopy of forest and, as they drew closer, they could see that they were tethered in place by long, thin strings that disappeared into the treetops.

"The look like pangifrangi flowers," exclaimed Toonie who had noticed one hanging out of Rangi's mouth when the baloomerangs first dropped down to them at the basket house. "I didn't know they grew in the sky and had such skinny stalks."

"They don't," said Is. "The snollygosters decorate kites with them so any passing baloomerang will stop for a nibble, but the flowers have hooks in them so when the baloomerang takes a bite, they're hooked and pulled down."

"Bird fishin'. Bird fishin'!" squawked Hobnail even though she knew that no bird would ever fall for such a trick (except maybe a silly bower bird who just couldn't resist), but wasn't at all sure about balooms or baloomerangs.

As they drew closer, more kites drifted up through the canopy until they were everywhere about them filling the whole sky with the wonderful odor of pangifrangi perfume. The balooms and baloomerangs were almost intoxicated with the fragrance but they understood what was happening and kept their heads about them, and deftly avoided the weeping cryacinths that were scattered among the others. But since all the flowers were on kites and the people on the ground saw they were being ignored, they started to dive, dart, and swoop about in an effort to snag one of the passing creatures. But Rango and Rangi were quicker than kites (and a lot smarter too) so they bobbed about and weaved in and out and missed them all, while happily honking to each other.

"This is like a minuet," said Toonie who wasn't exactly sure what a minuet was but had seen a movie in which gaily dressed people had been bouncing up and down and bowing to each other after spinning around and smiling and having a fine time in a great big room with mirrors on the walls (which made the room look even bigger and filled with a lot more people) and crystal chandeliers hanging from the ceiling and a little orchestra of men wearing white wigs and stockings playing violins and cellos and tubas (although she wasn't really sure about the tubas), one of whom had a baton like the Wundur-phul's fan, who tapped it on his music stand and told everyone else to do the minuet. But her reverie was interrupted by a popping sound coming from below which sounded (to her) like champagne corks going off (which also happened when people did the minuet). She looked over Rangi's side in time to see what appeared to be several rough brown baseballs coming up at her, which then slowed down and fell back.

"Uh-oh!" exclaimed the Itofit. "They've brought out some seed shooters."

"Should we go higher?" asked Toliver who had never been shot at before but knew the trick was to get as far as possible away from whoever was shooting at you, unless, of course, you were shooting too, in which case you tried to get as close as possible without being seen.

The Itofit wet the tip of his tail with his tongue and stuck it straight up in the air as if checking which way the wind was blowing, then stuck up both thumbs of his left hand an arm's length in front of his eyes (of which he squinted one and closed the other) and moved his hand in and out until he was looking down his forearm at where the seed shooters were shooting from. "Probably not. They can't shoot this high, and Rango and Rangi have to work pretty hard to take us higher."

The Itofit's evaluation was correct because none of the seeds got as high as they were (although one hit a pangifrangi flower kite and the whole thing tumbled down tail over tea kettle and crashed into a tree).

Hobnail leapt into the air and flew nervously above the baloomerangs. Her sharp eyes and jungley instincts gave her an excellent feeling for what was really going on below them and without even thinking about it, she began whistling *The Symphony for the Sons of Nam*.

"I think we'd better turn back before it's too late," said Toonie apprehensively as the minuet in her mind turned into a dirge. But the Itofit, who always tried to be a calming influence when he noticed others getting jittery, pointed out they were well above the range of the seed shooters and, in any case, the baloomerangs knew all about snollygosters and their tricks and would stay ahead of the game.

They were almost past the kites when a new, different kind of flower box kite swam into view. It was a lot bigger than all the others and climbing very rapidly and instead of having pangifrangi flowers on it carried what looked like a clump of bamboo.

"They've sent up a seed shooter," cried Is. "We'll have to be careful now!" Even as she spoke, the kite recoiled violently and they heard three pops in quick succession: Pop! Pop! Pop! and three seeds came flying at them. Rango dodged one way, Rangi the other, and the projectiles flew harmlessly by, but below them more kites swam into view, all of them lifting from the tops of the highest trees in the canopy. The snigglesnorfs, who until now had been thoroughly unconcerned with anything going on except their own games, peered over the side of Rangi (where they happened to be at the moment) and squeaked out dire warnings in unison, then Snorf jumped to Rango, ran up the Itofit's tunic and buried his face in the soft fur of It's back while Snorfa did the same with Is.

"They're sending up octopuses too," screamed Whizlet pointing at yet another new kite, this one covered with vines with thick leaves all along them, and several quivering stems, each with a big, hairy pod at the end.

"Uh, oh!" cried the Itofit. "That's a sticky creamy pod popper grafted to a whippy twinevine slinger."

"And it's loaded with ripe cream pods," added Is.

"We'd better get out of here," yelled It. "Rango and Rangi, get your jets ready." But even as he was calling out the danger, Snap! Whap! Sca-boom! One of the stems snapped and a slinging twinevine slung a pod in their direction. The pod streaked across their heads, only to burst a few yards further on in a great white shower of sticky cream.

"Oh my," exclaimed Toonie throwing her hands to her head, "we're being sca-boomed!" She felt the crane's white feather in her hair and quickly put it in her blouse for safekeeping, then grabbed the cat and held him tight.

Snap! Whap! Sca-boom! went another twinevine, and another pod sailed so close to Rangi that Toonie, Boogie, and Is had to duck and Hobnail, who was driving through the air above, only avoided being scaboomed by the most dexterous maneuvering.

Suddenly, sailing up at them as though it were a canvas wing came a pair of pants, or at least a huge back pocket from what looked like a pair of Levis but the leather patch above it didn't say Levis, it said Air Pocket, and everything around it got rough and Rango had to swerve one way and

Rangi the other, which almost forced them into some other traps, which they managed to avoid only by honking with their proboscises and then throwing them over their backs (and impolitely over the heads of their passengers which is why they honked) and let out blasts of air to jet them ahead.

"Those must be high pockets," yelled Toonie who preferred dresses herself except when they went to the woods like today and sometimes had to shinny up things. "But thank goodness we're not in still in the lake or they'd be pool pockets and we'd be all wet or at least getting rained on."

"Keeping jetting," screamed Whizlet who knew the better part of valor was a good set of rollerblades, but before anyone could answer, two more: Snap! Whap! Sca-booms! One from either side, rang out and two pods streaked toward Rangi. Hobnail avoided them by dropping in a heap and ducking under Rangi just as the two pods struck each other above her and burst into a cyclone of sticky white cream. All of the flittering balooms were showered with the goo and fell to Rangi's back where they squizzled and squirmed but were stuck fast where they landed, and everyone else looked like they had marshmallow topping poured all over them. Toonie tried to scream but her lips were stuck together; and Boogie, who wanted to snap his tail on Rangi's back to make an even louder sca-boom sound, couldn't because it was already stuck there; tasted what had plastered his ears down and decided it wasn't cream at all but yukky plant juice; and Rangi felt it oozing down her sides, gumming up her wings, and sticking her flappy ears to her cheeks. And before anyone really knew what was happening, poor Rangi, who could only manage a gooey-sounding Honka-helpa-honk-honk, started to go down.

"They've been guano'ed!" screamed Whizlet who wasn't exactly sure what guano was (though he had a pretty good suspicion) but knew what it did to you in *Bat Monsters of Guano Cave* and realized they had a serious problem unless they could get to the Wizard's Wand Waterfall really fast.

"We've got to help!" cried It, but Rango already knew that and was diving toward his falling companion while dodging seeds from the seed shooters and pods from the twinevine slingers at the same time, and got there just before Rangi lost all control.

"Honka-here-here-honka-honk-honk!" he trumpeted as he dove in front of her.

Hearing Rango's call, Rangi shook the sticky stuff from her eyes and with a great effort unrolled her cream-covered proboscis with which she managed to reach out and grab Rango's tail. Rango strove to regain altitude while dodging to one side, then the other while pods, which were now coming fast and furiously at them, burst all around and seeds screaming past, one of which Rango caught with his trunk and whipped back the way it had come. It slammed into a bamboo shooter, snapped its string, and careened off to burst a still unfired pod on a nearby slinger. The pod exploded dragging its kite to oblivion, and the other kite, now an untethered maverick, dove wildly into two others before plummeting with them to the ground. This caused so much confusion that Rango managed to get ahead of all the other kite-traps, and was almost safely away before the nastiest kite anyone had ever seen darted up toward them. It looked like a devil's head, whose horns were thorn trees on which everything had been miniaturized except the thorns, which glinted at the end of willowy branches and swirled around the kite, readying themselves to throw.

"A two-horned thorn thrower!" gasped It, but before Rango could react, the tree took aim, whipped several of its branches, and three thorns flew off, screaming toward them. The first hit Rango in the ear, going right through and pinning it to his neck; the second slammed into his shoulder just above his wing muscle; and the third whooshed right between Toliver's and Whizlet's legs and went deep into the baloomerang's side.

"Eck! Ouf! Ouch! Honka! Honk!" cried Rango, who realized the perilous danger they were in and felt three terrible stingings and itchings in his ear, neck, shoulder, and side. For a moment he lost control, not only of his pinned ear, but of his left wing as well, and with Rangi in tow began to go down.

"I'll help!" yelled Whizlet who reached down and grabbed the thorn behind his leg and started to yank it out so he could throw it back at the thankless thorn thrower, which had ambushed them and certainly needed a taste of its own medicine.

"Don't!" cried Toliver ,who heard a hissing sound coming from the wound and was afraid Rango might bleed really badly.

"Don't!" cried the Itofit who hadn't seen what Whizlet was doing until it was done and knew exactly what would happen if he did it. But both cries were too late for Whizlet had already pulled the thorn out and was about to sling it back when all the air inside poor Rango started rushing out through the wound. Rango spun around so quickly that his tail pulled away from Rangi's grip, the thorn flew out of Whizlet's hand, and Toliver was almost thrown off. But the Itofit quickly leaned forward and put his arms around both Whizlet and Toliver while simultaneously squeezing his knees as tightly as he could to keep his seat without being thrown off himself (which only made the air in Rango whoosh out faster, but that couldn't be helped under the circumstances.) And poor Rango, just like a balloon that someone blew up and then let go without tying off its neck, zoomed up and down, then over and around and around and around again, and over and under and upside down and downside up, and zoomed far away from Rangi (just like a whooshing balloon will zip off into the next county if you've blown it up full enough), and Rangi, without Rango to hold onto anymore, was once again sinking down toward the looming canopy of jungle forest and its horrid, mouth-wetting, bushwhacking, and waiting snollygosters.

By the time all the air had whooshed out of Rango, he had kareemed and karbobbled, spliffed and zooked so far away that all the kites were just little specks in the sky behind him and Rangi and her passengers were no more than a weeping white dot slowing spiraling down. And poor Rango himself was as skinny as a dry leaf that had flopped over on its side and was flittering to earth (or to Alabramble, which is worse). The Itofit, Toliver, and Whizlet scrambled to the upper side where they were able to grab hands full of loose skin and rode him like a not-so-magic carpet, which could only manage a feeble honka-honka-help-help-hurt. Pretty soon they flittered to the treetops and broke through the canopy of leaves after which Rango bounced from branch to branch before landing in a particularly large fork between two branches. As the riders clamored off his back (or rather his side since that's where they had ended up) Rango reached up with his proboscis and very feebly pulled his draped carcass up to a less precarious perch.

The Itofit, though dizzy himself, managed to hang onto Toliver with one hand, Whizlet with the other, and the branch with his tail until all their heads quit spinning around like the insides of washing machines. "Wow!" stammered Whizlet who realized he'd probably never get another ride like that even in next year's super stereo version of his virtual reality *Cyclonic Rocket Ride.* "What do we do now?"

"First things first," said the Itofit. "And then second things before we do third things…and the first of the first things is to take care of Rango!" The deflated baloomerang was draped over the branch looking completely disconsolate and a big tear was in the one sad eye that was on top looking at them.

"How do we do that?" asked Toliver who was always ready to stop everything else to help a friend, even if, and sometimes particularly if, it was a new friend.

"Let me see," said the Itofit scratching his brow with a scratching whisker. "First, we'll pull out all the thorns, then put salve on the wounds and make leaf bandages, then we'll get him as comfortable as we possible can, and then we'll run away."

"Run away!" exclaimed Toliver who was so loyal it often made him late for dinner. "We can't do that!"

"We have to," replied It, who was very pleased with Toliver's determination to stand by Rango but also knew why they couldn't. "First, because we have to help Is, and Toonie, and Rangi, and Spit, and Hobsong, before the snollygosters do something awful to them; and, second, because if we just stay here the snollygosters will find us, and Rango too, and then they'll have him for dinner."

"Yipes-a-doddle!" cried Whizlet. "Do snollygosters eat baloomerangs?"

"Only when they're damaged," continued It. "Otherwise they make dray-slaves out of them and harness them to their snollywagons so they can pull them around Smugsmog City where everybody will ooh and ah at them. But with all of us sitting here, they're bound to find us, but if it's just Rango lying quietly on the branch with leaves all around him, he'll probably be all right until he heals up."

"How long will that take?" asked Toliver who never liked to stay in bed a moment longer than absolutely necessary unless it was a rainy school day or he had the mumps or measles or something ghastly like that which made your body not want to move at all, and made it hurt if you did and even if you didn't.

"Not long if I can find some elpful ealing erbs down there," replied the Itofit pointing to the ground which was still a long way beneath them through lots of branches and flowers and hanging creepers, "and some creek clay and mushroom mulch to mix them with, and maybe even some pangifrangi flowers so Rango can nibble on something to get his strength back. But first we'll pull the other thorns out."

The Itofit steadied himself in the fork of the branch by Rango's head and scratched his friend on his tear-stained cheek. "Hold on tight, old fellow," he said. "This will hurt just a little but then it will feel a lot better than it does now." He dropped his tail so Rango could hold it with his proboscis, and the tail and trunk wound round and round each other until they looked like a candy can, and the Itofit took hold of the thorn in Rango's ear and with a mighty pull yanked it out.

He laid the thorn on the branch by his leg but Whizlet grabbed it and was about to throw it as far away as he possible could, saying angrily: "Let's get rid of this nasty thorn before it hurts somebody else.

"Don't do that yet," cautioned the Itofit taking it back from him. "Some things that are nasty sometimes can be helpful other times so lets keep it until we figure out what we need." He bent to pull the other thorn out of Rango's shoulder but it was so deeply embedded that he couldn't get a hold on it at all."

"Maybe you can use the first thorn to pry that one out," opined Toliver who had been listening carefully to what the Itofit had just said, but also knew how useful weird things could be.

"What a good idea!" exclaimed It, and before anybody knew it, except Rango of course, who was feeling it all, he'd popped out the other thorn too and laid them both aside.

Suddenly, there was a twittering and tweeting and a medley of miniature honks and honkas from above as a flight of fifteen or sixteen balooms came down through the canopy. They were the ones who hadn't gotten stuck to Rangi and had hurried off to where Rango had blown away and watched carefully to see where he disappeared in the forest. Now they swarmed around saying all kinds of nice and consoling things to Rango and even managed to make everything sound so nice that Snorf ventured out of the Itofit's tunic to see if somehow they'd all gotten back home.

"I'm glad you're all right and all here," said It, "and we really need you to find us some pangifrangi flowers for Rango, and if you find them, Snorf can run up and bring them back while I go down to the ground."

"What can we do?" asked Toliver who didn't want to be unused even though he had never felt so perilously positioned before in his life and knew that hanging on was probably a full time occupation.

"For the time being, the best thing is to stay with Rango and let him know we're all doing our best for him." He thought for a moment realizing that everybody had to have something to do or they wouldn't feel like they were helping as much as they probably could. "But let me see your spyglass, because if I can see where some elpful ealing erbs are from up here, I won't have to waste time wandering around on the ground looking for them. And Yipes can pull on that vine next to him to make sure it's sturdy enough for me to climb down."

Toliver reached in his pocket and was very happy (and just a little bit proud) to give his spyglass to It who scanned the jungle below, occasionally exclaiming: "There's one. Oh, yes, some of that too. Oh, good, look at that. Wonderful. Yes, yes, that will do excellently!" He slid the spyglass back into itself and returned it to Toliver. "Now if I just had something to carry them in, I'd have everything back in a spiffy jiffy or two!"

"Will this help?" asked Toliver who pulled a large plastic bag with a zip top from his pocket. "I've used it a lot, but it's still good."

"Wonderful!" exclaimed It, who put it in his mouth so he could hold it with his teeth and then jumped off the branch.

"Yipes-a-gluebblle." stammered Whizlet who was so startled by the Itofit leaping off into space and the vine being pulled from his hand that his tongue got all twisted around in his mouth. But the Itofit (who, after all, was an arboreal acrobat who could have gotten a job with Barnum & Bailey just doing what he often did when he slept) was quite all right and going rapidly down through the trees using both arms, both legs, and his tail with such aplomb that Hissofer, who was still wrapped around his hat brim, decided that he was undoubtedly descended from a Precambrian tree boa.

Snorf, who was every bit as at home in the jungle as It, ran up the trunk and from branch to branch, wherever the balooms called him to collect pangifrangi flowers. He was soon back with twenty-four handsfeet full and tucked them carefully into a knot hole in the branch where Rango could get at them any time he was hungry. A moment later, It's face reappeared next to him with Toliver's plastic bag still in his mouth but this time full of leaves and flowers and roots and two handfuls of red-yellow mud from a stream bottom. He sat himself on the branch and with Rango's trunk across his lap began mixing everything together and was even shaving one of the roots with his fingernail when Toliver offered him his penknife (actually a real Swiss army knife with three blades blades, two screw drivers, a magnifying glass, tweezers, scissors, a toothpick, and a corkscrew for scratching his name on things) which It was very happy to use and even employed the awl to stir his concoction. When he was finished he had a green-brown salve with specks of colored flowers in it, which smelled very much like a medicine cabinet. Using a rubbery leaf, he spread it thickly over Rango's wounds and covered them all up with aspirin leaves which stuck everywhere except where the thorn had gone clean through Rango's ear.

"I guess we'll just have to leave that uncovered," sighed It, "and hope it doesn't dry out too fast."

But Toliver started pulling things out of his pocket, his spyglass and some roofing nails, his string and Scotch tape and paper clips and shoe horn, chewing gum wrappers (some with chewing gum still in them; one chewed but carefully rewrapped for mending holes in things or sticking things together), a spool of thread with three needles stuck in it, and then a Band-Aid still unused and in its wrapper although pretty wrinkled. "Here, try this," he said brightly.

The Itofit was not sure what it was but when Toliver showed him how it worked he was delighted and carefully put it over the wound. Next, after Rango was made as comfortable as possible, the Itofit called all the balooms to him and told them to go down through the jungle and leave a maze of false trails. "If the snollygosters come with wiffer-sniffers," he explained, "we don't want them to find Rango. And even the best wiffer-sniffer can't tell a baloom from a baloomerang, so leave the most confusing trails you can, and if you find some stinging red ant nests, lead them right to those." Then he hugged Rango around the neck and slid his head under the baloomerang's big, flappy wounded ear and whispered something that neither Toliver nor Whizlet could make out (and probably wouldn't have understood if they did because it was in Itian anyway). But Rango's ear wiggled, his tail quivered, and he lifted his proboscis long enough to say: "Honka-honka-hope-hope-happy," then looked at them all with his big hopeful eye and waved good by with his tail.

The Itofit lifted Whizlet to his shoulders and showed Toliver how to sit on the base of his tail and hold onto his fur just like a little Ittle or Isette then took hold of a vine with both hands and swung out into the jungle. "We'll have to be very careful," he said, "because the Snollygosters will be looking for us."

They landed in another tree three trees away and three or four branches lower. This was a monkey puzzle tree, but even at its worst and most tangly, it couldn't puzzle the Itofit, who bounded down through its twisty branches and soon had them safely on the ground. "How will we ever find Rango again?" asked Whizlet who surveyed the dark jungle floor with long streamers of sunlight pouring down through the foliage and flowers as though they were stained glass, and everywhere he looked it seemed like a great silent cathedral with bell rope vines and great tree arches reaching upward in every direction, and he was already lost and feeling very, very little.

"I'm not sure we'll be able to," confided the Itofit. "But if the snollygosters don't find him and he gets better, he'll be able to fly home…except…" and here It wiped a tear from his eye, "…he won't go without Rangi and I'm afraid the snollygosters will eat her for supper if we don't hurry."

"I know what to do," said Toliver, pulling a little cardboard lined with neat rows of thumbtacks from his pocket. "I'll leave a trail of thumbtacks stuck in trees so we can find our way back and help him." And he stuck one in the tree right next to him where it stood out like a headlight.

"I'm afraid that won't do at all," said the Itofit. "If the snollygosters see them, they'll know what we've done and will follow them right back here."

"Snorf-snorfa-snorf-snorf," said Snorf, climbing out of It's sleeve and looking up expectantly.

"What a good idea!" exclaimed It, taking the pad of tacks from Toliver and giving them to the snigglesnorf. "We'll let Snorf run along in the branches and leave the trail up there where only we will know where to look for it." Snorf jumped to the nearest tree and disappeared above them while the Itofit, testing the air with his tailtip and sniffing the faint breeze to get his bearing, took off walking through the bushes at a fast pace. "We'll have to be very quiet," he whispered, "because the snollygosters will certainly be coming this way looking for us. And we'll have to be very careful too because we don't know what might be lurking around in a jungle like this just waiting for unwary people like us to pass by."

They moved in single file, trusting to the Itofit's jungle instinct to lead them to where they were going. The Itofit's furry feet made no sounds at all, and Toliver and Whizlet tried very hard not to step on any twigs or crinkly dry leaves, and they'd pretty well gotten the hang of it when their silent progress was shattered as Toliver yelled out then stifled it as quickly as he could. "Ouch!" he cried. "Something just bopped me on the head!"

"Owwww!" called Whizlet. "Something just slapped me on the nose."

"Watch out!" cried the Itofit, perhaps a moment too late, as he turned and pointed at a nasty looking bush that seemed to be glaring back at him and relishing the encounter. "It's a five-stemmed philobopaslapapokentripodendron… although we just call them philobopodendrons for short. It will bop you or poke you or slap you or trip you up, all of them if it can, and then insult you too by laughing at you while it does it."

The nasty-looking bush at which he was pointing had four different stems all branching from a thick central stalk. The middle stalk was topped by a large disheveled flower with tangled red and yellow petals and black seeds in the middle, many of which were missing like missing teeth, which seemed very much to be quivering with glee. The stem that had bopped Toliver had a big pod hanging off its end, while the one that had slapped Whizlet on the nose ended in a wicked-looking leathery leaf. Another looked like a sniggly black whip and the final one could have been a skinny arm with a closed fist on the end. The flower was consumed with mirth and while everybody stared speechlessly at it, the whip stalk whipped out at the Itofit's legs and tried to trip him up, but It jumped up just in the nick of time to avoid it. Simultaneously, the fist shot out and almost poked Whizlet, but Whizlet was on guard too and leaped to the side. But instead of retreating as the plant expected, since everything else in the jungle ran away from it in terror (often into the arms of a nearby rhodoclobbodendron which was its cousin). Whizlet stood his ground. The plant couldn't stand such effrontery and slapped at his ear.

"Yibble-yabble-kaboom!" yelled Whizlet.'yibble' as he jumped to the left, 'yabble' as he feinted right, and 'kaboom!' as he leaped at the plant and grabbed the slapping branch by the stem-throat. As the stem tried to pull away, the whip stem snapped at his feet, but Whizlet was ready for that. He lifted his foot and brought it down so quickly he caught the second stem under his shoe and immediately bent over and grabbed that too. When he stood up he had a quivering stem in either hand, and a look of fierce determination on his face.

"I can play this game too!" he exulted feeling like he'd finally got his hands on the controls of the Thunderfighter in the master's version of *Renegades of Sky Dome VII*.

"Be careful!" yelled It. "All the stems are connected so when one moves they all do something else."

Whizlet's lips almost disappeared as he rolled them back into his teeth, his jaw tightened, and his eyes glazed with concentration as he started to manipulate the two stalks in his hands to control the other two which, until that moment, had been trying their best to bop and poke him. But very quickly, those two stalks, instead of threatening anyone else, were squared off against each other while Whizlet made them dart and feint, throw punches and sling pods back and forth. The flower-face was no longer giggling but rather making a very seedy grimace which gave out a yowl as Whizlet got the hang of it and bopped it right on top of its flower-tangle with a bopping pod.

"Ouch!" screamed the flower but before it could say anything else, the poking stalk poked it right in the seed-mouth, jarring loose several seed-teeth. "Owww!" it screeched, then "Ouch!" again, then "Oooh! Oooh! Oof!" as Whizlet continued to force-feed it some of its own medicine. And very quickly, with something of a whimper, all the stems went limp, the central stalk hung its flower-head and let out a sigh of defeat.

"My goodness" exclaimed the Itofit. "That's the first time I've ever seen anyone get the better of a philobopodendron. Where did you learn to do that?"

"Ah. Gee," said Whizlet modestly. "Any kid could do that who grew up with *Cassius Ali and the Gladiators of Tiberius King*."

"What's that?" asked Toliver in a low voice. He wasn't trying to detract from Whizlet's moment of glory (which he knew Whizlet had surely earned) but he knew they were in a precarious position and thought he heard something suspicious coming toward them.

The Itofit's ears poked up and swiveled around until both pointed the way they had been going. "Sssssh!" he cautioned. "It's the snollygosters or some of their tagalongs coming this way. We'd better hide up in the branches with Snorf." And quick as a wink he hoisted Toliver up so he could pull himself onto a large branch and roll over in time to help Whizlet who was thrust up quickly behind him. From there they both scrambled upward while the Itofit seemed to fly past them and helped them again, this time into a tangle of leaves and branches where they all hid in the foliage and didn't move at all so their hiding place wouldn't wiggle and give them away. A few moments later they could hear several creatures of one sort or another passing beneath them but nobody dared look for fear of being seen.

But It listened carefully and when he knew it was safe again, he motioned for Toliver and Whizlet to climb on his back. "That smelled like a snollysollijer and two cotton-headed syffers," he whispered.

"What's a snollysollijer?" asked Toliver who didn't like the sound of that one bit.

"What's a cotton-headed syffer?" asked Whizlet who knew he had to sigh for himself sometimes (although not as much as Toonie did), but didn't want to be called one if it meant being cotton headed and had anything to do with snollygosters.

"A snollysollijer is a tagalong who gets to wear a uniform and play with seed shooters and thorn throwers without a license," responded It, "and a cotton-headed syffer is a really unfortunate tagalong who, in exchange for things to do, a place to sleep, and as much crackahol as he can consume on his days off, lets the snollygosters give him a free puntal bolotomy."

"Bolotomy blobs!" stammered Whizlet who'd heard of some pretty weird people in his day. "They sound worse than the Déjàvu Dead in *Doctor Zygote's Zoombie Battalion.*"

"They probably are," agreed It. "The snollygosters drill little holes in the middle of their foreheads and put a bol weevil in. The bol weevils weave whatever they find inside into cotton balls and after that, every time a snollygoster blows his screechy whistle, the cotton-headed syffers start to vibrate and do whatever they're told." He looked over his shoulder to make sure that Toliver was firmly settled on his back. "But we're in the middle of them now, so we'd better stay in the trees. That way we won't be so conspicuous, and can move faster if you can hang on tight, and we can probably run away faster too, if we have to." Very quietly, the Itofit took off through the trees with Snorf darting ahead and falling behind to leave a tack wherever he thought one should be left. Occasionally, the Itofit would stop to test a vine, at which time Snorf would climb on top of his hat (since Toliver and Whizlet were where he usually rode), and the whole assemblage would swing far out into the jungle and land smartly on another distant tree. Twice more they had to hide among the foliage while other groups of snollygosters and their tagalongs clamored through the jungle below them, and once they caught a glimpse of a lumbering figure, which made Toliver agree with the Itofit's assessment that snollygosters weren't very pretty at all, although they were big. Being on It's shoulders and not having to watch where to put his hands. Whizlet was in the best position to see ahead so he was the first to notice, far away and off to their left, a glint of light through the trees. Soon he saw another, and then another and another, and whispered in It's ear while pointing to them: "What's that?"

"It must be Mucky River," replied It, "with the sun sparkling on its surface or sparkle-flish jumping in the air, except there aren't any sparkle-flish in it anymore, so we must be pretty close to where we're headed. We'll rest here for a moment and listen very carefully, and maybe we'll hear something that will tell us the way to go next." And the Itofit's ears swiveled 'round and 'round, first one way, then the other, and sometimes both directions at once, all of which was so fascinating that Toliver forgot to listen at all and just watched It's ears instead. Finally, after It had also sniffed the air very carefully, he moved off again slowly and stealthily through the branches, with Snorf tip-toeing and toeing and toeing and toeing beside him, until they had almost reached the river.

The Itofit stopped, took Whizlet from his shoulders and put him on a branch by his ear and let Toliver climb off and sit astride another branch as though he were riding a horse, while he moved further along until he parted some leaves before his face and peered ahead. They were on the edge of a clearing in the jungle leading down to Mucky River. Moored to the shore was a rather large boat to which thirteen huge alligator-like amphibian creatures were harnessed but were now basking on the shore in their tethers.

"Uh-oh!" exclaimed the Itofit under his breath. "There's a tallagator tugfloat, and all the tagalongs who go along with it; and there are some snollysolijers on deck; and…" Whizlet scooted out along his branch and parted two leaves to look for himself, and Toliver did the same by stretching out on his branch and looking out below. "…and that means that somebody who thinks he's important is around somewhere."

"Maybe that's why they shot us down," said Toliver who generally equated importance with having a lot of people do what you told them to do to other people.

"We were probably a target of Opportunity," agreed Whizlet who wasn't exactly sure who Opportunity was or how he picked his targets, but knew he was important, and was either a good friend to have or a bad enemy, depending on whose side he was on.

"Shsssh," cautioned It raising his tailtip and moving it softly from side to side in front of Whizlet. "I think I hear something coming…"

"Look!" gasped Toliver pointing to the other side of the clearing. Neither the Itofit nor Whizlet could see his finger, but both saw what he meant for a column headed by the fattest man they'd ever seen was emerging from the jungle. The man looked like a bowling ball from which arms and legs were hanging, on top of which was a softball with a face sculpted on it. He was wearing the purple and green uniform of the snollysolijers, but his had a Rob Roy belt across his shoulder and around his waist with a huge brass buckle glinting in the middle. He also wore high leather boots coming above his knees and a helmet that looked like an upside down slice of cantaloupe with a grapefruit perched on top. In his hands, were a pair of leather gloves with which he beat out time by slapping them on his thigh. Directly behind him was another man, as skinny as the fat man was fat, dressed the same, except the grapefruit on top of his cantaloupe helmet was replaced by a tangerine, his boots ended in mid-calf, and he had no gloves to mark time but walked bent forward at the waist and marched to the beat as though he was a syncopated beanstalk.

"Wow," whispered Toliver who was almost at a loss for words (though not images.) "He looks like a pair of parentheses around the word (FAT)!"

"Followed by an upside down exclamation point!" exclaimed Whizlet whose only exposure to grammar was a game called *The Sins of Syntax* which his Aunt Mathilda had given him for Christmas and had fascinated him for fifteen minutes until he discovered it was schoolwork.

Snorf took one look and immediately retreated down the Itofit's tunic because he never liked crowds (especially when they marched to the same drummer) and he could see that the two strange figures were not alone, for immediately behind them were four snollysolijers with clubs and spears. Next came tagalongs carrying platforms on which were mounted seed shooters, thorn throwers, and creamy pod slingers, followed by other tagalongs rolling spools of creeper string or carrying pangifrangi flower kites. Then, to everyone's horror, Rangi, still covered with goo, stumbled into the clearing. She was flanked by whip-wielding solijers and had a chain around one leg, a muzzle on her proboscis, and a cable around her neck. Behind her Is and Toonie, with their hands tied behind their backs, were linked together by a chain between collars around their necks; and behind them were a bamboo basket and a thornbranch cage dangling from a pole suspended from the shoulders of two tagalongs. In the basket were a whole caboodle of cream-covered baloms huddled in a corner and quivering uncontrollably, while the cage held what looked like a wound up, whitewashed hose that could only have been Snorfa. Next came a burly tagalong pulling a cage on wheels in which, orange-yellow fur plastered to his body, green eyes blazing, and fang-toothed mouth spitting through the bars (from which a claw tipped paw, like that of a wild, enraged tiger, was slashing out at the flanking solijers) was Boogie. More armed snollysolijers followed and then came a palanquin carried by four tagalongs on which a lady of very ample proportions was reclining on a large pillow and fanning herself with the gossamer wing of a jolly giant jasmine flutterby mounted on a pinstick. Finally, taking up the rear, were more snollysolijers with whips, spears, clubs, and swords, followed by a lone corporal marching backward to his own drummer and keeping an eye out behind. Then, as the procession moved to the middle of the clearing, the ample lady cocked her head and looked up as she caught a haunting sound from high above and far away, which only Toliver and Toonie recognized as Hobnail's moody and mournful rendition of *The Serenade in Vain.*

The ample lady had a golden chain around her neck from which was suspended a silver whistle. This she lifted delicately between her thumb and pinkie, placed it carefully between her heavily painted lips, and let out with a terrible shriek. Everyone stopped in mid stride, or at least as soon thereafter as momentum would have it. The skinny snollysollijer who was second in line leapt into the air, kicking one leg forward and the other just as smartly to the rear, while saluting the back of the fat man's head with both hands at once. The rotund man, for his part, spun around and saluted the skinny man's belt buckle (which was directly in front of his face because the thin man had jumped so high) and clicked his heels together which, because they had hollow castanets cleverly concealed in the leather, let out a very loud, almost alarming, 'Clickoom! Clickoom!'

The ample lady smiled and wiggled enticingly on her pillow. "You tagalongs," she said pointing to some of her entourage with her fan and then motioning to their captives, "wash them off." She rolled up her fan and used it to swat a bug that had gotten stuck in her rouge. "The rest of us will wait here until the District Inquisitor gets back with the others."

"What others?" whispered Toliver apprehensively.

"Gulp!" gulped Whizlet who was afraid he knew the answer.

"Not us," said the Itofit fiercely, "because we have to save everybody."

The everybody, he was referring to, were pulled, dragged, and carried to the bank of the river where a large water pump was set up. Three tagalongs grasped each handle and began pumping water from the river through a hose to a nozzle held by two snollysolijers who directed the stream toward poor disheveled Rangi, who usually loved to play in the water, but now was shrinking away from it even though it was cleaning all the goo off her pretty body.

The ample lady stepped from her palanquin and waved to the fat man. "Major Dhump," she called. "Tell Sergeant Struddel to tell Corporal Porporal to load the artillery on the tugfloat and have some of your people bring a large fan, an icy glass of lillylotus syrupwater, and tell that nice looking, young tagalong to get down on his hands and knees so I can sit on his back."

"Yessir, y'r missessness," snapped back the major saluting and clicking his heels once again. For a moment he looked like a traffic cop. His hand with the gloves pointed at the thin sergeant and snapped up, while the other waved a young tagalong to come to him; then the first hand, swooped over the weapons' platforms, did a little twirl, and ended pointing at the tugfloat, while the other hand pointed to another tagalong on the boat, made a gesture as though drinking from a glass, and waved him over. The young tagalong ran up and got quickly to his hands and knees, but the lady had changed her mind and was going off to inspect the captives. Toliver couldn't help making comparisons, for while the major looked like a bowling ball, the ample lady seemed more of a cinder block, or perhaps four of them glued together, with a watermelon on top on which a face, rather than being sculpted, was painted. She was wearing a bright yellow dress with orange and blue flowers all over it, golden sandals, and her black hair was in a bob, her nose was in the air, and her mind was on the dinner party she was already planning for the evening. She went first to Rangi and pinched her on the belly, causing Rangi to shy away. The lady smiled, then put her finger into the cage of balooms, smacked her lips, and murmured: "Ah, yes! Delicious, delicious."

"Spit-grrrr-koff!" growled Boogie from his cage.

The block lady stepped back then glared at him. "And you for dessert," she snarled. "Whatever you are."

She turned away and walked to where Is and Toonie, dripping wet, were standing by Rangi who Is was trying to comfort. The block lady smiled wickedly as she stared Is in the eye, but her face took on a more quizzical expression as she looked Toonie up and down. She pointed a pudgy finger at a nearby tagalong who had a little round plug in a hole in his forehead, then twirled her finger three times and ended up pointing at a clump of wishy-washy flowers growing in the shallow water by the riverbank.

As the syffer hurried to do her bidding, Is whispered to Toonie. "Don't let her make you smell those flowers. They're weeping cryacinths. Before the snollygosters crossed them with xoc pepper plants, they were only sibilant sighacinths that just made you nostalgic for home, but now…"

"Shut up," snapped the concrete blockness coming closer. "I'll do the talking. You stick your tail in your mouth, and you…" she glared at Toonie, "don't even wiggle."

The syffer who had been directed to the riverbank came back holding a cluster of flowers at arm's length. The lady screwed up her face and took them from him. "These are past their prime," she snapped. "You stupid, stupid person. Are you too ignorant to watch what you're doing? How would you like a salad of these for yourself?"

"Yes, y'r missesness; maybe, y'r missesness; probably, y'r missesness; no, y'r missesness," returned the syffer who stood at attention and looked right past her without blinking even once.

She turned back to Toonie. "But I suppose they'll work…let's see." She pushed the bouquet into Toonie's face. "Here, smell this," she said sweetly.

Toonie screwed up her face like she did anytime someone played a mean trick on her and turned her head away. But she couldn't turn far enough. The woman grabbed her hair and turned her head back and pushed the flowers over her nose. Toonie tried not to breathe but couldn't and snorted just a tiny breath that filled her nose with a really nasty odor. And before she even knew what was happening, she started to cry. And once she started, she couldn't stop and, in fact, just kept crying harder and harder as if something awful had happened or like when ole Yeller died or like she did sometimes for no reason at all except it was maybe Tuesday afternoon and nobody had been nice to her all day. While she was crying, great big tears ran down her cheeks, and the woman's pudgy finger wiped one off, conveyed it to her watermelon-like head whose mouth opened to allow an equally pudgy tongue to dart out and slurp it down.

"Just as I suspected!" she gloated. "You leak salt! We'll be able to mine you while you're in gaol."

"In jail!" wailed Toonie who now had a reason to cry. And across the clearing, Toliver's eyes bulged out of his head and he almost exclaimed the exact same words except It's tail wrapped around his head and sealed his lips.

Suddenly, there was a commotion on the tugfloat as the door to the cabin burst open and another round figure sped through, raced to the gangplank, and hurried ashore, screaming all the while. This one looked like a cross between the major and the woman for he was almost as round as the first but blocky like the second. He was wearing short purple pants, an untucked lavender shirt with a large, floppy, orange and green bow tie, a dark green jacket a size too small, and a matching green cap. By the way he ran, the florid pink flush to his flesh, and the screechy high voice, which was doing nothing but calling attention to itself, it was obvious that he was a child. And behind the child, running down the gangplank, came an I-beam of a man dressed all in black, with a black string tie, black shoes, and black fingernails. "Stop! Stop!" he yelled. "You haven't finished your lessons! You've got your Begats all wrong, you're hopeless on the miracles of Milhouse, and your left shoe is untied!"

The boy took no heed whatever and waddled as he ran along the shore toward his mother and the strange assortment of prisoners. "Come back!" shouted the man, this time stopping long enough to stamp his foot for good measure. "Or I shall erase your name from the Book!"

"Odiferous," called the block lady sweetly. "Do as the Revered End Mister Beeble tells you or the Swinglowsweet Chariot will flatten you instead of picking you up."

"I don't hafta," answered the child stopping a few feet from Rangi and glaring at his mother. "Poppa pays him which means someday I'll pay him which means I don't hafta." He stepped forward, grabbed the end of Rangi's tethered proboscis, twisted it sharply until Rangi let out a little cry, then pushed it away. "Where's the other one? The Dujge has two so we have to have two too otherwise poppa will get steam-ears again."

"Your father will be bringing it shortly," she replied. "Now be a good little boy for momma and do what Mister Beeble wants, and get back on the tugfloat."

The boy ignored her, swept his eyes past the basket of balooms, and fixed it on Boogie who, having just been rinsed off, looked something like a wrung out dishrag, except unlike most dishrags, he was mad as a hornet: first for being in a cage, second for being dosed with river water and unable to make his hair stand up, and third because everybody was watching him and he wanted them to know what catness was all about, and to watch out when he got out!

"What is it?" said the boy taking a bamboo pole from a nearby tagalong. "I want it."

"You can't have it," his mother said. "It's dessert, unless Cookie decides it will make a better appetizer."

"Nyaaa," cried the boy. "I want it." He poked the pole through the bars into Boogie's side to which Boogie responded with a judo cat twist, three quick clawings at the pole, and a clamping on it with his jaws so when the boy tried to pull it out he couldn't, and when he tried to lift it, couldn't either because Boogie was too heavy for him, so he pushed it instead driving both pole and cat across the cage and slamming them into the bars on the other side. Boogie let out a yowl, rolled to the side, and leaped to the far corner, hissing, spitting, and growling all at once. "See," continued the boy taking the pole out to examine the teeth and claw marks on the bamboo. "He likes to play with me. And with a muzzle, collar, leash, and whip, I can teach him tricks."

"No, Odiferous, you may not!" said his mother more firmly. "He's already spoken for, and Fasada Dorque will drool green envy that I got one first. Ha-ha! And if your father has his baloomerangs to show off too, the Dujge will have a fit, Fasada will have a snit, and we'll have a perfect evening!"

"Nyaaa," screamed the boy again, but this time he slammed the bamboo pole on the ground and threw himself behind it, stamping his feet and pounding his fists in a terrible tantrum.

"Oh now, Odiffy. Stop that. All these people are watching you. Be a nice boy. Mister Beeble, help poor Odiffy, he's having a coughing fit. Come, come, Odiffypoo, momma'll think it over and talk to poppa. Perhaps we can just cut off its tail for soup."

"Yipes-a-doddle," gasped Whizlet.

Toliver, whose mouth was still stopped by the Itofit's tail, was as horrified at the spectacle as his friend, but equally frightened that Whizlet would give away there whereabouts. He threw his hand over his shoulder and waved it frantically in Whizlet's direction, hoping it said: "Shut up!" or at least a very firm "Be quiet!" to Whizlet, but Whizlet wasn't even looking at it so it didn't matter what it was saying. Instead, Whizlet was staring through the leaves behind them all, having been prompted to do so by a very peculiar sound as though a whole Chinese restaurant full of people were clicking chopsticks together. And what he saw to prompt his outburst was a square face with squinty eyes staring down at him and what looked like brown snakes and stickerbushes crawling along the branch toward him.

The Itofit, who was very good at sensing what was happening behind his back (except, like now, when he was completely distracted by what was in front), knew something was very wrong with Whizlet, so he rolled over quickly and jumped agilely to his feet. But before he could do anything, Whizlet was pinned where he sat, and a whip-like armicule was wrapping around both Toliver and the branch on which he was lying. Toliver felt it before he saw what it was and would have yelled out except he had just told Whizlet in no uncertain hand terms to Be Quiet! so he didn't dare, but an awful chill went down his spine then bounced back up and made his hair stand on end. And when he did look over his shoulder, he saw the same horrible face that had confronted Whizlet but could also see that it belonged to a snollygoster standing in a slippery-looking green pulpit with a pink canopy over the top that made it look like an wide open, grinning mouth with its tongue stuck out. He could also see that more armicules than a pod of octopuses had tentacles were threading everywhere; that two of them were wrapping about the Itofit, and that Whizlet was trapped by a stickerbush.

"The Itofit, I presume," sneered the snollygoster. "I knew when we snagged the Is that you'd be someplace nearby. How convenient of you to find us first!" And a portion of the stickerbush that had Whizlet pinned to the branch, leaped over, and pinned the Itofit's tail as well.

"Gurgle-gurgle-splash-splash-sploosh!" said something diabolical from below the tree.

"Yes indeed," responded the snollygoster. "We've caught them all, Gorgoncha. Good work, you ugly, insatiable beastie…"

"And who are you?" asked the Itofit rather crossly since the stickers were hurting his tail, but he realized that the first thing he had to do was find out who he was dealing with so he could deal with him properly, or if not properly, at least quickly and thoroughly.

The snollygoster had a whip in one hand and a lectric stick in the other.

He put the stick under his arm and slipped a brown-tinted monocle into his left eye, which had the effect of making it look bigger and more threatening. "I am Lutarious Roorback, District Inquisitor of Tallagator County, Smugsmog City, and all points below. And you are thieves."

"We're not thieves!" exclaimed the Itofit.

"Of course you're thieves," continued Lutarious Roorback. "You are breathing our air without a license, you are unvawfully hiding in our trees and concealing bark beneath your feet, and you are using our language without permission. Vicious crimes all, so I declare you, Prisoners of War!"

"War," snapped It angrily. "There's no war going on."

"There is now," sneered the District Inquisitor. "You declared it when you trafficked in our sky!"

"You don't own the sky," responded It.

"Oh yes we do," continued Lutarious, "and if you want to keep breathing from it, you'd better shut up or I'll also charge you with forming impermissible words with our air."

"Is that you, Lut?" called the block lady from across the clearing in her sweetest, most syrupy voice.

"Yes, my canary, and I've snagged the rest of the traffickers, so you, Odiffy, and the rest of Alabramble can rest easy tonight." Without turning on the juice in his lectric stick, he reached out and tickled what looked like an overhanging cabbage leaf. "Move along, Gorgoncha. Back to the tugfloat and I'll give you that net full of flish we dragged up this morning."

The monstrosity in which Lutarious Roorback was riding pulled its three victims from the tree and lumbered out into the clearing with them dangling from armicules. Toliver and Whizlet were both hanging upside down so their first view of the giant stomping clomping egregious capricious malicious duplicitous heinous spry trap was skewed indeed but nonetheless horrible. In fact, it was the most frightening creature that Toliver had ever seen, and even Whizlet, who was quite used to megabytes of frightful creatures, was aghast. Towering above them and swaying from one twisty vine foot to another was a great green barrel covered with thorns, from the bottom of which came four long twisty vine legs. It could stand on three of them, or two of them, or only one of them if it happened to be anchored to something substantial, and use the others to whip out and trip up its victims. Above the trunk was grafted a giant ocotillo cactus from which a score of willowy armicules slithered out and which the heinous spry trap used to snag its prey, lift them high into the air, and drop them past the pulpit in front (which looked like a gaping mouth but wasn't) splash into its funnel mouth below (which looked like a bulgling belly unzipped on top) filled with slurping digestive juices. Some of the armicules ended in stickerbushes; others in barbs; and still others in clusters of noxious nettle fingers. Atop the burl was a huge cabbage-like head with a red beet nose, ears of corn (although the left ear had become a cauliflower because of all the fights it had been in), and two protruding tuberous potatoes, one xoc, the other red, each with a hundred eyes looking everywhere at once, and sprouting from their tops were disheveled clumps of scraggly potato vines. The pulpit, hanging securely in front and at least ten feet above the green, slippery funnel mouth, had a velvety pink canopy above (which looked like a tongue sticking out of a misshapen mouth), and a small armicule of its own that acted as a sentient seat belt for the occupant.

The Itofit, who was hanging inverted with one of the spry trap's armicules wrapped around his waist and another around his left leg, was being bobbed up and down as he dangled over the clearing so everyone could see and admire what Lutarious Roorback and Gorgoncha had caught. Angry but unfazed, It tried twisting and turning to get loose but to no avail then called softly to Snorf who was quivering on his chest:

"Jump down, Snorf! Wheel away as fast as you can. We can take care of ourselves but they'll surely take care of you first, so get away as quickly as your handsfeet will take you."

Snorf poked his snout from the Itofit's tunic and his three eyes looked wildly around.

"Go ahead," prompted It. "Don't think about it, just go!"

The snigglesnorf squiggled from It's tunic, hung briefly by his last handsfeet, then dropped to the ground. The spry trap saw him jumping down (with two hundred ogling eyes it didn't miss much that happened around it, especially if it was tasty) and slapped at where he landed with a twisty vine foot. Snorf avoided the first slap, then ran right under the spry trap and out the other side, dodging other vine feet and armicules as he went. He was so quick he soon outdistanced the spry trap, then hesitated just a moment to see what else awaited him. The tagalongs and snollysolijers were all over the clearing but the snigglesnorf spied a way out and proceeded to do the most amazing thing that Toliver or Whizlet, both of whom were watching it all while still hanging upside down from the spry trap's armicules, had ever seen. Snorf started running then rolled up until he looked like a loose tire, with his tail and ten sets of handsfeet around the periphery, and all three eyes sticking out from the center, two to one side and one to the other, and it was a complete mystery how they could see anything at all as they spun 'round and 'round as the snigglesnorf, picking up speed all the time, wheeled toward the opening. Before he got there, however, the skinny sergeant rushed to fill the breach and stood with his arms outspread holding a net. Snorf wheeled about and hot footed-footed-footed it the other way, dodged the spry trap on the way back, and headed for the river. But somehow his spinning eyes saw the tallagators (or perhaps his ears, one of which projected from either side like fancy protuberances on a wheel's axle, heard the hungry mouth-snaps ahead) and he spun about at the last moment and hurried back. By now the circle of tagalongs and snollysolijers had closed in upon him, and Major Dhump, who looked more like a bowling ball than ever, rolled into the circle, waving two other snollysolijers toward Snorf. Both of these solijers wore horrid looking masks and had tanks on their backs with tubes from them leading to nozzles in their hands.

"Watch out, Snorf," yelled the Itofit. "They've got flabber gas…"

Snorf scooted left, then right, then back again, around in two little circles, and off to the side where Sergeant Struddel blocked him with his net toward the masked solijers, both of whom squirted him at the same time. Right before everybody's eyes, Snorf's tire seemed to unroll (not at all like a real tire would do when experiencing a blow out) and flopped and bumped to a stop, with all the little handsfeet on top quivering and shaking uncontrollably and the three eyes, one lolling left, another right, and the third, spinning ever more slowly on the end of its stalk, collapsed atop the snigglesnorf's twittering snout.

"Oh how horrible," cried Toonie trying desperately to throw her tied hands across her breast. "He's been flabber gassed!"

While the spry trap and its leering pulpiteer were intent on slapping, stepping on, stickerbushing, or otherwise kalumphing the wickedly wheeling snigglesnorf, the Itofit had wrapped his tail around one of the armicules that encircled him. He grasped the other with two hands and his free foot, and with a mighty push, broke loose from them both and dropped to the ground. The spry trap snapped at him with two armicules and whipped at him with a twisty vine foot, but only managed to snare his hat, which it threw up into the air where it flipped over and over again before landing atop its cabbage head. The Itofit rushed the snollygassers, did a hand spring as he came upon them, seemed to fly through the air and hit them both in the masks simultaneously, one foot planted firmly in each mask, somersaulted to his feet behind them, scooped up Snorf, and bounced immediately to the shoulders of the startled Major Dhump and off his backside, pushing him forward onto his face as he passed. Being so perfectly round, the major rolled twice before toppling back onto his feet, then swung around with his gloves pointed at the Itofit's tail, and called for artillery. The seed shooters, thorn throwers, and sticky pod slingers, which had all been pulled back to the tallagator tugfloat, were set up like ten, twelve, and twenty-four pounders lining the rails. They all turned to zero in on the Itofit and, as he ran past them, began firing in order. It ducked three seeds, jumped over four low-fired thorns, rolled past another volley of seeds, then caught a sticky cream pod right in the face. It exploded all over him, knocking him down, and plastering him spead-eagled to the ground with the still flabber gassed Snorf at his side. Gorgoncha lumbered over and loomed above him.

"Oh you miserable creature," spit out Lutarious Roorback to the supine and groggy but still struggling It. "Surely you didn't expect to outwit me with your futile acrobatics. But you leave me no choice but to charge you with attempted escape from vawfilled authority and I'll get the Dujge to hit you with another ten years." He tapped the spry trap with his stick and snapped his whip in the air. "Down, Gorgoncha!" An armicule reached into the pulpit and lifted him carefully to the ground. "Major Dhump," he called out, pointing at the Itofit, then waving the back of his hand at the still hanging Toliver and Whizlet. "Wash this thing off after you tie it up, and collar it to these others… then put them all in the cage on my tugfloat."

"Oh Lut," said the block lady hurrying up. "What a wonderful catch!" She winked at him and smirked happily. "The Dujge will be delighted."

"Diddle the Dujge, Leuna!" said her husband pompously, "I'm delighted. I've snagged the Itofit himself along with two of his henchboys and another snigglesnorf."

"Didja get the other baloomerang too, poppa," said Odiferous pushing past his mother.

"Not yet, Odiferous, but we'll come back tomorrow with a brace of wiffer-sniffers and track it down."

"Odiferous! Get back on the tugfloat this instant," said his mother severely.

"I want to see those," replied the child pointing to Toliver and Whizlet.

"Go back, I say," said Leuna. "There are all sorts of nasty things in the jungle, including those worms you're pointing at and the others your father and I have apprehended this morning."

Gorgoncha dropped Toliver and Whizlet to the ground at the feet of three snollysolijers with collars and chains while several others came with buckets of water to unstick the Itofit and Snorf. The child pushed past the solijers with the chains and kicked Toliver. "Hummph," he said. "They're skinny and probably stupid too."

"Odiferous! Do as I tell you," persisted his mother, "or I'll send you off to Tallaghetto to live with the little people." The boy made a rude face at Leuna, prompting her to continue, "And you'll have to pay taxes too!"

The child ignored her and ran to where the Itofit was being dragged to his feet by the snollysolijers. "Can I pull his tail, poppa?"

"Of course, you can, Odiffy," said the District Inquisitor, but when the Itofit snapped his tail away and glared at the child, he added, "But you'd better wait until he's tied up."

"But I wanna do it now," cried the child jumping forward and reaching for It's tail, but as he went past, Toliver put out his foot and tripped him up.

"Yooowll!" screamed Odiferous. "He kicked me! That dirty person kicked me!"

"Oh, let mummy help you," cried Leuna hurrying over and picking up the crying child. Then, very coldly, she said to Toliver. "You nasty little creature. You'll regret this." And, pointing her pudgy finger at him, called out: "Gorgoncha! Eat this!"

No sooner had she spoken than one of the spry trap's armicules sprang out, wrapped around Toliver, and before even the Itofit could respond, lifted him high in the air, swung him over his cavernous trapmouth, and began to drop him in.

"Stop!" commanded Lutarious Roorback snapping his whip in the air. Gorgoncha hesitated, then turned around and hid its tasty morsel behind a cauliflower ear, and tried to sneak Toliver down to its mouth without the District Inquisitor seeing it. But Toliver grabbed the ear and hung on for dear life. "Put him down!" commanded Lutarious again, this time both snapping his whip and waving his lectric stick, now turned on so it sparked as he shook it at the twenty or so potato eyes that were eyeing him appraisingly. "Everything in Alabramble is done according to the vaw, so you can't snack until after we convict him this afternoon." Then, much more quietly to Leuna: "He's got to be worth more alive than as spry trap fuel. We could at least grow his hair for bombsights."

"Convict us!" cried Toonie who tried to run over to help the helpless Toliver and was only prevented by the collar around her neck and the leash being held by a snollysollijer. "We're not guilty of anything."

"Not guilty? Ha!" responded the District Inquisitor. "You're as ignorant as the others. Of course you're guilty. I wouldn't have arrested you it you weren't guilty. And as soon as we get to Smugsmog City, Dujge Dorque will prove me right by paragraphing you all to Brablug."

"That's Bramblethorn Rehabitualization and Brain Laundering Uber Gaol!" sneered Odiferous who had squirmed from his mother's arms, wiped the tears from his eyes, and squinted evilly at Toonie. "Just in case you have a brain worth laundering."

"That's right, m'boy", agreed Lutarious. "If they're so not guilty, why aren't they showing us their air breathing licenses?"

"Our what?" asked Is as politely as she could under the circumstances. She had heard all kinds of terrible stories about how cruel and unusual Alabramble could be, but knew nothing of air breathing licenses.

"Ha! You don't have one, do you?" gloated Lutarious. "And you probably don't have the others either." He snapped his whip in Is' direction. "In Alabramble you have to have a license to do anything, especially anything that's against the vaw. Of course, that doesn't mean you can break the vaw just because you've got a license, unless you've worked it out with the Dujge beforehand, but when you're arrested, if you don't have a license, you are arrested for that too."

"If you don't have a license to steal," broke in Odiferous who knew he'd make a wonderful Dujge himself one day, "you get five years in Brablug for stealing, and ten years on top of that for not having a license to do it properly!"

"Let me see," continued his father, warming to his favorite subject. "I don't suppose you have a license to smell our flowers, walk on our ground, look at our beautiful women..." He pinched Leuna on the cheek until she giggled and turned slightly jaundiced from the excess of yellow blood the pinch brought to her face, "…or have a permit to think what we know you're thinking! Ha-ha! I know all about you people." He waved his lectric stick at the snollysolijers and barked, "Take them away!"

Two snollysolijers jumped to collar the Itofit and Whizlet together, a third scooped up the still groggy Snorf, and another growled at Gorgoncha who was still holding Toliver behind his ear hoping everyone would forget about him for a moment so he could drop the now angrily wiggling tidbit into his trapmouth. Reluctantly, the armicule dropped its prize to the ground while the cabbage head quivered with frustration. But then the red beet nose began sniffing one way and the other, then down, then up; an armicule uncoiled out and scratched the cabbage chin, another scratched behind a cauliflower ear, and all two hundred eyes looked everywhere at once. Suddenly, another armicule pointed straight up in the air, wiggled happily, and grabbed the Itofit's hat from the top of the cabbage head. It brought it down to the beet nose, which sniveled rapidly over Hissofer, and then began unreeling itself from the hat in order to drop it and its snagged and hapless snakeband into the gurgling trapmouth.

At that moment, Lutarious turned around to see how well his instructions were being carried out and noticed what Gorgoncha was up to. "Stop!" he roared. "Give it up! A hat will give you indigestion anyway."

The spry trap grumbled and pulled the hat away, then put it back on its head, hoping the District Inquisitor would let him have it, at least as a hat.

"That's much too small," said Lutarious. "Besides a nice hat is wasted on a cabbage head."

Gorgoncha, who didn't feel anything was wasted on it, glared down at his master.

"Give it up!" roared Lutarious igniting his lectric stick, but only as a threat, since he prided himself on being able to bribe anybody (or anything, for that matter) to get what he wanted. "When we get home, I'll give you an algae and swamp water cocktail." He waited as the spry trap thought that over, "…and a plate of worms and slugs." Gorgoncha gurgled, hesitating, "…and a termite log for dessert…" Gorgoncha put the Itofit's hat into the District Inquisitor's outstretched hand and burped.

"May I have my hat back?" asked the Itofit as Toliver was collared to him and Whizlet.

"Of course, you may not," said Lutarious. "It's confiscated, that is, it will be confiscated after the trial. Now it is merely state's evidence, duly impounded according to the vaw." He turned away and smiled at Leuna. "What a fine hat the dummy was wearing, he must have stolen it somewhere, look at this beautiful weave, and such an interesting little flap for ventilation."

"Yes," agreed his wife. "And what an exquisite hat band. The Dujge will drool." Hissofer looked her right in the eye without her even knowing she was under surveillance (since his head was tucked comfortably under his tail), stuck his tongue out at her (which she did notice but thought it was a pretty black feather), and decided to take a nap.

The Dujge put the hat jauntily on his own head, then snapped his whip, almost taking off one of It's ears. "That was just to let you know I know what you're thinking, and it won't work," he sneered.

"He doesn't really know what we're thinking, does he?" whispered Toonie who knew it was a woman's prerogative to change her mind as many times as she liked and figured she could even stay a change or two ahead of someone as cocky and sure of himself as Lutarious Roorback.

"I'm afraid he does," answered Is. "He knows we want to escape and won't think of anything else until we do."

Lutarious strode up the gangplank to the tugfloat and climbed to the whipping bridge followed by Leuna and Odiferous. The Itofit, Toliver, and Whizlet were pulled to where Is and Toonie were collared together and made to wait while Snorf was thrust into the thornbranch cage and Major Dhump lined up his solijers along the shore. On the bridge, Leuna scribbled a quick note, which she put in a bottle and stuffed into the huge mouth of a funny looking flish that she'd taken from a large jar by the helm. "I've written a communiqué to the Dujge telling him of our success and asking him to meet us at the dock in Smugsmog City to dispose of the legal formalities as quickly as possible," she said and threw the flish over the side where it splashed into the water and swam off at an extremely rapid wiggle downriver.

"Oh, diddle the Dujge!" exclaimed Lutarious who knew he would make a far better Dujge himself. "If he meets us at the dock he'll take all our booty for himself and we'll never get to show it off."

"I don't think so," said Leuna letting a cunning smile play about her pudgy lips. "Because I've also invited him and Fasada to a picnic after the trial, along with the Mayorling Piddlepuddle and Lativia. We'll have a baloom bar-be-que."

"Yes!" agreed Lutarious, brightening considerably. "If we invite old Piddlepuddle, the Dujge will be out gunned, out ranked, out manned, maybe even out vawed, and won't dare interfere. Write a note immediately and send it by flagonflish!"

"Excellent idea," said Leuna who always congratulated Lutarious for her suggestions.

"Oh, goodie," chimed in Odiferous. "Can we have skewered snigglesnorfs too?"

"Of course," responded his mother licking her lips, "and if you behave yourself and do as mommy tells you, I'll have Cookie make manxed meat pie of that spitting creature's tail...and you can have the rest of it for target practice."

"What's she doing up there?" asked Whizlet of no one in particular. He'd been keeping his eye on the bridge because he knew that's where the control handles had to be and if anybody was going to win this game they could only do it by getting hold of the joysticks. "She just threw something in the river."

"A flagonflish," said Is. "She's probably sending it ahead to tell the people in Smugsmog City we're coming and to get ready for the trial."

"A trial," wailed Toonie who still couldn't believe what was happening to them. "But we're not guilty of anything."

"I'm afraid we're guilty of being in Alabramble," said Is.

"Yes," agreed It. "And now it is our duty to escape."

"But if they think we've broken a law," argued Toliver who knew that laws were good and lawbreakers bad and since trials were always fair, they'd be quite all right, "we can explain we didn't and they'll have to let us go."

"But we did break their stupid old laws," said Whizlet who was not as naive as Toliver because he'd spent a lot of time in dungeons with demons for nothing more serious than turning on his computer.

"Quite true," said It. "And you mustn't obey bad laws, because that will make you crazy and if everybody is crazy, nothing works anymore."

Is nodded her agreement. "And pretty soon you can't tell right from wrong anymore either, and when that happens, you forget how your heart works, and the next thing you know...why, you'll do anything any stupid person tells you to do."

Lutarious snapped his whip and pointed to the prisoners who were quickly pushed and prodded to the tugfloat. Rangi went first and was dragged to the fo'c'sle where she was chained to the anchor cable where everybody would see her as they sailed into Smugsmog City. To either side of her were cleats and bits with the harness cables for the tallagators going out through paired scuppers ahead. Behind the fo'c'sle was a large cabin surmounted by an enclosed bridge on top of which was the whipping bridge from which a flag pole with the District Inquisitor's Emblem of Officiousness was hanging limply in the stagnant morning air. Behind the cabin was a cargo shed aft of which the artillery was lined up along the rails to either side of the parade deck, and beyond that was a large bamboo and barbed thorn cage. The fantail was an open cargo hold filled with manure in which Gorgoncha rested while they were underway, digging his twisty vine legs deep into the nourishing night soil, and from where he could dangle his stickerbush arms in the tugfloat's wake to snag any flish unwary enough to let a tugfloat pass above it and unfortunate enough not to have been snapped up by a tallagator first.

The prisoners were unshackled from their collars and thrown into the cage. The pole with the basket of balooms, and the cage of shivering snigglesnorfs (who were tangled together holding eighteen or twenty handsfeet and only looking out with one anxious eye each), was hung from a corner post of the cage to a stanchion by the rail, and Boogie's box was placed in back where no one else was liable to go (and endanger themselves from his fury) and Gorgoncha could keep twenty or thirty eyes on him at all times. Gorgoncha climbed over the fantail railing, settled on his manure pile, and probed vainly for worms. Major Dhump ordered some of the snollysolijers to set up a camp on shore and await their return in the morning, then he and Sergeant Struddel led a detachment onto the tugfloat and lined them up smartly on the parade deck. Lutarious, Leuna, and Odiferous watched from the whipping bridge, and Mister Beeble, who tired quickly of being the pebble in any of their shoes, went into the cabin for his Book and took it aft to the cage where a new and captive audience awaited his ministrations.

Mister Beeble was brave in his own way and knew the value of a dramatic setting, so he was on his way to the fantail side of the prisoners' cage where Gorgoncha would form a fitting backdrop for his performance, but as soon as Toonie saw him coming, she ran to the side of cage and accosted him directly.

"Here comes the teacher," she called to the others, then demanded of him. "Why have they done this to us?"

Mister Beeble looked kindly on the little figure and smiled as sweetly as he could. "I'm afraid, my child, you were in the wrong place at the wrong time with the wrong people doing the wrong thing for the wrong reason. And everyone knows that five wrongs leave you no rights at all. Besides, you don't know anyone in Alabramble, and you have a baloomerang, so you're guilty on all counts."

"We are not either," stammered Toonie stamping her foot as she always did when she couldn't think of a smart retort.

"That isn't true," agreed Toliver trying to sound sensible since he knew teachers always made good character witnesses, except with principals.

"None of the above!" shouted Whizlet from across the cage because he knew reason never worked with shady characters, and the Revered End was as shady as anyone in *Doctor Dementia's Dungeon*.

Mister Beeble's face darkened, his unencumbered arm arose slowly, and the finger at the end of the long, pale hand snapped out to point directly at Whizlet. "All of the above," he retorted, "and if you don't watch out, young man, the Satin Diabola will get you and roast you for dinner every night forever and ever, Ahem!"

"If you were a real teacher," said Toliver who, instead of getting intimidated when he was intimidated, got mad, "you'd help us instead of trying to scare us."

Mister Beeble walked along the cage, glaring at them all, and letting his finger bounce from bar to bar as though it were a picket fence and he was on a bicycle with a stick. "If the Satin Diabola doesn't scare you, little man, I wouldn't bother to try."

"The Who?" asked Toonie.

"No," responded Mister Beeble turning from Toliver and smiling again at Toonie. "The Satin Diabola. The Who are just one of his voices!"

"I love *Tommy!*" cried Toonie.

"See!" declared the Revered End. "He knows exactly how to get you. The Satin Diabola is smoother than silk, and just like silk, he's a worm at heart!"

"I love silk too," pouted Toonie as she rubbed her cheek on her shoulder so she could feel the wonderful texture of her pretty paisleyed foulard blouse.

"Wormcloth!" thundered Mister Beeble. "The Satin Diabola dresses all his friends in wormcloth, so when he rubs them with his rubber wand, their hair will stand up so he can grab them, and they'll cling to him forever!"

As he ducked under the basket of balooms, Hark Beeble tapped it and shook his head admiringly. "You're smart people, or creatures, or throwbacks, or whatever," he said to the Itofit, "teaching your lunch to fly along with you like that. Have you ever thought of raising them commercially? I'll get together with you when you're in Brablug…perhaps we can work something out with the Dujge. He'll deal if you're not greedy, and he has a weakness for baloomburgers."

Behind the cage, he glanced quickly at Boogie who was staring at him with undiminished hostility. He took off his coat and threw it casually over the box, but not before pulling a dead mouse from his pocket and tossing it high into the air. Gorgoncha whipped out a dozen armicules and snagged it with a barbed armiculenail, then dipped it several times into his trapmouth before gurgling with pleasure and rearing up as a backdrop for Mister Beeble. Hark smiled at the creature, then turned suddenly to face the group in the cage, all of whom had now come to the back bars to see what he was up to. He stood on the raised edge of the manure pit so he was above them and stared down on them with a look somewhere between sanctity and surrealism in his eyes. His timing, however, was impeccable for just as he lifted his arm to command their attention, a sound like a shot rang out as Lutarious cracked his whip over the whipping bridge. The solijers on the parade deck snapped to attention, two tagalongs by the gangway pulled the gangplank aboard, and poor Rangi on the fo'c'sle cringed against her cables. Mister Beeble shook his head and threw it back so his hair flew out behind just as a second shot resounded across the river, arousing the tallagators from their basking stupors. A third whip crack directed above their backs sent them slithering and slipping into the water, and Odiferous, manning the flish slinger on the whipping bridge, slung twenty dazed flish to the front where the tallagators lurched after them, dragging the tugfloat with them. Mister Beeble caught his balance by stepping backwards into the manure pile, then nonchalantly kicked his shoe to clean it off.

A fourth shot sounded to direct the tallagators into the river's current, and, with Gorgoncha looming behind him, the Book in his hand, and a glint in his eye, Mister Beeble threw wide his arms and began to declaim:

"I am the Revered End Hark Beeble of the First Smotherin' Paptist Turch of Smugsmog City…" he paused to allow his words to sink in, "…and I bring you the Good Ebbings of the Great Paptist!"

"The Who?" asked Toonie again.

"No!" said Mister Beeble sharply. "I already told you that. They only sing…the Good Ebbings are shouted with glee, for they are the true message of the Great Paptist, the Smothered One, the Bringer of the True Pap!"

"Oh," responded Toonie somewhat intimidated. "Is that a breakfast cereal?"

"It is the only food you need," continued Hark.

"Well, I could use some right now," said Toonie who suddenly realized she hadn't eaten anything since the bowl of sherburr in the tapioca-'n-bun treehouse.

"Then listen!" stormed Hark Beeble, "for the Smothered One offers eternal flourishment to those who feed on his Holy Pap!"

"That must have a lot of vitamins in it," exclaimed Toliver.

"Not vitamins. Vitality! Life after death after this life of death, as demonstrated conclusively by the Great Paptist when he let his hair and nails grow for three days and three nights after the Great Smotherin'!" Mister Beeble held his breath for a full thirty seconds while sucking up his diaphragm so his eyes bulged out like squeezed balooms. These he fixed on his audience with critical intensity, and when he had their undivided attention, continued: "It's all explained in the *Smotherin' Paptists' New Addendum* to the *Only Unburnable Book in This Wicked World of Woe*, along with its *Codicils*, *Commentaries*, *Critiques*, and *Claptrap*, of course, which also tells you everything you need to know about everything else, and if you just happen to know anything besides what's in the Book, forget it as quick as you can or you'll be in big trouble with the Great Paptist."

As though the rest of the world existed only to punctuate his pronouncements, three more shots rang out as Lutarious snapped his whip over the top of the unruly tallagators, two whom were lunging at each other. With the whip snapping at their snouts, however, all thirteen of them surged ahead jerking the tugfloat behind them. Mister Beeble was upended and sat with a thud onto Boogie's box from which he leapt a moment later as a single, well-aimed claw pierced his coat and the seat of his pants as well.

"How can we get your book?" asked Toonie, who was always a soft touch for a hard sell and an easy mark for a difficult delivery. "Do we send in boxtops?"

"No-o-o," thundered Hark rubbing his revered rear end. "As a matter of fact, you don't even need that Book anymore because it has been superseded by another, much more timely Book: the New, Improved, and, as of today, One and Only Required Unburnable Book for This Wickedly Woeful World of Ours, of which I have a collector edition right here. It's not only tried, true, blue, green, and yellow, not to mention crimson, pink, and angel wing white, but it makes everything else ever written obsolete, untenable, or beside the point, and it's printed on waterproof asbestos paper so it can withstand either hellfire or the Deluge, whichever comes first!" He thrust the Book he was holding over his head with both hands and shook it down at them, while behind him Gorgoncha, as though on cue, raised up to his full height. A hundred and fifty potato eyes stared down at them with terrible intensity, and a menacing gastric grumble issued from its trapmouth. One of it twisty vine feet slithered out to wrap around Mister Beeble's foot and an armicule wound itself delicately around his waist.

"Don't you even think of it," roared the Revered End over his shoulder, "or it's a salad bar in Smugsmog City for you!" But then, when Gorgoncha sulked into the far corner of his manure pit and sat down so he no longer formed a frightening backdrop, Mister Beeble changed his tone completely. Turning about, he said: "Did I hurt the peelings of the District Inquisitor's favorite icky, tricky, victory vegetable worm-armed monster? You know I didn't mean to do that, Gonchy. You can come back now, but behave yourself." He took a cockroach from his pocket and dangled it enticingly. The heinous spry trap arose again, gurgled something unintelligible, and lumbered back, taking the roach and weaving its armicules behind the Revered End in a pantomime of purgatory and perdition.

Whizlet always got angry when he felt put on (or put off for that matter.) "Why are you called a Revered End?" he demanded, presuming it was because Hark got to share the back of the tugfloat with Gorgoncha and the manure pile.

Hark Beeble puffed out his chest and spoke directly down at Whizlet.

"I, along with my Brethren in the Book, stand at the living end of a long tale that has veered again to the straight and narrow Path of Pap: therefore, we are the Revered Ends!"

"Ha!" scoffed Toliver under his breath to Toonie. "I think he sounds more like a big, dumb jacka."

"Don't say that!" cried Toonie. "Or you'll have to you wash your mouth out with soap, and I bet you don't have any of that in your pocket."

"Soap?" said Hark Beeble who was very quick to pick up cues from his audience. "Pap is soap for the sole and hope for the hellbound!"

"There's no hell," exclaimed Whizlet who knew that even the 7th Bottomless Pit in *The Hell Worlds of Hellonaca* had a secret trap door leading to Jacob's Elevator.

"Of course, there's a hell," stormed the Revered End Hark Beeble who liked being contradicted less then anything else except being ignored. "What do you think is across the river from Yew Nork, across the bay from Fran Sanfisco, and across the salt flats from Mormoan's City, not to mention atop the hill in Warpington?"

"I don't believe that," said Toonie who always, or almost always, backed her cousin in arguments with strangers.

"That's because you've never been to Yew Nork!" stormed Mister Beeble who had. "Those heathens nork you just for the hell of it!" And then, to add authority as well as finality to his pronouncement held up his Book again and concluded: "And not a single living, sinning, singing, dancing, boozing, kissing, cruising, cussing, cursing, thirsting, bursting, breathing, bleeding one of those Sons of Satin is in here!"

He thrust the Book at them so all could see the embossed gold letters on the fiery red cover: **THE SAVED AND THE LOST** and in much smaller letter: Cloud Assignments for the First Going After the Second Coming for the Third Generation of the Fourth Reich's Fifth Column (6th Impression; 7th Edition; 8th Wonder of this Wicked World of Woe).

"What's a cloud assignment?" asked Whizlet who was afraid it had to do with homework.

"It's your seat number in heaven," said Hark Beeble. "If you're lucky enough to have one."

"You mean people have reserved seats in heaven?" asked Toonie who felt that was probably a good way to handle the crowds.

"Not everyone," said the Revered End throwing open the Book for all to see. "Only the Saved. Which means only Smotherin' Paptists because only we can be saved; although others can be helped out if we put in the Good Word for them."

"Maybe because you're the only ones who need saving," opined Toonie. "I only need saving when my inner tube leaks."

"Ha!" stormed Hark Beeble. "It's the leak in your inner sole that should worry you, little lady, along with the fact that you're not in the Book!" He pushed the opened Book under her nose. The first page was three columns of names and addresses; each carefully numbered (except for #13, of course, which was reserved for people not in the Book). All those listed on the first pages, moreover, were Revered Ends. Hark Beeble's name was on page seven, quite near the top, and, in his copy of the Book, was highlighted in flaming pink.

"It looks like a phone book," remarked Toliver who, if the truth were known, considered the phone book the most boring book in the world, even ones with yellow pages.

"Very perceptive, young man," said Hark. "It's Heaven's Phone Book for Those Who've Gotten the Call."

"But why is your name in the front?" asked Toonie who was having a rare attack of logic. "If you're a Revered End, you should be at the back of the Book."

"No, no, my dear," said Hark Beeble with just the slightest bit of modest condescension. "In the Holy Happy Hierarchy of Heaven, as everyone who has studied the matter knows, the first shall be last and the last first, so the Revered Ends are the very first of all." He fanned through the pages of the Book. The first third were filled with names and numbers; but the last two-thirds were blank.

"It looks like it's mostly empty pages," said Toonie who was always looking on the bright side of things. "That means there's room for lots more people."

"Oh no, it doesn't," replied Mister Beeble sharply. "The blank pages are all for the Lost. There is no need to write down their names since they're not coming with us, so we just use empty pages to keep track of them. As you can see, the numbers of the Saved are engraved forever and nobody else need apply, give or take a few here and there who might make a sizable donation or have a deathbed conversion of debentures, so the Saved are already saved and the Lost are, as we occasionally have to remind the backsliders and bankrupt, Kabloomie!"

"How do you know that?" demanded Whizlet who knew that every game had an override switch built in somewhere or at least a restart button.

"Because the Revered End Ferry Jawell, the immortal founder of the Moral Misology, calculated it exactly with his secret formula," replied Hark, "upon the occasion upon which he was wafted up to Heaven on a Golden Pillow and had his Immaculate Vision of the Great Paptist's Throne."

Mister Beeble grasped the Book to his breast, his eyes rolled heavenward, and he let out a huge sigh, while Gorgoncha belched a fountain of juices into the air behind him. "The Revered End Ferry Jawell saw the seats for all the Saved ringed around the Throne of the Great Paptist, the Inner Circle of plush couches with purple velvet for the Revered Ends, then the pillowed easy chairs for the Elect, then the rings of straight backed chairs for the Elders of Alabramble, and receding into the distance, the benches for everybody else, and the Revered End Ferry Jawell saw that the radius of the concentric waves of bowed heads was a Great League, and he Squared the Circle and multiplied by Pi in the Sky, divided by Parthenogenesis, subtracted his commission and added an itinerary, after which his secret formula was complete, and Lo!" the Revered End Hark Beeble threw out his arms with the Book grasped firmly in his Right Hand "He knew, He Knew, HE KNEW that 53.9% of everybody were the Saved because that's how many seats there were for them, and he knew, He Knew, HE KNEW that everyone else was Lost and would have to stand in hell, and he proclaimed Us not only the Immortal Misology but the Immortal Majority as well, and We Are...Forever and Forever...Ahem!" Mr. Beeble's eyes rolled completely into his head. He gurgled an anguished moan and fell backwards onto a waiting crisscross of Gorgoncha's armicules, which lifted him again to his feet.

"That's awful!" exclaimed Toonie who was referring to Mister Beeble's left shoe, which had a hole in the sole which showed he wasn't wearing any socks.

"But it's the True Pap!" responded the Revered End. "53.9% constitutes an Immortal Majority in anybody's Book whereas the rest of you, 46.1% are Lost so you don't count."

"But if we don't count," inquired Toliver who could be very persnickety when dealing with numbers, "how can we be 46.1% of it?"

"By default," responded Hark with barely a ruffle. "And default is yours!"

"But if we're the minority," put in Whizlet, "why do we have so many more pages in your dumb Book?"

"That should even be evident to an ignoramus like yourself," replied Mister Beeble curtly. "The Lost all have big, bloated egos so they write their names very large and hancock up all the space so we reserve more pages to make sure none of them get away. And they won't get away...no! No! NO! They most certainly won't. We know who every one of you is by name, zeal ranking, and socialized maximum security number."

"How do you know that about everybody?" demanded Toonie who felt a ranky zeal number was probably worse than a maximum security number any day.

Hark Beeble huffed loudly, stiffened his jaw, and turned away to stare someplace else, then looked back over his shoulder with fire (or its heavenly equivalent) in his eye. "We know exactly where you stand in the Line of the Lost, little lady, by virtue of the Second Secret Formula which determines your Humanistic Evil Lascivious Lust number, your HELL number for short, which was revealed in a hot flash of insight to the Revered End Gimme Stagart when he was carrying out his top secret bottom research in human awfulness; research so secret even its methodology is still in the classifieds, which ranked everybody by their index of rank!"

"That sounds pretty suspicious to me," said Toliver who didn't like to be suspicious but really couldn't help it when he was. "How can you be sure about it if it's so secret nobody knows what he's up to?"

"Very easily," replied a totally unperturbed Hark Beeble. "First of all, all Revered Ends are, itsa facto, Certified Saved Persons, and all snollygosters are too, as long as they tithe in time, of course". Hark glanced quickly toward the whipping bridge where the District Inquisitor and his family were sitting on their cushions amusing themselves by watching the tallagators ravage the river, then bent over and put the back of his hand to his mouth, "...except that Leuna Roorback has registered a secret reservation about Fasada Dorque, but that will just have to be worked out through the seating arrangement in Heaven. After that, if you're a paying Smotherin' Paptist, you're a C.S.P. as well, and, as everyone knows, if you're not a Smotherin' Paptist, you're a terra hick, and terra hicks can't be saved, only upped, and then just a little."

"Upped what?" asked Toonie who'd heard of being one upped and bottom upped and seven upped and hiccuped, but never terra hicked up.

"Upped on downers," continued Hark Beeble who felt he was probably being contradicted again so decided he'd better do it himself.

"That doesn't make sense…" started the Itofit who knew a psychobabble when he met one.

"I'm not speaking to you!" snapped Hark Beeble angrily. Then to emphasize his displeasure at the interruption, he bent over to speak directly to Toliver and Toonie while holding his arm with a clenched fist above him whose index finger popped out and pointed at It and whose pinkie popped out and pointed at Is. "Don't listen to them. They're hopeless cases. Beyond the pail and out of the bucket." He thrust his Book to the front and used it to shield his mouth as he continued in a whisper. "People with tails get a blank page all to themselves!"

Whizlet, of course, heard none of this because his attention span for theological discussions was only a minute and forty-seven seconds, and he had long since turned about and gone to the other side of the cage to look out at the snollysolijers who were standing at parade rest on the parade deck. The (FAT) major and the sergeant were completing an animated discussion in front, after which the sergeant stamped his feet, gave a two-handed salute, stepped to the side, and jumped to attention. The major selected one of his gloves, raised it to his mouth, and blew into it so hard that his cheeks puffed out as though he was Dizzy Gillespie doing a blue note. The glove unrolled like a New Year's Eve party popper, its middle finger punched straight ahead, and a noise somewhere between the bellow of a bull moose in rut and Howard Cosell in Las Vegas cut through the dank air, snapping all the solijers to attention. Sergeant Struddel was so long and lank and Major Dhump so ruddy and round that when they stood next to each other they formed a perfect **10** and therefore considered themselves the one and elliptical epitome of policeness. In fact, they were so taken with their image that they loved (either alone or together) to quote Pulcan the Whipwielder to the effect that the police state was the best of all possible states, or (even more frequently) Pallace the Pallpacker's observation (made to the Revered End Billy Someday on the occasion of his First Diatribe Against the Natural

Religion of the Native Alabramblians) that an obedient policeman was the Right Handcuff of God.

"A-10-shun!" shouted Sergeant Struddel redundantly (since the solijers were already as stiff and straight as starched napkins) but allowing him nonetheless to prove the logographic necessity of his appearance with the major. "Major Dhump will now instruct you on the finer fine points of po'lice work beginning with the most important important points and working therefrom and downwards to the grosser gross points which are nevertheless fine points to get stuck in your mind. So listen up and dress down! If you understand the overview, you won't underestimate the overhead, or overstep your underlings, or undercut your overalls, or overrun the underdog, or overheat your underwear, or override your..."

The major cut him short with a wave of his gloves. He was holding the gloves firmly in his right hand and began to slap them rhythmically into his left palm, then, as though to awaken his oratorical genie, struck himself smartly across the cheeks, and began to declaim:

"Syffers, tagalongs, snollysolijers: lend me your spears! I come to bury greasers, not to haze them! The evils men fear chase after them; their goods are often impounded by the Dujge. So let it be with us!"

He spun on his heel and stood with his legs apart, arms akimbo, staring to the stern of the tugfloat where Gorgoncha was giving him the undivided attention of seventy or eighty eyes. To him the monster seemed so perfect an example of Alabramblian might that when he turned again, he was bleary-eyed and overcome with emotion: "We hold these truths to be self-evident, that all men are up to something and therefore arrestable; that they are in awe of cretin rites, especially in aliens; and that among these are reason enough to give life to libbers for the pursuit of happiness."

He stomped to the edge of the deck, slapped a thorn thrower with his gloves, spun again on his heel, and went on. "When in the course of human events, it becomes necessary for some people to kick the stuffing out of other people, a prudent regard for the opinion of mankind demands we be the kickers and not the kickees. Besides, it is an excellent way to keep your boots polished, not to mention your buckles, knuckles, apples, and teeth, and we all know that polish is the pride of the superior sollijer, the gleam on his spearpoint, the vanity of women, and the adornment of the Vatican."

"No, no, no!" whispered Sergeant Struddel quickly. "That's Polish, not polish."

"Of course," continued the major without missing a beat, "a pole is the best thing to shinny up, slide down, and use to hit people on the head, not to mention tax voters with and take with a grain of salt."

He spun again on his heel, now looking down the length of the boat to the seething white water caused by the thrashing of the tallagators. He grew agitated thinking what a capital punishment it would be to give prisoners a four tugfloat head start, then pursue them with a brace of two year old 'gators. He jumped into the air and saluted the flagpole, then went on excitedly: "Ask not what your country can do for you, do it to somebody else first! When sneaking up on them, walk softly and carry a big stick, then drop them from behind. We have nothing to fear but fearsome fellows, which is why we're armed to the teeth and taught to seek them out before they get to enjoy themselves. But remember, men: If the hand that holds the dagger thrusts it into his neighbor's back without a court order it's a felonious monk unless the Dujge is your uncle or Uncle is your employer."

He grew pensive, as he always did when reflecting on the unconscionable restrictions placed on himself and his cohorts in their zeal for vaw and ardor. Next he grew restive, then poetic:

On catching a felon be sure that you tell him
That he has the right to remain
Either silent or breathing
The choice you'll be leaving
To him, and he'll squeal if he's sane.

The thought of unreported felons or unrepentant fellows always incited the major to a state of far righteous indignation. He knew the problem was the panderdandering of prisoners decreed by the Neandercrats in Warpington when, on that day that will live in infamy, they got the Supine Court to agree to mollycoddle nonsnollygosters. But being a fully accredited, dutiful officiousness himself, he sounded a warning for his troops:

When breaking down doors make sure that you roar
To startle the people within
And if there are children
Be sure that you fill them
With fright, so they'll learn not to sin.

Snorting loudly, he took up a boxing stance in front of Corporal Pororal and threw a quick one-two at his chin, but pulled the punches a whisker shy of their target. The corporal didn't even wince but did gulp inaudibly, then shouted: "Yes, sir!"

"Good man!" muttered the major twirling his gloves, and then, as he turned away, slapped the corporal across the cheek with his patented Patton backhand. "Alertness, men! That's what and why we're all about here! Keep your eyes on everybody, your noses in everybody's business, and your hands in everybody's... On second thought, keep your hands to yourselves. Struddel and I will take care of the details. And always keep in mind, men: Four score and seven pounds of merry mota is a good night's haul, and if you even hope to get into the Good Knight's Hall in Heaven, make sure you inventory everything twice, then burn the inventory. But..." he cautioned:

> when doing your duty make sure that the booty
> Is turned in to Struddel or me
> We'll see that the divvy
> Is fair to the givee
> And fairer in fairness to we!

"No, no, no! Us!" whispered Struddel.

"What?" said the major.

"Us," repeated the sergeant. "Not we, us, fairness to us."

"That's what I said," said the major. "Fairness to us two who are we too." He slapped the sergeant across the shoulder with his gloves, then whispered: "Yes! Us two, who are we to complain, eh, sergeant? there's enough to go around the Dujge, the D. I., me, you. "

He stalked behind Struddel, raised his gloves, and continued: "And if they complain, sergeant." He made his point by swinging his gloves like a hammer to the sergeant's head, so when they knocked his helmet down over his eyes, the impact sounded like a cracked bell and the sergeant wheezed like Leuna's whistle. At the sound, all the solijers began to cheer wildly, which had an immediate effect on the major, transporting him in an instant to the great victory in reverse psychology achieved in Niet Vam. The blood rose to his face and he jumped into the air, clicking his heels with a resounding Clickoom!

> Always attack with the sun at your back
> And run (if you must) up a hill
> Pursuers are lazy

It drives them quite crazy

To have to arise for the kill…

"No, no, no!" whispered Sergeant Struddel impatiently as he righted his helmet. "That will never do! That's advice for the tsarmy, not the po'lice!"

"What?" cried Major Dhump, still carried away "The tsarmy! Of course! Charge and Be Diddled! Stand and Be Riddled! Ladies first and officers to the conference room! Into the Alley of Meth Road the six blundered! Man the seed shooters, men! Prime the thorn throwers and cock the cream pods! Fire when your guns bear fruit!" He rushed to the nearest seed shooter and spun it round and round looking for a target before making himself too dizzy to stand, whereupon he gillespied on the spot, and rolled off the parade deck.

Sergeant Struddel stepped to the front, pulled off his helmet, and rested it on his breast: "Old solijers never die," he intoned with a tear, "they just roll away. At ease, men, and once more into the bleachers!"

SMUGSMOG CITY, BLUES, and BLACKS

As the tugfloat passed the drab and barren areas that had been clear-cut on either side of the river, Leuna pulled down slatted shades so she and the DI wouldn't be bothered by the desolation. Beyond the devastation, she rolled them up again to catch the breeze. As they approached the city, the river got wider and wider, the water muddier and muddier, and the air dirtier and a hazy yellow-gray color. They stayed to the middle of stream because the tallagators got distracted near the shores and even though partially muzzled (to keep them from taking more than nips out of each other) they snapped at everything. There were also large branches overhanging the river that could scrape along the awning over the whipping bridge and the insects were denser and more ferocious near the shore. On the whipping bridge, Lutarious Roorback reclined on his captain's cushion with his lectric stick holstered to his belt, his whip and new hat laying at his side, and a glass of lillylotus syrupwater in his hand. Leuna was curled at his side fanning them both with her jolly giant jasmine flutterby wing and occasionally popping a smarshmallow bellyjean into her mouth. Odiferous was in front throwing stones at the tallagators to get them to bite each other, when he suddenly jumped up and down excitedly and pointed ahead toward the riverbank where a commotion in the branches of a tree overhanging the river caught his attention.

"A nonkey fight! A nonkey fight!" he yelled. "Can we go over and knock them out of the trees with your lectric stick for Gorgoncha and the tallagators?"

"No," said his father. "It must be something else. Nonkeys don't fight, at least when there's a chance they might fall into the river and catch something they weren't angling for."

"They just do unspeakable things that little boys shouldn't watch," said his mother, "so we won't go near them so you can."

"Well, maybe it's an eep or even a grrrrrilla." retorted the boy. "Gorgoncha would really like that! Can't we go poppa? Can't we? Please, please, please..."

Lutarious was about to yield when Leuna tapped him on the temple with her fan. "No, no, let's not," she said. "It's probably just a dribbegull or some other dirty creature that will make a mess of everything."

"Waaaa!" cried Odiferous. "Gorgoncha likes birds too."

"I said No!" said his mother.

"It's no problem, Leuna," said Lutarious. "Humor the lad and he'll grow up to be just like us." He picked up his whip and stood to direct the tallagators to the tree when something fell from its branches and splashed into the water. The tallagators saw it, swerved to the right, and spurted frantically ahead. Lutarious fell back, Leuna was knocked from her cushion, and, on the fantail, Hark Beeble was upended into the manure box.

"Yipee!" yelled Odiferous as he grabbed the railing and pointed ahead at a tiny head and two flailing arms churning toward the shore. "It's a nonkey! It's a nonkey!"

Lutarious regained his feet but even his angry snapping of his whip had no effect on the tallagators (except, perhaps, to drive them on faster) who had joined the race and were gaining on the poor creature. In the bamboo and barbed thorn cage, everyone was thrown back against the bars. Toonie was horrified at the spectacle. "My goodness," she exclaimed, "I've never seen a monkey swim so fast before."

"Or swim with his tail in front of his nose," rejoined Whizlet who was gauging the speed of the little head and its twirling arms against the thirteen thrashing tallagators, "but he's got it made if the bank's not slippery."

Whizlet's calculations proved correct for the monkey gained the shore and flew up a tree with his tail (and everything else which was now in front of it again) still intact. The tallagators consoled themselves by snapping at each other and swarms of mosquitoes, and Lutarious managed to reestablish control. He turned them back down river, but as the tugfloat passed under the overhanging branch, something leapt from the foliage and landed with a Plop! in the middle of the awning. A moment later, a vawyer climbed from the awning and slid down one of the stanchions supporting it.

"How do you do, sir!" said the right mouth to Lutarious as the vawyer approached with his shaking hand thrust up and to the fore. "Sorry to get your attention like that, but I'm Toppenbottom and I understand you have a problem, or perhaps two or three, maybe even five aboard."

One of his left hands pulled off his hat, his head nodded to Leuna, while the left mouth continued: "Good day, milady. I trust I didn't startle you, but I knew you needed help."

"We don't need any help," snapped Leuna who hated to be dropped in on unexpectedly. "But you might if I sic our spry trap on you!"

"Oh, goodie," shouted Odiferous. "Gorgoncha would love a stuffed vawyer."

"It would probably give him indigestion," scoffed Lutarious who had more experience with vawyers.

"Now, now, gentle people," said Toppenbottom's left mouth. "Look at the trouble you're already getting yourselves into just because you don't have a good vawyer. If you feed me to the beast you'd lose your spry trap license, anger the gods, and get three nuisance suits a week from my partners for the rest of your natural lives, give or take two years for extenuating circumstances."

"Wow, poppa!" exclaimed Odiferous. "With three new sun suits a week, you'd be the best dressed officiousness in Smugsmog City."

Lutarious patted his son on the head. "No, no, Odiffy, not the kind of suits that are pressed with an iron, but the kind that are pressed with vawyerly zeal for rasputniks."

"A nice distinction, neatly expressed," said the left mouth. "You missed your calling card, sir. And here's mine."

"I bet he doesn't have a Tugfloat Boarding from an Overhanging Limb license," persisted Odiferous, "so you could throw him to the tallagators. The Dujge wouldn't mind unless he owes him something."

"I have a license for everything there is," said Toppenbottom's left mouth matter of factly, but the right mouth continued so softly that only Odiferous could hear it: "Even one for eating little boys for supper sopped in mushrooms with an apple in their mouths."

"Yowl", screamed Odiferous who quickly ran behind Leuna's ample behind, and stood there clinging to her skirt and sticking his tongue out at the vawyer.

"Come, come, sir," said Toppenbottom's left mouth. "I know you have a problem because I saw your flagonflish going downstream, and you wouldn't send a flagonflish unless you needed to talk to the Dujge, and nobody needs to talk to the Dujge unless he has a problem." He stomped about the whipping bridge and looked over the tugfloat until spotting the cage beyond the parade deck. "Ah-ha!" he continued. "So there's the problem…well, I'll make them my problem, and I'll be your problem, and we'll be the Dujge's problem, and everybody will be happy with his own problem, unless we don't get paid in advance which would be a real problem."

He ran down the ladder, jumped over Major Dhump who had been upended again by the tallagator race, and hurried across the parade deck where Hark Beeble was just coming around the cage covered in manure. "Howdy Hark!" said the left mouth jovially while the right mouth was muttering under its breath, "Step aside, goofball. It's my turn now." His lower shaking hand thrust out then pulled back as the vawyer noticed the condition of the Revered End's exterior. "You must have done a good morning's work, Hark." said the left mouth blithely "You look like the Satin Diabola's rubber wand!"

He side-stepped Mister Beeble, put his briefcase on the deck, pulled his handkerchief from his pocket with a flourish, and used it to polish his spectacles while examining the District Inquisitor's latest catch. "Relax, everyone," he said, pulling off his hat with another hand and bowing to the group. "It's Toppenbottom to the rescue. Here's my card, here's my diploma, here's my hat…oops!" He noticed that everybody's hands were tied behind them so no one could take what he was busy using four hands to shove through the bars.

"Are you Mister Toppenbottom of Phister, Blister, Nister, Twister, &

Toppenbottom?" asked Toonie excitedly because she was always excited when she remembered something complicated, especially if it rhymed.

"No, I'm not," said the left mouth. "That's my cousin. I'm with Schuster, Brewster, Rooster, Booster, & Toppenbottom."

"Use us, not them," said the right mouth, cutting the left short. "We're arch rivals. They're arch fiends; we're arch angels. I'm Archy Toppenbottom; my cousin's Itchy, but even being scratched in the fifth didn't help him."

"We don't need a vawyer," said Toliver who was still mad at Gorgoncha for catching him, at Hark Beeble for intimidating him, and madder still at still being tied up. "We need a knife."

"And a fork too, I'll wager," said the left mouth. "And a spoon…probably a whole place setting. And how do you expect to get all that without a vawyer? Hmmm?" He almost glared at Toliver except he never glared at prospective clients unless they haggled too long over the bill.

"All tied up with your problems and still think you can do without Toppenbottom?" said the right mouth. "Think again, young man."

The left mouth chimed in. "You do have a license to think, don't you?"

"I don't need a license to think!" exclaimed Toliver.

"Ah-ha!" cried the right mouth. "So you think thinking is license enough all by itself, do you? No wonder you're in trouble in Alabramble! It's licentious and insentient to be a nonlicentiate here! If you take license with thinking, what else will you take, eh? Answer me that!"

"What's that?" gasped Toonie pointing up in the air with her nose. She was much too polite, usually, to interrupt people, or even vawyers for that matter, even though she was now quite convinced they weren't people, unless she was very startled, or somebody pinched her, of if she suddenly thought of something very interesting to say. And right now she was very startled because the smog had cleared for a moment and she saw a huge, malevolent face staring down at her from the sky. A gust of wind swirled the smog further and a gigantic fist could be seen behind the head holding a whip handle with the whip itself curled out in a great coil surrounding the head and descending into the smog.

"Yipes-a-doddle," screamed Whizlet who tried to throw his hands up in front of his face but because they were still tied behind him only succeeded in spinning himself around till he was looking at Toliver who also had a horrified expression on his face. The smog cleared further and massive iron shoulders came into view, followed by a naked chest. Over one of the shoulders and across the chest was the strap for a great seed bag hanging to the side, and the figure's other hand was scattering what appeared to be medicine ball size iron seeds. A great belt woven of thorns with a huge buckle that looked like a seed shooter encircled the waist. The belt was holding up a short kilt and hung from its side was a lectric stick the size of a telephone pole. Below the kilt, his right leg was wrapped in vines and his bare feet were in sandals, the right leg striding forth, the left on its toes behind.

"That's the Statue of Pulcan Smugsmog," said the Itofit.

"Pulcan the First," said Is.

"Pulcan the Whipwielder!" added the vawyer.

"My goodness," gasped Toonie. "Is he coming for us?"

"It's just a statue," replied the Itofit, "of the man who led the first snollygosters to Alabramble after they'd used up Hellonaca."

"You mean there really is a Hellonaca?" stammered Whizlet fearing the worst.

"There was," corrected It, "until it was washed and blown away."

"Now it's the Great Granite Wasteland," added Is.

"And so the snollygosters came here and are doing the same thing to Alabramble!" exclaimed Toliver who knew how to put two and two together, subtract them like politicians, and get nothing.

"I'm afraid so," responded Is. "After Pulcan became the first Emptor Caveat of Alabramble, the snollygosters started turning it into rasputniks as fast as they could."

"Smart people," said Mister Toppenbottom's left mouth. "You've got to give old Smugsmog credit. He came to Alabramble with nothing but a hope in his heart, a promise on his lips, and a pocket full of thorn tree seeds, and pretty soon he was selling sandals to the natives like they were going out of business. He got the Smotherin' Paptists to teach them religion so they'd know they'd need snollygosters to save them, then taught tagalongs how to tag along and syffers how to quiver. He was a genius, a great man. He even wrote the Three Books of the Vaw: one for snollygosters, one for tagalongs, and one for everybody else, which inaugurated the Golden Age of Vawyers!" The vawyer swept off his hat, threw his arm across his chest, and bowed to the towering statue.

As the tugfloat came around a bend in the river, a gusty breeze further dispersed the smog. The gargantuan figure was standing on a rocky promontory atop a hill covered with a teeming jungle of foliage that was writhing in the wind. "Once he discovered the value of nasty plants," said Is, "he made it his mission to cultivate as many noxious things as he could."

"He was a genius, all right," continued the Itofit, "a heinous genius. They call the area for a mile around the statue Pulcan's Paradise because that's where he built the Brambleham Boological Gardens, his Experimental Thistle, Thorn, Nettle & Sticker Plots, to carry out his experiments."

"And Pallace the Pallpacker, the Second Emptor Caveat, built that ten story statue of him right in the middle of the gardens so everybody in Smugsmog City would remember who's in charge," said Is.

"At night they shine lights on his whip so it looks like he's snapping it over the city." said It.

"And they spray diluted flabber gas from his nose so it wafts down on everybody and reminds them how bad things could get if they don't behave themselves." said Is.

"And it smells even worse than the smog so people don't notice how bad that is," added It.

"And it keeps everybody at everybody else's throat, so they all need vawyers," gloated Mister Toppenbottom. He slapped his hat back on his head. "Let's face it, folks: A contentious society is a vawful society! And Alabramble is as vawful as they come!"

"That's the ugliest statue I've ever seen," said Toonie who'd already been to three museums and seen lots of books with dozens of pictures of pretty statues in them.

"Yes," agreed Is, "it's said to be a very good likeness."

"Whatever happened to him?" asked Toliver who never liked to be left up in the air, especially about things that were up in the air.

"Nobody knows," answered the Itofit. "No snollygoster will admit it, but I've heard his heinous spry trap turned on him one night, plucked him out of bed, and fed him to a pack of tallagators. But all anyone knows for sure is he just disappeared, and Pallace the Pallpacker became Emptor."

"In Is, we heard that he was toisoned by his fourth wife, Penelope the Pivyperson," added Is, "who was Pallace's mother…"

"…by a previous engagement…" interjected It.

"…and she was the one who fed him to the tallagators…"

"…which is why they're so mean," concluded It.

"Does he have a statue too?" asked Toonie who didn't want to be startled again if she could help it.

"Not a statue," replied Is, "but he does have a monument called Tallaghetto…"

"Tallaghetto is only incidental," cut in Mister Toppenbottom's left mouth. "His real monuments are Brablug and the Codex of Cunep."

"Cunep." gasped Toonie almost hiccuping the word because it set so badly with her.

"That's the Second Emptor Caveat's Codex of Cruel, Unusual, Nasty, and Entertaining Punishments," said the right mouth with a bit more relish than Mister Toppenbottom usually displayed. "One of the most appealing, in the vegal sense of the word of course, of the Pallpacker's jurisprudential strokes of brilliance. We can keep 'em dancing on hot coals forever with that one. Nobody important gets hurt; everybody important gets rich; and everybody else gets entertained, except for the dancers, of course, but they wouldn't be dancing if they'd retained a good vawyer before knocking heads with the Codex."

Mister Toppenbottom concluded by glaring knowingly at the Itofit but was hindered from saying more by the snapping of Lutarious' whip. The tallagators turned toward shore where a complex of rundown buildings, dilapidated houses, and sewer pipes emptying into the river emerged from the grimy air. "That's Tallaghetto there," said Is, "where everybody but the snollygosters live."

"That's as ugly as Pulcan's statue," said Toonie who liked to make comparisons even if they weren't particularly nice.

"That's certainly true," agreed Is, "but when people with dirty minds are in charge of things, everything else gets dirty too."

"And pretty soon you have another Hellonaca," added the Itofit whose nose was twitching uncontrollably from the rancid air even though he was holding the fluffy end of his tail in front of it to filter the smog. "That's why in It we only vote for people who've volunteered to let the Assembly of Elder Ethicists approve their qualifications."

"In Is," said Is, "we know it takes well-educated people to run things correctly, so we train the people who want to lead us until they know how to do everything right, and since nothing is secret and we all discuss everything carefully, things get done the way they should."

"Poppycock," exclaimed Toppenbottom. "People are poor, nasty, brutish, and short, the last being the only virtue they possess, so they can't possibly run anything without a vawyer to argue with everybody else's vawyers about whatever it is you're talking about."

Beyond Tallaghetto the river was lined with docks and tallagator pits. The tugfloat moved past these till coming to a series of ornate wharves fronting a large square containing the stalls and booths of a busy open-smog market surrounded by warehouses and dark, dingy buildings. The docks were concrete enclosures where the tallagators climbed up ramps into cages filled with rotting meat, leaving the tugfloats behind bobbing against the wharves. Lutarious, Leuna, and Odiferous came down from the whipping bridge while two tagalongs slid the gangplank ashore. A crane operator dangled a dead rat from its tail to lure Gorgoncha from his manure pile to the wharf where he rumbled about while two palanquins were brought from the cargo shed for Leuna and Odiferous. Major Dhump directed Sergeant Struddel to direct a detachment of snollysolijers to recollar and uncage the prisoners and line them up on the wharf. Hark Beeble, who didn't have a palanquin, was in the cabin washing himself with cologne and waiting for the others to leave. The procession started off with Lutarious in Gorgoncha in front snapping his whip to clear a way through the square, followed by Major Dhump and his guard leading Rangi followed by the palanquins, followed by Sergeant Struddel and his solijers leading the prisoners, followed by the bearers carrying the cage of balooms and snigglesnorfs, followed by a syffer pulling a rope at least twenty feet long at the end of which was Boogie's cage in which Boogie was laid out regally like a lion. He disdained to look either to the right or left and did no more than swish his tail at any bystander curious and bold enough to dart in for a closer look before being brushed out of the way by the contingent of spear wielding solijers taking up the rear of the column. Behind them was Toppenbottom waving to everyone with the two hands, which weren't carrying his briefcase or passing out his cards, while his smiling face was talking to the crowds on either side from both mouths at once. And following all this, high in the air and completely camouflaged by the intervening smog, was a small gray bird with bright red shoulders and very sharp eyes who was surveying everything below and whistling *The Suite from Batman* softly to herself.

Before they had passed the middle of the square, however, Hobnail changed her tune. Some in the crowd felt a sense of foreboding and looked upward upon hearing the haunting strains of *The Mephisto* Waltz but none could see the intrepid parrot and the music seemed to hang on the air unsupported by anything more substantial than its own melody. Toonie heard it and stared ahead apprehensively, then let out another gasp and might have fainted on the spot except the collar around her neck would have hurt. Coming toward them into the square was a procession of more spear toting, sling carrying, sword wielding snollysolijers completely surrounding another heinous spry trap, even larger than Gorgoncha.

As the two processions approached each other, Leuna called back to Odiferous: "Sit up straight, Odiffy dear. Here comes the Dujge in Hydraplop. We mustn't let him think you're a languid lump, now must we?"

"Oh, diddle the Dujge," said Odiferous mimicking his father, and he slid even further down on his cushion until he looked like Nero at a cocktail party, much to the discomfiture of his mother.

"Sit up," she snapped, "or I'll diddle your doddle!" But the only thing he moved was his tongue, which he stuck out at her and burped at one of the tagalongs carrying his palanquin.

Leuna had no more time to waste on him for the two processions had met with Gorgoncha and Hydraplop facing each other in a sea of tagalongs and snollysolijers, with Gorgoncha standing on his taproots and stretching his ocotillo neck stalk in order to look taller. While Leuna daintily waved her flutterby fan at the Dujge, Lutarious slapped his rolled up whip to his breast, nodded his head (without, of course, taking his eyes from his opponent), and spoke formally: "Good Tidings, Your Onerous. In the name of Pulcan the Whipwielder, I am pleased to place before the Imperious High Courtex a cowardly cabal of sky-traffickers charged with multiple high crimes, misdemeanors, missteps, mistakes, missed popportunities, and failures to be licensed criminals."

Hydraplop sissed a steam burp at Gorgoncha, but the Dujge reached up with his whip handle and scratched his pulpit's canopy tongue until the siss became no more than a contented stomach roll. The Dujge smiled at Lutarious but said nothing. Instead he stretched out and looked past the other spry trap at what followed in its wake.

"My goodness," murmured Toonie who was often apt with appraisals, "it looks like a walrus caught in a whale's mouth."

"Or maybe Doctor Dementia himself," opined Whizlet wishing the escape button was near at hand.

The snollygoster, who glared down upon them from the heights of Hydraplop, was wearing a black velvet robe with scarlet trim and a high black collar which framed his chunky head. He had a mat of manicured gray hair and a huge, matching mustache, between which his porcine eyes squinted out like puckers in a grape and below which was a permanently drooping, half-opened mouth that sported a great iron tooth, so that, when he simultaneously snapped his whip and jaws, there was a crack like thunder and sparks of lightning flew from his lips. Now, however, those lips merely formed words, and these somewhat languorously: "M'yesss…I see success has crowned your endeavors with favors and fortune…m'yess, perhaps too fortunately for a District Inquisitor's limited budget…m'yess, baloomerangs can be expensive…often sickly creatures…m'yess indeed, bring it to my stables at the Courtex…my veterinarian has a great deal of experience with them…m'yess, my stablalongs know how to discipline them to the chain and halter…"

Before Lutarious could object to losing his prize, Leuna jumped to her feet and directed her tagalongs to raise her palanquin high into the air, from where she waved her fan and called out to an approaching vehicle: "Yoo-hoo! Yoo-hoo! Mayorling Piddlepuddle. Over here, over here." as though the mayorling could possibly have missed the confrontation between Gorgoncha and Hydraplop or even heard Leuna's summons amidst all the commotion.

The crowd scattered before the mayorling's coachman's whip and an open carriage drawn by two harnessed baloomerangs drew alongside the column. The man within and his three secretaries, as well as the two grooms trotting along behind, all ignored the prisoners and admired Rangi. But the prisoners could not ignore them. "Oh dear," gasped Is, "That's Loom and Loomi. They were baloomernapped from Is several moonspans ago but nobody ever knew who did it!" Loom, even though muzzled, managed to low honk a few reassuring words to Rangi, and Loomi did the same with womanly eye-talk, but the coachman prodded them with his pike and they had to desist.

"Congratulations, Mister Roorback," said the mayorling. "I see you've finally gotten a dray-rang for yourself. Now we all have the fun of them: my two large ones, the Dujge's two little ones, and now you have one too. I'll send you a bushel of pangifrangi flour to mix with slop, one scoop per bucket, or they'll starve, you know. They're very finicky, but certainly worth all the slop and inconvenience... Oh, good morning, Dujge Dorque. How exemplary of you to meet our Inquisitor after his triumph." He then spoke to one of the secretaries. "Make a note of the Dujge's dutifulness, my dear, and enter it in the Daily Duhlpers." He whispered ahead to his coachman who drove off through the crowd, but turned as they left and called back. "And of course we accept your invitation, Missessness Leuna Lativia loves bar-be-qued baloom, and be sure to skewer a snigglesnorf medium rare for her. She'll want at least three dozen legs."

The Dujge glared after him, then turned to Lutarious: "I accept the felonious flotsam you've drug from the river, as well as all the charges lodged against, before, and atop them in the hallowed name of Pallace the Pallpacker who paragraphed all poltroons to the purgatoria of Brablug in accordance with the Codex of Cunep, and declare the Imperious High Courtex of Alabramble now in session, and further order we adjourn forthwith and immediately to the High Courtex to convene our disciplinary deliberations under a proper roof so we can get on with the bar-be-que."

"I object!" said Toppenbottom's right mouth as he stepped forward and swept off his hat. "As the plaintiffs have not yet had a popportunity to confer with their vawyer and decide on a proper payment schedule."

"Objection overruled," said the Dujge even before Lutarious could object to the objection. "Payment schedules must be adjudicated on your own time and not that of the High Courtex." The Dujge reached out and slapped Hydraplop on the side of the pulpit. The spry trap whipped out its twisty vine legs, scattering the crowd in every direction, turned about, and started back through the square. Gorgoncha, somewhat miffed but like his master master of his own expression of outrage against superior strength, followed by the rest of the procession which snaked its way out of the square along an avenue leading toward the heart of the city. More on-lookers came in from side streets and gawked at the prisoners. The people seemed well fed, even somewhat overstuffed if one looked closely, but the children were all scraggly.

"Why are the kids so skinny?" asked Toliver.

Is shook her head sadly even though the collar rubbed. "The snollygosters believe in eating six times a day themselves, but have convinced the tagalongs that it's a waste of their tax money to feed the children."

"They say if they don't feed them, they'll learn to fight for everything and that will somehow make them smarter," added It.

"I thought people went to school to get smart," said Toliver who certainly hoped that was the case in his case.

"The schools here are the worst anywhere," replied Is.

The Itofit nodded his agreement. "They only teach enough arithmetic so people can figure their taxes, enough reading so they can read the signs telling them what they're not supposed to do, and enough made-up history so they won't know how bad everything is in Alabramble compared to everywhere else."

"There's a school now," said Is nodding to a warehouse-like building with little barred windows high up on its sides, chains locking the doors, and a sign over the entrance saying: PS. #13, The Jack Horner School for Conehats & Cornersitters. Plastered on the wall were a number of signs that appeared to be the winners from some kind of competition: "Happiness is Doing What You're Told" said one. Another read: "Don't Hurt Your Eyes Reading; and still another, "A Liberal Education is Subversive." The apparent winner, above all the others, read: "Knowledge Breeds Confusion" and below them and off to the side, a more permanent sign with an arrow pointing down to a cellar entrance said: "Burn Books Here >"

"That's awful," exclaimed Toonie. "What in the world would you do in school if you didn't read?"

"Mostly they just teach the boys to play tootball," said the Itofit.

"And the girls to cheer them on and clean up after them," added Is.

"What's tootball?" asked Whizlet who was afraid there was a game he might actually have missed.

"That's a contest where they let a little pig out on a field between two teams and all the players rush about bumping into each other and tripping each other up or otherwise knocking each other down until somebody catches the pig and runs to the end of the field, or throws it to someone else who runs to the end of the field, where whoever has it kicks it into a tree." explained the Itofit.

"It got its name," added Is, "because all the people who watch it toot for one team or the other, and I believe the winner is the one whose fans toot the loudest. Otherwise, I can't imagine why they'd bother to toot at all."

"Maybe Toot Glibrich invented it," opined Toonie who tried to imagine a house chasing a pig.

"No, he plays hardball," said It, "which is another game where all the players dress up like insects and run to a Fly Ball, take off their gloves, and strike out at bats, which they call an inning instead of an outing, which is also curious."

"I thought they dressed up like chickens and went to a Fowl Ball," said Is.

"No, that's softball," replied It, "and the Glib is never soft, especially on crime, unless it's white-collar crime, in which case he puts the starch in his upper lip; or welfare cheats, unless their welfare is a sizable subsidy, or fuzzy thinkers unless they think right, or better yet, far right, or neandercrats unless they're southern neandercrats, in which case they'll take his pitch to the Fowl Ball where they're all softies for each others' pigs."

The procession turned down a narrow street that led to a small square. Across the square was a huge, foreboding building with a belfry on top from which a large, cracked bell tolled the tidings of the vaw. A wide stairway led to imposing metal doors that looked like the mouth of a cavernous demon, to one side of which was a sculpture of Pulcan's Prototypo Spry Trap and to the other a blindfolded statue, or rather a statue that looked like an executioner whose hood had no eye holes in it. In one hand the statue held an ax, and in the other a scales, neatly balanced, one plate of which held a pile of coins and the other the Three Books of the Vaw. Hydraplop went around the building to one side, Gorgoncha to the other, and the prisoners were led up the stairway and taken into the building. Above the doorway, chiseled in granite, were the words: The Imperious High Courtex of Alabramble: *Leave All Hope Behind, Ye Who Enter Here.*

Inside was a large marble foyer with curved stairways going up to either side and another set of doors ahead, these of black lacquered wood. Snollysolijers in full regalia, including flabber gas masks, stood to either side of the doors, each holding a long spear, hilt to the ground. When the doors behind were closed and the ones in front opened, the prisoners were untied but not uncollared and prodded into the Great Chamber of the High Courtex where a cage of gilt bronze awaited them. A side door to the chamber was opened and Rangi was led in, still muzzled and harnessed, to another metal cage, while the basket of balooms, the cage of snigglesnorfs, and Boogie's box were placed on an adjacent platform with a sign announcing "Evidentiary Detentiary" facing the room. Snollysolijers took up their places standing along the walls, and, as the cage door slammed behind the prisoners, side doors to the Great Chamber opened to allow Toppenbottom and a crowd of curious spectators (for whom this was the only public entertainment in the city) to enter and fill the room. Across the chamber another door opened to admit Lutarious, now in a blood red robe with silver trim and wearing the Itofit's hat, followed by Leuna and Odiferous who took their places around a massive wooden table with a throne facing the front and plush chairs to both sides. The chamber's high ceiling was crisscrossed with rafters above which hung the great Fiberty Bell of Alabramble. Except for the openings in the belfry, there were no windows in the room, but four chandeliers festooned with flasks of luminescent algae hung from each quadrant and dangled above the spectators casting a viridescent glow across the room. The bell rope led to the side where the bellman stood on a raised platform, and the belfry itself was centered above the spectators so when the bell was rung to announce the proceedings to the city, the sound was deafening within the room and rained down upon the cages like the blast of a fallen angel's horn, but was less horrific in front where the Dujge and District Inquisitor had their places. The Dujge sat on a high dais behind a huge rostrum while the District Inquisitor's table and throne-like chair were below and to the right. Across from him, in front of the prisoner's cage, was a smaller, railed area with a metal table and chairs to which Mister Toppenbottom repaired and opened his briefcase.

The bellman ascended his platform, took hold of his rope, and sounded three bongs on the Fiberty Bell which, since the crack in it went jaggedly from top to bottom, sounded like a dissonant elephant bellowing his discontent with whatever he was discontented with.

"A cracked bell can't toll the truth," whispered Is to the others, "so we'd better expect the worst…"

"…and hope for the best," added Toonie hopefully.

"Didn't you read the words over the door?" asked Toliver. "There's more cracked in here than the bell."

No sooner had he spoken, than a door behind the dais open and the Dujge stepped into the room with *The Third Book of the Vaw* under one arm and a glass of julep honeywater in his hand. Now that he was no longer in the pulpit of his spry trap, he appeared to be a huge head supported by a pole pushed up through his robe, with equally gaunt arms arrayed to the sides. The District Inquisitor turned to the spectators and raised his hands, whereupon the courtroom erupted into a round of applause for the Dujge. Lutarious twirled his right arm and pointed at the gilded cage with a long stabbing finger and the spectators booed and hissed until Lutarious' left hand moved downward, seeming to pat the air, and the jeers quieted. During this ceremony, while the attention of everyone was directed to the Dujge and his dujgables, Hobnail flew in through one of the openings in the belfry, circled in the musty gloom among the rafters, then landed on the green-glowing algaelabra above the District Inquisitor's table.

The Dujge picked up his gavel and struck it sharply on a sounding board atop the dais whereupon everyone became quiet and the bellman announced from his platform: "The Imperious High Courtex of Alabramble is now in gestation as the Short Circuit Courtex of the Tribunal Kangerroon in the flagrant case of five sky traffickers and assorted evidentiary addendums duly assembled for Trial by Trapment preceding the Dujgement of Doom as detailed in the Codex of Cunep; Dujge Dealding Dorque, presiding. The District Inquisitor will now call forth, assemble, impanel, impound, hot seat, and short sheet a jury of peers who will peer into the matter and render his verdict."

Lutarious rose grandly from the throne, took off his hat, and turned to the spectators. "Hear Ye! Hear Ye: All ye citizens of Alabramble who have contracts with Smugsmog City, arise!" Eighty or ninety people in the audience stood up and threw out their chests. "You, you, you, and you," said Lutarious. "Come ye forth, take your places, and do your duty in the Jury Rig of the High Courtex."

"I object!" piped up Mister Toppenbottom's right mouth, "on the grounds that employees of Smugsmog City have better things to do."

The Dujge picked up a little silver bell standing by his left elbow on the dais and rang it. As the tinkle sounded across the chamber, all the spectators except Major Dhump who drooled, and Sergeant Struddel who barked, jumped to their feet and began to salivate, booing and hissing as they did so. "Overruled," said the Dujge, "by popular acclamation of the afflicted workers."

The chosen four came forward and took their places in a comfortable enclosure with twelve well padded arm chairs: "All retired snollysolijers, tax collectors, and other pensioners. Arise!" continued Lutarious, and when a hundred or so people rose ponderously to their feet, he chose four more from among them.

"Objection!" cried Toppenbottom's left mouth. "On the grounds that they're already asleep."

"Overruled," said the Dujge, "In deference to their deferments."

As the second four came forward, the District Inquisitor called out: "All those in imminent need of city services, arise!" But when everybody in the audience got up, Lutarious quickly went on: "And are related to Mayorling Piddlepuddle, members of the City Consul, the Dujge or myself." Fifty or sixty people remained standing and Lutarious picked three more and motioned them to the box.

"I object!" cried Toppenbottom's left mouth. "On the grounds that relative justice is not absolute and therefore too appalling to be worth my appealing."

"Overruled," intoned Dujge Dorque. "Relative justice is as speedy as light and therefore absolute."

The vawyer gasped and hung his head. He lifted it with his two upper hands while his lower left hand thumped to his breast and his lower right hand pointed upward to the Fiberty Bell. "Your Onerous," he intoned. "What is justice? I ask you? What is just as it is? and what is just as it isn't?" The District Inquisitor gave him a quizzical look, which didn't bother him at all since he was very used to quizzical looks, but the Dujge gave him a very dark look which did bother him. "But remember," he continued quickly, "it's just us who must contend about justice and just us who must decide if just us are just or just jesters, but it's you, Dujge Dorque, who knows what just us are and what justice is saying."

"I object," cut in Lutarious, "on the grounds that canned histrionics are hysteric and therefore inadmissible in a sound Courtex."

"Sustained," said the Dujge. "The vawyer for the guilty parties will confine himself to sharp points of the vaw and leave justice alone and just us as we are."

"Finally then," continued Lutarious glaring at Toppenbottom, "I wish confirmed by acclamation that the Fiveperson of the Jury shall be the dedicated, impartial, and everywhere respected, Leuna Roorback, Missessness of the Blood Red and Silver Robe."

The solijers along the walls thumped their spears on the floor and the audience yelled their approval but as the tumult quieted down, two lone voices could be heard: "We object!" yelled Toppenbottom's right and left mouths.

"To what does the vawyer for the guilty parties object this time?" asked the Dujge in glacial tones.

"I object to the naming of the Fiveperson," replied Toppenbottom right mouth as a left hand wiped his brow, "on the grounds that the jury should be anonymous as well as unanimous and co-animus, so I respectfully submit…" and the vawyer bowed deeply to Leuna "…that the name of the lovely, distinguished, and impartial Leuna Roorback be stricken from the record, and that the Lady Herself be impaneled with her fair fan but without fanfare."

"Overruled!" thundered the Dujge. "The whorey Alabramblian precedent of publicly recognizing, recompensing, and otherwise rewarding outstanding citizens is upheld." Then, much more mater-of-factly, to Lutarious, he continued: "State the stated state charges against the guilty parties."

Lutarious cleared his throat. "All are charged with violation of Alabramble Puerile Code, Section 23-636, Subsection 412, Paragraphs (f) through (gg); Smugsmog City Ordinance 1844 for entering the city without a permit; and…" he pointed directly at Toliver, "…battery, attempted murder, and child abuse for bodily attacking a member of the apprehending posse party."

"What did I do?" asked Toliver more surprised than discomfited.

"He attacked me!" cried Odiferous jumping to his feet, "when I wasn't looking, and he tried to get away, but I subjued him and happrehended him myself."

While everyone in the audience was looking at Odiferous, Toliver reached in his pocket and pulled out a big rubber band and one of his particularly fine, pre-rolled spitballs. And while the audience (here and there prodded by a snollysolijer's spear) applauded Odiferous' manhandling of the situation, Toliver, hiding just below the Itofit's elbow, let fly. The projectile hit Odiferous in the ear just as he was taking a bow. "Ooow!" he cried out. "I've been bitten!" And he fell to the floor clasping his head and groaning audibly.

"No!" shouted Leuna who couldn't bear to see their decorum depleted or their face lost before the people of Tallaghetto. She hurried over, pulled him to his feet, and rubbed his face in her ample bosom. "You've been smitten, with the affection of the people."

Odiferous had to stop crying since he couldn't breathe at all, and in order to help things along, the Dujge jumped to his feet and waved his arms. All the spectators began to cheer wildly again, making Odiferous perk up, puff out, and forget completely that his ear hurt.

"I accept your adulation," he said wiping the tears from his eyes and bowing repeatedly to the audience.

"Let me have one of those too," whispered Whizlet to Toliver. And as Odiferous was bobbing up and down, left and right, to the assembly, Whizlet let fly with another spitball that caught Odiferous in the back of the head.

"Ouch!" screamed Odiferous. "I've been stung!"

"No," cried Leuna, smothering him again, "you've been flung." And she threw him up in the air just as though he was an infant again. He was so startled by this turn of events (as well as perspective since he was spinning), he stopped bawling and gasped instead. But Toliver, who was very quick to see how things really worked, took aim at the Dujge's little bell and loosed another missile. As soon as the bell sounded, the people in the audience jumped to their feet booing and hissing, and the Dujge had to pound his gavel on its sounding board to restore order.

Whizlet took aim at the Dujge's iron tooth, but Lutarious who trusted no one and always tried to keep his eye on everybody, saw what was happening: "Stop!" he commanded. "The prisoners are armed and dangerous, possibly venomous and vituperative too! Disarm them!" The two snollysolijers standing by the door to the cage rushed in and collared both Whizlet and Toliver.

"Empty their pockets too!" demanded the Dujge who didn't know how close he'd been to being struck himself, but didn't want Lutarious to get all the credit for seeing the danger. However, so many things were taken from Toliver's pocket that another solijer with a wheelbarrow had to be called to take them all to the Evidentiary Detentiary Table.

When order was restored to the chamber, the Dujge glared down at the prisoners. "How do the guilty parties plead?" he demanded.

"Not guilty by way of madness!" declared Toppenbottom's left mouth. The vawyer climbed on his chair which, being a swivel chair, allowed him to swing around, first to the Dujge to whom he bowed, then to Lutarious at whom he grimaced, then to the audience with whom he hoped to establish rapport by lifting his chin and stuffing a right hand in his jacket, and then (after passing quickly by the prisoners' cage) back to the Dujge. "Innocent by virtue of insanity, Your Onerous," he said fearlessly. "Since no one in his right mind would be here in the first place!"

"Objection," declared the District Inquisitor. "The guilty parties committed their malfeasances with felonious forethought and mischievous malevolence; therefore they are sane and slated to remain so for the rest of the trial."

"Sustained," said Dujge Dorque. "Replead the guilty parties."

"Innocent by reason of ignorance," retorted the vawyer's left mouth immediately. "Since no one has ever been able to read the entire Alabramble Puerile Code, much less understand it."

"Objection," said Lutarious, stifling a yawn. "Ignorance of the vaw is no defense except for government employees who don't have to read."

"Sustained," said the Dujge. "Replead the guilty parties."

"Not guilty by virtue of not being at the scene of the crime," said Toppenbottom's right mouth doggedly. "Since they were in the sky and the sky can't be seen, they couldn't have been seen at the scene, and are therefore only presumed guilty until seen to be unseemingly otherwise."

"Objection," retorted Lutarious. "And if the vawyer for the defamed doesn't desist, he'll be charged with aggravated alliteration."

"Sustained," said the Dujge. "Replead the guilty parties."

"Guilty!" piped Toppenbottom's right mouth. "And we throw ourselves on the mercy of the Imperious High Courtex, hoist ourselves on our own petard, or gore ourselves on our own ox, whichever pops up first on the slot machine of the vaw or is most pleasing to the Dujge."

"No!" cried the Itofit from the cage. "We're innocent by being innocent by-passers innocently enjoying the sky and criminally interfered with by... aargh!" He gagged as Sergeant Struddel hurried to the cage, grasped the line to his collar, and yanked it from behind, then held it tight until poor It had to sit down to take a gulp of air.

"I object!" said the vawyer's left mouth.

"Cork it, Toppenbottom," snapped Lutarious in a fit of exasperation.

"But I must object," said the left mouth, "on the grounds of..."

"Don't say that!" cut in the right mouth.

"I have to!" said the left swiveling up its lips with as much dignity as they could display.

"No, you don't either," answered the right mouth sharply.

"I do too," replied the left. "It's in the best interest of our clients."

"The best interest of our clients is best served by not contradicting this best of all possible Dujges," continued the right mouth, after which Toppenbottom turned to the bench. "Sir! We rest our case."

"Overruled and accepted," said the Dujge pounding his sounding board. "Do the jury concur?"

"We do," said Leuna waving her hand briefly toward the other members. "We find them guilty of everything and anything else Your Onerous might add too, and recommend confiscations, incarcerations, arm twisting, and invitations to a bar-be-que for the miscreants' balooms, snigglesnorfs, and other disreputably delicious creatures."

"I'll take this to the Courtex of Appalls!" cried Toppenbottom's left mouth. "And even to the Supine Courtex if we have an Appalling failure!"

"What's the Courtex of Appalls?" asked Toliver who didn't like the sound of it one bit.

"It's where we could go next," responded the Itofit, "but its decisions are always appalling."

"But it does give us some time, at least an hour or two," added Is.

"And with time, anything can be made to happen differently," continued It.

"Time is like clay," explained Is. "You can mold it into anything you want as long as you're careful and know how to handle it right."

But before they had time to confer with the vawyer, or at least with the part of him that seemed to be on their side, Toppenbottom's right mouth declared: "Oh no, we won't. I've checked everything in the wheelbarrow", pointing to all the things taken from Toliver's pockets, "...and there's not a single rasputnik there. That's appalling enough for any vawyer, so we won't take this case any further, and shouldn't have taken it this far either, and wouldn't have if we'd known, and both of me agree on this completely." He snapped his briefcase closed and stormed toward the door.

Just then a piercing scream resounded from the twilit heights of the room. A feeling of doom swept through the chamber and everyone looked up timorously but none could see the angry gray bird circling among the rafters, though some later swore they saw two red eyes weaving about the Fiberty Bell, and consequently attributed what happened next to none other than the Satin Diabola himself. The scream ended in a rousing rendition of *The Devil's Trill*, and two large dollops of toothpaste materialized out of the air, one dropping with unerring accuracy to the tuft of black hair atop Mister Toppenbottom's head, and the other, equally well aimed, directly toward Leuna. She saw the dollop coming an arm's length above her head, angling for the spot between her eyes, but her eyes could do nothing more defensive than cross as they followed it to its inevitable splat.

"Eck!" screamed Leuna. "Those nasty, nasty bats in our belfry are battering their betters with butterbatter again!"

The Dujge leaped to his feet and raised his gavel to ward off any unseen adversaries but only succeeded in stimulating the spectators who broke out with wild cheers and applause.

"No!" cried the Dujge pounding his gavel on his thumb. "Ooow! I paragraph everybody to three weeks in purgatoria, and to hell with the Codex, I'll do it in camera myself!"

The chamber quieted immediately. As everyone settled down except Leuna (who was cleaning her eye with the tie of the man sitting next to her) and Odiferous (who was giggling so hard he had to be held down by Lutarious), the District Inquisitor continued with his vawscript: "I move you paragraph the pusillanimous poltroons," he intoned while silencing his son with some difficulty, "so we can get on to the bar-be-que."

"Good! I mean bad!" said the Dujge. "Bad for them; good for everybody else." He pointed his gavel at the prisoners' cage, glared at them with a terrible frown, and snapped his jaws so sparks flew from his mouth. "I paragraph you, you, and you..." He pointed his gavel at Toliver, Toonie, and Whizlet, "...to the treadmill salt mine in Brablug until you produce fifty pounds of salt each, and an extra twenty pound stint on the stairstep for Pockets for attempted attempting; and you and you..." He shifted his gaze to the Itofit and Is, "...to ten years with nose and tail clamps in a cell without horizontal bars, flowers, music, or fresh air. Take the snigglesnorfs to the cutting board, the balooms to the baloomicatessen, and that thing..." He grimaced menacingly at Boogie, "...to the zoo."

"No, no," your Dujgeboat," called out Leuna sweetly. "He's part of dinner too."

"That's what I said," snapped the Dujge who couldn't stand to be contradicted, especially in public or when playing shards. "I paragraphed him to the zoop."

"And don't forget the confiscations," whispered the District Inquisitor.

"Confiscations!" stammered Toliver who was always ready to lend anything he had to other people but also knew that people who took things without asking usually broke them so all they accomplished was to bog themselves down with things they couldn't use. "Are they going to steal all are stuff too?"

"They're grabby because they're greedy," replied the Itofit.

"And greed is a form of madness," said Is. "It turns time into stickerbushes and life into lusting without hope of happiness."

"As for the confiscations," continued the Dujge. "M'yess, let me see…I confiscate the baloomerang for the District Inquisitor whose prior claim was established by trickery which will be overlooked but not forgotten. I confiscate everything in the wheelbarrow for the Smugsmog City Museum of Maudlin Art. And I confiscate that hat…" He pointed at the Itofit's hat, which was sitting on Lutarious' table, "…as the professional pillage of the High Courtex since it's obviously a pillagebox hat."

"I object," exclaimed the District Inquisitor, "on the grounds that this hat is not confiscatable since it has already been tendered as a bribe to the District Inquisitor; a bribe which can be vegally accepted because it wasn't effective; by the ex-defendant and now convicted felonious It. However…" Lutarious pointed directly at Toonie, "…that feloniousness is further guilty of concealing a white crane feather on her person, so I suggest the High Courtex confiscate that for himself." Lutarious waved to Sergeant Struddel who hurried into the cage and plucked the feather from Toonie's blouse and brought it to the table.

"I don't want a feather," snapped the Dujge, "without a cap to put it in." He snorted, clapped his jaws at the ceiling, and became more reasonable. "M'yess. Let me see. At least, give me the hatband. Then we'll call it even Steven even if Steven isn't involved at all. M'yess…he's got too much already anyway."

"No," replied Lutarious slapping the Itofit's hat on his head. "To the victor belongs the spoils, and I'm spoiled. I mean victor, and this is spoils of war, and warring over it spoils it, so I'll wear it as a spoiled victory, and the next hat we pillage is yours." He twirled the feather and stuck it into the hatband, which made Hissofer quiver with a repressed giggle because not even a snake can resist laughing when anyone, even a District Inquisitor, tickles him with a feather. Of course, when a snake has a belly laugh it is at least three feet long, so Lutarious' new hat began to tremble with mirth. Lutarious, however, had no idea what mirth was, so he didn't notice it at all, but the spectators went off with the distinct impression that the Satin Diabola had somehow infiltrated the D.I.'s new hat and was rocking and rolling around his head.

"Toll the tidings," intoned the dampened Dujge to the bellman. Then, as the Fiberty Bell sounded three cracked notes, summoned the major: "Major Dhump, carry out the paragraphings and the prisoners…but, hmmm… m'yess, let me see…take those two…" He pointed his gavel at Toonie and Is, "…to my chambers for further internment, interrogation, and indoctrination in our 'Just Say Mo' dogma."

"Don't let your duties interfere with your dinner, Dujge," called over Leuna. "The mayorling and Lativia well be arriving in an hour and dear, dear Fasada wouldn't want to be late."

"M'yess. Fasada mustn't be derailed, must she? Major, lock those two in my private holding cell. M'yess, and keep an eye on them yourself. I'll be back after lunch for the bunch. M'yess, m'yess, and put the others in the dungeon under Struddelvision until they can be sent hidebound and headlong to Brablug."

The Clickoom from Major Dhump's heels resounded through the building and he saluted so smartly that he hit himself in the brow, snapping his head back. "Yessir, Y'r Dujgeboat! Aye aye and ahoy! Sergeant Struddel, quick, quick, doubletime and triplespace, off with the Brablugians to the dungeon while I off the others to the Dujge's chambers. And Corporal Porporal place y'rself at the disposal of the Missessness Roorback, and away with her confiscations and confections without confabulations or concessions but with all necessary concision and coercion…and hip-hip away thems that gets in y'r way."

Sergeant Struddel leaped into the air, kicking one leg forward and the other back where it caught in the bars of the cage and twisted his foot, while his two handed salute, rather than touching his forehead (since he'd jumped so high) reached only to his upper lip, swelling it further. But he pulled his foot out (losing a boot), ignored his lip, and waved to a contingent of solijers along the wall. Together they collared the collared prisoners, collected all the cages and baskets, took hold of Rangi's tethers, and proceeded out through the High Courtex to the foyer in front. Major Dhump and six solijers took Toonie and Is up one of the curved staircases, while Sergeant Struddel and the rest of the contingent pulled the Itofit, Toliver, and Whizlet through a small door beneath the staircase and down to the dungeon in the basement. Leuna appeared outside the front doors on her palanquin and motioned for Corporal Porporal to follow her and Odiferous with her new livery and lunch and hummed herself a tune as she reflected on how fortunate and fortuitous the day was proving to be.

"Oh my!" wailed Toonie when she and Is were locked in a bamboo cage in the Dujge's chamber. "I'll never sniff another flower as long as I live."

"Don't blame it on the flowers," responded Is patting Toonie on the shoulder and pointing her tail at Major Dhump. The major and a gruff looking solijer had remained with them and were sitting at a table by the door of the room, playing a game of chocolate checkers whose pieces were candy, and each time they jumped one of the other's pieces, they ate it with a great deal of lip-smacking glee. "Flowers just remind us what Mother Nature is telling us about ourselves in the nicest sort of way. It's people who don't smell flowers that you have to worry about."

"Or people who grow bad-smelling flowers just to trick other people," replied Toonie who was trying to apply everything Is said to her to her own way of thinking. "And I suppose that flower was telling me to blow my nose more often, but I can't see how that will help us now, even though it might feel good." And she blew her nose rather loudly and wiped a tear from her eye. "But what else can we do?"

"For the moment, we'll have to wait," replied Is, "because sometimes time meanders a bit before it decides what to do next and all we can do is meander along with it, while staying ready, of course, to move ahead just as soon as it does."

Toonie had blown her nose again while Is was speaking, so only caught the very last words. "Do you think what It does will help us?"

"I'm sure anything It does will help us," replied Is, "because taking care of things is what It does best and at the moment we're the most important things for It to take care of."

Is, of course, was right for the Itofit was thinking of nothing else except how to get out of the dungeon he and Toliver and Whizlet had been put into, and finding out where Is and Toonie were, and rescuing them, and then all of them together finding their way to the kitchen of Lutarious Roorback and saving their other friends, and do it all before dinner time, and maybe even sooner if they could, or at least not later. But when he looked out through the bars of the dank dungeon cell at Sergeant Struddel and the syffer who were guarding them, and at the heavy iron door beyond them, and at the single, high barred window, much too small for anyone to crawl out of, which was across the room facing into a window well in an alley behind the High Courtex building, he knew, deep down in his heart, that he'd have to think very hard, and very quickly, about their predicament and then do something really smart right away.

"Can you do your whistle in here?" he whispered to Toliver, because he remembered it sounded very much like Leuna's, only nicer.

"Sure," replied Toliver and he took a big breath and put his fingers into his mouth.

"No, no, not now," cautioned the Itofit, "but keep it ready in case we need it."

Sergeant Struddel and the syffer were sitting at a table in the center of the dimly lit, dingy stone room with its single dusky flask of tired old algae dangling from a wire above them, and dripping, slime covered pipes crossing above their heads, and chains with collars and cuffs hanging from the walls. Heaped high on the table between them were all the things taken from Toliver's pockets, which, to the solijers, were a glistening treasure of exotica. Sergeant Struddel lifted up Toliver's compass and looked at it carefully. "What time is north o'clock?" he asked the syffer while holding the compass to his ear and shaking it.

"Twelve hours after south o'clock, sir," answered the syffer who had discovered Toliver's flintstone and steel and was busy shooting sparks at a particularly large cockroach on the wall.

The sergeant gave up on the compass, ruffled through the pile, and picked up a large wad of waxy paper. His face took on a puzzled expression as he bounced it up and down, weighing it in his hand.

"Don't open that!" cried Toliver who'd never heard of reverse psychology but did know how it worked.

Sergeant Struddel knew exactly how to ignore Brablugians while letting them know exactly how completely they were being ignored, so he studied the package from one side, then the other, held it to the light and then at arms length to the window before unwrapping a big wad of still-squooshy, pink, only slightly chewed bubble gum with the practiced flourish of the trained investigator and poked it sharply with his finger which immediately got stuck. When he pulled his finger back, a thin pink strand kept him attached to his prize. As he pulled it further out, the gum slipped out of its paper and onto the palm of his other hand whose thumb and forefinger immediately arrested it before it could flop to the floor. When he tried to open them, more pink strands appeared so he used the other hand to help free them. But as he brought it back into play, the long strand, he had already pulled out, looped down and caught on his shinny belt buckle. Noticing what had happened, for he was well trained to observe events carefully, although, at the moment, tending toward exasperation, he reached down to pull it off but only succeeded in adding two more strands to his growing cat's cradle which looped around the lower buttons on his shirt, so he angrily pulled the other hand away, which added an additional four strands, at which point, one of the sparks which the syffer was aiming at the cockroach went cockeyed (which they're very liable to do if the styffer is not a trained flint and steel man) and instead struck the fuse to one of Toliver's cherry bombs that had rolled from the pile and was poised innocently before the sergeant. Seeing the sizzle, the syffer slid into action and leaned over to do something (although he wasn't exactly sure what) and only managed to put his face directly in front of the now reddening face of his sergeant. Consequently, when the firecracker exploded and Sergeant Struddel, who somehow had not noticed this development at all, leaped into the air, slapped his hands to his ears (which crisscrossed his horrified expression with a pink webbing and glued his lips together), and tried to let out a screech of surprise, he blew a large pink bubble instead which also exploded (with a lesser pop but greater consequence) all over himself and the very startled face of the syffer who fell back and threw his hands up which only managed to get all his fingers involved in the sticky mess until both he and Sergeant Strudel collapsed into their chairs staring horrified at each other through a truly treacherous, treacley pink web that bound them together.

"I told you so," said Toliver who had never been known to be smug, especially since arriving in Smugsmog City, which would cure anyone of that affliction, but did know how to call attention to the consequences of a lesson unlearned.

Whizlet, however, had no such compunction. "Yipes-a-doddle!" he gloated. "They look like they fell into the hyper-viper-piper-wiper in *Reptilian Republic!*" Then, more contritely and even quite wistfully, he added: "I sure wish Hissofer was here to see this."

Hissofer Booshocks, of course, was still wrapped around the crown of the Itofit's hat which was perched atop the leaden gray head of Lutarious Roorback who with Leuna and Odiferous had just gone into the downstairs kitchen in their modest mansion below the municipal smogfan in the suburbs of Smugsmog City to tell Cookie exactly how they wanted the bar-be-que prepared. The basket of balooms was hung from a hook in a rafter next to the cage of snigglesnorfs where both Snorf and Snorfa, having become accustomed to their captivity and, like all cornered creatures, ready and willing (but probably not able) to take on all comers with fifty or sixty quick (but very short) right jabs, were peering down defiantly (or at least as defiantly as they could with six little eyes on telescoping stalks that much preferred to look at dancing flutterbys.) Below the cage was Boogie's box on the cutting board from where he appraised the butcher knife with a professional eye, hoping against hope that it was no match for twenty claws.

"First, of all," said Lutarious pointing at Snorf, "skewer the snigglesnorfs and let them bleed into the kettle, then boil the blood and throw in the balooms, after breading with anjimyma flour, of course, and sizzling them in the frying pan until their noses uncurl and bellies deflate. Then fillet their flanks, marinade the round rib roasts in fickle pickle juice, dice the hearts and livers for the soup."

"And float their eyeballs in the soup too," cut in Odiferous who was already drooling.

"Now, now," said his mother, "we'll let Cookie decide on the soup as long as that lovely nasty thing". She pointed at Boogie who returned the compliment by spitting at her so vehemently that she involuntarily took a step backward, "...is in it, and save his tongue for me and give his rear end to Fasada Dorque."

"Nyaaa!" cried Odiferous. "You said I could have it for target practice."

"Momma changed her mind, Odify dear. But you can feed stink weed to the Dujge's baloomerangs instead, but make sure no one is looking."

"Good idea," agreed Lutarious who, when Leuna had jumped back from Boogie's feint, was forced to step aside and was now standing directly under the snigglesnorf's cage. "And make sure the Dujge gets some of that rear end too."

While Cookie was repeating the instructions, knowing full well she'd do it her way anyway, and showing off the polished skillet she'd use for braising the balooms, Hissofer quietly unwound himself from the Itofit's hat and stuck himself straight up in the air until his chin reached the bottom of the thornbranch cage where he was quickly pulled inside by Snorf and Snorfa.

The major-domo appeared at the top of the stairs leading to the kitchen and announced that the livery of the Dujge and Missessness Dorque had arrived at the foot of the esplanade and inquired which type of reception was desired: The Royal, in which all the servants lined the outer stairway while the red carpet was rolled down and the servants bowed to the ground; The Lesser Princely, in which the major-domo and downstairs staff stood to the side and bowed formally; The Plebeian, in which the major-domo waited for the door chimes to sound, then send the downstairs maid to attend to the matter; or the Blacklist, in which the gardeners would ostentatiously block the door with their wheelbarrows and then quickly disappear around the side of the house.

"Oh, the Royal, I suppose," replied Lutarious chortling to himself, "as a sort of booby prize."

"But hold the carpet," added Leuna, "since Fasada will undoubtedly be wearing those atrocious spike heels of hers."

"Can I stay and watch them skewer the snigglesnorfs?" asked Odiferous who knew that nobody was likely to skewer the Dujge or his missessness, at least until after the next election.

"No, you mayn't," said his mother. "The Dujge likes you and Fasada would think you were up to something. So shut up and come along."

As they went off, the major-domo waved to Cookie, who was gloriously fat, and her two scullery maids to hurry along and take their places on the steps. Cookie grumbled but went, helped up the stairs by the maids, one of whom pulled and one of whom pushed, leaving all parts of dinner securely cooped and caged to contemplate the terrible fates that awaited them. The balooms were clustered in a protective heap in the far lower corner of the basket whimpering among themselves and wringing their little trunks together like fingers on a pair of thoroughly dismayed hands. Snorf and Snorfa were none too happy either but had rolled up with Hissofer between them so no one could see him. As soon as everyone was gone, Hissofer slipped his first third out of the basket and carefully investigated the heavy snap latch securing the lid. A snigglesnorf with its strong little handsfeet might have been able to move it but a poor snake with only his tongue (or perhaps two tongues depending on how far back you start counting) to work with and a too easily dislocatable jaw couldn't cope with it at all. So he went out through a hole in the bottom and, as Snorf held on to his tail, stretched down to look at Boogie's cage, but it too had a heavy latch.

At the front entrance, the major-domo and Cookie along with the upstairs and downstairs help, the gardeners and stableboys, the scullery maids and chimney sweeps, the kitemen and algeaboys were lined along the stairway and applauding politely as the Dujge's calash pulled by a brace of baloomerangs about half the size of Rango and Rangi came to a stop. The Dujge waved to Leuna and snapped his tooth at the stableboys who loved to watch the sparks, and Fasada, who was wearing a matching calash on her head, except rather than being open, all the ribbed sections were pulled down over her face so she wouldn't have to offend her eyes by looking at anything. She rolled back her hat and smiled at the coachman whose hand was extended to help her from the vehicle.

"The Dujge and Missessness Dorque," announced the major-domo in his third most impressive voice and all the help bowed to the ground as the guests ascended the stairs to where Lutarious, Leuna, and a scowling Odiferous awaited them.

Leuna stepped forward with both her hands extended, grasped Fasada by the forearms, and jerked her up the final step. "Fasada!" she said almost breathlessly as though it had been herself rather than Fasada who had just worried her way to the top of the stairs.

"Leuna!" answered Fasada, who was indeed wearing heels so precariously spiked that her feet wobbled, and, above the collar of her designer mu mu, her face was caked with enough make-up to make Tammy Fay Bakker look like an Amish schoolgirl.

"Fasada!" said Leuna pulling the other woman forward, almost tipping her over, and kissing her on the cheek.

"Leuna!" replied Fasada, reciprocating the peck but baring a tooth.

"Fasada!" said Leuna turning her head slightly to protect her throat.

"Leuna!" said Fasada as she pulled away, veiling her eyes behind their blight of mascara and their accustomed sheen of incomprehensibility.

"Fasada!" said Leuna turning ever so slightly so as to put a protective shoulder between Lutarious and the Dujge.

"Leuna!" breathed Fasada accepting the gambit and lifting her nose just enough in the direction of Lutarious to indicate she thought him an envious, backbiting, lecherous low life but smiling sweetly to conceal her thoughts.

"Fasada!" countered Leuna wiggling her posterior at the Dujge like a wasp before the sting.

"Leuna!" continued Fasada flickering her eyelashes as she did when slapping mosquitoes.

"Fasada!" gushed Leuna stroking her throat with her longest fingernail.

"Leuna!" sighed Fasada, but before she could say anything more, the Dujge became annoyed.

"Fasada," he said imperiously. "The Dujge is waiting." He spoke as though someone else was standing in his shoes and he was hovering impatiently in the space above their heads, a habit he'd picked up while whiling away dreadful hours atop his dais.

"Oh, diddle the Dujge," said Fasada. "This is girl talk."

The Dujge stomped past her and let Lutarious take his arm as they went into the foyer. "I see you've hidden away that hat band I wanted," he said. "Afraid I might pull rank and make an epaulet out of it or maybe an earring for Hydraplop?"

"What!" cried Lutarious pulling off his hat and staring at the crown with its missing ornament. "Odiferous! Come here!" And when the boy sidled up to him. "Come clean, Odify. Where is it?"

Odiferous had no idea what his father was referring to but being quick to seize any advantage took in the situation in a glance. "She took it," he said quickly, pointing to one of the downstairs maids who always poked a handkerchief into the keyhole of her bedroom door.

"I doubt it," said Lutarious who had his own designs on the girl. "Go to your room and look for it. It probably fell off when I was helping you with your tie, your shoelaces, and your begats."

"No!" screamed the boy who knew he could always win a shouting contest if his father was preoccupied with something else or liable to be embarrassed.

And he also thought, quite wrongly, that this was a good time to impress the Dujge with his independence.

"Go!" roared back Roorback pointing at the ceiling. "And don't come back without it!"

"Der District Inquisitor ist hafing a disquisition," mumbled Cookie to the scullery maids as they hurried by, "so ve vant to not raddle his ribcage except vit der vittals. Zo efrybudy ged der dinking caps on. Vat shud ve do furst? Vat shud ve do secund? Hmmm... I tell you. I tell you...Furst ve snaggle the snifflesnorts...den ve magk der zoop...den ve bast der balooms...den ve... hmmm...vat den ve do, hmmm?...ya...ya...ya...den ve barb der Que und vorry aboot dersert later...zuch a habby kitshun...zuch a habby kitshun..." She hurried down the stairs with a great smile wreathing her face, plucked out her butchering knife, and after checking it daintily with her thumb, pulled out the sharpening stone and danced about the kitchen swooshing the knife one way and then the other along the stone as though she was conducting an orchestra of kettles and pots, of ovens and stoves, of hanging spoons, singing sinks, and tin pan alleys. "Vat ve do furst?" she sang out. "Vat ve do furst... fillup der belly...or schlaken der thirst..." She stabbed the knife at Boogie, "...sliver the liver or..." she tapped the snigglesnorf cage with the sharpener "...snoddle a snort?" She swung around and around, sharpening away, "... coddle der kidneys...or twiddle der torte...? Ya...ya..." she cried, stopping in mid swing and pointing her knife like a sword at Boogie's cage: "Vat furst... vat furst...?...der spit-noodle zoop mit onyuns und zumplings...?" then the other hand with the sharpener like a flintlock pistol at the balooms, "...or der frizzled balooms mit zumzing like pumpkins? No, no, nooo!" And she advanced on snigglesnorf cage with a look of triumph in her eye. "Brink der climbup," she called out to the scullery maids. "Furst, ve snuffle der snorfs und powder dem till zum sticks, den ve cut dem all oop into ninety-six drumsticks!"

Outside, having been properly reprimanded, Odiferous went off to sulk but not to his room, and while his parents, the Dujge, and Fasada stepped into the Quartering Room for hentails of jin and scramooth, he ran out to the driveway to throw stones at the birds in the fountain and plot how he could lure the Dujge's calashmen away from the stable. He heard the snap of a coachman's whip and fearing the worst began to run away but then saw it was only the Mayorling and Lativia Piddlepuddle's phaeton rounding the corner with six grooms trotting behind and the Stablemaster on a four man palanquin taking up the rear. The stablemaster lifted a bugle to his lips and sounded *The Approach of the Coach*, followed immediately by *The Arrival of Highville*, and, as they rolled and ran up the esplanade, completed his trio with an enviable rendition of *Hail to the Chief's Teeth*.

"You and Fasada wait here," said Lutarious to the Dujge, "Leuna and I will do the honors."

"No, no, let's all go," said Leuna who worried about the silver.

"Yes, yes, let's all go," said Fasada who wanted to see if Lativia got a red carpet.

"Oh, phooey," said Cookie in the kitchen who had gotten the ladder under snigglesnorfs' cage. "Bud ve be bock, shishkaboobs. Doonchu vorry!" And she blew a kiss to the poor creatures and wobbled to the stairs.

As he and Lativia came up the stairway, the mayorling slipped a handful of peanuts to the major-domo, then grabbed Lutarious by the elbow and shook his hand firmly. "Great catch, today, Lut. But my sources tell me there's another baloomerang out there somewhere. Are you going back after it tomorrow? I could use a spare when one of the others get tired."

"It's mine," said the Dujge who could be quick as a fink when events dictated. "I'm running up in my tugfloat in the morning."

"Don't bother. It's hurt and sinking fast," replied the District Inquisitor who could also play the game. "Probably only good for baloomerang steaks, wallets, and piano keys, so we'll just have to wait and see. I'm going back this evening myself with Doktor Quacker and a patch kit."

"Lativia, what a lovely frock," said Leuna. "I'm sure it cost an arm and a leg. I wonder whose."

"What?" said Fasada, checking her gloves and stockings.

"Oh, it's a nothing-at-all," smiled Lativia, "just a little spring something I sprang upon while springing for lunch the other day with the grovenor's wife."

"Inside everyone," gushed Lutarious. "Hentails for the ladies and tarminis for the wicked, eh boys? And snacklettes or dherbs for everyone. Dinner will be ready in a jiffy, give or take a baloom or two. Ho, ho, ho."

With the arrival of the mayorling's phaeton, Odiferous ran off to disable the municipal smogfan so the stabbleboys and coachmen would be sent to fix it and he could sneak a bushel of stinkweed to the baloomerangs, but while he was waiting for the smog to accumulate sufficiently for anyone to notice and do something about it, he decided to run to the kitchen in hopes of getting in on the snigglesnorf skewering and perhaps even talk Cookie, who was easily flattered by someone who knew her weakness for fat fritters fried in tallagator grease, into letting him throw darts at the furry creature before she dropped it in the soup. But first, he decided, he'd better pass through the Quartering Room so no one would associate his absence with the failure of the smogfan and also give him a popportunity to swipe his father's hat with which he could make a dashing impression on Cookie's new scullery maid. He hurried around back and, straightening his tie, went into the Quartering Room through the French doors, nodded to the mayorling, smiled at his ugly wife, explained to his father that he'd probably lost his hatband in the kitchen, but that he, the Dutiful Child, would retrieve it forthwith, then backed out of the room with the Itofit's hat in his hands behind him.

"Noise," said the mayorling as Odiferous hurried off. "It's all about noise. Make enough noise and the people will vote for you."

"And they'll listen to you too," agreed the Dujge, "especially if you have a sounding board and bell."

"Agreed," agreed Lutarious. "Whoever makes the most noise wins."

"That's true, of course," said Leuna belching loudly, "which is why we've soundproofed Odify's room so he can learn his lessons at the top of his lungs."

"He'll make a fine Inquisitor some day," opined Lativia, "if he plays the crowds as well as he does Beeble."

"Life is just a game of tootball," added Fasada selecting another dherb, "where the little piggy is always someone else."

Odiferous took off at a run, hoping he wasn't too late for the excitement, which was, in fact, about to commence. Cookie's assistants had placed the step ladder below the snigglesnorf's cage and Cookie, who was much too fat for this sort of thing and should have known better but just couldn't not do it herself since she loved the feel of terrified snigglesnorfs using their furry little handsfeet to get out of her stangulating grasp, had started up the ladder. One step, and take a breath. Two steps, and take two breaths, and the third step with both scullery maids behind her holding her steady with four hands and her nose just above the bottom of the snigglesnorf cage door which she opened with a flourish and, smacking her lips, thrust both arms inside. But what popped out directly between them, right in her beaming face no more than a hairs breadth from her nose, was the most frightening thing she'd ever encountered. A huge mouth, wide open, with teeth all over it, and two jet black tongues darting out, and all of this attached to a spring-loaded yellow, red, and black tube of terror, reared up and snapped at her nose.

"Yowl!" she screamed as her eyes popped out and her body toppled backward. She flew from the ladder right on top of the two scullery maids who were squished to the floor beneath her. Fortunately, they cushioned her fall so she was hardly hurt at all, but, unfortunately, she had flattened her help so there was no way she could get up (which she was quite incapable of doing by herself even if her legs weren't all tangled in the ladder). And while she watched in horrified fascination, not one, but two little snigglesnorf faces appeared over the sill of the cage door, and one of them climbed out until it was hanging by its very last handsfeet and the other climbed down it until its back legs were held by the first one's front hands, and the two of them together reaching all the way to her shoe. And then, horror of horrors! the awful tube of terror wound its way down both snigglesnorfs to her foot, then crawled like the finger of death up her leg and over the huge mound of her stomach to coil there and stare her right in the eye again, and just as it leisurely opened its ghastly mouth one more time, she let out a squeak and fainted dead away. Snorfa let go of Snorf who dropped to Cookie's foot and climbed quickly to the cutting board while she pulled herself back up and ran along the rafter to the basket of balooms who were lined up like spectators at a picket fence watching an unlikely wrestling match between Andre the Giant and Barney Google with Barney on top and the Giant bamboozled. Using ten pairs of handsfeet and a mighty body wrench, she opened the basket so all the balooms, gibbering and jabbering among themselves and thanking her profusely, flew out and headed for the open window.

Snorfa would have followed right behind them but she heard something coming down the stairs to the kitchen and turned her head to listen more carefully, before calling down a warning to Snorf who was already atop Boogie's cage and had managed to pop the latch so Boogie could push the door open with his nose. Snorf heard the same noise, for it was quite noisy by this time and even singing an off-tune song to itself, and Boogie of course heard it too since his ears were almost as sharp as his eyes and nose, and sometimes sharper, and knew it was Odiferous coming because he recognized the wheezing, and Hissofer too listened with his whole body and then slid down from Cookie's belly and right across her, fortunately for her, unconscious face.

Odiferous bounded into the room with the Itofit's hat at a jaunty angle on his head, but came to a sudden stop and his mouth dropped open as he surveyed the chaotic scene before him where Cookie and her girls were heaped on the floor and the snigglesnorfs were not only loose but one was on top of the baloom cage and the other on the cutting board, and neither was yet skewered and both were staring at him, and not in fear but rather in what might be called delightful anticipation. Then two things occurred so quickly that he couldn't even comprehend what was happening to him. The spitting creature, who he hoped to use for target practice, was standing not two feet away from him with all its fur standing straight out, its tail swooshing back and forth with a terrible, menacing rhythm, its mouth open and its jaw chattering, its claws all out and its back legs taut as steel springs ready to explode, and all of it aimed at him as though it was about to use him for target practice. And even more horrible yet was his father's hatband which had just slithered off Cookie's face and now, as he watched, frozen and terrified, coiled up in front of him, reared back, and quick as a flash, with a wide open mouth, flashing eyes, and kniving as well as forking tongues, struck at him. And Hissofer, who really did know how to frighten people when he wanted to, scared him so badly that Odiferous let out a terrible scream and jumped straight up in the air causing the Itofit's hat to fly off and roll across the floor. In fact, Odiferous was so frightened and jumped so quickly that his shoes stayed right where he had been standing and his socks flew off as he went up, followed by his pants, and he propelled himself so high that he hit his head on the door jam and knocked himself out.

"What's that awful noise," cried Leuna in the Quartering Room. "Somebody's molesting poor Odify!" She ran out followed quickly by the District Inquisitor. Overwhelmed by her maternal instinct, she rushed toward the kitchen but just as she came to the top of the steps, Boogie appeared charging at them and without the slightest hesitation ran right between her legs. Startled (but hardly intimidated) she stopped on a dime and, for the barest flicker of an instant, weighed the alternatives of flying to Odiferous' aid or catching the nasty spitting thing that probably had a hand, or at least a claw, in whatever mischief was occurring, but before she could decide on either course of action, Lutarious ran into her backside and the two of them tumbled down the stairs and ended in a heap on top of Odiferous. Leuna looked up in time to see the last five pairs of Snorf's handsfeet (and his tail) disappearing out the window.

"Oh, poor Odify," she cried getting to her knees and cuddling her child. "He's been spit upon and snigglesnorfed!"

"It doesn't smell like spit to me," grumbled Lutarious climbing to his feet and brushing himself off. "But at least he found my hatband." He picked up the Itofit's hat, straightened Hissofer who had once again wrapped himself around its brim, and plopped it firmly on his head.

Just then Odiferous came to his senses, let out a wail, and groaned to his mother. "Poppa's hatband bit me!"

"Poppycock," said Lutarious bending over his son. "No stories this time. Give us the straight skinny. What didyado to Cookie?"

But Odiferous did not hear his father at all. He saw only Hissofer's tongue sticking out at him, those mesmerizing, unblinking, lidless, staring eyes, and that quivering tail; all no more than six inches from his nose, and before Hissofer even had to open his mouth, Odiferous' eyes rolled up into his head and he fainted.

"Help me," sobbed Leuna. "We must get Odify to the fresh air and away from here before he wakes up and is frightened again."

"Fresh air won't help," replied Lutarious. "He needs to be deodorized. And where's my feather?"

"Over there," said Leuna angrily. "And bring me some licorice water to sprinkle on him. No one will notice the smell. They'll be much too concerned for poor Odify."

After replacing his feather and sprinkling Odiferous liberally from a bottle of licorice water, Lutarious took the boys arms, Leuna his legs, and together they carried him to the Quartering Room and laid him out on a couch.

"What's going on here?" demanded the Dujge. "First, all those screams, then the zoop ran out through the French doors, and now this...what kind of a bawdy house are you people running here?"

"The hatband, the hatband." moaned Odiferous.

"Now, now. Don't worry yourself," said his mother. "Momma's little hero found daddy's little hatband and everybody's happy again."

Odiferous looked from his mother's woebegone eyes to his father's frown to the abomination around his father's head which had just scared the pants off him, gulped audibly, and lifted his hand, but whether to point at something or ward off an expected blow no one knew, for while all eyes were riveted on the boy, Hissofer pulled his head from under his tail, opened his mouth widely, and mimed a hissss. Odiferous let out a choked gurgle and passed out again.

The mayorling, who thought Odiferous had been trying to point at something behind them, spun around, looked out through the French doors, and let out a scream of his own. There, rising up through the smog and framed perfectly by the doors, were a cloud of balooms and five baloomerangs, two of which had snigglesnorfs hanging around their necks busily removing the muzzles which were all that remained of their tethers and harnesses. "My God," gasped the mayorling and everyone twirled around to see what he was gaping at.

"My livery!" cried the Dujge.

"My dinner!" screamed Leuna.

"My prize!" croaked Lutarious.

"My goodness," said Fasada who was so near sighted she couldn't see what was happening and assumed everyone had had one tarmini too many.

Behind them, running across the lawn, was the Dujge's maître d'stable who let out a feeble cry and burst through the French doors looking as pale as Fasada's eye bags. "Your Dugjeboat," he cried falling to one knee. "They've escaped! A gang of baloomersnatchers armed with snigglesnorfs raided the stable after sabotaging the smogfan to lure us away and made off with your Dujgeboat's livery."

"I'm not blind!" thundered the Dujge. "Don't just stand there kneeling, you dundersnort, bring me Hydraplop! There's more than one way to sniggle a skewersnorf, and at least three or four ways to bag a rangerbloom. I mean, ring a bloomerbag. I mean, oh phooey, do whatever I'm talking about! And hurry a get on!"

Lutarious grabbed his whip and lectric stick from the mantelpiece and ran out through the doors calling for Gorgoncha, for portable seed shooters, for six contingents of snollysolijers, for sharpshooting syffers with slings, for Corporal Porporal to run, not trot, to alert Major Dhump and Sergeant Struddel of the terrorists afoot, or aflight, and for Leuna to get a contingent of tagalongs to coddle and guard Odify since the villains were obviously nidkappers too."

"And send runners to the Imperious High Courtex," yelled the Dujge who suddenly remembered his later appointment with Is. "Tell them to quadruple the guard, battle the manments and winnow the widows. I mean man the battlements and women the windows, and cordon off my chambers." He too ran from the room following Lutarious onto the lawn just as two baloomerang muzzles dropped out of the sky and flopped over their heads like straightjackets.

"What's that peculiar odor, ladies?" asked the mayorling while gazing at Odiferous with a suspicious eye. "It smells like flambe d'fennel, but let's not worry about it. I suppose that's what happens when the smogfan fails. I think we could all use another termini, perhaps a double to soothe ourselves and prepare for any coming ordeal that might disturb the tranquillity of the city and render our services not only necessary but perhaps crucial to the continued maintenance of vaw, order, and civility in moments of crisis, don't you? Now, where has the major-domo gone when we need him? Major, major-domo," he called, "Come quickly! We need refills."

As Boogie ran back through the city streets the way he had been taken from the High Courtex, his friends were in a deepening gloom, not only because the algae lamp was failing but because Sergeant Struddel and the syffer, who had finally gotten all the bubble gum off themselves, were still rifling through Toliver's treasures and had found his skeleton key which, being in the compendium of proscribed objects, things, substances, and attitudes in the Third Book of Cunep, had immediately been reconfiscated and hung on a hook beneath the high window on the far side of the dungeon, completely out of reach. And upstairs, Major Dhump and the snollysolijer were already into their twelfth game of chocolate checkers and becoming cross with each other because of all the sugar they'd eaten. Major Dhump was ogling Is because he always liked to do what his superiors did (when they weren't around) and wondering how far he dared go, when the voice of Lutarious Roorback rang out from the outer room.

"Major Dhump!" thundered the voice.

Major Dhump leaped to his feet and saluted the wall. "Yessir!" he responded sharply, clickooming his heels.

"The city is under attack. Hurry to my tugfloat and throw the seed shooters overboard."

"Yessir," responded the major hurrying toward the door, then skidding to a stop. "No sir… that is, I mean, yessir I would sir but no sir I can't sir, because the Dujge sir told me to remain with the prisoners sir until he arrived this afternoon, Sir!" He clickoomed his heels again and spun around, now saluting the solijer who jumped to his feet and saluted back.

"Oh, diddle the Dujge," said the voice.

"I can't do that, sir!" gulped the major. And then, much to his horror, the District Inquisitor's missessness, who was known in the ranks as Never-Forgive-an-Insult-or-Leave-a-Stone-Unthrown Leuna, snapped: "Do as we say or I'll diddle your doodle, major."

"Yessir ma'am sir…I mean, yes ma'am sir sir," stammered Major Dhump who now felt virtually helpless and so outmatched that he ran from the chamber and out through the outer office before the District Inquisitor called again: "And take this solijer with you or you'll have to do it all by yourself!"

"Yessir ma'am sir sir," snapped the major who called his cohort who was only too happy to tag along rather than be left with the D.I. and his missessness. He hurried out behind the major and the two of them ran off much too confused by the sudden change in orders to even glance about the room to see where the voices had been coming from, and, indeed, all that was to be seen, blended like doom into a gray curtain, was a stately staring but nonetheless grim, ungainly, ghastly, gaunt and ominous bird of lore sitting on a pallid bust of Pallace above the chamber door.

"We'll do it in a trice!" cried Major Dhump over his shoulder. "When shall we return, sir?"

"Nevermore!" quoth the maven but the two solijers were too far gone to notice that the voice drifting after them was now none other than that of Vincent Price.

As soon as their footfalls died away, Hobnail flew into the inner office whistling Mr. Strauss's *Child's Play Polka* only to find Is and Toonie securely locked in the Dujge's private cage.

"Oh dear," cried Toonie, "so close and so farrago! If only we had Toliver's key."

Hobnail had flown round and round the High Courtex building looking in every window so she knew where the others were imprisoned and that all of Toliver's things were spread out on a table. She flapped her wings excitedly, warbled a hurried rendition of *The Thieving Magpie* by Mr. Rosini, and dashed out the window through which she had come. She dropped like a stone through the alley behind the building, braked herself at the last possible moment, and stepped to the ground by the dungeon's high window. She peeked around the corner, noticed that Sergeant Struddel and the syffer were still pawing through Toliver's things, and because she had such excellent eyesight, also noticed that his skeleton key was not among them. Very carefully she stuck her head through the bars and looked around only to find the key right there beneath her beak, hanging on a hook, from which she silently lifted it, and flew back to the Dujge's chamber. But just as she was leaving, Boogie came around the corner, saw her climbing into the smog, and, since cats are insatiably curious, ran straight to the window she had just left, and peeked inside.

When he looked in, he saw exactly what Hobnail had just seen, except that not being gray and nearly invisible but bright yellow-orange, Toliver saw him. The only thing Toliver could think to do, however, was hunch his shoulders and put his finger to his mouth to tell Boogie to stay very quiet, which Boogie interpreted as a signal beckoning him to come. He squeezed his head through the bars, gazed first at the floor ten feet below him, then at Sergeant Struddel and the syffer who were pulling on either end of Toliver's roll of silly putty, and who were standing directly between him and his goal. But above his head was a pipe that crossed the room and went directly into the cell, so Boogie squeezed the rest of himself through the bars, stood on his hind legs and put his front paws over the pipe. Pulling himself up wasn't very easy, even for a determined and acrobatic cat, because the pipe was all slippery and slimy, but he managed anyway and began tip-toeing, or pointy-clawing his way across the room, much to the consternation of Toliver who looked on in horror as the cat took one agonizing step after another. The Itofit noticed that Toliver had quit breathing and quickly saw the reason why, and then Whizlet, who was generally aware when people stopped breathing around him (since he often stopped breathing himself when battling dragons or groblets or enemy rocket ships), caught on and also stopped breathing, hoping thereby to help Boogie who had reached the center of the room and was directly above Sergeant Struddel's head. Instead of watching his next step, however, since cats' insatiably curiosity is even heightened when they're in harrowing positions, Boogie was watching the tug-of-war so he didn't notice the particularly drippy piece of slime upon which he stepped and which flew out from beneath him. He fell to the pipe and since it was very slippery slipped all the way around it until he was hanging upside down with his fore and hind legs wrapped around the pipe but sliding fast. He lost the battle with the pipe just as the dislodged piece of slime hit the sergeant on the ear causing him to look upward. Cats always land on their feet so Boogie twisted automatically in midair and what the sergeant saw is hard to imagine since it was a twirling ball of yellow-orange fur plummeting from out of space and clamping onto his face with twenty extended claws and a horrible spitting noise to go with them.

Sergeant Struddel gasped and let go of the silly putty, which zinged to the syffer's side, slapping him in the nose, and alerting him to the situation. Horrified, he watched while his sergeant tried vainly to dislodge whatever had attacked him. Then he grabbed his club and readied himself to strike at the assailant.

"Watch out," screamed Toliver who had starting breathing again just in the nick of time for Boogie was so intent on the flailing sergeant he didn't notice the syffer about to strike, but heeding Toliver's call, detached himself and leaped to the side just as the syffer let fly a mighty blow which bonked Sergeant Struddel on top of the head and knocked him for a lollapalooza.

The syffer gasped but had no time to worry about what had already happened so as the sergeant spun to the floor and the flashing ball of spitting, hissing yellow-orange ferocity ran between his legs, he rose his club again and took careful aim.

"It's time for your whistle," called the Itofit to Toliver.

Toliver gulped another breath, thrust his forefinger and pinkie into his mouth, and let fly with a super high C. The syffer froze in mid swing and began to quiver wildly, and, as Toliver continued magnificently with his best whistle ever, began to bounce up and down across the cell; his one eye looking left and up, the other right and down; until he came within reach of the Itofit's tail which flashed out, caught him around the neck, and reeled him over to the cell. With Toliver still whistling and the Itofit pinning the syffers arms behind him against the bars, Whizlet reached out and grabbed his key ring, pulled it off his belt, and reached outside the cell to unlock their door. He ran out first, grabbed the syffer's club and tripped him up with it so that as the Itofit let loose and Toliver finally took a breath, the syffer collapsed into the cell. And while the Itofit and Whizlet, one on each leg, pulled the now cuckooing Sergeant Struddel in behind him, Toliver ran to the table and scooped up all his things.

"Don't forget your key," called the Itofit who remembered it had been hung on the hook. "We might run into more locked doors on the way out of here or on the way into where everybody else is." But when they looked to the hook, the key was missing, which certainly seemed very mysterious but was not something they had any time to cogitate about.

"I've got these," shouted Whizlet holding up the syffer's key ring as he jumped out of the cell, slamming the door behind him.

Boogie was already scratching at the door of the dungeon and as soon as the Itofit opened it, ran down the dingy hallway and up the stairway at the other end, only to be stopped again at a locked door at the top. Fortunately, the second of Whizlet's three keys fit the lock, and since he was the first behind Boogie, he kicked the door open, and they continued running down another hallway and up another twisting flight of stairs until they came to the locked door to the foyer.

"Be careful this time," the Itofit called after them. "We don't know what's on the other side so let's peep before we sneak." They opened the door slowly and peered out into the dim, empty foyer with only a single algeaflask chandelier casting a green glow over the marble walls. Whizlet ran to the huge iron doors, key to the front like General Sherman's sword, and stabbed at the lock, then stabbed and stabbed again.

"They don't fit," he cried, now pushing on the doors as hard as he could. "And they're as solid as gigabyte of granite."

"That's all right," replied the Itofit, "there are sure to be other doors, and we can't go until we find Is and Toonie anyway."

"You don't have to find us," said a voice from the dim recesses above the circular staircases, "because we found you first."

"And I have Toliver's key," added Is, "because Hobnail brought it to us."

"We thought you gave it to her," said Toonie who suddenly appeared sliding down a banister, followed almost immediately by Is who had never slid down a banister before but decided she certainly wanted to do so again (although not just now and probably not on this banister either.)

"Where have you guys been?" asked Whizlet who liked to keep track of everybody, just in case.

"We've been in a high dudgeon!" exclaimed Toonie. "But Hobnail talked us out of it."

The Itofit took Toliver's key, which fit the lock in the iron doors. He turned the key then pushed very hard and opened one of the doors just a crack so they could peer out into the afternoon's smoggy pallor. Except for an old lady pushing a rusty shopping cart full of rags and five or six people sleeping on the sidewalks, the square in front of the building was empty.

"It must be siesta time," remarked Is, peeking over It's shoulder.

"Where should we go?" asked Toliver.

"We still have to rescue Rango and Rangi and Snorf and Snorfa and all the balooms before bar-be-que time," said Toonie.

"Me-ow-me-out-of-the-coop," said Boogie, elaborating on this terse reply with his tail.

"They've all gotten away," said the Itofit, "but the Dujge and the District Inquisitor are sending the tsarmy so we'd better hurry and get out of Smugsmog City as fast as we can."

"But we don't want to look like we're running away," cautioned Is, "or people will wonder what we've done."

The Itofit threw out his chest and patted his hair (or the fur atop his head) down with his tail. "We'll just look like we belong and walk through the city as though we have business someplace around the next corner."

But as they went down the steps in a businesslike group, Hobnail, who'd gone back out through the window rather than down the stairs with Is and Toonie and was now high above surveying the city in every direction and seeing what they faced, called down to them in no uncertain terms not to linger on the order of their going by singing a few wild bars from *The William Tell Overture.*

"Heigh-ho Silver!" cried Toliver jumping ahead and taking off at a gallop.

"High! Oh Silver!" cried Whizlet chasing behind.

"Hi, Ole Silver!" cried Toonie looking about for a horse.

"My, Old Silver must be a stalking groblet," said the Itofit taking Is' hand and hurrying after the others.

Directly across the square was the way they had come from the tugfloat but the Itofit didn't want them to get trapped between the tallagator pens and the river so he motioned them down a side street and they hurried on to the next crossroads. Some people were walking ahead so they turned right and ran on, crossing several other streets, until coming upon a group of men in ill-fitting white uniforms all chained together by the legs. Some were using picks and shovels to dig up cobblestones and put them in a cart, while others were taking other cobblestones from another cart and putting them back down. Resting against the buildings to either side were snollysolijers with their hats pulled down over their eyes and clubs at their sides. Some of the prisoners saw the escapees coming and waved them off before the solijers could notice them, forcing the Itofit to turn quickly and lead the others down the nearest alley. At the far end of the alley were three curving roads fanning out like fingers. They stopped for a moment, hesitant over which way to go, but the Itofit was never one to puzzle long over puzzlements when action was called for, so he led them toward the street most directly ahead. But no sooner had they started than Hobnail began whistling Mr. Mozart's *Requiem* and Toliver threw up a hand, stopping them: "It's a dead end," he exclaimed. "We have to go another way."

The Itofit skidded to a halt and turned quickly to his left but Hobnail changed her tune to the opening strains of Mr. Shubert's *Unfinished Symphony* and Toonie stopped short. "We can't go that way either," she cried. "We'll never get through."

"There's only one other way," said the Itofit turning on his heel, and he led them off along the right fork. This took them to Executioner's Square whose park was ringed with confectionery stands and whose center was dominated by the ancient hanging tree with the public gallows built around its base and row after row of benches (much like in the Revered End Ferry Jawell's vision of heaven) spread out around it. The Itofit turned right but Hobnail sounded a warning. He turned left only to hear the same restive plaint so he stopped in his tracks and scratched his ear with a scratching whisker. But even then Hobnail kept warning them for she was not only looking at all her friends but at three different contingents of snollysolijers, each coming down a different street, one behind them, one from the left, and another from the right. Hobnail could see no way out, so she dug into her repertoire and dusted off Mr. Berlioz's *March to the Scaffold*.

"How awful!" cried Toonie throwing her hands to her face.

"We're trapped," cried Toliver looking about wildly.

"Circle the wagons." Cried Whizlet spinning around.

But Boogie ran into the square and under the benches, then flew up the stairs of the scaffold, leaped to the trunk of the old hanging tree, and ran up it as fast as his sharp little claws would take him.

"What a good idea!" exclaimed the Itofit who was always quick to acknowledge somebody else's smart thinking. "Let's do that too!" They all ran to the scaffold from the top of which, Is, who was extremely agile, leaped to the lower branches and turned around. The Itofit boosted Toonie up to her and, as the two of them climbed further into the tree, leaped to the branch himself with Toliver clinging to his back. As soon as Toliver scrambled off, the Itofit hung down by his tail, scooped up Whizlet, and pulled him into the cover of leaves just as the first and second contingents of solijers turned into the square and ran into each other. And, while they were sorting themselves out, the third contingent ran into them, and while all of them were picking themselves up, Sergeant Struddel, with an enormous bandage around his head, staggered into the square himself (aided by the syffer who had done him in), surveyed the situation, and made for the gallows in order to rally his men.

He banged his helmet (which he was carrying instead of wearing since it wouldn't fit over the bandage) on the railing to get everyone's attention and when they looked over to see what the racket was all about, waved for them to come closer. "They've escaped," he yelled. "The cowardly cravens are loose in the city. They're armed, legged, and dangerous! They have secret flying yellow perils and cohorts from the outside who outnumbered, overwhelmed, and underdone us, but we'll get them all back as soon as we're organized by names and ranks, not to mention files and serial numbers, and everybody knows that I'm in charge."

"Oh, no you're not!" came a furious voice from the edge of the crowd. "I am!" And a very red faced Major Dhump pushed through the solijers, mounted the platform, and hurried to the center. He spun on his heel, pushed Sergeant Struddel away, and threw up his right arm with his right hand closed and his index finger extended and pointing directly at the Itofit who, along with the others, was concealed in the foliage only a few feet above him. Knowing that another moment of glory had arrived, he held the pose for just long enough to etch it deeply on all his men's memories, then began to exhort them: "Onward! Heroes of Alabramble! Great things and glory are about to befall us!"

But before he could explain exactly what great and glorious things were in the offing, Sergeant Struddel, who had skidded to the railing, grabbed the executioner's lever to steady himself and inadvertently opened the trap door beneath the major. So, instead of his heroic pose, what was imprinted on everyone's mind was Major Dhump's still red but now startled face and his arm upraised with its finger pointed toward the sky plummeting from sight. And as he disappeared, from the very spot in the smog to which he had been pointing, came a haunting rendition of Mr. Saint-Saen's *Dance Macabre* and all the solijers looked up anxiously, hoping the strange music wasn't meant for them, but fearful that the Satin Diabola was somehow loose again over Smugsmog City.

Sergeant Struddel was down on his hands and knees peering through the trap. "Help the major," he cried. "He's been dumped but he's bounced back before and he'll bounce again, and, remember men, a dumped Dhump is doubly dangerous, so roll him out and he'll redouble his redoubtableness, and we'll all strike again before the iron's hot and the flish are out of the kettle!"

Helped by a squad of snollysolijers who half carried, half pushed him back to the platform, a dazed Major Dhump took up where he left off. "Sergeant Struddel," he cried. "That way!" and he pointed the way the sergeant had come from the High Courtex building. "Take Contingent Two. Check the alleys and in the garbage cans, under the dumpsters and over the transoms, in the cubbyholes and out and about." He steadied himself by grasping the railing with both hands, then lifted his gloves and pointed down a side street. "Corporal Porporal! Take Contingent Three and do the same. Roust the roustabouts and lampoon the lallygaggers all the way to the smogfan. I'll take Contingent One to the river and we'll sound them out if they're there and drown them out if they're not!"

"But what if they went that way?" asked Sergeant Struddel pointing across the square and down the one street that no one would be covering.

"No one in his, her, or It's right mind would go to Pulcan's Paradise," scoffed the major. "Or is that right brain? No, left brain. No, that's not right either unless it's left behind, or maybe it's the right behind, but if it's right behind you, it'll cross you up every time until you're left with nothing but a bad case of ambidextrose confusion. No, no, sergeant, if the Brablugians go to the Boological Gardens, Pulcan's Pulpy Protectors will bop them or poke them or slap them down or change them into weeping idiots and all we'll have to do is pick up their peaches later."

Major Dhump put his gloves to his lips and blew "Charge", and all of the solijers ran off as directed until Executioner's Square was as quiet as what comes after it for its main attraction. The Itofit's head popped out of the foliage and looked about. "They're gone," he whispered, "so we'd better be too." He jumped to the scaffold and turned around to catch the children as they leaped to his arms followed by Is, with Boogie catching a ride on her shoulder.

"Which way should we go?" asked Whizlet who hadn't any idea where they were, much less where they were going, but knew that three ways were blocked and the fourth unthinkable.

"I guess we'd better go that way," said the Itofit pointing the way Corporal Porporal had gone, "since the smogfan is outside the city and we want to be gone before everybody wakes up from siesta." But they had not even reached the edge of the square when they all stopped horrified for Lutarious Roorback riding in Gorgoncha had just turned a corner ahead of them and was bearing down on the park.

"Oops!" cried the Itofit skidding to a halt. "Not that way. This way." He pointed the way Sergeant Struddel had gone with Contingent Two "...and we'll double back through the alleys."

"Yipes-a-doddle!" cried Whizlet as they started off again. Mesmerized, he ran ahead, gaping over his shoulder at Gorgoncha as the beast rose to its tippy-vine toes and shifted into a galumphing garden gait, and plowed into the back of the Itofit who had skidded to a second halt.

"Not that way either." cried It, but before he could explain why, a terrible shriek sounded from above and before them as Dujge Dorque in Hydraplop spotted them coming and blew a Summons All Syffers on his whistle.

"To the river" called Toliver remembering his encounter with Gorgoncha. "We're better off with Major Dhump and the tallagators than a Dujge on a Diddle!"

But Major Dhump heard the call too, so he to-the-rear-marched his men and was now bearing down on them with the fierce determination of one doubly done in.

"To Pulcan's Paradise," cried Toonie, "maybe they have some hideacynths or at least a hydrangea to put on so we can put them off." And she ran off toward Whipperwithawill Avenue and the infamous Boological Gardens with the Experimental Thistle, Thorn, Nettle & Sticker Plots of Pulcan the Whipwielder, while high above, Hobnail drove them on with a cacophonous concatenation of Mr. Ravel's *Balero*.

When Lutarious Roorback caught sight of them turning toward Pulcan's Paradise, he reached into his bottle of cockroaches, threw a handful into Gorgoncha's heinous spry mouth, and snapped his whip for overdrive. The Dujge sparked his tooth furiously, waved Sergeant Struddel and Contingent Two on with his lectric stick, and reached into his bag of stunned mice for some octane for Hydraplop. Major Dhump had wheezed his way to the head of his men and was, once more, where he felt he belonged, except he was slower than everyone else so being in front was not really a good idea, and only resulted in Contingents One, Two, and Three, along with Hydraplop and Gorgoncha, all arriving at the junction of Executioner Square and Whipperwithawill Avenue at the same time causing another clash of confusion which gave their prey a few precious moments to reconnoiter the scene ahead.

Before the fugitives was the foreboding fence and spiked iron gate of Pulcan's Paradise and just inside were signposts with signs pointing left, right, and up Pulcan's Hill. They slammed the gate behind them and dropped its locking bar, then stared in confusion at all the choices confronting them. To the left was a pole with five signs on it. The topmost said: "Little Bo Creep's Kiddie Garden," followed by "Thorn Throwing and Seed Shooting Gallery [Brablugian Moving Targets Must Be Taken in Back Entrance], and below that: "Mushroom Madness Sanitarium" and further down: "Tuber Traps & Ankle Daisy Chains"; and finally: "Frightful Fungi Factory." To the right, the signs read: "Crossbreeding Contumelies & Other Disconubia [Follow the Colored Arrows], and below this were individual signs, each with a large colored arrow pointing off along different trails: by the red arrow it said: "Pricklepoke & Stinging Nettles"; by the blue arrow: "Funnysuckle & Toison Pivy"; by the green arrow: "Snapdragons & Tallagator Weed"; by the yellow arrow: "Lassoing Kudzus & Cowpoke," and by the purple arrow: "Lady Fingers & Chokeweed." Straight ahead facing Pulcan's Hill was an archway in whose arch, in large iron letters, was written: "Pulcan Smugsmog, Caveat Emptor I," and hanging from one of the side posts, a neat little sign that looked like it was done in embroidery (but it was really a barbed wire weave) saying: "Penelope's Plot for the Culinary Adept."

"Which way should we go?" asked Whizlet who could hardly make sense of all the rigmarole.

"Remember what Major Dhump said," said Toliver whose only confabulation with honest to goodness (or badness if you prefer) military persons had been that morning with the snollysolijers of Alabramble. "Up the hill, because pursuers are lazy!"

"Right!" responded Whizlet. "Let's drive 'em crazy!"

"And make them arise in a kiln," cried Toonie shaking her fist at the archway, "and we can punch 'em down like they're puffed up and doughy."

The wide path on the other side of Pulcan's Archway divided into a number of smaller pathways all going off in different directions up the hill, so the slope before them was a maze whose various walls were all different sorts of nasty bushes and shrubs.

"But which way should we go now?" wailed Toonie whose camaraderie faded as she looked in horror at the menacing maze.

We don't have time to think about it," said the Itofit looking over his shoulder at Hydraplop and Gorgoncha surrounded by a horde of snollysolijers and syffers who, having sorted themselves out, were surging up to the gate, "so we'd better boogie with Boogie and go that way." He pointed to the narrowest, least inviting trail along which Boogie's tail, stuck straight up in the air, was disappearing.

"But that looks like the worstest way of all," exclaimed Toonie whose grammar often matched her confusion.

"Yes it does," answered Is, taking Toonie's hand and heading them off after the cat on the presumption that if the ladies didn't go first, no one would. "But we have to expect the snollygosters to make the safest way look most dangerous."

Since Boogie, now moving stealthily as the yellow-striped, green-eyed, and lean-mean Spitpurrkoff was descended from a long line of jungle cats who were never known to put up with any nonsense from bushes, trees, vines, and creepers, much less mushrooms and flowers. He moved quickly on his little padded feet, hissing at anything that even remotely tried to bother him, going this way and that, up one trail and then switching to another, until he came to a small pond choked with weeping cryacinths that, as he stuck his head through to peer across the pond, caught him unaware and squirted him with sobbing spray . Toonie stopped and shook her fist at the now chortling cryacinths, then called to Toliver: "Give me your plastic bag and a clothespin."

Toliver was about to protest that they didn't have time for diversionary tactics, but when he saw the look in Toonie's eye, he did as she asked. She put the clothespin on her nose, ran to the edge of the pond, and filled the bag with juicy pods and flowers of the cryacinths, which she then crushed and squeezed until the bottom of the bag filled with juice. She couldn't help crying, of course, and the clothespin made her speech sound like a lallation, but that didn't matter at all because no one could doubt her determination. "Gif me yur waterpithol," she demanded.

Toliver rifled his pocket and pulled out his water pistol, whereupon Toonie opened the bag and filled it with the juice. "Juth in cathe," she lisped, "an' even if they catcth uth in the middle uf the pond, they'll haf to cry all the way to the bank!"

"You shouldn't cry now," said Whizlet sympathetically. "They haven't caught us yet."

"I'm not crying," cried Toonie. "I'm juth practithing what I'm gonna do to Lutariouth Roorback when I get 'im in my thights!"

The Itofit scooped up Boogie who was still wheezing and sneezing and tearing all over himself, and circled the pond. "We'd better go that way," said Is pointing at a narrow, winding trail. "Those are lying lilies and a bed of chokeus, but they only attack if you're resting, and those little bushes are pink asailyas but they never fight when their blushing, so as long as they're blossoming we'll be all right."

"And those long spindly things are night-blooming scareus," added the Itofit, "so they're asleep now and won't bother us either." They hurried along the trail to another clearing carpeted with grab grass, so Is cautioned the children to high step across it. Several pathways led off the other side. The Itofit didn't hesitate in choosing the one that looked nastiest, but no sooner had they started off than Hobnail shrieked down at them to go another way around an ambush of creeping thorn throwers and jumping chortle cactus which were lying in wait beyond the a bend in the trail. Once she had their attention, she guided them through the maze, safely avoiding matched sets of philobopodendrons and rhodoclobbodendrons, camouflaged mushroom mines, smilax sticker traps, and a whole glen of orchid ogres (not to mention the deceptively alluring Plot of Penelope the Pivyperson where Pulcan's wife, who was renowned for her toison pivy hentails, witch hazel shakes, and black widow spider plants, had spun her web of deception), until they came out below the great iron toe of Pulcan's statue. And little did they know as they pushed ahead into the shadow of the huge, looming monument that they were also pushing into Alabrambian history for the Battle for Pulcan's Toe was about to begin.

Neither Hydraplop nor Gorgoncha could follow them directly to the statue for the paths were too narrow for the veggiebeasts, so the Dujge turned left and the District Inquisitor right to where access roads wound up the hill. Contingents One, Two, and Three, however, pushed ahead with each taking a different pathway and fighting their way through Pulcan's Protectors toward the top. The carnage was catastrophic but Major Dhump, Sergeant Struddel, and Corporal Porporal drove their men on and regrouped as they reached the promontory. The gigantic statue of Pulcan the First, Whipwielder and Emptor Caveat, was striding forth among a field of boulders with both feet on pedestals, his whip snapping above his head, and his left hand throwing out iron seeds (which were attached to his fingers by thin iron rods so they looked to be sprinkled in the air.) His crown was of spiked iron and below the spikes was an observation deck of squinched and spandreled arches. The crown was reached by a winding staircase within the statue lit by little barred windows along the way. The baroque entrance was in the back pedestal through an elaborate set of polished doors at the head of a short flight of steps, and led, presumably, to the staircase inside the goliath. The pathway to the entrance led between two boulders directly below Pulcan's Big Right Toe with its pointed iron toenail curving down over the trail, to either side of which were the largest, meanest, and most feared philobopaslapapokentripodendrons in all of Alabramble. Beyond the hundred year old sentry plants, the path led through a garden of herbamorphs and skirted a puddlepond directly beneath the statue in which baby tallagators were nursed and trained to the harness and razor-mouthed ripanha flish had their teeth sharpened on saw weed and emery grass.

Boogie dodged between the philobododendrons and screeched to a halt in the face of all the basking, snapping tallagators, then turned and ran to the top of Pulcan's Toe up a meshwork of wines that wrapped around the statue's foot and went up to his thigh like an argyle legging. Everyone else stopped too, not because of the tallagators, which they hadn't gotten to yet and were quite small anyway although they did have big mouths, but because the philobopaguardians had been alerted by Boogie's passage and now smelled them coming. But rather than looking dangerous, both of them were trying to entice the visitors into their embrace by waving their arms alluringly. Toliver jumped to the fore and confronted the one to the right, while Whizlet did the same to the one to the left and eyed it as though it was the Mirrored Medusa in *A Gargoyle's Grotto of Demented Doric Demons.*

"Ready?" called Toliver who was a quick study even when the teacher was only a younger cousin of his best friend.

"Ready!" responded Whizlet.

Then, perfectly syncopated and without missing a beat (as though they'd been practicing this all day), they yelled in unison: "Yibble yabble kaboom!" first feinting left, then jumping right, then leaping ahead into the middle of the philobopodendrons which, having never been so accosted before, were totally unprepared for the assault, and before they could respond, felt the little human creatures astride their innards, each grasping two of their nasty arms and using them to force the other arms to bop and slap and poke, not only their own central face-stems, but the other's as well, just to let them know who was in charge.

With the sentry plants subdued, Toonie ran by them and then, as quickly as she could, past the puddlepond where she jumped off the path and continued on beyond Pulcan's Left Foot expecting to run down the other side of the hill, but skidded to a halt at the top of a sheer cliff which formed the backside of Pulcan's Promontory.

"This will never do!" she cried to Is as she looked down on a canopy of glistening bramblethorns and gristly pricklepoke. "We're wrapped in a cul-de-sackcloth!" She turned and ran back to the pathway and looked wildly about. The ornate doors to the pedestal, with their easily reached, big brass handles, polished wood panels, and stained glass fanlight above, beckoned. A bronze plaque to the side said: "To Pulcan's Crown - Visitors Welcome." Toonie hurried up the stairs and reached for the handles.

"Don't go in there," called Is from behind.

"Why not?' called back Toonie. "It's the only place left and maybe we can find something inside to help us. Besides, the sign says we're welcome so nobody'll mind."

"That's what's wrong," responded Is. "Never trust anything snollygosters tell you…at least not until you've checked it out very carefully yourself and find out why they're doing it." She quickly looked around the area beneath the statue. The puddlepond was in the middle and boulders blocked the sides, but she noticed some scuff marks in the sand by the back of the other pedestal beneath Pulcan's right heel. "This way," she said. "Let's see what's over here."

Together they ran to the other wall. From a distance it looked like solid stone, but when they got closer they could see that there was no mortar between some of the blocks, which might have formed a door. Toonie put her eye to the crack and peered in. "It looks like a latch," she reported, "but I can't see how we can do anything about it from out here."

"Let's see," replied Is looking around. "Emery grass and saw weed are thin as a slats and sharp as files. Maybe if we're careful we could cut through the latch and get inside." She went to the edge of the puddlepond and chased away some miniature snapping tallagators, then pulled out clumps of saw weed and emery grass and wrapped their roots (which weren't sharp at all) as handles around the lower end of two of the toughest blades. "I'll saw from the top," she told Toonie as she handed her one of the pieces, "and you file from the bottom, and we'll be through it in no time at all."

The latch was no match for their determined efforts and soon fell away. Toonie pushed on one side of the door but nothing happened, so Is pushed on the other side and the stone panel swiveled open. Inside was a curved stairway going up Pulcan's leg and disappearing into the gloom above. They hesitated just a moment for their eyes to adjust to the half-light, then stepped inside and mounted the stairs. The first little window was by Pulcan's knee and as they looked out they could see the first of the snollysolijers organizing above Pulcan's Protectors and readying themselves for a charge at the monument.

The Itofit ran to the edge of the puddlepond where feeding baskets were hung from the gatorcorral, snatched up one of the baskets, and jumped about among the tallagators, grabbing them by their tails, and dropping them in the basket. When it was almost filled he dashed to the vines where Boogie had run up Pulcan's Toe and scrambled to the top. Boogie was down on his haunches, whiskers and ears laid back, jaws chattering and tail swooshing behind, spitting at the attacking solijers. Because of the boulders, the solijers could only come two or three at a time along the pathway where they were forced to confront the philobododendrons now manned by Toliver and Whizlet. Their clubs and spears were no match for the long, bopping, slapping, poking arms of the sentry plants, but driven on by Major Dhump from the rear, and Sergeant Struddel and Corporal Porporal from either side, they kept up the assault, certain to tire their antagonists with wave after wave of servile syffers. Two tried to climb a vine up Pulcan's Toe, but Boogie's slashing right paw took off the first helmet to appear over the top and knocked the solijer down upon the other until both tumbled back. But another quickly followed. As his grizzled face peeked over Pulcan's Toenail, the Itofit sidearmed a tallagator which bounced toward him, slapped him in the face with its tail, and grabbed hold of his nose with its snapping mouth.

"Youch!" screamed the syffer, toppling back into the arms of those pushing him from behind. Falling in agony, he pulled the tallagator from his nose and flung it into the air where it turned over and over again (which only succeeded in making it angrier and angrier since tallagators, who don't have to worry about falling over themselves, never get dizzy) until it landed on another syffer's shoulder and immediately bit his ear.

The Itofit jumped to the snarling cat's side and began, with calm assurance and deadly aim, to cast the rest of his tallagators at the attackers. The little gators were enraged from being summarily plucked up by their tails and dropped into a basket full of themselves, so they were slapping their tails and snapping their jaws wildly at anything they could. The Itofit was taking them out one at a time, twirling them above his head, and letting fly at the enemy where they snapped onto arms and shoulders and ears, or fell to the ground where they jumped about and bit at ankles. But still the snollysolijers kept coming as more staggered from the legions of Pulcan's Protectors, caught their breath, and charged. As the ones in front fell back from the barrage of branches and fusillade of gators, Major Dhump, to awaken the best in his men, blew Reveille on his glove and motioned for Sergeant Struddel to lead a charge. The sergeant leapt into the breach. He ran ahead with his cantaloupe helmet skewed precariously on his bandages, but jumped to the side by Pulcan's Toenail and yelled for Corporal Porporal to take over. The corporal looked over his shoulder and waved his club for his men to follow, then turned, lowered his weapon, charged at Toliver, and was immediately bopped on top of the head for his trouble; a bop that flattened the kumquat atop his helmet, squashed the helmet onto his ears, and pushed it down over his nose. He collapsed to the side and ended up sitting against Pulcan's Pedestal with his eyes spinning around like tennis shoes in a clothes drier and his tongue sticking out from the corner of his mouth.

Toonie and Is gazed down upon the melee from the window in Pulcan's Belt Buckle at what was, for all its initial success, an almost hopeless contest. Before their eyes and partially blocking their view, the scattering of Pulcan's iron seeds swayed in the breeze. "I wish we could bop 'em with those beans!" said Toonie.

"Maybe we can," responded Is. "Let's go out into Pulcan's Arm and see how they're attached to his fingers." The hurried up the stairs into the rotunda of Pulcan's Chest where the main stairway continued toward the crown, a ladder went up his right arm, and a narrow walkway angled down to his left hand. Is led the way to his fingers where the thin iron rods holding the seeds were anchored to the floor by bolts.

Toonie grabbed a bolt but couldn't turn it at all. "Oh, I wish I was a wench," she cried, "then I could turn it!"

"Maybe we can cut through the rods like we did the latch," suggested Is, who quickly got down on her knees and began sawing away. Toonie crawled into the adjacent finger and started filing as hard as she could. The iron was old and brittle so the saw weed and emery grass dug into it with a fury and soon the rod on which Is was working snapped at the cut. As the seed fell, the rod snaked up the finger and out beneath Pulcan's Fingernail. Neither Is nor Toonie could see what effect their strategy was having, but a roar from below hinted at what was happening. The first seed fell from Pulcan's Hand, bounced from a boulder, and careered down the hillside, whipping the rod from side to side as it bounded along and scattering terrified snollysolijers in every direction. A moment later the second seed hit nearby with similarly devastating effect. Major Dhump looked up in horror at a third and fourth seed, which were vibrating and shaking wildly at the end of their rods and destined to drop down upon them at any moment. Horrified, he threw his glove to his mouth and sounded Retreat!

The snollysolijers were only too happy to escape the quintuple threat into which they had been driven and fell back down the hill, only to be brought up short at the upper line of Pulcan's Protectors where all of the abominable assemblage of plants were now wide awake and thrashing about on their stems, just waiting for anyone to come within range of their nastinesses.

Boogie clawed at the air behind the retreating figures, the Itofit rushed back to the puddlepond to refill his basket before the next, inevitable charge, Toliver and Whizlet took breathers while inducing their philobododendrons to do a high five, and Is and Toonie, who couldn't tell how successful they'd been, loosed the last two seeds which bounced down the hill behind the fleeing troops. When the last rod had been cut, they went back to the rotunda then up toward Pulcan's Crown but stopped when they reached the windows in his eyes and gazed out in horror as Gorgoncha lumbered across the field of boulders toward Pulcan's Toe.

"Uh-oh," yelled Toliver catching sight of the heinous spry trap and its even heinouser pulpiteer.

"Yipes-a-doddle," responded Whizlet, taking a firmer grasped on his philobobojoysticks, "I don't think we can yibble-yabble-kaboom Gorgoncha."

Boogie saw the monster too and retreated up Pulcan's viney argyle legging and hid among the leaves to watch for an opening. When the Itofit returned to the top of Pulcan's Toe with a fresh basket of tallagators and another basket of ripanha razor flish he had scooped from the puddlepond (both of which he hung from the end of his tail as he climbed) Major Dhump had regrouped his solijers who, being inspired the arrival of the spry trap, heeded his call and charged again.

Gorgoncha threw one twisty vine foot over a boulder, used another to slap away a pesky rhodoclobodendron, and anchored a third to the tangle above Pulcan's Toe. Seventeen potato eyes watched Boogie's progress up the leg and an armicule flashed out to snag the tasty morsel, but Boogie saw it coming and did a backflip over its nettle fingers. Once in the air he did a Louganis, an upside down, inside out, over and under double half gainer, with a triple twist to the top of the pulpit's canopy. The canopy snapped down like a diving board, bopping the District Inquisitor on top of the head, then sprang back, throwing the cat all the way to the red beet nose of the startled spry trap. Boogie hesitated not a moment, but ran upward and leapt to a potato and began scratching out its eyes as frantic armicules slapped all about. Gorgoncha spit a stream of icky awful spry juice into the air and would have diverted all its attention to the little demon except that Lutarious

Roorback snapped his whip and pointed his lectric stick at the Itofit, who was so involved in throwing ripanha flish at the new wave of syffers that he had not yet seen the danger looming above. But the Itofit also heard the whip and as the spry trap slapped at him with its fourth leg and three armicules, he too leaped to the veggiebeast and ran up the thorns along its side as though they were a ladder. Passing the pulpit he slung a tallagator which snapped by the ear of the District Inquisitor and dropped indignantly to the bottom of the pulpit where it flopped about until Lutarious trapped it under his foot. The Itofit continued to the top of the cabbage head, sticking ripanha flish into Gorgoncha's cauliflower ear as he passed, and from his new bastion continued to rain his teeths of terror on the solijers below.

Is and Toonie had gone back down to the window in Pulcan's Knee and were watching the battle close-up in helpless fascination. With two of his enemies firmly ensconced on his head and right eye, Gorgoncha's attention was riveted on dislodging them, so he raised two twisty vine feet to aid his armicules, and, to maintain his balance, leaned against Pulcan's Leg. Even Lutarious Roorback realized the danger above. He leaned far out of his pulpit and uncoiled his whip so it hung down Gorgoncha's barrel chest, took careful aim at Boogie (who was well within striking distance), and was just about to disable the cat with a stinging, stunning lash when Hissofer Booshocks, who had been watching the pursuit through the city and the battle around Pulcan's Toe with the keen interest of the professional predator, knew that the moment to strike had come. He pushed six inches of himself off the Itofit's hat brim, flopped down and doubled back until his upside down face was directly in front of the District Inquisitor's nose, hissed a horrible challenge which reverberated through the pulpit, and threw wide his jaws. Lutarious was so startled that he fell back into the pulpit and dropped both his whip and his lectric stick, but while the whip fell away outside, the stick dropped into the pulpit where it bounced about spitting angry sparks in every direction. In trying to escape his own weapon, Lutarious loosed the tallagator under his foot, which immediately bit through his shoe and into his toe.

Hissofer, who had done his work well but who was now in a compromised position, knew the time for a prudent snake to escape was at hand. He rapidly unwound himself from the Itofit's hat until only enough of his tail was hanging on for support, and pushed three quarters of himself out like a quivering tendril toward the window in Pulcan's Knee. Even though the spry trap was leaning against the statue's leg, the window was too far for Hissofer to reach, but Is saw him stretching out and quickly threw him her tail to help. As Hissofer and the tail entwined, Is pulled back and both the snake and the Itofit's hat sailed off and flew from the District Inquisitor's head, while the pretty white crane feather fluttered off and lodged in the vines. "Ye gads, Sir!" cried Major Dhump who had been watching these developments from below. "A hat attack, Sir! Your hatband is making off with your hat!"

"My hat's possessed," screamed Lutarious grabbing for it with his now free whip hand. But he was a moment too late for his hat was six feet below him and hanging by its hatband which was hanging from a furry tail hanging from the barred window in Pulcan's Knee. In a rage, Lutarious grabbed his lectric stick and, as Is reeled Hissofer and the Itofit's hat to the window, leaned out to lectrifry them all.

"Oh no, you don't!" screamed Toonie who stretched her arm out with Toliver's water pistol gripped firmly in her hand and pointed it right at Lutarious Roorback's face. Squirt! Squirt! Squirt! Squirt! Four times she pulled the trigger just like Wyatt Slurp at the OK Soda Fountain and a stream of weeping cryacinth juice splashed all over his furious visage.

"Yowl!" yelled Lutarious as he fell back into the pulpit clawing for his gas mask canister. Gorgoncha, sensing rather than seeing the danger by his chin, pulled the two twisty vine legs that had been slapping at the Itofit from his head, regained his balance, and pushed away from Pulcan's leg. Boogie, realizing it was time to boogie, leaped from the potato eye just in time to catch a clawful of the argyle vine and pull himself toward the window. But Gorgoncha was in a fury and threw three armicules toward him, which threaded their way among the vines chasing the cat until one of them succeeded in snagging his left leg and pulling him back.

"Watch out!" screamed Toonie to the pinioned cat.

The Itofit heard her call and, thinking she was directing it at him, swirled around looking for the danger. He saw Boogie in trouble and leaving his baskets behind jumped from the top of Gorgoncha's head to the springboard of the pulpit's canopy and somersaulted through space to land on the vines next to the cat. But Gorgoncha threw out four more armicules, two of which snagged the Itofit just as he managed to pull Boogie away from the other. Lutarious Roorback, who had been dazed when Boogie sprang upon his canopy, discombobulated when the Itofit snipped his ear with a tallagator, and befuddled byToonie's squirts, pulled himself back to his feet, this time wearing his flabber gas mask, and screaming for Gorgoncha to move him close enough to stun the Itofit with his lectric stick. Gorgoncha gurgled a gastric response and leaned forward, now lifting a twisty vine leg to further ensnare the Itofit and snag the little nastiness that had scratched out thirty-six of its right eyes.

Is reached for It but he was too far below her and, as the vine foot and more armicules writhed about him and fastened again on Boogie, everything seemed lost and the situation hopeless. The District Inquisitor waved his stick with delight and Gorgoncha spit a triumphant gob into the air, while Major Dhump, in a paroxysm of rapture, blew a flourish on his glove.

Toonie gasped and Is blanched, but then, from high above, came the ominous opening strains of Mister Beethoven's Fifth Symphony: Boom, boom, boom, BOOM! Boom, boom, boom, BOOM! Followed by a screeching whistle that sounded all the world like a bomb streaking down from the sky.

Lutarious twisted his head upward in time to make out, circling like a mosquito before the grim and ghastly grimace of Pulcan's Face, a little but very fierce looking gray bird who had just loosed one of two icky sticky cream pods it was carrying in its talons. The bomb, with pinpoint accuracy, hit the top of Gorgoncha's left potato eye, splattered in every direction, blinding the left potato, and sending a particularly large dollop right at Lutarious who, before he could duck or turn away, was struck full in the face and knocked down into the pulpit with the still snapping tallagator and his sparking stick. The enraged spry trap forgot all about the Itofit and Boogie and pulled its armicules away from them to swing wildly at the sky-demon. This was enough to upend the baskets that the Itofit had left atop its head, spilling their contents in a rain of snapping jaws and razor teeth on the solijers below and splashing two ripanah flish into the pulpit. And even before Gorgoncha could zero in on its swooping antagonist, the second bomb splashed into his other potato blinding it completely.

From the window, Toonie, who was very excited and until that exact moment had never known what these words meant before, cried: "Custard's last stand, and good riddance to puddinghead too!"

Dazed, the spry trap spun away and staggered across Pulcan's Toe. It steadied itself with two twisty vine feet in the puddlepond and another on the path while Lutarious wobbled to his feet and scratched vainly at his flabber gas mask, which was now glued to his head, while shaking his left hand wildly in a vain attempt to dislodge a ripanha flish.

Gorgoncha, maddened as he'd never been before, used his fourth vine leg and all his potato vines to wipe the sticky pod juice from his eyes while his armicules thrashed wildly above his head. The bird, however, having loosed her missiles, sped away and as Gorgoncha spun around in a spry trap frenzy, the agonized voice of a seemingly wounded Itofit called from the side.

"Help me!" he cried. "I'm trapped in the vines."

Hearing the voice of his accursed antagonist, Gorgoncha lurched to snare him, dash him to the ground, and stuff him into his spry mouth. But as he gurgled toward the voice, Lutarious pulled off his mask and gazed in horror at the panorama unfolding before him. "No!" he screamed. "Back beast! Back I say!" But he was too late, for the enraged spry trap having zeroed in on the Itofit's cry, was already stepping off the sheer cliff of Pulcan's Promontory with nothing before it save a tiny parrot, madly flapping her wings to hover just beyond reach, and crying like a wounded It.

The spry trap tumbled into the abyss taking Lutarious Roorback with it in a mad plunge to the canopy of bramblethorn and pricklepoke below. But as it fell, the twisty vine foot that had vainly sought to clear the potato eyes, snapped reflexively into the air, showering splashes of sticky cream pod juice in every direction, one of which slammed into Hobnail, fouling her wings, beak, and tail. And with no one to see what had happened, she fluttered helplessly behind her gargantuan victim to the jungle below

Boogie scrambled through the bars to the window in Pulcan's Knee but there wasn't enough room for the Itofit to squeeze through, so Is called to him to go the way they had through Pulcan's Right Heel but avoid the fancy entrance. "And bring the others," she cried, "as quick as you can because things are getting even worse." Toonie's horrified expression and bulging eyes alerted the Itofit to what Is meant. He swung around and steadied himself in the argyle vines as Hydraplop, whipped on by Dujge Dorque, lumbered toward Pulcan's Toe. The veggiebeast reared back on two twisty vine feet and used the others to reach out and slash at Toliver and Whizlet who, both unaware of the new danger, were valiantly fighting off more snollysolijers with the slashing arms of their philobopodendrons.

"Watch out!" yelled the Itofit but his warning was lost in the roar of the battle, and Toliver only realized the threat when a twisty vine leg reached in and plucked his philobododendron's bopping arm clean off. He slapped at two encroaching armicules with his slapping branch but the armicules tied it up like Mike Tyson in a clinch while another vine foot plucked the central flower face clean off its stem. Knowing an untenable position when he found himself in it, Toliver jumped from perch and yelled for Whizlet to do the same. Whizlet heard the call but, confident of his abilities and loath to abandon his station, pulled his bopping and poking arms up like John L. Sullivan posing for a daguerreotype and prepared to give battle. The Dujge snapped his tooth, slapped his whip, and sparked his lectric stick all at once, and leered down at Whizlet with an imperious high chortle. The ensuing entanglement was as quick as it was decisive. One twisty vine foot slapped down on Whizlet's bopping arm, three armicule enmeshed his poking arm, and another vine foot snaked up, wrapped itself around the whole lower trunk of the sentry plant, and yanked it completely from the ground.

"Yipes-a-doddle," cried Whizlet. "time to boogie!" and he leapt to the rear and raced after Toliver who skirted the now depleted puddlepond and was racing for the entrance to the monument behind it. The Itofit, however, who had scampered around through the argyle vines in escaping the seven armicules Hydraplop had deployed to snag him, now steadied himself with his feet and tail, stuck both thumbs of his right hand into his mouth, and blew as hard as he could. The resultant whistle was a very strange but very loud shriek that caught Toliver's attention just as he reached the handles of the polished doors. He spun around; saw the Itofit hanging by his tail, and using one hand to whistle and the other to frantically wave him away from the doors. And below him, running around Pulcan's Toe was Whizlet, and behind him, now looking like an upside down question mark because he was all bent over trying to grab Whizlet from the rear, was Sergeant Struddel hot on his tail.

"Over here," yelled Toliver stepping to the side and grabbing a door handle. Whizlet saw him and ran as fast as he could for the entrance but as he streaked up the steps, Toliver yelled again: "Yibble-yabble-kaboom!" and threw open the door. Inside was an ambuscade of Alabramble's latest secret weapons: a plot of lilies of the Valkyries, a spiked bed of night stalks, and a hanging box of snapping torch gingersnaps. Whizlet responded in a flash. He feinted left, jumped right, and spun around just as Sergeant Struddel stumbled past him into the ambuscade and Toliver slammed the door behind.

The Itofit was now stabbing his arm downward to show them where the secret door was and preparing to follow as quickly as he could when a twisty vine foot wrapped around Pulcan's Leg and snared him around the waist. Three armicules followed and ripped him from his perch. Hydraplop was already astride Pulcan's Toe with two vine legs steadying it below the pedestal and the fourth hanging onto Pulcan's Toenail. With both sentry plants disabled, Major Dhump and the remnant of victorious snollysolijers surged around Hydraplop and cheered as the spry trap triumphantly pulled the Itofit into the air and dangled him above its trap mouth.

"Ha ha!" gloated the Dujge. "Succulent justice, if I do say so myself. You'll feed Hydraplop for a week and make him an Itabane forever!"

As Hydraplop waved his prize for the solijers to admire, Toliver and Whizlet ran back to the puddlepond. Seeing the awful danger the Itofit was in, Toliver reached into his pocket and pulled out his magnet. He kissed it, then reared back and let fly. It sailed through the air right at the Dujge who didn't see it coming until it homed in on his iron tooth and smacked him in the mouth. He let out a roar of surprise, fell back, and in grasping for whatever was attacking his mouth, dropped his lectric stick right into Hydraplop's trap mouth where it sparked and sizzled causing Hydraplop to dance about as though it had swallowed an electric eel. It pulled its three armicules from the Itofit and dipped them quickly into its trap mouth like someone trying to pick a penny out of a pot of boiling water. It snagged the stick and tossed it into the air while its three other twisty vine feet, which, in its mad dance about the battlefield, had dispatched a number of the less agile solijers, stabilized it below Pulcan's Toe in puddles of the icky sticky cream pod juice that had splashed down from Hobnail's attack on Gorgoncha. The Itofit, who was now held only by the fourth vine leg, was swinging madly from side to side and even the Dujge had to hold on to the sides of the pulpit to keep his balance.

As the swaying of the veggiebeast subsided, the Dujge, who had never been more angry or self-righteously dujgemental in his life (except perhaps at Fasada when she told him to go diddle), pulled the magnet from his tooth and threw it back at Toliver. "You're next," he cried, "and your sidekick too! So watch and see how Hydraplop got his name while he plops your friend into his watery gulpit!" Hydraplop, who was thoroughly choleric now, steadied the Itofit once again above his mouth and prepared to dip him three or four times as an appetizer. He burbled a belch and, while the solijers, this time conducted by the gloves of Major Dhump, began a victorious crescendo of cacophonous cheering, lowered the Itofit toward a gastric doom. But just as the twisty vine leg was about to dip him in, the spry trap lurched to the side.

Hydraplop staggered crazily for a moment trying to regain his balance. The Dujge grabbed the lip of his pulpit to steady himself and looked wildly around for the source of the disturbance. He saw only the terrified faces of the surrounding solijers who feared the spry trap might topple upon them, and Major Dhump whose expression was one of utter astonishment.

"What happened?" screamed the Dujge as he scanned the horrified faces.

"Sir. Yessir, sir, y'r Dujgeboat, Sir!" shouted Major Dhump who had seen the whole episode with his own eyes but couldn't believe it at all (and decided right then, in the middle of all this confusion, never to eat so many chocolate checkers again at one sitting.) "It's a sneaker attack, Sir, a terrible toe'd terrorist, Sir, an enemy foot solijer, Sir, an insolent insole fighter, Sir, a mucilaged…"

"Shut up and tell me what's happening," screamed the Dujge bending over the lip of his pulpit.

Yessir, sir, Sir," retorted the major saluting Hydraplop's thorny belly, then pointing his gloves at one of the spry trap's now amputated vine feet. "Sir! That mossy rock just rolled up the hill, Sir, and bit off one of y'r Dujgeboat's heinous spry feet!"

The mossy rock, since it carried its own carapaced citadel on its back and was therefore unconcerned with soft solijers bonking themselves with beanpoles, ignored everyone, licked its lips, and murmured happily to itself. "Hmmm! Not bad at all, and marshmallow topping too." Delighted with this latest treat in his march across this strange land, the turtle turned to another of the vines hanging (as far as he could see) from two potatoes and a cabbage in the sky, and bit it off as well. Hydraplop sat with a thump onto Pulcan's Toe and the Dujge, finally recognizing the terrible mossy rock disguise the Satin Diabola had taken to torment him, reared back with his whip to snap the creature into oblivion, but as the far end of the whip trailed out behind him, it came within reach of the Itofit who grabbed it with his tail and yanked as hard as he could. The Dujge, holding his whip handle with a demented death's grip, was pulled backward out of his pulpit and fell like a stone into

Hydraplop's gurgling mouth, splashing heinous spry juice over the thronging solijers.

"Yowl!" cried the Dujge who, if he hadn't splashed almost all of the juice out of the spry trap's mouth, would have been digested on the spot.

"Burp," expostulated Hydraplop who realized immediately that it had never had so large or so fine a meal before (something like a Christmas stuffed goose) and, for a moment, even forgot about the terrible toe torment that was dining on it.

The turtle, however, kept on his merry way, turned to the third twisty vine leg, and bit off another tender tip. Hydraplop lurched again throwing its fourth vine leg into the air and, since it now needed it desperately for support, let loose of the Itofit who sailed over Pulcan's Toe and landed with a splash in the middle of the puddlepond. The fourth leg, while the others danced about on their now stubby tip-toes, grabbed wildly for something to anchor itself on. It slashed out desperately and wrapped itself tightly around the first thing it found. This was Major Dhump who, since his arms were pinned to his sides couldn't sound Retreat! nor call for reinforcements, went down like the Hindenburg. And because they were on the rather steep slope of Pulcan's Hill, Major Dhump did what he always did when upended, and began to roll down the hill. Hydraplop pulled back to anchor itself, but rather than stabilize the tottering creature, Major Dhump rolled up the twisty vine leg like he was a rebounding yo-yo running up its string, and the heinous spry trap, completely unbalanced, tumbled to its side and bounced down the hill. The terrified snollysolijers threw down their weapons and, rather than face any more of the horrors at Pulcan's Toe, followed in a rout behind the avalanching spry trap, preferring to take their chances with Pulcan's Protectors.

The devastation as Hydraplop crashed cabbage headlong through the Experimental Plots (dragging Major Dhump behind like a can behind a bride and groom's car) was horrendous. It cut a swath through Pulcan's Protectors, uprooting many as it went, all of whom tumbled with it, snapping, tearing, and slicing at the spry trap as they went until the whole mess came to rest by arched iron gateway to Pulcan's Hill with one potato eye jammed under the arch and the other impaled on the spiked fence beyond, and the whole of the veggiebody shredded into smorgasbord. Major Dhump was cut loose by a snapping sissorsplant and crawled to the Dujge who had been thrown clear of the trap mouth, bedraggled, besplattered, and benumbed, with his robes digested off.

The Dujge shook his fist weakly at Pulcan still grim visage high above. "Call in the tsarmy," he wheezed, "and bring on the cloud worms!"

When the Itofit sailed over Pulcan's Toe and splashed down in the middle of the puddlepond, Toliver ran to the edge and threw his emergency reserve piece of beef jerky into the water which immediately attracted the razor toothed ripanha flish long enough for It to stroke for shore and pull himself onto the bank where Whizlet was clearing a space among the remaining tallagators with the Dujge's lectric stick. Since they couldn't see what was happening on the other side of Pulcan's Toe, they raced to the secret door and slammed it behind them, then, since the latch was sawed in two, used the lectric stick to bar it firmly.

"UP HERE. Up Here, up here!" echoed Toonie's voice through the iron statue but they needed little encouragement to mount the winding stairs two or three at a time. Toonie had come back to the rotunda in Pulcan's Chest and was carrying the Itofit's hat and holding her finger to her lips. "Shssss!" she whispered. "Is is having a quiet time. But here's your hat. Hissofer saved it by not letting go when he scared Lutarious Roorback by torpedoing him in the nose and then saved himself by squiggling to Is' tail which Is had thrown out the window for him to climb up because she saw he needed help and he did so we've got it."

"Hissss," confirmed Hissofer rising up, and seeing all the world like a periscope sticking up from the conning tower of a submarine.

"And here's your feather," replied the Itofit taking the white crane feather from a pocket of his tunic. "A good feather is a fine thing to tickle your ear or rub your cheek with or scratch your chin when you have to think very hard about something."

"What's up there?" asked Toliver who always liked to get to the top of things he'd already gotten to the bottom of.

"Just the observation deck," reported Toonie, "and the barrels of flabber gas the snollygosters squirt out of Pulcan's Nose at night, but Is said we can't use that, no matter what they threaten to do to us."

"I agree," replied the Itofit, "but let's go up to the observation deck too. We can see what's happening with Hydraplop and all the solijers, and maybe see the best way to go so we can get away from them."

"Hydraplop's coleslaw," announced Toonie, "and the solijers are all running away, so we should be able to go any way we like, except every way is still in Alabramble." And her lips turned down and she started to sniff.

"Where is Is?" asked Whizlet who knew the only way to keep Toonie from pouting over their situation was to change the subject as quickly as possible. But as Toonie kept sniffing (even while she was fixing her feather back in her hair), Whizlet pushed past her and continued up the stairway. Is was standing with both hands on the railing of the observation deck with her eyes closed and her tail thrown over her shoulder. At her foot, calm as a Cheshire napping at noon, was Boogie purring loudly and washing his whiskers. Whizlet stopped and waited for the others, then whispered to the Itofit: "What is she doing?"

The Itofit, of course, knew exactly what Is was up to, but also knew it would be hard to explain to people who didn't. "She's looking for help so we'll know what to do next."

"How can she look for help with her eyes closed?" asked Whizlet who was afraid she might be looking in the wrong direction.

"She can see further that way," explained It. "And she can even sort of whisper to what she sees if they know how to listen."

"Look!" cried Toonie who had gone over to stand by Is. She too put both hands on the railing but she didn't close her eyes and couldn't throw her tail over her shoulder (but only because she didn't have one), so she'd thrown Boogie over her shoulder instead. She pointed where she was staring and everybody else (except Is who seemed very far away indeed) looked where she was pointing at six tiny objects still far in the distance.

"What are they?" asked Whizlet sounding just slightly apprehensive because he wasn't sure if what he was seeing were friendly flying saucers from *Alien Fandango* or an attack of blob dwarfs from *The Planet of the Amoebaemorphs*.

"Baloomerangs!" exclaimed the Itofit with a great deal of excitement slipping out with the word. "Is put a call out to our friends and somebody must have heard."

The baloomerangs grew larger until it was clear that the two in front were pulling away toward them, and that one of the ones in back was holding on to the tail of another with his proboscis and being shepherded by the last two to either side.

"Oh my goodness," said Is, opening her eyes and looking where the others were staring. "It's Loom and Loomi in front, and Rangi helping Rango."

"Who are the two little ones?" cut in Toonie excitedly.

"Why, it looks like Oom and Ome, the Oomer twins. They disappeared from Is just after Loom and Loomi and no one knew what happened to them either."

There was a happy honking of baloomerangs and balooms (since the six large creatures were accompanied by the flock of balooms who had come with them from It), and Snorf and Snorfa were running around on Loom and Loomi's heads respectively, then standing on their six pairs of back handsfeet and waving their upper ones to those on Pulcan's Crown. As soon as Loom and Loomi hitched their trunks to the railing, the snigglesnorfs ran off and jumped to Is and It's shoulders, sniggling and snorffing happily. Is, Toonie, and Boogie quickly climbed to Loomi's back while the Itofit, Toliver, and Whizlet clamored onto Loom. And quicker than a snigglesnorf can turn his (or her) eyes inside out, the baloomerangs had turned loose of the tower and started away.

"Where shall we go now?" asked Toliver gazing down in wonder at the carnage and confusion at the foot of Pulcan's Hill and at the sea of bramblethorn and pricklepoke behind.

"Oh my!" exclaimed Toonie throwing her hands to her cheeks. "We can't go anywhere yet. Hobnail isn't with us!"

In all the excitement, the poor little bird had been forgotten about, but now everybody looked around, scanning the sky for their heroic companion. Toliver took out his spyglass. "The last we saw of her, she was fighting Gorgoncha, and look! Down in the bramblethorns!" He focused his glass on the area of flattened jungle just below the precipice, "...that looks like what's left of Gorgoncha there."

"But where's Hobnail?" wailed Toonie, fearing the worst.

But before anyone could answer her plaintive cry, a mournful rendition of Mr. Ravel's *Pavan for a Dead Princess* wafted up from the tangled canopy below the cliff.

"Look behind where Gorgoncha crashed," said Toliver handing his glass to the Itofit. "It looks like a marshmallow on a stick."

The Itofit looked where Toliver was pointing. "It's Hobnail, all right. Stuck to a branch with cream pod juice."

"But how can we get down in there?" asked Toonie, who couldn't see what they were looking at so knew it had to be somewhere under the roof of brambletrees. Before anyone else could figure what to do, Snorf called to Snorfa, then to Oom who glided over and let the snigglesnorfs jump to his back. He peeled off like a navy bomber at the Battle of Midway and dropped to the canopy of forest, then steadied himself just above the upper thorns while the snigglesnorfs ran down his proboscis, one after the other, and Snorf hung from Snorfa until both of them disappeared into the canopy. A moment later, Oom backed off like a helicopter and rose up, with two snigglesnorfs and ball of goo dangling from his nose.

He caught up with the other baloomerangs as they headed away from the horrid iron head of Pulcan's monument. "Poor Hobnail," sighed Toonie with motherly concern but a great deal of relief. "How can we wash all that awful icky sticky stuff off her?"

"I don't think we'll have to worry about that," replied the Itofit pointing to a roiling mass of black clouds driving through the sky ahead of them. "It looks like we're all in for a soaking."

ROOTING for the FLOWER

The baloomerangs closed up into a tight formation with the flock of balooms bobbing about among them, squeaking their excited honklettes back and forth. "Can baloomerangs fly in clouds?" asked Toliver who wasn't sure if they needed a special license.

"They love the clouds," answered Is, "because clouds are all wet and bouncy. So we'll all have to hold on tight and let them bounce along with what's happening."

"Will we get lost?" asked Toonie who didn't want to, at least no more than they already were. "'Cause I think we should go back to It. At least it's safe there."

"It may be safe," replied Toliver who had a stubborn streak wider than Mucky River when his righteous indignation was righteously raised by indignity, "but it's wrong. We can't let those stupid snollygosters stop us in our search for Ludgordia. If we do, we'd be as dumb as they are, only in a different way."

"I think we should talk to Mister Wun-dur-phul again," offered Whizlet. "He warned us about trouble when we left so he'd probably know how to steer us right too."

"I'm afraid we'll have to go where the wind takes us," said Is, not wanting to put a damper on their discussion but not wanting the others to be disappointed by coming to an impossible decision either. "Because we'll have to make it as easy as possible for Rango."

"And right now we probably don't have too much to say about it anyway." added It who had just gotten hit on the nose by a very large raindrop. "But at least the clouds will hide us from anybody who might be chasing us and might even blow us out of Alabramble, of course…" and the Itofit only added this because he considered every possibility when thinking ahead, "we won't know where we are then so we might just fly back without realizing it."

"But the baloomerangs won't let that happen," said Is quickly. Hobnail was still stuck to Snorf's handsfeet so Is reached her tail over so the parrot could perch on it during the storm, then brought her tail to rest on Loomi back between herself and Toonie. In front of Toonie, Boogie settled down with all of his claws firmly griping the saddlemat, and Is leaned forward to put her hands on Toonie's shoulders.

"Hang on tight," called the Itofit putting his tail around Whizlet's waist and his hands over Whizlet to Toliver's shoulders. "It'll be bouncy, jouncy, and flouncy, and we don't want it to be trouncy too."

"Yipes-a-doddle," cried Whizlet adjusting It's tail like a seatbelt in an assaultmobile. "This'll be more fun then the purple pumice cloud in *Volcano Blizzard*."

"Or maybe less," said Toliver who had never played *Volcano Blizzard* and didn't think the swirling black clouds that now enveloped them fit completely with his idea of fun. Loomi was still right next to them but he could hardly see her through the swirling mist and the light was failing fast. He pulled his piece of string from his pocket and threw one end of it over to Loomi so it dropped down in front of Toonie. "Hold on to this," he yelled, "so we don't get separated."

The clouds got thicker, darker, and bumpier, and soon Loomi was completely lost to sight. Sometimes Toliver's string went up and sometimes it went down; sometimes it pulled his arm out straight, and sometimes went slack; and once it went up over his head and came down on the other sides, and then went down again and started to go underneath, when Loom, who felt it tickling his belly, reached over his shoulder with his proboscis and took it from Toliver. Every now and then (and sometimes even quicker) the murky darkness was sizzled to brilliant white by a flash of lightning followed by a horrendous clap of thunder, one of which knocked Toliver forward onto Loom's neck, and might have thrown Toonie completely off Loomi except that Is was holding her so tightly. And once the clouds thinned for just a moment and Toliver looked up, only to see Toonie looking down at him, and their heads were pointed at each other.

"You're upside down!" he cried excitedly.

"No, you're upside down," she yelled back, "because if we're upside down so is that duck." And she pointed at a duck who was flying between them totally unconcerned, it might be noted, because ducks take to clouds like, well, ducks to water, so whether it's up in the air or down in lakes hardly makes any difference at all, and was, as far as Toliver could make out, flying upside down too (which ducks never do). But then Loom did a barrel roll to come down alongside Loomi again, so when they finally broke out of the clouds, their little formation was still intact except there was the duck between the Oomer twins surrounding by a flock of admiring balooms. All the icky sticky cream pod juice had been washed off Hobnail, so when she peeked out between Is and Toonie and managed to stretch her wings again and shake herself off with a wonderful shivering, she felt as good as new, and whistled a few bars of Mr. Elgar's *Sea Maiden* to let everybody know how she felt.

Before anyone could ask, much less decide what to do now, the duck peeled off to the side, let out a raucous good by, and headed, of all things, toward another cloud bank some distance off.

"He's a glutton for polishment," said Toonie, quite happy they had emerged unscathed but also happy they weren't going that way themselves, even if these clouds were white.

"What's a loon?" asked Whizlet remembering what the Wun-dur-phul had told them but not sure what it meant.

"A loon is a duck with a loony voice," replied Is, "and if you're thinking what I think you're thinking, I think you're right."

"He never knows what he's thinking," said Toonie quickly who also remembered the Wun-dur-phul's parting words, but couldn't recall if he'd said 'Trust a loon' or 'Distrust a duck', and really didn't want to go back into the clouds, at least not quite yet.

"I think you're both right," agreed the Itofit, who leaned over and whispered in Loom's ear. "At least he seems to know where he's headed which is more than I can say for us, so let's trust him to be our guide for awhile."

The baloomerangs caught up with the loon just as they entered the new escarpment of cloud. This time the vapor was all white so the wonderful colors of the balooms and baloomerangs turned to pastel washes and lovely watercolors, and the bumps, when they came, were gentler and more like the ups and downs on a country road, so even Toonie was quite happy to enjoy the fun their steeds were obviously having. Two or three times they lost sight of the loon but each time their guide called out with his wonderful voice and the baloomerangs answered in song and altered course to follow. After awhile, the air grew colder and everybody's breath added a little more vapor to the chowder through which they flew, and once or twice the clouds thinned sufficiently for them to see great icy walls looming up to either side and disappearing above. And when the loon called out encouragement, her voice came from ahead but echoed from both sides as well so it sounded like a whole orchestra of very strange instruments playing counterpoint to each other. But when the air warmed again and the clouds finally fell off behind them, their guide was nowhere to be seen, but the land below was a lovely canyonlands with streams of water cascading down from the icy mountains and forming into little ponds with waterfalls at either end, and lush, pretty vegetation all around them.

The canyons led to an area of forested hills where the cataracts settled into more gracious streams winding through the landscape. The air was fresh as well as clear and even Rango seemed to perk up considerably and wiggled his tail rather smartly when the Itofit called over to him and asked how he was holding up. The Itofit, of course, was delighted (since he loved new places, especially when they were clean and beautiful); Is was elated; Toliver was feeling invigorated; Toonie, transfigured; Whizlet was whistling a Hobnail tune which made Hobnail happy; Hissofer was snoozing; and Boogie, blissfully oblivious of everybody else, had become beguiled by his tail which he was trying to wash but which, having a mind of its own, kept escaping from his grasp and darting out toward Snorf and Snorfa who were romping up and over and back and forth across the backs and bellies of the twins. Behind them the clouds rolled off showing the icy purple mountains through which they had come, forested and deep green lower down, spotted with blue lakes and streaks of white waterfalls, red cliffs, indigo shadows and glades of golden grass, and yellow canyons with their wild torrents of white water like beautiful feathers, and ahead a ridgeline with a tall grove of old craggy trees bedecked with pangifrangi flowers thrust up and waving in the breeze like the fingers of a hand welcoming them to the new land.

The Itofit pointed to the grove of trees and Is nodded, then leaned over and whispered in Loomi's ear. Loomi raised her proboscis and called out with a marvelously musical baloomerang songcall and the other baloomerangs circled behind her and descended to the high trees. Rango, Rangi, and the twins settled in some especially lush branches (where Snorf and Snorfa scrambled off and chased each other down the trunk like squirrels) while Loom and Loomi took their riders all the way to the ground. Now that they were safe again, or at least in a very beautiful place (which is almost as interesting and probably better for you), Is fussed over Loom and Loomi, fondled their proboscises, rubbed their necks, and whispered in their ears, telling them how happy she was to see them again and how wonderful they'd been in helping them all, especially Rango, and that there was no need for them to delay their return to Is any longer (because she knew that the worst thing of all for baloomerangs was homesickness). Then everyone else said thank you too and waved good by as they rose up among the branches, sang out a little encouragement to Rango as they passed, picked up the twins, and climbed above the trees where their sensitive proboscises picked up the scent of distant Is and started them off in that direction.

While Is had been tending the baloomerangs, the Itofit had been reconnoitering the ridge on which they had landed. When he came back, he called everyone together.

"I don't see any trails here," he told them, "but I believe I've found a very small footprint in the damp moss over there pointing as though whoever made it passed this way just a little while ago and went off toward that fern forest below us, so I think we might go there too. If we find whoever it was, he or she might be able to tell us where we are…"

"…and what we're doing here too," cut in Toonie who had sort of forgotten herself and knew a little help would be welcome.

"What about Rango and Rangi?" asked Whizlet who, now that he knew about baloomernappers, felt honor bound to worry about them.

"They'll be fine until Rango heals completely," replied the Itofit.

"With all these pangifrangi flowers they'll be very happy too," added Is.

"But how will we find our way back?" asked Toliver who was busily running through his pockets. "I've already used up all our thumbtacks and I don't have enough string to take us very far."

"This time we don't have to worry," answered It. "Is can always find Rangi because they have interactive intuition that lets them know where the other is any time they need one another, so while Rango is recuperating, we can explore this wonderful new place and see what it's all about and maybe even where it is."

"Isn't it here?" asked Whizlet suspiciously, slightly alarmed that maybe this was just a super virtual reality and if someone turned off the switch, Poof! they'd be someplace else altogether.

"It is indeed," responded the Itofit who always kept his feet on the ground (except when he was in the trees or riding Rango). "And so are we but it would still be nice to know where that is in relation to everything else which is how we know where we are in the first place."

"Here's another footprint," called Toliver who had followed Boogie to the mossy patch on the edge of the ridge, "and it's pointing toward that fern forest too." Above them, Hobnail had stretched her wings and taken to the air, and was now circling the fern forest and singing one of her favorite tunes, *The Waltz of the Flowers* from Mr. Tchaikovsky's *Nutcracker Suite*. The music was so light and lively that the whole group, happily united once again, danced down the hill with the Itofit, Toliver, and Whizlet in front and Is and Toonie right behind holding hands and laughing. They entered the fern forest hoping to find more footprints, but the fallen fern fronds were very springy and not good for showing any marks at all, so mostly they just kept going on instinct and hope (and that secret, happy feeling that tells you you're doing the right thing) until they came to a little pool below a spring where clear water bubbled up from the ground and ran off down the hill into a tangle of smaller ferns. Sitting by the pool was a little man with very large ears and eyes, wearing a green suit and holding a fishing pole, who, when he heard them approaching, jumped to his feet and turned around. As he did so, he pulled his line out of the water and Toliver noticed that there was no hook but rather a pretty stone neatly tied on the end. Just then a very large fly flew over the water and a big fish came to the surface and snapped it up.

"Pardon us," said It, stepping forward. "We didn't mean to surprise you. I'm the Itofit and these are my friends and we hope you might help us."

"How do you do," said the little person. "My name is Toodle Lou and I must be going." And with that he turned and hurried away, following an ant path along the stream and quickly disappeared around the next bend.

"How peculiar," said Toonie. "He ran off before we could ask him where we are or even where we're going."

"Yes," agreed Is. "Perhaps we should follow him since he certainly seemed to know where he was off to."

The little group followed Toodle Lou but he was nowhere to be seen around the next bend, so they just kept going until they came to a clearing in the fern forest, and there he was again, sitting beneath a tree with his line this time going up into the branches.

"Hello again," started the Itofit. "We didn't mean to startle you back there."

But before he could say anymore, Toodle Lou jumped to his feet and pulled his line out of the tree. "Starlings are startled and hamsters are hurried; robins are robbers and ferrets are furried, but I'm Toodle Lou so it's time that I scurried." And he ran around the tree and disappeared again into the forest. And just as he left, a very large nut fell out of the tree and a little furry animal with squinty eyes and a shovely tail popped out of a hole in the ground and scooped it up.

"I suppose we should keep following him," opined the Itofit, "since he does seem to be going somewhere, even if it's only someplace else." They set off once more and not too much further along they saw the little man again, this time sitting on a rock by a hole in the ground with the line from his pole disappearing into it. Everybody stopped and no one said anything because nobody wanted to scare him off again. Toodle Lou seemed oblivious of their presence, so while he gazed off happily into space, Whizlet crept forward, slipped into the hole in the ground, and grabbed the rock at the end of the fishing line.

"Oh dear!" cried Toodle Lou awakening from his reverie. "Something's caught me!" He dove into the air and, following his fishing pole, disappeared into the hole. When everybody came to the hole and looked down, he was standing next to Whizlet, and only coming up as high as Whizlet's elbow, and Whizlet had put the stone into his mouth, and Toodle Lou had put the fishing pole down the back of his green shirt. "Well," he said, "I must be going." And he started to climb out of the hole with Whizlet in tow.

"Can't you stay and talk to us for a moment?" asked Is.

"Oh no! I'm Toodle Lou and I have to be on my way."

"Well, you may be Toodle Lou to everybody else," said Is very politely but very quickly too, "but to us you're someone else altogether so you can stay."

"And who else might I be," asked Toodle Lou, not crossly but not with much curiosity either since he was mostly engaged in trying to pull his stone from Whizlet's gullet. Hobnail landed in a tree, cocked her head for a better look, and began whistling Ms. Beach's *Gaelic Symphony*, which perked Toodle Lou right up and he did a little jig on the spot. The Itofit, who could never resist a lively dance, joined in, and Is continued:

"All the Little People I've ever known have been named O'This or O'That or O'Somethingelse, so I think you must be Al O'Ha, which means you can either stay or go, whichever you please."

"How very interesting!" exclaimed Toodle Lou. "I've always wanted to be somebody else just to see what other people are like, so perhaps I will try it on, but just for a moment, now, unless I like it a great deal, of course, and then maybe longer, but not too long or I might forget where I was going, even if I wasn't going anywhere. What can I do for you?"

"Are you a leprechaun?" asked Toonie in amazement and already looking about for a rainbow.

"I've never leapt a can in me life," said Toodle O'Ha, "though I have been known to roll out a barrel or crack a cask, and I'm always one to tipple a tun if there's a tun to be tippled about."

"We're trying to get to Ludgordia," explained Is. "And we hoped you might be able to tell us how to go." Al O'Ha scratched his chin, then rubbed his nose, then pulled on his ear.

"I don't think I can do that at all," he said, "since you're already there, even though you may not be, but that's only true if you don't know that being here and being there are quite different things, because you can be here without being there, but not vice versa."

"That sounds very confusing," said Toonie who was generally both here and there and really didn't see a whole lot of difference.

"It's only confusing if you're confused," continued Al O'Ha, "but if you're not confused, why, you're most definitely there."

"That's very reassuring," said the Itofit, "but while we're here and there, we were hoping to speak with the Ludgord."

"In that case," replied Al O'Ha, "you'll have to speak softly and carry a big trick, because the Ludgord only lets himself be disturbed by nice people who know the trick."

"We're nice people," exclaimed Toonie. "And we're not disturbed at all. I mean except by not being where we're s'pposed to be, and I don't like people who play tricks because they're not nice."

"Not that kind of trick," responded Al O'Ha shaking his head and pulling again on his string. "A real trick."

"I know what your trick is," said Toliver who had been studying the situation very carefully and putting it all together. "You fish without a hook so you can enjoy it without having to throw the little ones back and you only catch big ones who want to be caught, and prove it by swallowing a rock."

"Oh, I'm not fishing," responded Al O'Ha. "I'm just having lunch with my friends. Anyone who kisses my kigamstone, which is a chip off the old Blarney block, gets a wish fulfilled."

"My goodness," exclaimed Is, staring at Whizlet who still had the stone in his mouth. "Whizlet must have a very big wish to make."

Whizlet's eyes got as big and as sparkling as saucers of champagne and his mouth fell open.

"Of course, I do." said he, pulling the stone out by its string, and dangling it in front of everybody. "I wish…"

"Don't say it!" exclaimed Toonie. "Until we all get to vote on it."

"But it's my wish," said Whizlet, "and I wish…"

Toonie clapped her hand over her cousin's mouth so he couldn't say anything more. "What do you think we should wish?" she asked Is.

"I think it's his wish," replied Is, "so we must let him use it as he wishes."

"It's our wish!" stammered Toonie, who often felt other people's things were hers if she really needed them, and right now she knew they really needed the right wish. While she was arguing, Boogie, who was a very curious cat, in more ways than one, snuck over to sniff the pretty stone and just couldn't not lick it too. And quicker than he could snap his claw pads, a little bowl full of chicken livers and tuna fish sprinkled with kibbles appeared in front of him.

"It works!" cried Toliver pointing at the cat who was happily munching on his snack.

"Let me try that!" cried Toonie grabbing the fishing pole and pulling it from the back of Al O'Ha's shirt. But she pulled it so forcefully that the line flew up in the air and the stone landed right on the top of the Itofit's hat where Hissofer Booshocks, who was still snoozing on the brim, stretched up and flicked his tongue out at what had landed in the middle of his dream and almost bonked him on the head. And even before the Itofit, who immediately felt the new weight on his head, could respond, a sun-warmed flat rock with a sunbeam shining on it through the trees appeared on top of his hat, and Hissofer slithered onto it and wound into a contented coil.

"My turn!" screamed Toonie yanking the pole and pulling the rock to herself.

"I wish you wouldn't be so grabby," said Whizlet, who didn't like it at all when Toonie gave him orders or stuck her hand over his mouth.

"Oh, I'm very sorry," said Toonie contritely. "I really shouldn't be so anxious all the time, but I'm sure it's a fault I could overcome if you'll all help me be nicer. Is, why don't you kiss the stone?" She smiled prettily and handed the pole to Is.

"I'm afraid it won't work anymore," said Al O'Ha who watched as an inner luminescence in his kigamstone faded away. "It has to be recharged after every eleven wishes."

"How do you recharge a stone?" asked Toliver who was always curious about technological things but didn't see any prongs on the stone or a plug anywhere to plug it into.

"Let me see, there are several ways," answered Al O'Ha. "The quickest way is to set it on the Stepping Stone to Elsewhere in the Chamber of Lord Sunstar atop the Halidome in Arigon where it was originally made, and when the morning sun is reflected from the lake through the Arch of the Condiment it will sparkle with new power, but you have to be there to do that, and if you're not there, you have to do something else."

"Wow!" said Whizlet apologetically. "That sounds like a lot of work. I'm sorry I put it in my mouth and drained all its kigam away and then made a silly wish. Can I do anything to help you fix it?"

"Yes, you can!" said Al O'Ha as he untied his stone from the line. "You can take this stone as a present to remember when I got my new name, and then help me look for another one to replace it with."

"You mean one that's already all charged up? Where do we look and how do we know when we find it?"

"We don't and we do," answered the little man. "You never know where to look but you always know when you find it, because the Ludgord lets you know."

"You know the Ludgord!" exclaimed Toonie. "That's wonderful because that's who we're looking for because we're lost because the turtle ate our flower and we have to get home and the Wun-dur-phul said we should and Rango got hurt in Alabramble where the rest of us almost got brablugged if not worse and the wind blew us here, so I guess we're lucky."

Al O'Ha looked at her with such a peculiar expression on his face that Toliver thought he might change his name back to Toodle Lou and run off again, so he quickly interrupted: "If we can find the Ludgord by looking for your stone, we'll all be happy to help you, so why don't you go first and show us what we have to do."

"Do? You don't have to do anything at all to find the Ludgord," replied Al O'Ha. "In fact, it looks like he's found the Ludgord already." He pointed at Boogie who had just finished his tuna and chicken liver snack and was now rolling on his back with all four paws stuck up in the air. He was stretching his neck to either side and snapping his tail happily on the ground, but when he noticed everyone looking at him, he became suspicious, then concerned, then alarmed, and then so anxious to be someplace else that he jumped to his feet and ran off through a hollow log by his side.

"Oh my!" exclaimed Toonie slapping both cheeks at once. "Let's hope that's not one of the six gates to Ludgordia because I don't think the rest of us will fit through it and I'd get my dress all dirty and there are probably worms in it anyway."

"Gates?" asked Al O'Ha still somewhat puzzled by Toonie. "There are no walls in Ludgordia so how could there be gates?"

Whizlet was quite sure the Wun-dur-phul hadn't fibbed to them so he quickly came to his cousin's defense. "But the Wun-dur-phul said there were…" He held up three fingers on his right hand, "…three gates to the Lud…" and throwing up the same three fingers on his left hand, "…and three gates to the Gord. And that's six gates…"

"And then the Ford," added Toonie who was remembering very hard, "but he didn't tell us why the Ludgord needed a car."

"How very peculiar," replied Al O'Ha who was quick to see when he might have offended anyone. "The Wun-dur-phul always tells the truth so he must be right. Maybe I just went around them, or didn't notice when I went through, or maybe my mother did it for me when I wasn't here yet, or perhaps I was asleep when it happened and dreaming something else, but now I think we should follow your friend because he must know where he's going or he wouldn't have gone." He jumped over the hollow log and hurried after Boogie.

The others quickly followed because they didn't want to lose sight of the little man who, without a wishing stone on his line, might not stop at all. Hobnail leapt from Is's shoulder for more aerial reconnaissance and banked sharply to the right as she saw the yellow tip of Boogie's tail weaving through the tall green grass of a little meadow on the slope below them. Since she was able to see where the cat was going (even if he wasn't, because the grass was so high) and was able to move more quickly, she crossed the meadow and landed on a branch in a tree on the far side to await his coming. While she was waiting, her sharp eyes gazed about. Ahead, through the lower branches, she saw a flower filled glade in the woods where another figure, draped in a xaalu robe, was seated upon a rock talking to some birds who were fluttering about.

Boogie had not seen Hobnail soaring above and stopped under the tree where she sat to wash the pollen off his whiskers (and wait for the others because he really didn't want to run away from them) and let out a plaintive Me-ow-I'm-here just in case. As the rest of the group came up to them Hobnail picked up the note Boogie used for his call and took it from there as a lead in to Mr. Bach's *Musical Offering*, then darted ahead to the edge of the glade.

The others were curious about what Hobnail might be telling them, so they followed as quickly as they could through the forest but stopped in amazement on the edge of the glade for an imposing figure was standing like a statue in a spot of sunlight watching them approach. He, or at least they assumed it was a he, was wearing a long xaalu robe woven of opalescent feathers with its hood pulled over his head so his face was in shadows, and his arms were crossed in front with each hand going into the opposite sleeve which were very large and hung down like cave mouths facing each other across a flowery glen. He pulled his right hand out and a wand appeared in it as if by magic and seemed to grow right before their eyes into a very long staff (much too long to have been concealed up his sleeve, or under his robe for that matter), for when he put one end on the ground, the other end towered above his towering figure. At the top of the staff, held within a twisting of gnarled roots was a bright blue jewel, so that it looked as if the staff, while still a young tree, had grasped the stone underground and once having made it its own, would never relinquish it again. The figure shook its head and the cowl of the robe fell away, revealing a craggy visage with silver hair and a beard to match, and piercing eyes so very blue (and even shining with an inner light) as to seem to be two more jewels matching the one in his staff. He threw up his left hand and the robe fell open about his chest revealing, or at least indicating since it only opened a little bit, that he was dressed as a harlequin, or at any rate in very colorful clothes.

"Oh my," stammered Al O'Ha stopping abruptly at the edge of the glade. "It's Makyo! Makyo the…ah…ah…Makyo the…ah…"

"Makyo the What?" whispered Toliver who noticed how confused Toodle Al seemed to be and was afraid he might run away.

"I'm not sure at all," responded Al O'Ha. "What day is it? Is it Bluesday or Thorsday? Because if it's Bluesday, he's Makyo the Musician, and if it's Thorsday, he's Makyo the Mighty."

"I think it's Hatterday," whispered Is.

"Oh, that's terrible!" cried Al O'Ha very softly, "because on Hatterday, he's quite mad."

"Maybe we could pretend it's Sunday," whispered Toonie who liked to pretend that pretending worked when she couldn't think of anything better to do.

"Hmmm," considered Al O'Ha rubbing his chin. "On Sunstarday, he's Makyo the Magnificent, but then he's not easy to fool. We'd be better off pretending it Scryday when he's Makyo the Magician and wrapped in illusions anyway, or Moonsday, when he's Makyo the Mendicant and takes all the help he can get."

"How about Wednesday?" whispered Toliver who never liked to leave a possibility unprobed or a day forgotten.

"Never on Whensday," responded Al O'Ha, "when he's Makyo the Menzaster spinning riddles and waiting around for things that never happen until something else does."

Makyo raised his staff, swung it around over his head; then thrust it to the fore so the blue jewel held by the gnarled finger-roots pointed directly at them.

Everyone felt a wonderful tickling as though something funny was about to happen that would make them all laugh uproariously. Hobnail, who loved shinny objects, flew to the staff and landed on the roots, and Boogie, who was getting curiouser and curiouser, ran up, stood on his back legs, licked the jewel, then dropped down looking for another bowl of treats.

"Hrumph!" said Makyo but before he could say anything more, another voice spoke up from the trees behind him.

"Oh Makyo," it said, "stop frightening the children." The voice was so lovely and so lilting that everyone peeped around Makyo to see to whom it might belong, but the owner of the musical tongue was still hidden in the forest.

Makyo too had an arresting voice, deep and resonant, with even perhaps a twinkle in it: "I am not frightening the children," he said. "I'm just tickling them to see how they glow. And just to show me how frightened they are, they're recklessly throwing their bodies at my staff and I haven't even swung back, but I shall now!" He lifted his staff once again, but not so quickly that Hobnail was unable to scramble up the bough so that, when it was once more upright, she was perched directly on top so the blue stone looked as though it was clutched in her talons. But instead of announcing her success with a triumphal aire, she peered off in the direction the second voice had come from, and sang a beautiful warbling of *The Dream of Columbine*, which seemed, by its own magic, to bring forth the person who had spoken so imperiously to Makyo. She was a tall and regal woman with long golden hair, also wearing a robe, although hers was a lovely vertul with a speckling of ivory, and opened at the front to show that she too was colorfully dressed. Instead of a staff, she was carrying a basket in which she had collected things from the forest: there were long stemmed flowers and mushrooms, three kinds of berries, some nuts still in their shells, wild apples and peaches, and little fruits that looked like dew melons. And along with all these were the furry heads of two little creatures very much like plump squirrels (just like the creature they'd seen earlier who ran after the nut from Toodle Lou's fishing tree), who helped her collect things from the higher branches.

"Oh my!" exclaimed Al O'Ha. "How fortunate for us! It's Ms. Ka'aba."

"Shishkebob!" coughed out Toonie who didn't believe that Makyo, however batty he might be on Hatterday (whatever that was), would skewer such a beautiful person on his stick.

"No no," repeated Al O'Ha. "It's Ms. Ka'aba - Trippytucatchup Ka'aba, the Lady of Ludgordia and Paragon of Arigon."

The beautiful woman came into the glade and smiled pleasantly at all of them but spoke to Al O'Ha. "Oh good-by, Toodle Lou," she said in her musical voice, "I didn't know you were here leaving."

"Yes, I'm not," replied Al O'Ha. "Because today I'm Al O'Ha, so I can stay and say hello if I like to, and I do like to, so hello to you two too." He bowed very formally, first to Trippytucatchup Ka'aba and then to Makyo.

"Why that is a lovely name," said Trippytucatchup Ka'aba. "And who are your friends, Mister O'Ha?"

Al O'Ha put his hand over his mouth and looked just slightly confused. "I really don't know, or at least I don't know their names, though I suppose they have names, but I just haven't sorted them all out yet, so perhaps we could give them all numbers, but that wouldn't do at all. They'd too soon disappear if someone subtracted accidentally, but I know they're baloomerang people who came in a flock and left a fraction nibbling pangifrangi flowers in a tallow tree, and perhaps…"

Before he could go any further, the Itofit stepped forward and took off his hat. "We're very pleased to meet you," he said. "This is Is from Is, and I'm the Itofit, and all these others are our flower friends…" He was about to start with Toonie and Toliver, but Hissofer rose three inches of himself from the center of his coil on the flat rock atop It's hat (which was growing cool in the shade) then wound down to the brim like a rainbow rolling itself up for the evening, much to the delight of Makyo and Trippytucatchup Ka'aba who observed him with a great deal of interest. As he put the flat rock on the ground, the Itofit lifted his hat so Hissofer could display his wonderful tongue. "And this is Hissofer Booshocks who is a tail to tell the truth and can attach himself to others when he wishes to. And this beautiful young lady is Toonie Petalpaper and her excellent friend is Toliver Manfellow and her cousin is Whizlet, the tamer of philobopodendrons, while the wonderful creature rubbing his sides around your legs, Ms. Ka'aba, is Spitpurrkoff, the fierce and fearsome fellow lately of the Dujge's dungeon, and the exquisite bearer of feathered song atop your staff, Mister Makyo, is Hobsong of the perfect pitch and thousand strange voices who has an unnamed egg inside who would not like to be overlooked either, and I certainly wouldn't want to overlook someone who wouldn't want to be overlooked even if they're not born yet."

"We're very pleased to meet you too," said Makyo nodding his head agreeably. "And welcome to Forests of Arigonia."

"Isn't this Ludgordia?" asked Toonie, suddenly quite fearful they might have been blown to the wrong place.

"This can't be Ludgordia," Whizlet reminded her, "because we haven't gone through any gates yet, and you know what the Wun-dur-phul told us."

"Have you met the Wun-dur-phul?" asked Trippytucatchup Ka'aba. "He's a very nice person and always perfectly honest, even with strangers and people who don't want the truth."

"Yes we did," said Toliver. "And he said we'd have to go through six gates to get to Ludgordia, but we haven't found any of them yet."

Makyo ran his fingers through his beard. "I think that is probably both true and perhaps not quite true too. As I understand it, you've already passed through a number of gates except you may not have known they were gates at the time."

"And there are really many more than six gates," added Trippytucatchup Ka'aba. "But if you get through any six of them, you know what they're like and never have any trouble recognizing the others."

"The only gate I remember," said Toonie, "was the door to the It-Fine below the tulip 'n lovable tree, and we wouldn't have gotten through that if Panoleon and Lamburtaine hadn't let us."

"And the gate to Pulcan's Paradise," cut in Whizlet, "but nobody'd go through that unless they had a screw loose or were being chased."

"Not those kind of gates," replied the Lady of Ludgordia. "These are gates in your mind that lead you to better and better places all the time."

"Quite true," agreed Makyo. "And you've already passed through the Gates of Courage and Perseverance."

"And Fairness and Trustworthiness, too," said Trippytucatchup Ka'aba.

"How do you know all that?" asked Toliver who was automatically suspicious of anyone who knew stuff about him when they hadn't even met before.

"Why, we can see what you're like," said Trippytucatchup Ka'aba. "You can't hide the colors that radiate from your body, although you can learn how to brighten them up, which you seem to have done, or make them vibrate and dance, or even play something like visional-optical music."

While Makyo and Trippytucatchup Ka'aba were explaining these interesting things, Toonie, who, unlike Toliver, was never suspicious of friendly people, had been counting on her fingers. "That's already four!" she exclaimed. "Only two more gates to go and we can talk to the Ludgord or, come to think of it, maybe we can talk to the Lud or the Gord right now since we already have more than three. Or I s'ppose we probably just have two for each and need one more for both, but how do we find the last two anyway?"

"That depends on what appears before you that needs doing and how you do it," said Makyo. "The gates appear in the most unusual places and could be most anything, and they always lead to interesting experiences…"

But before he could give a for instance, a sudden commotion disturbed the discussion. Boogie had stopped rubbing his sides on Trippytucatchup Ka'aba's legs and stood up to investigate her basket, assuming that was where the tuna and chicken livers must be. But when he tipped it toward his nose, the two little creatures jumped straight up in the air and dove to the bottom of the basket among the flowers and mushrooms. The Lady of Ludgordia stooped down to show him the basket but cautioned him.

"Be careful of my little collectivores," she said. "They're very shy and quite unaccustomed to anyone like yourself. But I'm not sure we have anything here a person of your tastes would find too interesting." The little collectivores, however, did interest Boogie so he dug down with his paw until he had uncovered them. Two tiny faces with very large eyes peered up at him as he stuck his nose down to check them out. Aware now that he was the center of attention, and knowing he shouldn't pounce on strangers in a strange basket, he hesitated just long enough for one of the creatures to grab his paw with its large, strong hands and yank so hard it almost pulled him right into the basket, while the other ran up his now outstretched arm, bopped him on the nose, jumped to the top of his head, and grabbed hold of both his ears. Boogie had undoubtedly lost the advantage of surprise by his polite hesitation, but now it was as if a bolt of lightning had struck, for he leapt into the air so vigorously that the creature holding his paw was thrown into the air and spun end over end until it landed on Trippytucatchup Ka'aba's shoulder, while the second one had the very good sense to let go of his ears and jump to the lady's sleeve and run up it to join its companion. But even then neither of them felt safe for Boogie was dancing around on his hind legs and spitting at them with all his fur standing out (so he looked three times larger than before), so they both jumped into the air, spread their arms and legs widely so that loose folds of furry skin opened like bat wings around them, and they glided to Makyo's sleeves and ran up inside.

Snorf and Snorfa, who had been watching all the excitement from around the necks of the Itofit and Is, began clapping with eight or ten handsfeet each until the two collectivores came out of Makyo's cowl by his chin, and stared over at them appreciatively.

"Come, come," said Makyo. "We mustn't start off by startling each other or we might not get over it for a very long time and miss all the fun we might otherwise have had together." He put his hand across his chest for the two collectivores to climb onto his wrist, while, at the same time, lowering his staff (slowly enough for Hobnail to scurry back down the shaft) until the far end was right above Boogie's head, then dipped it down so the blue jewel touched the cat's brow. Boogie felt the most wonderful feeling wash through his whole body. His hair flopped down as though someone had pulled its plug, and he sat with a thump upon the ground feeling utterly calm and complaisant. And while Makyo kept his staff above Boogie's head, the collectivores ran down it and jumped to the ground in front of the cat, then sat up, tweaking their bushy tails and making it so obvious that they wanted to be friends that Boogie was captivated by them (which was, of course, what collectivores did best) and soon rolled to his side and was frolicking with them when Snorf and Snorfa, who could never resist a good frolic themselves, ran down to join in the fun.

"You're a magician!" exclaimed Whizlet.

"Not really," replied Makyo. "But in Arigonia we understand the value of peace and friendliness, and we always try to avoid misunderstandings."

"I guess you've never been to Alabramble," said Toliver.

"Unfortunately, I have," responded Makyo. "Which is one of the reasons we're so careful here. Peace and perversity are like water and phosphorus. They can't exist side by side. Put them together and the phosphorus explodes, scattering the water everywhere. So to have peace you cannot be perverse."

"And you have to find peace in yourself first," added Trippytucatchup Ka'aba, "then you will also find it everywhere else."

"I s'ppose it's like your apples," mused Toonie looking in Trippytucatchup Ka'aba's basket. "If you have one rotten one it will spoil the others too." She reached in and took out a flower that looked like a chrysanthemum with golden petals. "What beautiful flowers these are, Ms. Ka'aba. They're so pretty and smell so nice. Are they for your hair?"

"No, though I do love to make bouquets and leis with them," replied Trippytucatchup Ka'aba. "We've collected these for our friend Fou d'Royant when he comes back."

"Oh my," exclaimed Al O'Ha. "Is Fou d'Royant off on another of his marvelous excursions."

"Yes, he is," replied the Lady putting her finger to her lips then pointing to a gnarled tree on the far side of the glade whose roots were all twisted and stumbling over each other above the ground. "He's been off to Ludgordia for a long time now and he's right over there if you wish to see him."

This sounded very strange to Toonie but she didn't want to sound silly by asking so she whispered to Is: "How can someone be here and gone at the same time?"

"Why that's quite easy," responded Is, also in a low voice. "It's like when you're reading a good story and you're both here and off in the story at the same time, or when you're very carefully knitting a sweater or shawl, why, the same thing can happen then, for while you're in your needles and lost in your design, you're also sitting in your chair smelling the pie baking."

"I've done that with my computer!" exclaimed Whizlet. "I can be in my bedroom and in hyperspace too, especially when I really have to concentrate on what I'm doing or get zapped all over the place."

"And I've done it while I'm running," added Toliver, "and pretending I'm Carl Lewis at the Olympics!"

"Of course," exclaimed Toonie, "I've done it." But before she could explain how, she was stopped by a lovely tune coming from the branches of the gnarled tree Trippytucatchup Ka'aba had pointed toward when mentioning Fou d'Royant. Hobnail had flown over, grasped two talonsful of thick, shaggy bark, and was perched horizontally, looking down among the knotted roots. She was softly singing the refrain from *The Child of the Enchantments*, a tune she usually reserved for herself, to whomever was below her.

The others tip-toed over and looked where Hobnail's dreamy gaze directed them. Sitting among the roots was a beautiful young man. His eyes were closed but he was smiling and he radiated a perceptible air of joyfulness and contentment.

"What's he doing?" asked Toliver in a low voice.

"Fou d'Royant is off exploring," replied Trippytucatchup Ka'aba, "but he's somatose now so we mustn't disturb him."

Toonie, however, was drawn to him and climbed among the roots to sit next to him. "What does somatose mean?" she asked.

"Why, he drank some glorningmory and 'sroom soma tea a few days ago and he's been off in Ludgordia ever since wandering through the magical reaches of his own mind and playing with the Ludgord."

"And when he comes back. If he comes back. He'll be able to tell us all sorts of wonderful things," added Makyo.

"If he comes back," exclaimed Toonie. "Do you mean he could get lost inside his own mind?"

"Not really lost," replied Trippytucatchup Ka'aba. "Just so completely enraptured with how beautiful it is that nothing else could disturb the wonderment he's feeling."

"You mean he might decide never to come back?" asked Toliver who was generally more responsible than that.

"After awhile he might just forget about his body altogether and it could drop away like a dry leaf from a tree," explained Makyo. "He's still young and quite new to this adventuring, so we like to keep an eye on him."

"We'll coax him back because we love him too much to let him go," said Trippytucatchup Ka'aba. "I suppose it is selfish of us, but he is one of the Treasures of Arigonia."

"Is Ludgordia in your mind?" asked Toonie who was trying to put it all together. "'Cause if it is, we've been looking in the wrong place."

"Ludgordia is your mind," said Makyo.

"It must be a virtual reality," exclaimed Whizlet. But when Al O'Ha scratched his ear and gave him a quizzical expression, he continued: "That's just, well, sort of a memory of a playtime somebody saved as numbers that wrap you up in their game and let you play it too just like it was as real as tomorrow and you were right in the middle of it."

"Ludgordia is as virtual as virtual can get," said Makyo, "and everybody owns it, or maybe nobody owns it but everybody has it."

"All they have to do is find the way in," continued Trippytucatchup Ka'aba, "which is why knowing about the gates is so important."

"Every gate has a kamijani guarding it," said Makyo. "They are spirit thanes with two faces, one looking where you came from and the other at where you're going."

"And as you pass through," said the Lady of Ludgordia, "for just a moment, you get to see through their eyes where you've been and where you're headed, so you can fix things even better than they might have been if you never passed that way."

"Couldn't we ask the kamijanis to send Fou d'Royant back?" asked Toliver who was always practical, even about very strange things. "They could show him us here waiting for him and he'd come back so you wouldn't have to worry anymore."

"And if he's been talking to the Ludgord, maybe he could take a message for us," opined Toonie.

"Fou d'Royant has already passed through all the gates," said Makyo, "so the kamijani are all part of him now."

"Well how can we get him back?" demanded Toonie who was getting such wonderful feeling just from sitting next to him that she really wanted to meet him and tell him all about it.

"I bet if we had one of Al O'Ha's kigamstones we could wish him back," said Whizlet. "But this one's worn out and I don't know where we'll find another..." But he stopped in mid sentence and gaped at Makyo, or rather at Makyo's feet where a beautiful stone was laying between them and sparkling with a warm radiance. He pointed at it excitedly. "Hey! Toodle Al, is that what we're looking for?"

Al O'Ha's eyes got very large. "Makyo," he scolded, "you've been hiding a kigam kissing stone all this time under your foot and if Whizlet hadn't seen it, we might have had to look all day long." He hurried over and picked it up. "What a beautiful stone," he exclaimed. "We'd have had to look all week for one as pretty as this."

Toonie jumped up and clapped her hands together. "O! Goody!" she cried. "Now I can wish for Fou d'Royant to wake up; and Is can wish us back home; and Toliver can wish all he wants for those awful Alabramblians; and Whizlet can say hello to the Wun-dur-phul as we pass; and the Itofit can wish Rango all better; and Hobnail can wish a song; and Boogie can..."

But before she could complete her wish list, Al O'Ha touched her arm and shook his head. "I'm afraid this will have to be incubated first," he said. "And that will take all day in a tree, so I'll change my name back to Toodle

Lou and go do it. But if Ms. Is doesn't mind, I'll keep Al O'Ha for special occasions when I meet more wonderful people." And he popped the stone into his mouth, waved good-by to Trippytucatchup Ka'aba, and climbed up the tree they were standing under. "Toodle-lou," he called as he disappeared among the branches above them. "I'll look for you in Ludgordia."

"Oh dear," sighed Toonie. "Ludgordia is up a tree too. I'm afraid we'll never find it if it keeps moving around like that." She shook her head sadly from side to side, then brightened as another thought struck her. "But we still have Fou d'Royant, so let's just shake him and wake him, and he can talk to the Ludgord for us."

"Shaking him won't help," said Trippytucatchup Ka'aba "But perhaps some music would. Fou d'Royant loves beautiful music."

"It might work," agreed Makyo. "But the mountain has been playing the Windfane every afternoon this week and Fou d'Royant hasn't responded yet. But perhaps if we…"

"What's a Windfane?" asked Toonie who often interrupted people when she became excited.

Trippytucatchup Ka'aba smiled at Hobnail who, at the mention of music, had perked up the feathers around her ears fluttered her wings, and sidled down Makyo's staff. "A Windfane is a musical temple played by the wind. Songbirds live nearby and always join in, and sometimes other animals as well, (We once had a passing badger play the bagflowerpipes) and the trees sigh and murmur in the background."

"The Ludgord loves novelty so he's always writing in parts for creatures passing by," added Makyo. "And Fou d'Royant loves to sing. He calls the Windfanes his concert halls and lets the Ludgord sing him too."

"Would it help if we made a little detour and went to the Windfane?" asked the Itofit.

"Where Hobnail could add her beautiful voice and maybe call your friend back," added Is.

"It might indeed," replied Makyo, "but it might be just a waste of your time too."

"We won't know if we don't try," said the Itofit, "so I think we should do it."

"Can you tell us where a Windfane is, or come with us?" asked Toliver who thought that would be the easiest way to start.

"Oh no," said Makyo. "The Windfane has to find you or it doesn't work at all, and we still have some others things to do here."

"But couldn't you give us a hint?" asked Toonie who knew that little hints were always fair when looking for hidden things.

"We already have," said Trippytucatchup Ka'aba. "And just by knowing Windfanes exist, you're more than halfway to finding them. All you really have to do is listen."

"In that case, I suppose we have two choices," said the Itofit thoughtfully. "Either we can keep going the way we were going, or go another way."

"What way were we going?" asked Toonie. "And how will we know when we get there?"

"We'll follow our intuition," answered Is who had such an interesting intuition herself that she liked to use it all the time just to see how much fun it would lead her into, and at the moment her intuition was telling her that whatever Makyo had up his sleeve was at least as interesting as his long staff with its pretty blue jewel.

Upon hearing about the Windfane, Hobnail had taken to the air and flown up above the trees. More dark clouds were rolling over the mountains, but they were still far off and she saw no need to worry about them since they wouldn't be going back that way in any case. Ahead were steep forested slopes but off to their right was a canyon snaking a tortuous way through the landscape. A narrow pathway led down through a maze of snarled trees to a large plateau whose further edge was the lip of the sheer canyon wall. The plateau was splotched with sandy patches and dotted with grass and flowers. Copses of wind-blown trees grew like stubble on a craggy face, and rearing up atop the far edge was a great pile of boulders that had avalanched from the mountain and seemed poised to tumble over the side. The boulders were stark and etched on the space behind like a haunted, castellated ruin. They were overgrown with vines and shrubs, and trees ringed the assemblage and pushed up from within. Hobnail soared over the sheer wall of the canyon, felt the refreshing breeze rolling through it, and noticed the strange formation below her. The trees were beginning to rustle in the wind, which moaned with a musical base chord as it swirled through the monument, so she called back her discovery to the others by singing *The Rock* of Mr. Rachmaninof.

"I think our intuition is calling," said Toonie who, since the Lady of

Ludgordia had told them to listen, had been doing just that, "so I s'ppose we'd better follow it."

Following the parrot's song, they wound through the maze along the narrow trail. As they came out on the plateau, they saw the pile of fallen boulders across the sparse, sandy upland, and heard a strange, low moaning as of someone calling to the spirits coming from its direction. Since the boulders seemed very much a place where a stealthy mountain cat might hang out, Boogie ran ahead to investigate, and Hobnail, who was certainly as curious as any cat, sailed above and landed in small tree pushing up among the boulders. The rest of them climbed down among the rocks strewn through the upland until they came to the perimeter of the ruin, which now took shape as a beautiful sculpture garden of windswept trees, boulders, shrubs, and flowering bushes.

"Oh look!" said Is. "Flute flowers and zither weed!"

"And tuba roses," said It.

"And harp vines," said Is, pointing to a mass of tangled foliage handing down the boulders above them."

"And basso bamboo, horn blossoms, and timpani woods," exclaimed It.

"Why there are even lyre bracken with plectrum thorns."

Both It and Is stopped with their noses twitching, grew quite serious, and used their tails to waft bits of air from several different directions to their nostrils.

"What do you smell?" asked Toliver who was also wiggling his nose but there were so many strange flowers about that all he could detect was a medley of perfumes.

"I think…" began the Itofit, "…and I'm right! Look!" He was pointing at a pair of tiny, stone-like figures who stepped from niches to either side of the pathway leading up into the boulders.

"It's Panoleon and Lamburtaine!" exclaimed Whizlet, then, upon looking more closely, "…or maybe their older brothers."

"And meaner brothers too." gulped Toonie who watched the smaller one pulling his club from his back and the taller one, whose grimace was becoming grimmer by the moment and whose menace was meaner still, spit on his spear tip and twirl his chain above his head.

"Where's the Escape button!" hollered Whizlet.

"I think we must sit down and show them we mean no harm," said Is.

"Because Panoleon and Lamburtaine only guard the It-Fine and never bother anyone who isn't bothering it." And without a by your leave she sat right down and smiled at the Fine Thanes. The Itofit sat next to her and the children huddled down to both sides while Boogie bored his way into the pile and Hobnail flapped above, completely speechless.

The Fine Thanes came up to them, the shorter went around to the left, the taller to the right and when they were both in front again, the shorter put up his club, the taller stuck his spear into the ground and hung his chain from the top, and both sat down and screwed up their faces into what might even have been smiles.

"Roink!" said the short one.

"Ribble-ribble," said the other.

"Wow!" said Whizlet. "I knew they were our friends all the time."

The Itofit's tail slid gracefully out in front of him and, along with his hands, wove a greeting in the ancient symbol language and asked if they might enjoy the Windfane.

The Thanes roinked and ribbled back for a good two minutes, punctuated here and there with more of the Itofit's waving motions. Is entered the conversation with a sweeping undulation of her tail that made everyone (at least everyone who understood the ancient language) laugh and then nod their heads up and down. Hissofer who certainly preferred this type of talk to making sounds (which his tongue was too narrow to do very well anyway) hung everything of himself (except enough wrapped around It's hat brim to keep from falling) from It's head and joined right in, which encouraged Boogie to come to the front, stand on his back feet (as he did when scratching his scratching post) and talk with his paws as well as his lovely tail which he even bristled once or twice to emphasize what he was telling them about Alabramble.

"What are they saying?" asked Whizlet who almost hated being left out of a conversation as much as he hated washing behind his ears or going to bed before the last of the groblets had been kerplunked for the night.

"They say they're Fane Thanes: temple guardians," replied Is. "The smaller one is Ponabarte and the larger is Mitour. They say the Windfane is only one of many different kinds of magical places in Arigonia." She looked carefully at the smaller one's small fingers, which were weaving their own beautiful patterns in the air. "There are also Terrafanes and Firefanes and Waterfanes and…"

"And Sunstarfanes!" shouted Toonie who just couldn't wait to remember something, "where the Lord Sunstar steps out with his stoned chambermaids!"

"Just like the Wun-dur-phul said!" exclaimed Whizlet who was glad his scaly friend had really known what he was talking about.

"Do they know where Ludgordia is?" asked Toliver who was trying to remain as business-like as he could.

"They say the Windfane is an entrance to Ludgordia," answered Is, "for those who know how to leave themselves outside and let the music take them in."

"It's a gate!" exclaimed Whizlet.

"Yes, it would appear to be," agreed the Itofit, "but Ponabarte says it is a gate to nowhere and that nobody goes through, which is why it leads to everywhere for everybody."

"And everywhen too," added Is, "so we must be on the right track. The wind from the mountain is picking up, so let's go further in and listen to this wonderful temple make its music."

Once Hobnail had ascertained that Ponabarte's net was not for her, she flew up to a harp vine and burrowed into it to where delicious looking gourds were hanging. She pecked tentatively at an especially ripe one, but jumped back when it resounded with a G-flat, then opened with a medley of overtones, and dropped seeds to a sounding stone below. Hobnail wet her whistle, as it were, with some delicious pulp-rind, listened to the rising wind as it coursed in tuning octaves through the Windfane, then sang out Mr. Mozart's *Magic Flute* so everyone would know something strange and wonderful was happening around her. The others needed no encouragement and started to follow Ponabarte and Mitour into the innards of the temple, when Is stopped and seemed to be listening very intently.

"I hear a cloth harp," she announced, "but I can't imagine who is playing such a strange tune."

Hobnail heard it too, and tried to match it to one of the Schonberg concertos she knew, but gave up the effort when the music turned minimalist and she realized how tasty the gourd was. As Is went ahead enthralled by the sounds, she disturbed a flock of balooms who had been hiding in the harp vines but now that the Fane Thanes had personally cleared the visitors, they took to the air and danced about, leading them further into the strange and beautiful temple. One of the largest of them noticed the Itofit and, knowing a twistle player when she saw one, twittered over and landed on his hat. She rolled and unrolled her proboscis several times, tweaking incessantly to the others, until she noticed that the Itofit's hatband was Hissofer Booshocks and jumped straight up in the air with a frightened squeak.

"What are they saying?" asked Toonie who noticed that the Itofit had cocked his head and was listening very carefully to every bit of the confused chatter. But before he could answer, Is called from the boulders ahead with such an ululation of surprised delight that everyone hurried to where she was. She was standing in a glade among the great rocks holding a tapestry that might have been woven by the fairy fingers of a goddess. It had wonderfully colored warps and rainbowed woofs with golden threads threaded among them and dappled silken cocoons hung all about.

"Why this is the most beautiful cloth harp I've ever seen!" she exclaimed, "and it was just draped over this bed of violalettes playing itself in the wind." She very lovingly rubbed it across her cheek and held it out for Snorfa to admire. The snigglesnorf was so thrilled with the new acquisition that she ran up to Is's shoulders and around her neck and down her back and around her side and back up to her chin and around her neck again and back to her shoulder where she gazed out at the cloth harp with twenty-four sets of handsfeet all quivering at once. As Is sat down and threaded her tail through the loops, she offered the other side to her accompanist. Snorfa took up her position on Is' breast and very delicately pulled on the lovely material and stroked the buzzing cocoons.

The excited balooms led the Itofit to a niche in the rock nearby. When he looked in to see what had them so up in the air, as it were, he too let out a cry of joy and brought out the most wonderful twistle he'd ever seen. It was a five baloom twistle with nine polished flutes of exquisitely worked diamondnut wood joined with golden bands, and silver frets adorned the gourd neck and the strings were purple twine vine. As Snorf took his position on It's chest, the first notes of the cloth harp wafted gently across the glade. The breeze picked up and swirled about, tuning the Windfane, and the balooms fluttered into position. For a moment, the Itofit listened enraptured, caught the tune Is was playing, and brought the twistle to his mouth. The melody was a light and lively variation on Hobnail's real name which Is had been looking forward to playing for her new friend, and which the Itofit, the snigglesnorfs, and the balooms picked up on immediately. Poor Hobnail who was sitting on a branch above Is' head was so surprised and delighted, and then overwhelmed, that she only managed to join in the first few notes, then fell over in a swoon. Fortunately, parrot's feet never let go of what they're holding onto, so rather than fall off the branch, Hobnail just toppled forward and spun around until she was hanging upside down with her wings dangling below and her whole face (since beaks can't do it by themselves) bedazzled with a smile, her left eye staring dreamily off into space and her right eye moving up and down, seeming to follow the dance of the extra balooms who were bobbing about the twistle.

The wind grew stronger and was channeled every which way by the marvelous sculpturing of the Windfane. It rushed through the resonant stone horns and across the vibrating vines, washed though the swaying branches and leaves of the trees and scintillated the expectant flowers, all of which began to pulsate together in a tuneful but almost discordant way until the cacophonous prelude was overcome with high joyful sounds. The rocks sang, organ pipe cactus rumbled with deep resonances, and all the unopened blossoms and brittle fingered bushes added their own special notes to the symphony. New melodies wove themselves from the vibrancy and the Itofit and Is picked up the marvelous harmonies with the twistle and cloth harp. Hobnail came out of her swoon and began to sing with her most beautiful voice, swarms of flutterbys rose from the flowers and danced on the music, and wonderful, fabulously colored birds dove and swooped in the wind, adding their own songs to the ensemble, as the Windfane displayed itself as one of the most extraordinary orchestras ever assembled, called into session by the Ludgord, conducted by the mountain, and played by the wind.

Toliver, Toonie, and Whizlet sat down and felt chills up and down their spines, while all manner of happy pictures and thoughts danced through their minds. And Hissofer, since snakes are famous for being deeply affected by music, bobbed his head and seventeen inches of neck up and down in syncopation with a baloom fluttering in front of the Itofit's hat; while Boogie sat mesmerized by the music, letting the rhythms swoosh his tail over the sand while he nonchalantly washed his whiskers, first with his left paw, then with the right, then with both at once so he looked like he was sitting up applauding (which he very probably was, but needed to disguise it because he never liked to do anything to make anybody mistake him for a human being.) The Itofit stopped playing for a moment to let the balooms change places, and Snorf, who loved cloth harp and twistle duets more than anything else (including iced sniggle bars), but had never been bedazzled by a Windfane symphony before, ran happily to the top of a nearby boulder to hear the music from there; then ran up a tree, then back down and out of sight behind a ledge of whistling wisteria. When he reappeared, Toonie was the first to see him (since, even when she was absorbed in something as wonderful as Windfane music, she like to keep track of where everyone else was), and he was sitting on someone's shoulders. The face next to him was so radiant with joy and wonder that it seemed to shine all by itself, so it took a moment and three cascading arpeggio refrains before she realized the face belonged to Fou d'Royant who had been aroused from his somatose rapture by the music and now, having found the source of it, was staring wide-eyed and in absolute delight upon them all. Toonie could hardly contain herself. She jumped to her feet and hurried to Fou d'Royant.

"Oh my goodness," she exclaimed. "We're so happy you woke up and could come. We've already met you, but you haven't met us because Shishkebob introduced us while you were home with Toes, whoever she is. So we had to come and ask the Windfane to call you so you could hear Is' cloth harp and the Itofit's twistle, and meet Snorf and Snorfa and Hobnail who are also musicians, and I'm Toonie, Petunia, really, but you can call me Toonie, and…"

Fou d'Royant's eyes were very wide and very happy. They stared directly at her as she spoke but when it seemed she might never finish, he put his finger in front of her lips. When she sputtered to a stop, he pointed first to her eyes, then to her ears, then wove his hand in a circle in the air and put it to his own lips.

"He wants you to watch and listen," said the Itofit, "because if everyone does that carefully, there isn't much need for words."

Snorf ran back to the Itofit to play the twistle again with the new group of balooms who had taken up their positions and were synchronizing themselves with the instrument and the other members of the orchestra. But now the wind had picked up and was become gusty and sharp. The sounds from the Windfane were dissonant, more brooding and ominous like a Shostakovich symphony, and even Snorfa looked quizzically at Is as she tried to keep pace with the now driving music. Is glanced at the Itofit who was himself looking at the children, all of whom were looking toward the mountains behind Fou d'Royant. Whizlet's jaw had dropped open, Toonie's eyes were getting bigger than umbrellas that someone had just popped in your face, and Toliver gulped as hard as he could to get the frog in his throat back down into wherever it usually hid. The Itofit looked over his twistle at what all the children were staring at and gulped himself. Pouring down from the mountains, through which they themselves had so recently come, were five fingers of black cloud that looked like they were attached to a hand, which was reaching out of the sky toward them. And popping out from under the fingernails of each finger were horrible wriggling creatures with stubby wings, all of which were descending toward the plateau.

The Itofit jumped to his feet. "Skyworms!" he cried.

The Fane Thanes leaped to the sides, weapons at the ready.

"What are skyworms?" quivered Toliver's voice.

"They're earthworms that get sucked up into the air by tornadoes and then get spun around and around and around until they get very long and thin, and they stay that way until a hurricane comes along and bloats them up into dirigiblobs. After that, they bore through the sky the way earthworms bore through the ground." said Is.

"And eat clouds and swallow lightning and sneeze thunder," added the Itofit.

"Are they dangerous?" asked Toliver, who knew that just because something looked frightening didn't necessarily mean it was, even it you ought to run away anyway.

"They weren't at first," said Is. "They were just shy creatures who only came by when everyone else was inside staying out of the rain."

"But then the Warpingtonians got hold of them and crossed them with ferocious fen slugs and changed them into killer dirigiblugs," added It. "And that's what these are because they aren't hiding in the clouds."

"…and they're in the flying tooth and jaws formation." added Is.

"Why are they coming after us?" wailed Toonie who had had quite enough fright for one afternoon already, thank you.

"The Warpingtonians sell them to anybody who promises to use them against people the Warpingtonians don't like." explained It.

"Or against people who don't have any rasputniks to buy their own." added Is.

"Or they give them to people who build belching smog factories at home but keep their rasputniks in Warpington."

"Or use Warpington vawyers to keep the Glibriches on their side."

"Like the Alabramblians," concluded the Itofit, "who must own these, 'cause look!" He pointed to where the skyworms had landed, opened their ghastly mouths, and were discharging phalanxes of armed and armored snollysolijers and syffers who were advancing toward the Windfane with maces and axes and whips, and clubs and spears and chains, and slings and arrows and bows, and nets and cages and cagues, and nasty, leering, spit-dribbling faces.

The Fane Thanes who were very much smaller than even the smallest of the advancing legion hurried out to meet the enemy without flinch, flicker, or fear. Hobnail fluttered above hoping to sing them some encouragement, but all she could manage was a falsetto rendition of Mr. Tchaikovsky's *1812 Overture* with hiccups for the cannon blasts.

"How brave!" swooned Toonie, "but how hopeless." And she buried her face in Is' silky fur and began to weep, thinking again of Brambleham Park, of Brablug, and a gleeful Odiferous. Fou d'Royant climbed to the top of a flat boulder and sat with his legs hanging over the side, still smiling, still wide-eyed, and also, thought Toliver, oblivious of the danger. But Toliver clamored up next to him anyway and, feeling better, sat down to watch.

The Alabramblians fanned out into a half circle and roared and screamed to distract the temple guardians while moving to encircle them. But the Fane Thanes stood their ground and only stepped three paces apart so they wouldn't get into each other's way during the fight.

"Roink!" said the smaller to the taller while rubbing his club on his thigh and checking the hitch on his net, which was slung over his back.

"Ribble-ribble," replied the taller, spitting on his spear tip and hefting his chain.

Suddenly a bugle call rang out, sounding the charge, and the attack came simultaneously from the front and both sides. It was coordinated by a colonel in back with a chest full of metals, gold draped epaulettes, a shiny silver helmet, binoculars around his neck, a baton in his hand, and a bugler at his side. He was surrounded by two lieutenant colonels, three majors, five captains, seven lieutenants, thirteen second lieutenants and the mess sergeant, all of whom also had binoculars around their necks except the mess sergeant who had a pitcher of tarminis. The first wave rushed in, only to be driven back by the wildly swinging club and whirling chain of the guardians; a second wave drove in and a third, only to be similarly driven back. The colonel barked at a lieutenant colonel who barked at a major who barked at a captain who barked at a lieutenant who barked at the moon while the second lieutenants did a war dance, the bugler sounded the Kamikaze Thrill Trill, and the mess sergeant poured everyone a drink. A contingent of syffers formed themselves into a Deathshead Wedge and charged again while the five captains threw their tarmini glasses at a rock pile that looked like a fireplace and ran back to the agitated skyworms. As the Deathshead engulfed the guardians a huge cloud of dust arose from the melee from which screams and groans and horrible shrieks issued forth. The dust formed into a swirling whirlwind by the twirling of Mitour's chain and the whirling bonking club of Ponabarte, and when it cleared the syffers had fallen back, only to make room for a light brigade of snollysolijers.

As the light brigade moved into position, the bugler trumpeted a call that sounded very much like an air raid siren, and the skyworms, each now commanded by a captain, took to the air and roared toward the guardians with their giant mouths agape and dripping with teeth. The bugle sounded again, and, coordinating its movement with the legions of the air, came the charge of the light brigade. While Ponabarte readied his net for the worms and his club for the solijers, Mitour glanced back at the Windfane. Fou d'Royant had gotten to his feet and was swirling his hand in the air by his ear, then threw it forward as though launching a spear. Mitour turned back to the skyworms, dropped his chain by his foot, and spit on his spear tip. And taking aim along his other arm, he cast his glinting javelin into the sky.

"Oh dear," cried Toonie who was still clinging to Is but watching too. "He only has one spear and there are five dragons! And look! He's missed them all!"

And she was right, for Mitour's spear darted through the air high above all the charging skyworms, but just as it reached its apex, Fou d'Royant snapped his fingers, and the spear exploded into a dazzlement of lightning and a ear-thumping clap of thunder. The shock was so great the worms could not possibly swallow the lightning or sneeze away the thunder, and shriveled instead until they were no larger than earthworms, which fell to the ground among the officers and bore their way into the earth as quickly as they could. The dust-devilish whirlwind at the site of the melee seemed for a moment to resolve itself into two gigantic figures, who looked like projected images of angry Fane Thanes in a towering fit with a perfectly coordinated club and chain slicing and swishing and slamming through the enemy. The phalanxes broke. The solijers and syffers, to the last frightstruck fighter, threw down the arms and rushed away from the battle, overrunning the colonel and his tarmini entourage who resisted for only a moment before joining the retreat and scuffling as quickly as possible in a rout toward Alabramble.

"Wow!" exclaimed Whizlet. "If you patented Ponabarte and Mitour you could probably put ole Warpington out of business!"

"Or at least until they got religion," added Toonie who thought that was probably a good thing to have for a rainy day when there might be some dirigiblobs around.

The Fane Thanes were busily gathering up all the discarded weapons of their erstwhile opponents and throwing them into a huge pile on the site of the battle.

"What are they going to do with all those awful things?" asked Toliver who figured the guardians didn't need them themselves and was hoping they wouldn't sell them to anybody else.

"They'll make a fire of all the wooden ones." explained the Itofit.

"And melt down all the metal ones." added Is.

"And drink the molten brew for dinner."

"And make a ball out of all the indigestible parts."

"And sling it all the way back to Smugsmog City where the people will take it to be a grim reminder of doomsday."

"And probably put it on a pedestal in Brambleham Park," concluded Is, "facing away from Arigonia."

Everyone had been so engrossed in the engagement they hadn't really heard the Windfane's martial music that accompanied the furious Fane Thanes into battle, but now the wind, which had dispersed the black clouds, grew more tranquil and played a pastoral to soothe its creatures and return its environs to the serene elegance of the mountains. Even Toonie felt calm enough to let go of Is and went up to Fou d'Royant.

"Excuse me if you don't want me to talk," she said as apologetically as she could, "but it's the only way I can say what I want to say since I don't have a tail." She hesitated to let that sink in and hoped that he wouldn't put his finger in front of her mouth again, then continued. "Thank you for waking up and coming over, but…ah…well…we're trying to speak to the Ludgord and hoped you could help us, 'cause Shishkebob said you and he are really good friends…"

"We're trying to get home," said Is who had come over with Toonie. "The Itofit and I would like to get back to It and the children are even much further than that from where they live…"

"So far that probably only the Ludgord can help," added Toliver.

"Unless we could borrow Ponabarte and Mitour and go back to Alabramble first," piped in Whizlet who hated to leave unfinished business behind, "and then talk to the Ludgord like the Wun-dur-phul said we should."

Fou d'Royant looked at them all, put his hand to his face, and nodded agreeably. Then he turned and led them to the far edge of the Windfane and pointed to the river flowing through the canyon below. He looked at them expectantly and when nobody offered any objections started off along a trail that headed down into the abyss.

"I think he wants us to follow him," said the Itofit. "But let me put this lovely twistle back in its niche before we go."

"And I'll put the cloth harp with it," said Is. "Because I wouldn't want to leave it out where it might get rained on."

Fou d'Royant came back and shook his head, then indicated with his hands that they were to keep the instruments. He went to the niche where the twistle had been, reached in, and brought out two goose-feather bags. He gave one to Is for her cloth harp and the other to the Itofit for the twistle.

"Maybe he's taking us to a Waterfane," suggested Toonie looking first at the waterproof bags and then at the steep trail to the river. "But I wish he'd invite some baloomerangs too to get us down there."

"It is a shame we don't have anything to give in return," said Is. "Because it would be nice to leave something that Ponabarte and Mitour could remember us by."

"I have a seed from your talapalodion tree," said Toliver rummaging through his pocket and pulling out the talapa nut he'd gotten at the basket house.

"What a fine idea," said the Itofit. "We can plant it on the site of the battle to commemorate the prowess of the Fane Thanes."

"And it will get bigger than all the other trees," mused Whizlet who remembered how huge the talapalodion tree was. "Maybe some baloomerangs will come to live in it and be company for Ponabarte and Mitour."

They went to the site of the battle and the Itofit explained to the Fane Thanes what he wanted to do and asked them to make sure it got enough water until its roots were deep enough to fend for itself. They were very excited by the idea and gathered up all the captured spears, then used them to construct a real picket fence around the spot where the seed was buried, and, when Is explained how big and how pretty the tree would get, roinked and ribbled their delight and invited everyone to come back and see how it grew.

Fou d'Royant waved good-by and led the others to the steep trail to the river, while Hobnail sailed above singing a calumpety, bumpety version of *The Grand Canyon Suite*. Although the air was fresh and the view magnificent, the trail was narrow, rough, and scary, and while everyone went in single file behind their guide, Toonie, who found it more awful than awe-inspiring, held onto Is' tail. And Boogie, who didn't mind the trail but saw the river ahead and hoped to change everybody's mind by being stubborn, sat down and washed his whiskers. When that didn't work (because everyone was too concerned watching where they were stepping to notice his defection), he hurried along behind, pretending he was a mountain lion and hoping he wouldn't have to be a sea lion too.

His fears were well founded, however, for the trail ended at a small, sandy beach tucked in between two towering walls of sandstone and granite. There was only room enough for a few canyon bushes and a tangle of wild grapes climbing the rocks, so it looked like a very peculiar place for Fou d'Royant to have brought them, until their silent guide motioned the Itofit into the bushes to help him pull out a giant pod-pontoon raft. The pods were closed long their upper sides and looked like canoes while the floor between them was a basket-weave of vines firmly affixed to their insides. Basket-like rails extended across the front and back and stem-posts for the passengers to hang onto jutted inwardly from the pods. There were no oars for any of the passengers, but a rudder and tiller carved from a single root was pivoted in the back and projected over the rail, and little root loops hung from the tiller for the steersman to put his wrist through. Fou d'Royant showed everybody where to sit and made sure that the root loops hanging from each post were securely around their waists while Hobnail found a perch in a large vine in front which stood up like the proud prow of a Viking prowler. Only Boogie refused to be tied by a vine and lay down between everyone in the middle of the raft, poked his head up like a sphinx, and dug his claws into the floor. After the Itofit and Fou d'Royant pushed them out into the stream, however, It took his seat and settled Boogie on his lap so they could intertwine their tails, which Boogie felt was quite the nicest way he'd ever been held, and Fou d'Royant took his place standing at the tiller.

The current was swift but smooth, the wind was at their backs, and Fou d'Royant seemed well practiced at the rudder for he kept them to the middle of the stream with the high cliffs pushing up like the battlements of a great castle to either side. Soon, however, waves began to form and the raft dipped and shot ahead as it surfed along their tops. The raft came to a cataract with large rocks projecting up on both sides with flumes of dashing water between them through which their helmsmen steered with great skill, and though they bounced about a great deal and got thoroughly sprayed by the cold water, the pod raft held its own until diving into a whirlpool and spinning around so violently the Itofit's hat flew around and around (almost unwinding Hissofer who was having a marvelous ride because he was experiencing the river as a great snake slithering through bumpy terrain) until It pushed his hat more firmly down and held it in place. Soon the canyon widened out again and seemed almost like a lake along which they gently drifted and Hobnail, feeling she wasn't needed in the parrot's nest (she refused to refer to such things as crows' nests) rested on Is' shoulder and enjoyed the breeze ruffling her tail feathers from behind. Whizlet asked if he could steer for awhile and Fou d'Royant stepped to the side and gave over the tiller. Toonie wiped the water off her white feather and Toliver took out his spyglass to look at the nests of canyon birds which were built on ledges and in niches of the canyon walls and from which curious nestlings gazed down upon them while their parents soared about calling to each other in the wind.

Soon, however, the current picked up again and from far ahead a roaring sound echoed from both sides of the canyon. Fou d'Royant took the tiller from Whizlet and tightened the root loops around his wrists. Toonie put her feather inside her blouse and the Itofit took off his hat and wrapped the root loop that Boogie had disdained around it. He wedged the hat firmly between his leg and the pod, right next to the cat who, being drenched already and therefore in no mood to be trifled with, looked with a baleful eye upon Hissofer who was having such a fine time that he had stuck himself up like a periscope and was staring down the river.

The terrible roar became louder and louder and Toonie, just before it got so bad she feared no one might hear her, yelled out to Is:

"That sounds like a waterfall. Do you think we're going to go under it… or…or…oh my goodness!" Her worried tone was brought on by the fact that she couldn't see ahead anymore for a mist rising from the agitated water was forming in the canyon and obstructing her vision; and the current was getting markedly swifter; and the water was bouncing along as though it was going over a washboard; and the air was roiling about like the turbulence they had encountered in the black clouds; and the noise was deafening; and Hobnail, now once more safely above them but only barely visible through the foggy spray, was bouncing about and wildly singing something she couldn't even hear. Fou d'Royant kept them to the middle of the river but it was obvious that he could do nothing else to save them from what was ahead, for their raft was now racing along at breakneck speed and plunging deeper into the angry, swirling fog. They all realized that the waterfall they were hearing was not coming down to either side but was, in fact, what they were about to go over, and they hadn't a chance in the world of going anywhere else. But Fou d'Royant stayed the course, and just as the roar became unbearable and the current shot ahead like it was blasting from a hose, the top of the pods opened and willowy, feather-like appendages streamed out and were caught by the now furious breeze.

The raft lifted from the surface of the river and sailed ahead with the wind. Below them they saw the water suddenly fall away and plunge in torrents into a great chasm just as they themselves were completely swallowed in the fog. From ahead and now below them they heard Hobnail whistling Mr. Janacek's *In the Mist* like she really meant it, but a moment later they burst from the fog as though stumbling from a smoky room. Behind them, the river plunged over the edge of a vast escarpment and fell for a thousand feet before crashing to a great ledge, then bounding into rainbowed spray that plummeted to a wide river below. And ahead of them was the most beautiful vista they had ever seen.

Far in the distance was a great blue expanse of ocean and the mountains from which they flew curved around to either side and descended in craggy ridges to the water. The valley between was a land of rivers and lakes, of rolling forests and grassy plains dotted here and there with great pinnacles of rock, which were thrust up like gnarly fingers through the sands of time. The pinnacles were sometimes sharp and steep with cuts and cleavages; sometimes rounded with soil enough for wind blown trees to cling to their sculpted sides and summits; sometimes veined like polished jasper or translucent like agate. Their raft-kite floated like a feather over the valley, dancing with every breeze, while Hobnail soared ahead singing *The Triumphal March* from Aida to a legion of resplendent birds who swooped and serenaded through the air around them. Occasionally a breeze would sweep up from below and raise them higher but they were continually driven forward toward a particularly large lake within which was an enchanted island. The island was a lush, jungly garden from whose center rose the largest and most beautiful of the valley's pinnacles. It was carved by the ages like fine jade and its top opened like a lovely flower to the sun. Beyond the lake, clustered between it and a small, rocky bay with a wide channel to the ocean, was a city of old stone and wooden buildings. The town was dotted with parks, and many of its streets were canals, all of which were lined with flowery walkways and arched bridges. The canals formed an island in the center of the town which was also a garden with strange and beautiful buildings thrust up among the trees.

The raft-kite fluttered toward the lake and settled in the shallows among a water garden of lotuses and lilies. Hobnail resumed her perch while singing Mr. Debussy's *Isle of Joy* but a moment later, when ripples among the lotuses told of the arrival of some underwater creatures, she leapt back into the air, circled the approaching denizens, and changed her tune to *The Golden Fish*. A moment later, the backs of the creatures could be seen by those on the raft, and they were indeed golden except it was an iridescent gold shimmering with medleys of colors. The fish pushed their heads above the surface and looked at those who were looking at them. Fou d'Royant smiled bouyantly and pointed to the beautiful island with its towering pinnacle. Several of the fish swam under the raft, lifted it on their back, and moved it carefully out among the flowers of the water garden, and then, more quickly, toward a beach on the island at which their guide had pointed.

"I wonder if that beautiful island and mountainrock is the Hallidome of Ludgordia," whispered Is.

"It could be," replied It. "The Most Able It said it rose from the depths and reached all the way to heaven with the Fanes helping everyone up."

As they approached the island, everyone felt very happy as though welcoming emanations from the magnificent pinnacle were overflowing inside them. Fou d'Royant and the Itofit pulled the raft onto the beach and the rest, following Boogie's lead, scrambled ashore. A combination of the sunlight and the breeze as they descended from the mountain had dried their clothes, so Toonie took out her feather and put it back in her hair and Whizlet, always enterprising, looked about on the stony beach for another kigamstone. Toliver stood looking at the great mountainrock that dominated the island and could see steep pathways up its side that often went into tunnels in the rock, only to come out again further up. The higher reaches of the pinnacle were wrapped in clouds and looked like a wonderful flower in full bloom with four petals opening out and what looked to be a diamond-tipped stamen poked up from the top.

Fou d'Royant motioned for them to follow, but they had gone no more than twenty or thirty yards through the lovely garden when Is' nose perked up. Toonie who was quick to notice things like that asked immediately what she had smelled. "I believe it is Ms. Trippytucatchup Ka'aba," replied Is, "for she was wearing that wonderful fragrance that seems also to be coming to us on the breeze. And look! There she is again."

"My goodness," exclaimed Toonie. "How did you get here before us? We steamed and flew almost all the way."

"Don't forget the Windfane and the skyworms," reminded Whizlet, seeing that his cousin had probably forgotten the delays they had undergone since separating from the Lady of Ludgordia.

"Makyo and I knew there wouldn't be room for us on the raft, so we came a different way," replied the lady. "but welcome to town of Arigon and the Isle of Blissful Blazes."

"Where are the fires?" asked Toliver looking around in some confusion. "I don't smell any smoke and everything looks too green to burn."

"There are many blazes on the island," said Trippytucatchup Ka'aba. "There are fires and flames sculptures in the Firefane inside the Halidome, and out here our sunstar sparkles in a thousand different ways and all the colorful birds and flowers are little blazes of energy too."

"And so are the lizards," exclaimed Whizlet pointing at a rainbow-hued creature which had climbed a tree behind the lady and was watching them curiously from an overhanging branch.

"Yes, we have flaming geckos, torchback chameleons, and many other kinds of friends you probably don't have names for, but you will find them all interested in you and interesting to talk to."

"Is Makyo here too," asked Toliver, "because we got attacked by skyworms and snollysolijers from Alabramble when we were at the Windfane, and he probably ought to know 'cause they're still running around somewhere up there."

"Yes, we saw them coming and watched what happened when they decided to bother the Fane Thanes. We've closed the passes so they won't be able to find their way back to Alabramble and after awhile, when they get tired and hungry, they'll stagger out and we'll pick them up."

"What will you do with them then?" asked Whizlet who sort of hoped that Arigonia didn't have dungeons too, but realized you sometimes needed them for people who hurt others.

"We'll send them home," replied Trippytucatchup Ka'aba, "on the condition that the Alabramblians send all the baloomerangs and other things they've stolen from others back where they belong, and promise not to bother us anymore."

"But what about us," asked Toonie. "I think they want us and we still have to go back the way we came, and that means…"

"You won't have to worry about that," said the lady.

"You mean we can talk to the Ludgord and he'll take care of everything?" stammered Whizlet excitedly.

"Why yes, that's exactly what I mean," replied Trippytucatchup Ka'aba, "because the Halidome is a place where it is easy to do just that."

"If you know the secret," interjected Toliver.

"There's no secret at all. You just have to be good-hearted and willing to listen. The Halidome will do the rest."

"Does the Ludgord live in the Halidome?" asked Toonie who felt that they might finally be getting somewhere with their explorations.

"Heshe lives everywhere," replied the Lady of Ludgordia. "The Ludgord is like the breeze. Although we can't see it, the trees weave its mystery with their branches, or like the air whose praises we hear by watching the birds riding upon it."

"Or like the beautiful Windfane to which you sent us," said the Itofit, "which makes music all the time, even when no one is there to hear it." He handed the goose feather bag with the twistle in it to Trippytucatchup Ka'aba. "We found these beautiful instruments among the boulders. Fou d'Royant indicated we should bring them with us, so I'm very glad we found you to give them back."

"Fou d'Royant meant they are yours to keep," replied the lady, "because they were made to belong to those who could play them so beautifully." She turned to Is. "And the cloth harp is for you and Snorfa for you've shown that it would not be so happy anyplace else."

"Why thank you," said Is. "I'm sure the cocoons have wonderful flutterbys. Perhaps, some we don't have in It." While she was speaking, one of the cocoons burst open and a lavender and vertul flutterby fluttered out, circled the group, and wafted off past Fou d'Royant's head. Fascinated, Fou d'Royant followed. Toonie, who was not about to let Fou d'Royant wander off by himself, hurried after. One of the collectivores from Trippytucatchup Ka'aba's basket jumped out and followed too, and Boogie went behind the collectivore knowing that anything was more interesting than standing around making noises.

Whizlet yelled "Yipes-a-doddle! Wait for me," and hurried after his cousin.

"I suppose we ought to go that way too," said the Itofit to Trippytucatchup Ka'aba, "or your beautiful friend might get lost."

"Fou d'Royant can't get lost," said the lady, "because it never matters to him where he is, and one place is as good as another, but he's going toward the Halidome anyway, so let's follow him."

Flutterbys neither leave nor follow trails but trust the breeze and visit what flowers they like, so the whole group was led on a wonderful wandering through the copses and glades of the Isle of Blazes. Here and there they saw animals that looked like little deer, antelope, and ibexes who stopped their grazing to watch them pass. At one point Fou d'Royant stopped abruptly, sniffed the air, and turned off to the side toward a dark thicket.

"Oh dear," cried Toonie. "That isn't the way we're going at all. The flutterby went that way. Fou d'Royant! Fou d'Royant! This way! This way!"

But Fou d'Royant ignored her call and kept on until he disappeared in the thicket with Boogie bounding behind, Hobnail gliding above singing *Scenes from Childhood,* and the two collectivores (who knew that Fou d'Royant had a wonderful nose for collectables) scurrying to both sides, picking up nuts and truffles which they stuffed into their cheek pouches. The collectivores were quite right about Fou d'Royant for even he stopped long enough to pick some beautiful flowers and luscious grasses and peel some orange lichen from a rock before going on. This gave everyone else time to catch up with him and follow him very quietly through the thicket (for he was moving on tip-toes and had turned back long enough to put his finger to his lips). He stopped when he came to a doe, who had just given birth to two fawns and lay with them in the grass. She was not at all alarmed when Fou d'Royant came up to her and put what he'd collected right by her head, and the collectivores did the same and, when their pouches were emptied, hurried off to secure more. The doe nibbled at the lichen and ate a truffle while the fawns stared at everyone with very large, trusting eyes.

Trippytucatchup Ka'aba took the nicest things from her basket and lay them on the ground.

"Oh my," said Toonie. "I should have brought something too!" She looked around then pulled the white crane feather from her hair. "Here," she said delightedly. "A present from the sky for your beautiful babies." She lay the feather on the ground between the twins.

"And they can have my kigamstone too," said Whizlet laying it down, then turning to the Itofit. "But tell them with tail-talk that they'll have to recharge it."

"I should have something too," said Toliver who dug down and rummaged around his pocket while his mouth twisted into a thought-compelling shape and his eyes crossed as though he was looking at a fly on the tip of his nose. But before he could find whatever he might have been searching for, the doe looked at Trippytucatchup Ka'aba and bleated softly. The lady picked up the feather and kigamstone and gave them back to Toonie and Whizlet.

"That was very nice of you and your gifts were very much appreciated by our friends, but they aren't the sort of things they can carry with them so she asks me to thank you and give them back because the feather looks so pretty in your hair and the touchstone is made for a creature with hands."

Fou d'Royant put his hand on Toliver's arm, shook his head, and motioned for him to follow. They started off again through the woods and he led them out of the thicket, across a flowery glade to the far side of a meadow where two gnarly old trees had grown up together; not just side by side but entwined and twisting around each other so that some of their branches had grown into one another and the bark from one melded into that of its neighbor.

"O! How very nice," said Trippytucatchup Ka'aba. "A beautiful pair of tolive trees with blossoms and fruit."

"Tolive trees!" stammered Toliver. "I've never even heard of such a thing." He bent over and picked up two ripe berries that had fallen to the ground. "Can we eat the fruit?"

The berries looked like crabapples with puckered skins. One was colored scarlet and the other purply-blue and both were firm and looked delicious. Toliver was about to taste the red one but Fou d'Royant touched his hand and shook his head.

"They can't be eaten until they've been properly pickled," explained Trippytucatchup Ka'aba. "They have to be put in a wooden cask of wine for one full moon cycle and then they're ready."

"What kind of wine?" asked Toliver who knew there were all kinds of fine vintages although he'd only tasted a few himself.

"Any wine will do," replied the lady. "But each gives a different result. A sweet wine does one thing, a dry wine another; red wines are pungent and saffron wines, lusty. Green wines are slightly sour and bubbly blue wines make them tangy."

"We'll need a lot of fruit to try all those," said Toliver. "Maybe I can plant these so we'll get enough to find out what everybody likes best."

"Yes you can. The red fruit is a boy tree and the purple fruit from a girl tree. If they are planted near each other they will grow together just like their parents and make the finest fruit imaginable." Toliver took his red bandanna from his pocket and very carefully wrapped the two berries together and put them safely away.

"Thank you, Fou d'Royant," he said, but the young man just smiled and turned away to climb over the tangled roots of the tolive trees. This time Hobnail had anticipated him and gone off that way herself. She was now some way ahead but they could hear her delighted whistling of Mr. Eldest Bach's *Fantasia* so Toliver was sure she'd found something quite extraordinary, and the collectivores, who had certainly never heard *Fantasia* before, ran up a tolive tree then jumped off to glide through the woods to be with the lovely bird who sang so sweetly. They too had lovely, cooing voices and called ahead for Hobnail (who they'd really taken a fancy to) to wait for them. The parrot, being a real bird and not just a creature lucky enough to be able to soar about on folds of skin, came back and did two loops and an Immelman around them, then fluttered before them and sang an invitation for one of them to land on her back and fly with her up above the trees where the great Halidome of Arigonia reached toward the sky. A moment later she came back for the other and all three of them glided about and were soon joined by other birds who had been attracted by Hobnail's song.

Fou d'Royant clapped his hand with delight watching them and hurried ahead to a clearing whose grassy slopes lay like a shawl about the shoulders of the Halidome. Makyo was there, sitting on a rock with his staff propped up by his side. Fou d'Royant sat down beside him and all the others did the same. The Itofit took off his hat and as soon as he laid it on the ground, Hissofer slide off and wound to the top of Makyo's staff to investigate the pretty blue stone. The collectivores glided to Trippytucatchup Ka'aba where Boogie had curled up on her lap with his chin on his tail, and Hobnail landed on Is' shoulder singing a very pretty rendition of *Love the Magician*.

"I'm very glad to see you all again," said Makyo. "As you can see, finding the Halidome of Arigonia was not so difficult after all."

"Arigonia," stammered Toonie sadly. "I thought it must be the Halidome of Ludgordia, but if it isn't, I suppose we can just keep looking."

"It is that too," said Trippytucatchup Ka'aba, "because Arigonia and Ludgordia are closely connected."

"There are many Halidomes of Ludgordia," said Makyo. "But only one of them is also the Halidome of Arigonia."

Fou d'Royant gazed at Toonie with his lustrous smile and with his hands wove a picture of what the Halidome was like. They started far apart then came together and spiraled up with the fingers on both sides moving in their own separate patterns, weaving a tapestry of finger-rhythms before her eyes, saying that the Halidome of Arigonia was as magical and wonderful a place as ever there was. His large eyes seemed to look so deeply into hers that she wasn't sure if he was him or another part of herself that she was just now discovering for the first time. Then he spoke, quite softly but everyone could hear, for his voice was as resonant as his face was radiant.

"Ludgordia is the Ludgord. They can never be separated. It is not a place like Arigonia or It or Is. Although it isn't different from any of them either, and is neither close by nor far away, for it is everywhere you are. It is much too wonderful for words so I couldn't possibly describe it, but when you learn how to get there…why, it has been right here all along."

"Ah!" said Toonie feeling wonderful herself because Fou d'Royant had finally spoken to them (and she'd been the one to get him to do it). "How do you learn how to get there?"

But Fou d'Royant just smiled again and very carefully put his finger to his lips.

Toonie looked so disappointed that Trippytucatchup Ka'aba whispered to her:

"Fou d'Royant once told me that our mind is like the sky in which thoughts are clouds," she said. "Most clouds are quite ordinary but some are really impressive. They're huge and filled with lightning and thunder, sleet and rain, while some are puffy and white, some gray, some black, but all of them, even the frizzy ice clouds way high up, are really quite close to the ground. Why, some of them are even on the ground and when we're thinking them we're in a real fog, but the sky itself goes on and on and on forever."

"Maybe Hobnail could understand all that," sniffed Toonie, "but Fou d'Royant didn't tell us what to do."

"I think he means you've already learned," said Makyo. "Since you've passed through two more gates, you know exactly how to go on."

"What gates?" asked Toliver.

"I bet the canyon was one of them," exclaimed Whizlet, "but Fou d'Royant and the flying raft got us through that."

"You went through the gates of compassion and loving-kindness," said Trippytucatchup Ka'aba. "When you put off your own search to help us awaken Fou d'Royant, and seemingly went out of your way to do so, you passed through a gate whose kamijani was so delighted she kissed poor Hobnail right on top of her head and almost knocked her off her branch."

"And when you gave up your gifts to the doe and her new fawns," added Makyo, "you showed us you understood your way through the other."

"What did the kamijani do there?" asked Whizlet

"Why she allowed us all to remember how wonderful it is to be born and made us realize how very precious our own lives are," explained Trippytucatchup Ka'aba.

"And how wonderful it will be when we're all mothers ourselves too!" exclaimed Toonie. "That's the most magical thing in the whole world."

"As magical as Toddle Lou's kigamstone?" asked Whizlet wonderingly.

"Or the Windfane and the music of the twistle and cloth harp?" added Toliver.

"Or Makyo's staff?" continued Whizlet.

"Or the flower that got us here?" appended Toliver.

"Better'n everything," said Toonie with a finality so imperious that all Toliver and Whizlet could do was look at each other in astonishment.

"In Arigonia everything seems to be magical," said Is.

"And everybody is a magician too," added the Itofit. "Which is what the Mostable It told us when he came back and tried to teach us how to be like them."

"Magic is just a way of being in love with life instead of things," said Trippytucatchup Ka'aba. "Because if you love life...why, it's like loving anything. Whatever you do makes it better."

"But what should we do now?" asked Whizlet who more or less loved everybody (except groblets) and was sure Makyo had at least one more thing up his sleeve.

"Well, if you ask me," began Toonie, who always said that when nobody asked her. "I'd wish that Toddle Lou...I mean, Al O'Ha was here with his new kigamstone all charged up so Makyo could use it to send us all home."

"Is that what you'd wish if you had just one wish?" asked Makyo who looked at her with his piercing blue eyes and seemed like he really wanted to know. Toonie was somewhat nonplused (or perhaps nonminused depending on how good you are at arithmetic).

"Well, hmmmm..." she said squinting one eye at Makyo in a very apprising way and twisting her mouth all out of shape. "Not really, I s'ppose... If I only had one wish, what I'd really wish for...was...let's see...I'd wish that every wish I wished would come true."

She was very pleased with herself but Makyo shook his head. "That would never do."

"Why not," demanded Toonie who was certainly nondivided in what she was thinking at the moment. "Wishing for more wishes is the only smart wish a girl could make."

"Not at all," continued Makyo. "First of all, if all our wishes came true, life wouldn't be any fun at all. We'd never get to see what wonderful things it had in store for us even though we'd never thought to wish for them. And second of all, I said you only had one wish, so even if you got all the wishes you wanted, you'd still only have one wish because every wish you made would be for more wishes, and all you'd ever get is more and more of what you already had too much of."

"And third of all," added Is, "if you had all those wishes then there wouldn't be any left for anybody else and that wouldn't be fair either."

"And besides," cut in Toliver, "if all you had to do was wish, you'd just sit around wishing all the time and would never learn how to do anything else."

"Oh, that would never do at all," cried Toonie who was now, if not deflated, at least nonmultiplied. "I'll just have to think about it, just as It always does."

"I know what I'd wish," said Whizlet very firmly, and before anyone could ask what, continued: "I'd wish Rango was all okay again because he's hurt and it's my fault because I pulled that thorn out of his side and made him go swoosh all over the sky and end up deflated hanging over a branch."

"That's a very fine wish," agreed Makyo who then looked at Toliver. "And what would you wish?"

"I don't think my wish is very smart," replied Toliver who, even when he was given something nice, liked to keep it mostly in case somebody else might need it. "And probably not very possible either. But I wish the people in Alabramble wouldn't be so mean anymore and would find out how much better everything is when you're nice to each other."

"That's an excellent wish too," agreed Makyo.

"I know what I'd wish now too," said Toonie with a great deal of excitement. "I'd wish we could all be best friends forever."

"I think you have that wish already," said Is. "Because that's something we can make happen just by being happy and considerate with each other."

"Well put," said Makyo. "But what do you wish, young Lady Isofit?"

Is took the Itofit's arm. "They all made such wonderful wishes that all I can wish is that they'll all come true."

"And what about you, far-seeing Itofit? Since much of what's happened today is all your doing, I'd like to hear your wish too." The Itofit eyed Makyo as carefully and thoughtfully as Makyo was eyeing him.

"I wish you'd tell us who you really are."

"Hmmm," replied Makyo appreciatively, "some wishes are harder than others, but that might be very difficult indeed."

"You mean you're not Makyo the Magician!" exclaimed Toonie.

"Or Makyo the Menzaster?" added Whizlet who hadn't figured out what that was yet but liked the sound of it.

"Or Makyo the Magnificent?" continued Toliver. "How can anybody be more than that?"

"Let's just say I'm Makyo the Arigonian and leave it at that," responded Makyo. "Since I've done what I've had to do and now, like you, I can go home and be pleased with today."

"What did you do except fool us all the time?" asked Toonie.

"I only fooled you in order to find out about you. That way I could see what you were like and decide what kind of people you were underneath."

"Underneath what?" asked Whizlet suspiciously because he knew there were all kinds of levels underneath each other, some of which you could only get away from by hitting the escape button or maybe even the off switch or, as the very last resort, by pulling the plug.

"Underneath what you're like when you think other people are looking," answered Makyo.

"But why did you go to all that trouble," asked the Itofit, "since you didn't really have to bother with us at all?"

"Oh, but we did," responded Makyo. "After you escaped from Alabramble, the Alabramblians put out an All-Tails Bulletin on you. They described you very accurately and said you might be coming this way. They wanted us to catch you and send you back because they say you're associated with a band of terrorists who invaded their country."

"Oh dear," coughed Toonie involuntarily. "That's not true at all!"

Makyo raised his hand to calm her. "They told us about the Battle for Pulcan's Toe and how you and an army of subversive sky-demons tried to capture Smugsmog City."

"But what would we want with their dirty old city?" cried Toonie whose eyes were huge and almost popping out of her head.

"No, no," hurried Makyo. "It's all right. We know what really happened but we still had to find out if you'd done anything wrong."

"I suppose we did violate some of their laws," said the Itofit who realized that being forthright with the Arigonians was surely the best way to be.

"That isn't what worried us," replied Makyo. "We judge by the heart, not by the tongue. A very wise man once said: "For people of extraordinary virtue there is no law.""

"But don't we have a duty to obey the law?" asked Toliver.

"If the law is virtuous, you certainly do," agreed Makyo. "But don't ever let that duty become slavery to foolishness in the name of virtue."

The Itofit scratched his brow with a scratching whisker. "You mean that anyone who knows the difference between right and wrong, who does what is right and honors the good, is above the law...because laws are made for people who cannot tell the difference and are unable to live their lives properly?"

"I almost agree," replied Makyo. "But if laws are rightly made they can mold everybody's conduct toward doing what is right, so that obeying them is the same as doing right, but if the laws are bad or biased or foolish, why then you're quite right, and the wise citizen is forced to judge for himself. But he must only disregard the bad laws and must never make a show of it, or those who are not wise will think they too can live as laws unto themselves which, of course, they cannot."

"You're a dujge too!" exclaimed Toonie.

"No, not really," said Makyo. "I may occasionally be called on to be a sort of magister, but never a dujge. There is quite a difference, you know. And I judge you've done nothing wrong, so we'll politely tell the Alabramblians that you've been caught, tried, and punished."

"Punished!" exclaimed Toliver who didn't relish any more of that and didn't think it fair either. "Yes, we're going to exile you to home."

"But how can you do that?" asked Toonie. "Since the turtle ate our flower...I mean he's a wonderful turtle and probably didn't know what he was doing and was certainly hungry, or at least he had a huge appetite, and he chomped it right down to the ground, and now it isn't there anymore, and..." Her face suddenly brightened, "...do you have another flower for us?"

"No, I don't," replied Makyo. "That wouldn't work anyway because you have to go back the way you came. But flowers grow back, you know, and yours has been doing just that all day."

"But how can we get back to the flower?" asked Toliver who was generally quite practical when he was lost. "Since we don't really know where we are..."

"We have the baloomerangs," said Is. "And Rango and Rangi always know the way home."

"But Rango's still hurt," said Whizlet, "unless my wish worked."

"I think it did," Trippytucatchup Ka'aba. "Because look, here come your friends now."

Everyone looked where the Lady of Ludgordia was pointing. Two baloomerangs and a flock of balooms were circling above them and honking and honkaing down to where they sat.

"But we still have to get over Alabramble," said Toliver. "And the wind that blew us here will be blowing against us now, and even if Rango's better, he probably should rest before we ask him to take us anywhere." He looked at the sky where the sun was dropping behind the Halidome and beginning to cast its long beautiful shadow over them. "And it's getting late and I don't know if we have enough time."

"There is another way to go," said Trippytucatchup Ka'aba. "Since you've passed through two more gates, you'll know how to use the Stepping Stone to Elsewhere in the Halidome."

"Will the Stepping Stone to Elsewhere take us to Ludgordia?" asked Toliver.

"It will take you through Ludgordia, since that is how it has always worked for us." began Makyo.

"Then you're the Ludgord!" exclaimed Toonie putting two fingers in front of her wide-open mouth as though to frame the truth she'd just uttered.

"Not really," replied Makyo. "But then again, really too…because everyone is the Ludgord."

"That doesn't compute," said Whizlet, "because it would all be a jumble."

"Oh, but it does, my young friend," continued Makyo. "Because the Ludgord appears as the very quiet voice inside all of us which tells us how to do things correctly, especially when we're being careful but don't seem to know what to do at all."

"I know that voice," said Toonie. "It told me how to stop fussing about unimportant things."

"And it sometimes tells me what to put in my pocket," said Toliver.

"And me too!" agreed Whizlet. "I had to think real hard, but it told me how to get out of the dragon's lair in *King Kludgeon's Keep*."

"That's the one," agreed Makyo. "But usually we're talking instead of listening so we miss what it says, even though it always says the right thing at exactly the right time."

"That must be why Fou d'Royant is always telling us to be quiet," announced Toliver.

"But what about now?" asked Toonie. "I'm listening as hard as I can and all I'm hearing is everybody talking."

"Maybe we should all listen quietly for a moment," said Is.

And they did. Everyone kept very still and even the flowers seemed to hold their breath, the tickle bees stopped buzzing, and the birds glided about silently. Above them the Halidome glowed and even its sharp rocky defiles seemed to sparkle with meaning.

Toonie looked down at the ground from which all the lusciousness about them was sprouting.

"That's it!" she exclaimed. "The ground is magical, and we could..."

"...use it for fertilizer," said Toliver

"And take it to the flower..." continued Whizlet.

"Which would grow right back... a whole new flower. I betcha it'd work!"

"What a good idea," agreed the Itofit. "Thank you Makyo." He looked around. "But what soil should be take. We must be careful not to take something that doesn't belong to us."

"Take a handful from the Windfane," said Trippytucatchup Ka'aba, "and sprinkle it with water from the Waterfane. You'll find them wonderfully magical."

"But where can we find another Windfane and a Waterfane?" asked Toonie. "And how can we carry them with us?"

"I have a plastic bag and bottle," said Toliver.

"There are five Fanes in the Halidome," explained Trippytucatchup Ka'aba. "You'll go through all of them to get to the Stepping Stone to Elsewhere which is at the very top."

Whizlet clapped his hands. "It's just like the Wun-dur-phul said. There are six gates to the Ludgord!" The Itofit ran his tail lovingly down Is' back.

"But what must we do to have the Halidome help us? Even magicians have to know what they're doing or it never works right, and we're not magicians."

"Just go to the top," said Trippytucatchup Ka'aba.

"And when you can go no further," continued Makyo, "just hold hands and concentrate very hard on a place where you've all been together before, and would like to be again."

"And let the Halidome show you how everything exists together in Ludgordia in the most marvelous ways," added the Lady of Ludgordia smiling so warmly at all of them that they understood exactly what she meant.

"Can't you come with us?" asked Toonie who really didn't want to lose any of her new friends, especially ones who were able to show her so many wonderful things.

"No, you must go alone," responded Makyo. "Then you'll know you can and will never have to worry about it again."

"But we certainly look forward to seeing you again," added Trippytucatchup Ka'aba, "so please visit us anytime you can, and as soon as you can."

"We'd like that very much," replied Is. "I'd like to bring you some of our flowers and flutterbys too."

"And perhaps we could take up where the Mostable It left off," added the Itofit, "and learn more about your wonderful ways."

"Thank you," said Toliver who was always polite when people were nice to him (and sometimes, although not always, when they weren't). "We'd like that very much too, but now the shadow is getting very big."

"Yes, we'd better hurry," agreed the Itofit. "For we still have to get to the top of the Halidome and that looks like a very long climb."

"One of the trails begins right over there," said the lady pointing between another pair of tolive trees. "You'll first come to a Waterfane. The trail will take you along its edge then up the side of the Halidome. Follow it through the other Fanes and you'll have no trouble at all."

"But don't tarry too long in any of them," cautioned Makyo. "Because the Fanes can be very beguiling."

"The Beguiling Fanes!" exclaimed the Itofit. "They must be what we remember as the Beguiling Thanes who told my grandfather's grandmother's great great grandfather how to build our It-Fine dwellings."

"So the It-Fine must be an Itfane," agreed Is. "And we can probably learn all kinds of new things by seeing more of what the Mostable It modeled them on."

Hissofer slid across Makyo's knee and back onto the Itofit's hat, while

Hobnail glided to Makyo's staff and cocked her head to look one more time at the fascinating blue jewel. She put her eye right next to it and while she was engrossed, the two collectivores ran up and jumped to her back. It had taken quite a bit of effort for her to lift just one of the little creatures so she swiveled her head to tell them she couldn't possibly take both. But they cooed back contentedly and settled on her shoulders. The blue jewel seemed to glitter between her talons and she felt a strange force tickling her belly and pushing her up. She opened her wings to let it play along their undersides and almost immediately found herself airborne and floating up without any effort at all. Soon the three of them were wafted higher than the treetops and were soaring up alongside the Halidome. The breeze was stronger there and from above she heard music that sounded as if it was emanating from another Windfane and both collectivores were chirping to her to join the song. She couldn't possibly resist such an invitation and a moment later found, much to her own surprise, that she was whistling a lusty version of Mr. Elgar's *Enigma Variations.*

The others said good by to the magician and his lovely lady and followed Fou d'Royant who led them between the tolive trees and along the edge of a marsh of tall grasses topped with golden yellow plumes. Beyond the marsh was a miniature lake of very clear water nestled at the foot of the Halidome. Fou motioned for Toliver to fill his bottle with the water, for the trail ahead was rocky and steep. They were soon well above the surface and able to look down into it as though it was a mysterious flower. What they saw was a remarkable underwater garden with clouds of beautiful fish weaving through it. There were deep holes and mysterious depths, cave entrances half blocked by flowing grasses, and the intricate shapes of a myriad long-stemmed, feathered, and gently waving water plants. The trail turned to the side then ended at the top of a flight of well-worn stone steps going down into the earth and curving out of sight. Following Fou d'Royant, they descended into the earth through a seashell-shaped tunnel with water-polished walls glowing like mother-of-pearl.

"Oh, my goodness! Look how beautiful this is!" exclaimed Toonie when they got to the bottom and found themselves in a long, curved chamber whose outside wall looked like a coral reef and whose floor was of abalone and oyster shell. The light was shimmering in blues and greens coming through the inner wall which was a crystal-clear membrane separating them from the depths of the lake. All sorts of bright colored and amazingly shaped fish and other extraordinary creatures swam through the water and walked on the bottom. The membrane undulated with the action of the water so it was often impossible to see where the liquid ended and the air began. The light cast its spell over everyone, and even Boogie, who had never seen so much raw tuna fish on the hoof before and at first felt they would probably be happy to be eaten to save them from having to spend another moment in such a wet and worrisome place, became almost mesmerized as he peered into the depths. Whizlet too was fascinated and ran right up to the apparent wall of water and stopped just inches before it. As he stood there a large, torpedo-shaped fish with a snout like a peeled back banana dashed right at his face, hit the barrier only inches from his nose, and pushed it out like it was made of cellophane, then bounced back into the pool blowing bubbles and seeming to laugh as well, before retreating behind a rock ledge to chortle to himself.

"Yipes-a-doddle!" screeched Whizlet leaping back. "You scared me, mister fish!" The flish, as though understanding his words, retracted his snout so the open peel closed around it and swam more slowly past, eyeing him sardonically with one huge eye that looked like a saucer filled with oil in which a sapphire was floating.

"This must be the Waterfane," said the Itofit who came up beside Whizlet and put his hand out and poked it carefully into the waterwall. A creature that looked like a watermelon with moth's wings wobbled up so the Itofit could stroke its back. Soon a host of other strange creatures, emboldened by the watermelon's audacity, came over too, bubbling and clacking among themselves, and offering their beautiful bodies for the others to stroke through the membrane. When Is came over, the Itofit took her hand and put it against the waterwall. "What a wonderful material this is," he said happily. "We'll have to find out what it is and get some for our lavatorium."

"It has a wonderful texture," agreed Is. "We might even be able to make bubbles with it and have our bird friends flying below the water."

"And Snorf and Snorfa would love to play with the flish," added It who needed to offer little encouragement to Snorf who scrambled down his arm and poked the first third of himself clean into the membrane.

"We might even be able to make suits of it," mused Is, "that would hold enough air for us to breathe while we swam underwater." While she was speaking, Whizlet, who had been keeping a wary eye on bananasnout, noticed his antagonist peeking around the ledge with the banana opening for another run. But before he could warn either Is or It (since he didn't like to interrupt other people's conversations), the torpedo launched itself again right at the Itofit's head. But Hissofer had seen what happened earlier and was also keeping track of bananasnout. As the creature dove for the membrane, Hissofer unwound himself like a taut spring from the Itofit's hat brim and flashed like a javelin into the waterwall. Bananasnout had never before gotten such a tit for his tat and when Hissofer appeared like a tongue of fury from his intended target's brow, the poor flish escalpurlated in fright on the spot, his bananahead peeled all the way back revealing his flaming red fright, then closed like an accordion. He let out a terrified bubble and dove like an arrow into a deep crevice in the reef, vibrating uncontrollably all the while.

"Wow, Hissofer!" exclaimed Whizlet happily. "You're my kind of a snakeperson. You scared the scales right off him!"

Fou d'Royant was amused by the whole spectacle and now that everyone's concentration had been broken, waved them to follow him to the far end of the chamber onto an escalator of woven grasses which carried them further along the waterwall while taking them slowly back to the surface. They stepped off on a ledge far above the water where Fou d'Royant bowed to them all, smiled radiantly, and pointed along the trail that continued to the Halidome. Then he sat with his legs hanging over the side and gazed down into the pool while the others gathered around and looked where he seemed to be staring. The afternoon sun sparkled on the dancing surface and glinted with patterns that hinted at secret and mysterious things. Woven among the pattern of lights were the watery depths below, pregnant with intimations of impending perfection, so that all of them upon viewing the living tapestry saw also the wonderful weavings of their own hopes and dreams. Their eyes turned inwardly and they saw themselves looking at their own seeing as it orchestrated itself with the flowings of the Waterfane whose ancient magic opened in wonder to those who were calm and quiet enough see it.

The Itofit was the first to emerge from the magical spell, so he motioned for the others to follow and continued along the trail winding up the side of the Halidome. Only Fou d'Royant remained behind, blissfully lost again in his exploration of the vast and limitless horizons within his own mind. Steps had been fashioned in the steeper parts of the trail and where it was narrow, rough stone walls or low tangled bushes acted as railings. As they mounted higher they came to a resting place and looked back the way they had come.

Fou d'Royant had stripped off his clothes and dove into the water and now seemed a glowing ball of light deep beneath the surface swimming among clouds of flish. Beyond the little lake they saw Makyo and Trippytucatchup Ka'aba still seated in the glade that now lay in the foreground of a vast and magnificent panorama encompassing the valley and icy mountains of Arigonia. They waved one last time and went ahead to the first of the cave mouths leading into the Halidome. High above, the collectivores launched themselves from Hobnail's back and glided past, cooing to the snigglesnorfs and clicking their teeth at Boogie. Hobnail was having a wonderful time soaring on the musical breeze but was such a curious parrot she couldn't resist seeing the secret chambers inside the mountainous rock, so she glided down, back-flapped her wings behind Is, and stepped from the air onto her new friend's shoulder. The Itofit stopped at the entrance wiggling both his nose and ears as he always did before entering a strange place, and Toliver, who felt that boys should go first in possibly dangerous situations, while girls should have the honor when it was a matter of etiquette, jumped to the front and went inside. Whizlet, who never liked to lag, was right behind him, and just behind him was Boogie who, though he was smelling water again, dared not wait for the indignity of being carried in Toonie's arms. Ahead was a faint murmuring of not quite intelligible sounds as might be heard when putting a shell to a straining ear, and when they stepped into the Halidome they were bedazzled by a wondrous sight.

Great clefts in the rock allowed sunlight to stream through in shafts of blazing light which reflected back and forth through an immense cavern festooned with stalagmites, chandeliered with stalactites, and walled with great slabs of resplendent crystal. The pathway was jasper stepping-stones winding through sparkling white sands toward a central pool of deep, clear water whose surface was so still as to form a perfect mirror. The aura of the place was of calm majesty and, though no one felt like speaking while they walked through it, Is whispered to Toonie:

"This must be the Terrafane, for I can feel it speaking to my feet just as the ground does at Is or It when everything is perfect and the day beautiful."

There was a terrace overhanging the pool where they stood silently and let the Halidome weave its enchantment. The illusion was perfect, the mirrored pool so fine they could not tell on which side they stood, and the Terrafane took them deep into the living core of the great world of which the Halidome was but a projecting eye-stem and planetary antenna. All of them felt the heart of the planet beating in their own breasts and they knew that this wondrous place was not only a living expression of a sentient world, but a place of which (for the moment) they were inseparable parts, for they felt its mighty intelligence merging with their own minds and probing their wonderment. Hissofer slid from the Itofit's shoulder, left his weaving signature on the glistening sands, and slipped into the pool of water. He swam to the center underwater looking like a chromosome of colorfully banded thought-images, then broke the surface and moved round and round, crisscrossing his own ripples, until the still water fragmented into a mosaic of lustrous colors and shapes. For each of those watching his wonderful performance, he composed a symphony of silent music that evoked memories of times long, long ago when others ruled on the surface of this world and beauty had a strange and reptilian sensuousness. When he finished his song, he slid from the far side of the pool and climbed a stalagmite by the pathway to await their coming. The Itofit had no words to say but saluted Hissofer with his tail and held his hat out for the elegant snake to resume his place, then they continued along the trail until coming once again out into the afternoon sunlight at a place where they could look down over the lovely town of Arigon and the restless sea beyond.

The trail climbed higher and took them to a flat plateau carved out of the side of the Halidome which they had been unable to see when they glided down from the mountains. The plateau was a garden of wonderful trees and bushes and great rocks sculpted into strange shapes, with hanging vines and flowers everywhere.

"Look!" exclaimed Is squeezing the Itofit's hand and pointing at all the pretty vegetation. "Why there are glorningmorys and roodwoses, yepote cactus and igoba bushes. How very lovely."

"And look over here," said Toliver who had found a mushroom garden thriving in the shadows of an overhanging rock. "All different kinds of toadstools. Toodle Lou would love it here." He poked his finger into the soft ground. "And the dirt is so rich and black I can take some of if for our flower."

"What beautiful merrymota plants," said the Itofit admiring a stand of tall, deep green bushes heavy with candle-like clumps of tiny flowers glistening with golden sap. Hissofer again slid from the Itofit's hat and wound his way among the fabulous plants, thoroughly enjoying the feel of the rocks and sand, the moist earth and tickly moss, the scratchy lichens and slippery leaves, until he climbed the tallest merrymota bush which bent under his weight and deposited again atop the Itofit's hat. Rango and Rangi landed in a clearing and the two snigglesnorfs ran over to pull on their proboscises then hurried back to the Itofit and sniggled and snorfed a request.

"I'm sure it will be all right," agreed It, who snipped off two of the larger clumps of syrupy flowers and gave them to the snigglesnorfs, who ran with them happily to the baloomerangs, who honked their thanks and nibbled them down.

"It sounds like another Windfane," said Toonie expectantly because the breeze was already tuning the marvelous instrument and Hobnail was fluttering and cooing on Is' shoulder. The music began as a low prelude to a marvelous symphony to which even the parrot listened without joining in and instead rubbed the back of her neck against Is' furry ear while learning the tune note by note and chord by chord. The music drifted down over Arigon and they could see people, very tiny now for being so far away, gazing up to see what was inspiring the Halidome to an afternoon concert. The balooms hovered around the Itians but the Itofit told them with his tail that they hadn't time to linger so they could not join in with the twistle and cloth harp, but Hobnail roused herself and took to the air to dance with the remarkable little creatures while the music conducted them through its polyphony as though it were scripting itself on the breeze with their antics. The deep, melodious vibrations spilling from the plateau were more than incredibly beautiful music for they created a haunting echo of the hidden structure of reality whose underlying, universal vibrance resonated through the bodies and minds of its audience.

Boogie, who was hearing the music in terms of wonderful growls, yowls, roars, shrieks, and purrs, danced through the Windfane and found the trail climbing out the other side where it disappeared among a stand of gigantic boulders. Whizlet saw the cat exploring ahead and ran after to see what he might have found. A few minutes later he hurried back and very anxiously whispered:

"Boogie's gone crazy!"

"Oh dear," gasped Toonie. "Did he eat a toadstool?"

"I don't think so," responded Whizlet, "but I followed him into another cave which is full of candles and fires and flames floating in the air. I don't know if he burned his tail or what, but he's running round and round the walls, and jumping from ledges, and spinning in the sand, and rolling on his back and growling at the ceiling."

Everyone followed Whizlet up the trail and into the next cave. Its door was shaped like a flame and its walls were of old silver textured into a thousand bas-reliefs and abstract designs. Candles in colorful holders were arranged in patterns and their flickering lights caused the frieze to pulsate, so what was seen among the shadows appeared as a moving mosaic of ferns and trees and strange, beautiful creatures. The floor was of burnished gold hammered into the rock, forming a winding pathway among wondrous and mysterious torch sculptures. The center of the room was a great hearth with a medley of fires upon it whose flames danced and fused with each other in a wildly colorful display. From the white heat of flashing phosphorus to the greens of many salts and the cool blues of phosphorescent washes, all radiated a welcoming warmth enveloped in a hundred fiery shades of red, orange, and yellow. There were no windows in the room but the ceiling was a dome of crystalline amethyst glittering with a panoply of reflected lights. Boogie was acting as Whizlet had reported, doing back flips and front flips, twirls and spins. His yellow-orange body danced with the firelight and he seemed a flame himself, but one able to dart through the chamber unlinked to any source of fuel except his own exuberance. At the far side of the chamber a pool of glowing lava sent liquid ripples across the overhanging rocks, one of which was a ledge of translucent carnelian projecting out between pillars of swirling fire. Boogie found the platform and settled himself between the pillars of flame and stared back at them with his eyes shining like blazing green emeralds in the half-light of the recess. His glowing, unblinking orbs were hypnotic and cast a spell across the Firefane suffusing his companions with the energy he felt, the immanent dance of creation, and they encountered their own lives as the vitality of that which powered the universe and they shared the cat-like vibrancy of his resonance with eternity.

"I don't think he's crazy at all," stammered Toliver. "I think he's... he's..."

"Enchanted," said Is.

"Ennobled," said It.

"Enthroned," said Toonie

"Yipes-a-doddled," agreed Whizlet.

"Mrer-ow-ow!" cried Boogie throwing his head back and calling out to the mysterious presence of the Firefane. His call jangled the candles along a golden wall which sparkled behind the crystal portals of their holders, the dancing flames of the hearth responded with a medley of flares, and all joined the music wafting up from the Windfane to create a vibrating spectrum of sound and prismed shadows thrown upon the walls. To Boogie the spectacle was of great cats rumbling in deep-forested jungle, while all those who watched the sensuous play of light on his fur and eyes were taken into their own deep yearnings and heard the music as a rumbling on the threshold of intelligibility where their own deepest selves communicated their code to their outer projections.

"It's the voice of the Beguiling Fanes," whispered the Itofit, hearing clearly what his grandfather's grandmother's great great grandfather had told of Arigonia to the generations, which followed.

"It's the Voice of the Mothers," said Is, stroking her tail down the Itofit's back and squeezing Toonie's hand with a womanly touch of shared intuition.

"It's magic," said Toliver, "but I bet we can figure it out."

"It's like drums and storm clouds at the beginning of an exciting movie," added Whizlet, "but I bet it's interactive so we can write it as we go along anyway we want."

Hissofer's eyes also gleamed and his tongue slipped in and out, tasting of the thermally agitated air, picking from each swirling eddy a molecule of flavor, all telling the meaning and memories of this strange room redolent of deep caverns where snakes and dragons met to writhe and winnow with the earth. Hobnail had remained in the Windfane as long as she dared, but now glided into the Firefane. To her the sounds were echoes reverberating through her musical memory, farewells told lovingly with the promise of return. But being clothed in combustible feathers, she was wary of all the flames so she swooped low along the golden pathway to where it ended on a platform of fire agate beyond the carnelian pedestal where Boogie rested. No signal was given but the others followed in her wake, walking slowly and silently along the path among the sculptures of flame. Boogie stole from his eminence and joined them on the platform, which then rose majestically toward the ceiling where a great sunstone swirled open from the center, allowing them to pass through to the Chamber of Lord Sunstar.

Rising from the muted depths of the Firefane, the Sunstarfane was at first too brilliant to be seen as anything but a bedazzlement of light, but as their eyes grew accustomed to the new surroundings they gazed at a beautiful portico that formed the top of the Halidome. Its walls were the jagged peaks of the Halidome's rim and stood as sentries around its periphery before whose ancient gaze they ambled as they wandered among its terraced gardens. Here and there wild, bonzaied trees and small tangled hedges complemented the space and everywhere framed vistas of fabled Arigonia. Swifts and swallows darted about calling to each other and the new arrivals, then diving to their nests in the clefts and cleavages of the great towering central feature of the Fane. Rising majestically from the center of the portico was the Stepping Stone to Elsewhere, the uppermost peak of the Halidome. Unlike the streaked and lovely granite below, it was a great aggregation of milk white and rose quartz fashioned by the wind and rain into a lovely summit, which was flattened on top and worn smooth by the feet of countless generations of voyagers. Mosses and lichens carpeted parts of the rock, which was itself veined with deeper colors and streaked with images reminiscent of its eternal origin. It projected above the walls of the Sunstarfane but was not its apex, for magically hung above it, seeming to be suspended in the air without scaffold or support, was a pyramid-shaped crystal, flawless and perfectly clear, which acted as a prism for the afternoon sun and flooded the sky chamber with a myriad scintillating lights. So ethereal was the pyramidion that none could tell if it was a real thing of this world or but a shimmering projection from some other which hung as a dream-image connecting the two.

"Oh, how beautiful this is!" gasped Toonie squeezing Is' hand. "What is it telling you through your feet, Is? It must be the nicest thing you've ever heard!"

"Take off your shoes and listen yourself," replied Is in her most musical voice. "I couldn't possibly explain it as beautifully as the Halidome itself."

The children sat down and removed their shoes and socks; Toliver even tied his laces together and hung his sneakers around his neck, then found his attention drawn to the soles of his feet which began tingling and tickling in a wonderful way. A moment later he could feel the energy of the Sunstarfane radiating upward through his feet, washing his whole body was a wonderfully purifying essence until he felt he was somehow identical with the Halidome and, indeed, with the whole universe with which it connected. Boogie lay down to feel the vibrations through his whole body and the Itofit put his hat on the ground so Hissofer could slide off and be enraptured by the marvelous force projecting from the rock. Hobnail lifted from Is' shoulder and soared about the Stepping Stone where the balooms and baloomerangs (with the snigglesnorfs gazing spellbound from their backs) bobbed happily in the soft breezes commingled with the Halidome's radiance. On the far side of the peak she found an irregular pathway of natural stone steps leading to the top of the great quartz monolith and glided back to tell everyone, but instead found herself singing *The Magnificat* in response to the orchestration wafting up from the Windfane.

The Itofit and Is walked hand in hand among the terraces while the children and animals danced along, too awestruck and filled with wonderment to do anything but listen and absorb the musings of the Halidome. They came eventually to the stone steps Hobnail had spied and followed the Itofit as he led them to the top, which was a shimmering shelf of rose-white stone veined with opalescent crystal. Everywhere they looked, from sea to icy mountains and across the exquisite terrain of the Vale of Arigonia was a vision all-encompassing perfection.

"This must be Ludgordia," whispered Toonie.

"Or perhaps a step before," responded Is.

"What do we do now?" asked Whizlet who was a little lost without a control stick.

The Itofit took his hand. "Makyo told us to hold hands and think of a place where we want to be where we've all been together before."

"But let's not think of that awful old Alabramble," said Whizlet making a fist and a grimace at the same time, "or Toot Glibrich either, but we could remember the Wun-dur-phul's umbrella."

"We all met at the basket house…" began Is.

"So we should think of it just as it was when we ate the sherburr and met Thomey and the baloomerangs," added Toonie hurriedly. "And we'll just see what happens." She took the Itofit's hand with her left hand and Is' with her right. The Itofit took Toliver's hand and Is took Whizlet's hand and Toliver and Whizlet took each other's hands, and Boogie wound his way between everybody's legs, rubbing first with his left side, then his right. Hissofer encircled the Itofit's tail which It rose so the snake could slide off onto his hat, and Hobnail landed on Is' shoulder and began preening her fur and cooing in her ear. Just then Whizlet remembered Toodle Lou's kigamstone and how it could be recharged atop the Stepping Stone to Elsewhere in the Chamber of Lord Sunstar and realized he'd have to take it out of his pocket except both his hands were being held and he wasn't sure where the Arches the morning sun had to shine through were anyway, so he decided not to worry about it and looked up at the diamond-like pyramidion above their heads which was glowing with a marvelous luminescence. It took his breath away and reminded him of things he couldn't quite remember, so he looked down instead to where everyone else was gazing at the top of the Stepping Stone, but what he saw was not rose-white quartz at all but what looked to be the very top of the Itofit's talapalodion tree. And it was getting larger and larger all the time, as though they were descending quickly toward it (or it was somehow growing right before their eyes) until he couldn't see anything else except all its leaves and branches and then the roofs of the basket house. It seemed so very real that he shook his head and closed his eyes tight, and when, a moment later, he opened one just a little bit to check. Why, they were all standing on the verandah of the basket house. He looked up in amazement only to see Rango and Rangi with Snorf and Snorfa hanging on their backs coming down through the tree amid a whole flock of balooms just as they had when they'd first met them that morning.

"My goodness," said the Itofit. "We're home again. Or at least some of us are."

"Yes, we almost are," agreed Toliver who really didn't want to go a step further himself but knew if he didn't, no one else would either. "And our flower is still a long way away."

"We can fly there on Rango and Rangi," said Is. "It won't take long at all, so I can pour us a glass of iced chi to go with a plate of sunseed tiscuits and we can rest just a moment to get our wits together after all this excitement."

"But Rango's hurt..." began Whizlet but stopped as he watched the Itofit carefully inspecting his friend.

"It isn't very far and it's all downhill," said It. "And Rango seems quite his old self again. The Halidome must work it wonders on bodies as well as minds and spirits, so I'm sure he could carry you and Toliver while Rangi carries the rest of us."

Toliver took the tolive tree seeds from his pocket and handed them to the Itofit.

"Since we planted a talapalodion tree at the Windfane in Arigonia, you should plant these in your It-Fine garden to remember the day we all met."

"But they're yours…" began It.

"I've got lots of stuff," countered Toliver, "and I'm always finding more."

"Besides we don't have any wine to pickle the fruit," said Toonie.

"Or Panoleon and Lamburtaine to guard them," added Whizlet.

"Well, in that case," said the Itofit, "we'll find a beautiful place and tell Kamirill to take special care of them."

"And when you visit again, we'll have a picnic under them," promised Is.

While Is and Toonie brought out a tray of chi and tiscuits, Hobnail flew to the roof of the basket house and pulled out some of its fibers just as though she was hoping to build a nest, and Boogie stalked around the railings looking out to make sure no sky worms or vawyers were descending on them. Hissofer disdained the treats but did gobble another talapa nut and settled very comfortably on the Itofit's hat brim with his snout on his tail and a lump in his belly, while the sun cast long purple and vertul shadows through the talapalodion tree's branches.

Rango and Rangi helped everyone onto their backs then jumped over the railing and glided off the way the Itofit pointed. Boogie spread-eagled himself on Rangi's head and Hobnail, who was quite exhausted from her long day of flying, rested happily on Is' shoulder and cooed her contentment. Rango was happy to be well enough to carry the boys and honked encouragingly to Whizlet who was sitting in front and rubbing him on his favorite spot just behind his ear while telling him how happy he was that Rango was feeling good again. Toliver was in back trying to look every which way at once so he'd be sure to remember everything he possibly could about the wonderful world of It. They flew across the mazeberry labyrinth and the arched bridge and almost immediately thereafter were circling down over the clearing in the center of which stood the remnants of the remarkable flower whose peculiar penchant for swallowing things had occasioned the day's adventures. As Makyo had surmised, it had grown back a bit and a new, but very small blossom stretched out at the end of a fresh stalk. Toliver took out his bag of soil from the Windfane and bottle of water from the Waterfane. He sprinkled the soil around the bottom of the plant and poured the water on top to wash it down, then stood back to see what might happen.

Almost immediately, the flower perked up. Its stalk grew thick and the little blossom swelled until it burst open into a beautiful white and blue trumpet tinged with vertul, with lightning bolt streaks, and two stamens pushing out like eyes that looked at them with golden, pollen flecked coyness. They stood holding hands for an awkward moment until Toliver, who liked teary good byes even less than spoonfuls of cough syrup, pointed to the red-orange sun now dropping behind the trees surrounding the clearing.

"We'll have to hurry," he said, "because we still have to get away from the island (if that's were the flower takes us) and then home through the woods. So I'd better go first and make sure." He stepped forward then turned to say good by to the Itofit and Is and tell them how much he had enjoyed spending the day with them and how wonderful he thought they were, but before he could say anything except "Thank you for everything." he was lifted up and pulled backward into the flower.

"Yipes-a-doddle!" yelled Whizlet jumping forward. "He didn't even get to say good by, but I will." But before he did, he too zoomed into the flower head first as though he'd taken a running dive into a pool, and the bulge he became became smaller and smaller as it disappeared down the stem.

Boogie was peering around from behind the Itofit's leg, not at all sure he wanted to undergo the indignity of being devoured by a flower twice in one day, but while he was being so intent on not letting it sneak up on him, Toonie did and snatched him up under her arm. No sooner had she done so than both of them were picked up and sucked into the beautiful trumpet with her looking back in amazement at the Itofit and Is, who were holding tails and waving good by. Hobnail was on Is' shoulder, preening Is' neck and watching the flower with one cagey eye while the other looked dreamily off in the direction of the talapalodion tree.

When Toonie dropped ingloriously onto her back at the bottom of the flower stalk, Boogie jumped from her arms and ran around in circles because they were on the island again and if he'd gone any other way, he'd have run into the water. Toliver was already pushing their log back into the swamp and Whizlet had found three neatly stripped and pointed poles lying nearby which they could use to pole themselves back to the mainland.

"We have to hurry," said Toliver. "It's getting very late." As he spoke the sun dropped below the trees and plunged the little island into shadow.

"He have to wait for Hobnail and Hissofer," replied Toonie firmly, "because we can't leave anyone behind." But even as she was speaking, and much to her horror, the flower, now deprived of the day's glorious sunlight, closed up its trumpet, folded its leaves in around it stalk, and dozed off for the night.

"Oh! My goodness!" cried Toonie slapping her hands to her face. "I think it's too late!"

"We can't wait any longer," said Toliver following Boogie onto the log (but not up to the captain's perch where the cat settled), "or it will be too dark to find our way through the woods."

"Yipes-a-doodle!" exclaimed Whizlet. "We'll have to go back tomorrow and get Hobnail."

And as they poled their way back to the other shore, they all agreed that that was exactly what they'd have to do.

(And that, my friend, is
The Endofit)